DEATH OF THE DEVIL

Further Titles by Caroline Gray from Severn House

BLUE WATERS, BLACK DEPTHS
THE DAUGHTER
GOLDEN GIRL
SHADOW OF DEATH
SPARES

The Civil War Series

SPAWN OF THE DEVIL
SWORD OF THE DEVIL
DEATH OF THE DEVIL

DEATH OF THE DEVIL

Caroline Gray

522587

This first world edition published in Great Britain 1994 by
SEVERN HOUSE PUBLISHERS LTD of
9–15 High Street, Sutton, Surrey SM1 1DF.
First published in the USA 1994 by
SEVERN HOUSE PUBLISHERS INC., of
425 Park Avenue, New York, NY 10022.

British Library Cataloguing in Publication Data
Grey, Caroline
  Death of the Devil
  I. Title
  823.914 [F]

  ISBN 0-7278-4698-1

Typeset by Hewer Text Composition Services, Edinburgh.
Printed and bound in Great Britain by
Hartnolls Ltd, Bodmin, Cornwall.

CHAPTER 1

"My lord!" panted my servant. "My lord! The Queen comes."

I was in my garden, pruning my roses. They seem to grow better in Normandy than anywhere else in France. Now I was forced to suppose that I was confronted by a madman, although Pierre had been a faithful valet of mine for the past five years. "You are gabbling," I remonstrated, mildly.

"My lord, a messenger has just arrived, to inform us that the Queen, being in this neighbourhood, has chosen to spend the night at the Château d'Albret. She is no more than a mile distant at this moment."

I realised that he was speaking the truth, at least as he saw it. And thus I became quite agitated myself. There was only one queen with whom I had any acquaintance. But that seemed impossible. "Are you speaking of the Queen of England?"

"My lord?"

His bewilderment gave me my answer. And some relief, as well. My acquaintance with the Queen Dowager Henrietta Maria, had been a good deal more than nodding. In this early autumn of 1650 she was, as far as I knew, languishing in exile in Holland while presumably still mourning the execution of her husband King Charles I. Our acquaintance had also involved endangering my life on more than one occasion, as being commanded to serve her by the late Cardinal Richelieu, I had been commanded *by* her to serve her incompetent husband in his war upon his own people.

1

But if it was not Henrietta Maria who had found her way back into her native country and now came knocking on my door . . . "My God!" I said. "You mean the *Queen*?"

"The very one," Pierre said, most reverently.

"Then prepare some clothes for me, oaf!" I shouted, and ran for the small staircase leading into the château.

At the top I encountered the Countess d'Albret. As I am the Count d'Albret, it may seem odd for me to refer to the lady of my house in such a fashion. The fact was that Marguerite le Gron was the Countess d'Albret in her own right, through her marriage with the previous holder of that title, now dead. I was the Count d'Albret in *my* own right, because of Cardinal Richelieu's grant of both the title and the lands that went with it, and although, additionally, Marguerite and I had tumbled and adventured together for some twenty years now, on and off, and had lived together as man and wife for the past six, we had never actually got around to being married. Nor were we likely ever to take such an irrevocable step, for although we enjoyed each other's company in the most Biblical of senses, we had never really liked each other. Pure chance had thrown us together. Mutual employment by Richelieu had kept us together. And a mutual determination to have done with the considerable dangers of the international intrigue in which we had dabbled for all of our adult lives was still keeping us together. Nothing more.

However, I threw my arms around her and gave her a most hearty hug and kiss. This was always a pleasure, for Marguerite remained very well endowed with all of those attributes that go to gladden a man's heart, beginning with flowing golden hair, – the dear girl was still only thirty-five years old – which surrounded somewhat pert features, and then passing, perhaps more slowly, to a formidable décolletage, to arrive at a very attractive body indeed. The whole, sadly, inspired by the most utterly shrewish disposition. "Have you not heard, you great lout?" she demanded, wriggling in my arms. "Her Majesty comes a-calling, and you are dressed like any common gardener."

I gave her another hug, against which her struggles were in vain. Marguerite was a sturdy wench, but she was like a babe in my arms. I have always been somewhat large, standing some inches over two yards in height, and built to match. Indeed, as the years had gone by – I was now approaching my fortieth birthday – my build could be described as having become a trifle excessive. But this had not diminished my lust for life in the slightest. I kissed her. "I am about to change."

"But what am I to wear?" she demanded. "It is at least a week since I had a new gown. And what are we to serve her? I am all of a tizzy, Helier."

She called me this because my real name is Helier L'Eree. Like her, I hailed originally from the Island of Garnesey, which is situated in the bay of St Malo, scarcely more than twenty miles from the coast of France, but belonging to the English Crown. I kissed her again, and set her on her feet. "You are speaking of woman's responsibilities," I told her. "See to yourself. I must make haste."

"Wretch!" she bawled behind me.

I ignored her as I hurried to my bedchamber where Pierre was waiting with water and clean clothes. Pierre was not a great talker, which was just as well, as I needed to think. It is not every day that a queen comes calling, and she seldom does so without having something on her mind. I had not even known that this Queen Dowager, who also happened to be the Regent of France, was in Normandy. I had never met this lady, who although she was a Spanish princess went by the name of Anne of Austria. However, both Spain and Austria being ruled by branches of the Hapsburg family, it was sometimes difficult to tell them apart. I did know, however, that

3

she had had what might be termed an interesting life. Married at a very early age to Louis XIII of France, she had rapidly found it necessary to understand that not all men regard women in the same light. Her husband had certainly preferred to regard young men rather than even his own wife, in *any* light and had, as soon as was convenient, sought the arms of a certain Duke of Luynes. He had, however, done his kingly duty and provided her with a necessary clutch of children, one of whom, known as Louis XIV, was now technically King of France under the regency of his mother.

But behaviour of this is sort often upsetting to the injured wife. It is more likely to be upsetting where the wife happens to be a Spanish princess, for the Spaniards are a proud and intolerant people. Left to her own devices, as it were, Queen Anne had sought her own path to pleasure. It was rumoured that she had numbered amongst her lovers the English Duke of Buckingham and it was widely accepted that she and her husband's chief minister, Cardinal Richelieu, had found it necessary to confer in the utmost privacy on every possible occasion. Now, as I have mentioned, this Richelieu fellow had been the employer of both Marguerite and myself, on the most secret and nefarious of missions. But how many secrets does a man keep from his mistress, especially when that mistress happens to be the Queen of France?

To further complicate matters, while Richelieu had now been dead for close on eight years, he had been succeeded, as chief minister, by an even more devious scoundrel, named Jules Mazarin. There were not lacking rumours to the effect that Anne of Austria had, in selecting Richelieu's replacement, merely moved from one cardinal's bed to another. Some even claimed that they were co-habiting as man and wife, a state of affairs which had only a couple of years previously caused a mini-civil war in France itself, or at least in Paris, known as the Fronde. Since my return to France following the

4

collapse of the Royalist cause in England after the Battle of Naseby, I had elected to keep out of the public eye so that I had not even informed the Cardinal of my existence. I was in an interesting situation, and one which aroused my curiosity as well as my apprehension.

I am bound to admit that my curiosity was equally aroused in another direction. I am a libidinous fellow – the circumstances of my life have made me so – and this Anne of Austria was reputed to be one of the most beautiful women in Europe. It may therefore be imagined with what eagerness I dressed myself in my best coat and breeches of crimson lake, with white sleeves and lace trimmings, and yellow decorations; my hose and shoe-bows were also crimson lake, and my shoes were black. I even donned a wig, of burnt umber colour, for the occasion.

Marguerite was no less resplendent in her overskirt of mauve and her underskirt of violet, with gamboge trimming, white lace and red gloves, her yellow hair worn loose and on her shoulders.

Together with our servants we waited at the portcullis of Château d'Albret, as the royal party came into view. There were more of them than we had expected, so that Marguerite had to issue orders to Jules, our butler, "Two more sheep to be slain, and make haste," ere she could arrange her features into a smile and sink into a deep curtsey before the woman who now dismounted in front of her escort.

I also bowed deeply to the Queen, sweeping the cobbles with the feather in my hat, while taking in her striking looks. Anne of Austria was now just past her forty-ninth birthday, but she could have been ten years younger. She was of medium height, for a woman, that is, more than a foot shorter than myself, although the feather in *her* broad-brimmed hat reached my forehead. Her features were a trifle too bold to be considered truly

5

beautiful, but they were certainly handsome and most attractive. The slight pout of the lips, the firm chin, the straight nose and most of all the somewhat languid dark eyes, all promised a great deal of pleasure to any man upon whom she should choose to bestow her charms. As she wore little powder, her hair, as loose as Marguerite's, could be seen to be a dark brown. As for her figure, the vagueries of feminine clothing, with its layer upon layer of petticoat below and corset above, acted as a proper concealment, but I formed the impression that it was everything that one might expect in a woman who was also a queen and a mother.

For her part, the Queen equally seemed pleased at what she was looking. "Count d'Albret," she said, her voice a delight, even if she still spoke French with a slight accent, which was the more attractive. "You are every bit as remarkable as you have been represented to me."

She gave me her hand to kiss, and I did so most fervently, while collecting my thoughts. "As do you make the sun but a pale imitation of light, Your Majesty," I ventured.

"Why, Count," she remarked. "Why are you not at court? And is this your pretty little wife?"

Why split hairs? "Indeed, Your Majesty," I agreed. "The Countess d'Albret." Marguerite was not looking terribly pleased at the Queen's description of her, but she had the good sense to give another curtsey and also kiss the royal glove. I escorted Anne up the steps to the knight's hall while some of her people followed, and others gave our people instructions upon what needed to be done.

"A fine château," the Queen remarked. "No doubt it has its tale to tell?"

"All old houses have tales to tell, Your Majesty," I said, not wishing to be drawn into a discussion either of how much blood had been spilt exactly where she

6

happened to be standing, or how I came into possession of this stately pile.

"If Your Majesty would care to accompany me," Marguerite said, "I will show you to your chamber."

"What I would care to do, Countess, before anything else, is have a glass of wine and something to eat." The Queen seated herself in one of the huge chairs which surrounded the table.

"Of course, Your Majesty." Clearly again put out, Marguerite waved at our servants, and a decanter and glasses were produced.

The Queen sipped, while we anxiously waited. She nodded. "Very good."

"Our own vines, Your Majesty," Marguerite gushed.

"How interesting," Anne said.

Servants were now bustling in with various laden platters, crockery and cutlery, which they arranged on the table. "I trust this meets with Your Majesty's approval?" Marguerite said.

"I believe it may," the Queen said. "Now I wish to speak with Count d'Albret. Alone."

The Queen Dowager looked around her, and her people hurried for the doorway, carrying our people with them; clearly they were used to obeying her every command without hesitation. Marguerite did hesitate, but I jerked my head and she left as well, barely keeping her temper under control. The doors closed, and I was alone with the Regent of France. I was more expectant than overawed. I had had *tête-à-têtes* with a queen before – this woman's sister-in-law – and I had also been closeted, on more than one occasion, with Richelieu: in this, no doubt Anne of Austria and I shared a bond.

The Queen indicated the decanter. "Will you not join me, Count? Or should I call you, General L'Eree?" I poured myself a glass while debating just how much she knew about me. I was about to find out. "Are those oysters?" she inquired.

"Cultivated on our own Normandy coast, Your Majesty."

"Then I will begin with those." I hastily placed half a dozen oysters on a plate and set it before her, taking a few myself. "Now sit you down," she commanded. "Here, close to me." I pulled a chair beside her, inhaling her perfume. The Queen lifted an oyster to her lips and sucked the flesh into her mouth. "Before he died," she said softly, "dear Armand told me so much about you. In fact, everything."

I could do no more than wait, concentrating upon my own dish. "He told me how you fled Garnesey when just a lad, because your mother was burned as a witch."

"It was a foul injustice, Your Majesty."

"I have no doubt of it, just as I can understand your grief and anger. Even if," she pointed out, having consumed two more of her shellfish, "your unnatural size leaves one in some doubt as to whether you are, indeed, a natural man. But that is something we can discuss later," she said, leaving me in some confusion. She finished her oysters, and licked her fingers; I hastily wiped her hands with a napkin, a pleasurable task, and then refilled her glass. "The Cardinal also told me how, I assume to keep you company in your self-imposed exile from your native home, that you abducted this woman you now call 'wife', she being then scarce nubile."

I would have liked to argue this point, as it is my opinion that Marguerite le Gron was virtually born nubile. However, the Queen was continuing. "And how, having seized the pair of you, he persuaded you to undertake a most dangerous mission for him, into the heart of Germany."

"Yes, Your Majesty," I said. "He did this by threatening to take the life of the Countess in a most unpleasant fashion."

"And of course you loved her too dearly to permit that."

"Well, Your Majesty, I did. I was very young. Besides, Your Majesty, what else could a gentlemen do?" I did not wish her to be in any doubt about my social status.

"What else?" she agreed. "Now, what is under that cover?"

I lifted it. "Mutton chops, Your Majesty, from my own flock."

"I think half-a-dozen of those would go down very nicely. But I also think a change of wine is called for. This stuff is very pleasant, but I need some body. Do you not have any Bordeaux wine?"

"Oh, indeed, Your Majesty."

"Then send for some."

I hurried to the door, outside of which there was gathered a considerable crowd, dominated by my, by now, extremely irate, "wife". However, the claret was brought, as well as some Malmsey for later, as I could tell this was going to be a lengthy meal. The Queen was tearing a chop apart with fine white teeth. "Richelieu also told me how you returned from the German wars as one of the most famous warriors of your day, and when he gave you an estate not far from here, how you preferred to retire to Garnesey with your then wife – a German lady, if I remember correctly – there to become a farmer. There was some talk of another woman, was there not?"

"Another woman," I muttered. I had just helped myself to some chops, but suddenly I quite lost my appetite.

"But not, I imagine, Mademoiselle le Gron," Anne remarked. "This was a highborn lady."

"She was truly a spawn of the devil," I whispered.

The Queen glanced at me while delicately dropping her chewed bones to the floor, where the dogs immediately cleaned them up. "That is something else we must discuss in due course. Refill my glass."

I obeyed, and took one for myself, feeling a trifle hot under the collar. Quite apart from my certainty that the Queen was leading up to something by this recounting of my past life, the mere hint of a memory of the Princess von Hohengraffen could make me sweat. However, she had now finished with her chops, and was again licking her fingers while I needs must attend to her with a clean napkin. "Then he told me how he had felt it necessary to recall you from your island hideaway to perform another task for him. The securing of the safety of the Queen of England, no less." She spoke with considerable contempt, and I recalled that Anne of Austria and Henrietta Maria had never got on. "And how, in the course of attempting to carry out his instructions, you became embroiled in the English Civil War. But then he died. And you disappeared. It was by chance that I learned you had returned to the second estate he had granted you. Lift that cover for me."

"Pigeon pie, Your Majesty."

"Capital. Serve some for me, and for God's sake take some yourself. I hate eating alone." I obeyed, forcing the food down. "So, will you not complete the tale?"

I drank some wine and swallowed. "There is little to complete, Your Majesty. As the Cardinal told you, I fought for the King, and when he was defeated, I returned home. I had pressing personal matters to attend to."

"Which brings me to my point," the Queen said. "The King."

"Your Majesty, I gave my all fighting for that man. The cause is lost, no matter how often men may raise their standards and shout, 'King Charles I is dead, long live King Charles II.' I can play no further part in that business. Besides, I have no intention of ever returning to England. I am under several sentences of death, most notably one issued by Cromwell himself."

"Are you acquainted with this man?"

"Very well acquainted, Your Majesty. It was my

misfortune to save his life, some years ago, before the war even started. Had I let him drown, the entire course of history may have been changed."

"And now he seeks your head? That is a strange form of gratitude."

"Well, we later differed over certain matters. He is no man to cross."

"But yet one who conforms to the laws of civilised society?" she suggested.

"Well, as to that, Your Majesty, he does so where he finds it necessary, or pleasing to his version of God."

Anne drank some more wine, and I hastily refilled her goblet. "Is that a treacle tart?" she inquired.

"Indeed, Your Majesty. Made by my own dear Marguerite."

"Serve me some, and you may pour the Madeira. What I need to tell you," she said, "must remain a secret between you and me."

Well, here was flattery, if you like. Besides, my curiosity was now greater than ever, in view of our last few exchanges. I placed the dish of tart in front of her, and added the goblet of sweet wine. "You may be certain of it, Your Majesty."

"Richelieu always said you could be trusted," she mused. "You were at Naseby?"

"I was, Your Majesty. It was one of the most botched affairs imaginable."

"The King fled. But he left his coach behind, and all his private papers. So I understand."

"Indeed, Your Majesty. And Cromwell and his friends have been publishing them ever since, as evidence of His Majesty's perfidy."

"They have not yet published *all* the papers," Anne said softly.

I frowned. I was not aware that Charles I had been secretly

11

negotiating with the French Government, although all things were possible.

"They no longer *possess* all of the papers," the Queen said, and abruptly rose from her chair. Naturally, I did also, but she gestured me back to my seat, while taking a turn up and down the room. "Many years ago, L'Eree," she said, "I did a singularly foolish thing." She glanced at me. "No doubt you have been equally guilty of youthful indiscretions."

"A dozen or more, at the very least, Your Majesty," I assured her.

"I was lonely, and thus I made a friend," the Queen said, returning to stand in front of me. "He was ever my friend, but he was equally ever the enemy of my adopted country, and in a position to do it great harm."

"By God!" I said without thinking. "Buckingham!"

Her chin came up. "Is it that well known?"

"It has always been but rumour, Your Majesty."

"Then it must remain rumour. Which is why I am telling you this."

"I do not understand that, Your Majesty."

"The Duke of Buckingham and I, in the course of his visits to Paris, both as official ambassador for the King of England and in a private capacity, occasionally encountered one another. Do you require me to say more than that?"

"By no means, Your Majesty. May I say that the Duke had to be the most fortunate of men?"

The Queen cast me a glance, but it was by no means entirely reproachful. "As a result of our meetings," she continued, "the Duke felt constrained to write me some letters. These, of course, I burned, as soon as I had read them. Sadly, in my youthful innocence, I felt obliged to reply, on the understanding that my letters also would be burned. Unfortunately, the Duke chose to keep them, as it appears, and indeed, they never left his person. I have no doubt that he *would* have burned them, in the course

12

of time. Alas, he was cruelly murdered before he had the time to do so."

"By the man Felton," I recalled. "But with respect, Your Majesty, that was twenty-two years ago."

"Quite." She seated herself again, or rather, threw herself into her chair in a most unlady-like fashion, so that her hat fell off. I retrieved it, but she made no effort to take it, so I resumed my seat with it on my lap, while appreciating her greatly enhanced beauty. "Thus while I wept for the gallant Duke, I presumed that the proof of our . . . friendship had long been destroyed. Now it turns out that I was wrong."

I leaned forward, my interest at last fully caught by what she had to say rather than her person.

"It appears," the Queen continued, "that the letters were on the Duke's person when he was struck down. They were found by the servants who stripped the body, and these fellows, being apparently sensible and loyal men, kept their tongues. Obviously they could not read the letters, as they were in French and these were common folk. But they delivered them to the King, and I have no doubt that *he* read them. I cannot say what his reactions were to the discovery that his chief minister was so close a friend of the Queen of France. However, it would appear that he also kept his counsel, and did not even show them to his wife – you may recall that at the time the Duke was murdered, Charles and Henrietta were not actually getting on very well. If he *had* shown them to her, there can be no doubt that she would have made them public. What the King appears to have done was bury the letters in the depths of his own most secret correspondence, and very probably he forgot they were there, with the various problems that pressed upon him."

"My God!" I said, quite forgetting my manners in the presence of royalty. "Do you mean they were in the King's coach when it was captured by the Roundheads?"

"It would appear so. Along with everything else."

"But again, Your Majesty, that was five years ago."

"Indeed. But there was, it seems, an enormous amount of papers and correspondence. Cromwell and his cohorts were obviously the most interested in locating all the documents that could be used to prove that King Charles was a traitor to his country. His correspondence with the Duke of Ormonde in Ireland and the Duke of Lorraine in the Low Countries, implored them both to invade England and help his cause. They were not, it appears, in the least interested in twenty-year-old love letters. I am quite sure that they would have *become* interested, in the course of time, but for the time being they gave the bulk of what they considered the irrelevant correspondence to various clerks to be sorted and classified and filed for future reference."

"And this task has now been completed," I mused. "And your letters found. May I ask who has made the approach? Cromwell himself?"

She shook her head. "You mistake the situation, Helier. My letters were never found by the clerks, for the simple reason that they were no longer there." I scratched my head, dislodging my wig to do so, but neither of us noticed. "It appears that some time after they were taken to London, and before the clerks had got to them, they were stolen from the accumulated documents."

"By whom? And why did the thief wait five years to contact Your Majesty?"

"I shall come to that in a moment. I do not think they were stolen by the principal herself, as she may well have been occupied elsewhere at the time. I imagine they were procured by an agent. Obviously the clerks who were classifying the various documents were not even aware of their existence, and so did not miss them. Then, the principal to whom they were delivered took some time to decide what to do with them."

At this point I felt called upon to interrupt the Queen.

"May I ask, Your Majesty, how, if no one knew those letters were in the general correspondence, did this person, this lady, as you say, find out?"

"Now that is a question that remains to be answered. But it is not relevant at this moment. At the time she obtained them, you see, Helier, my personal position appeared impregnable. All France was at my feet, and dear Jules ruled supreme. But then there came the Fronde. Did you not take part in that?"

"It was a Parisian business, Your Majesty, and hardly affected us down in Normandy."

"And you did not choose to offer your so famous sword in defence of the monarchy," she remarked, somewhat tartly.

"I have adventured enough, on behalf of the Cardinal, Your Majesty. Now I seek only the quiet life."

"Well, you will have to give up the quiet life, at least for a season."

"Your Majesty?"

"This female . . . I cannot possibly consider calling her a lady although she claims to hold a great rank . . . has recently written to me, indicating that she is considering publishing these letters."

"Blackmail," I remarked. "For a correspondence more than twenty years old? Your Majesty, why do you not tell her to publish and be damned?"

Anne of Austria was on her feet again. "Three years ago I could have done that, L'Eree. But now . . . sadly, since the Fronde, my stock has fallen. Not only with the people of Paris, but with the nobility. They seek, and would use, any means to bring me down. You should remember that when I was meeting the Duke, France and England were at war. The Duke was indeed assassinated. He was about to depart England with an expedition for the relief of the Huguenots in La Rochelle. Were those letters to be produced now, I could be accused of treason. Whether I survived such an accusation or not, the damage would be irreparable."

"I understand. Then the ransom must be paid, Your Majesty. May I ask what it is?"

The Queen sat down again. I observed that there were beads of sweat on her face. "The ransom is yourself, L'Eree."

I suppose there are times in everyone's life, fortunately few, when we are quite struck dumb. I certainly was at that moment. "I would imagine this woman has known you before, Helier," Anne said, "and wishes to renew her acquaintanceship. That is a considerable compliment."

"No doubt, Your Majesty," I muttered, while a thousand possibilities raced through my mind. "May I ask the name of this lady?"

"There is nothing to be agitated about, Helier," the Queen said. She took a letter from the bodice of her gown and unfolded it. "Her exact words are: *I would be more than willing to return these letters to you, should you wish them. However, I will release them to but a single messenger, a certain Helier L'Eree, sometimes known as the Count d'Albret, who is in possession of the d'Albret estate in Normandy. I ask nothing more than this. Send L'Eree to me, and I shall personally place the letters in his hands.*" She smiled at me. "Nothing could be simpler than that." The woman was demented.

"Her name!" I shouted, with a sad lack of deference.

"Why, she signs herself Richilde, Countess Culhaven. I do not know where that is, but I am sure you can find it easily enough. For she adds, beneath her signature: *the Count should seek my husband, who is in the service of the King, in Scotland, and who will bring him safely to me.* There you are," she concluded triumphantly. "Now, how soon can you leave?"

"Your Majesty," I said, as earnestly as I could. "I

cannot leave. Not now, not tomorrow, not next week. It is not possible."

The Queen's face hardened. "I had not expected a refusal in this small matter, Helier. Why, you shall be gone scarce a month."

"I shall be gone forever, Your Majesty. And so will your letters. This is the most obvious trap."

"How so?"

"Your Majesty, in the first place, I am, as I have explained, under sentence of death by the Commonwealth Government. I am sure you will agree that I am not the sort of man who can easily resort to a disguise. Therefore the very moment I set foot in England I will be arrested. There will be no necessity for a trial, as the sentence has already been pronounced."

"What exactly was your crime?"

"Why, that of changing sides, Your Majesty. Although I may say that I never fought for the Roundheads voluntarily, but was dragooned into doing so."

"Thus you sought to follow your own better judgement as soon as you were able. Well, that is all several years in the past."

"I would not like to advance that argument to General Cromwell, Your Majesty."

"But he will have to listen to you, if you go as my accredited ambassador."

"Your Majesty?"

"France of course already has an ambassador at Whitehall, as dear Jules considered it appropriate to recognise the *fait accompli*. While not approving of it, you understand. However, his business is matters of state. You will be my ambassador on a personal basis. You are no doubt aware that Prince Henry and Princess Elizabeth are both in the London Tower?"

"I knew they were in England, Your Majesty."

"They are in the Tower. Well, these Roundheaded people declare time and again that the Prince and Princess are well looked after and in the best of health, that they are not considered hostages for the good behaviour of the Prince of Wales, or Charles II as he now calls himself, and that their futures will be decided in due course. I consider it my duty, as their aunt by marriage, to ascertain for myself whether or not these claims are true. Does not my heart bleed for these two children, neither more than fifteen years old, kept in durance vile?"

It occurred to me that if the Buckingham letters *were* to be published, and the Queen to lose her crown, she would have very little difficulty in making a living, on the stage. But I had more important matters on my mind. "Your concern does you great credit, Your Majesty," I said. "But still . . ."

"As my ambassador," the Queen said "you will be accepted by the Commonwealth Government, and will be able to travel freely about the country. Cromwell understands that as I am Regent, to offend me means to offend France, and he cannot afford to do that. He is also well aware that his party has achieved its triumph solely because France has never thrown her weight behind the English royalist party, or indeed, never supported it in the least, save most clandestinely. Were we to do so now, were we to support this new King Charles, this usurping general would be well on his way to a hangman's noose himself."

I could have argued that point, but it was not relevant, in view of everything else I had been commanded to do. "That may well be, Your Majesty, but then there is the matter of the Lady Culhaven."

"Indeed. She is an old lover, I suppose, whom you abandoned? Dear Armand spoke of your philandering."

"Well, as to that, Your Majesty, if I am right in my estimate of her true identity, the lady and I have certainly, from time to time and some years ago, been as friendly as, shall I say, yourself and the Duke of Buckingham."

"I knew it," Anne said. "Well, you will have to resume

18

relations with her, if that is what she wishes, until you have got hold of those letters. She has made it perfectly plain that if I do not send you for them, she will publish them."

"You do not understand, Your Majesty. Lady Culhaven does not wish me to go to her as a lover. She wishes me to go to her so that she may kill me."

Anne regarded me for some seconds. "Is she, then, some female Goliath?" she inquired. "You, Helier, the most famed swordsman in Europe, afraid of a woman?"

"Your Majesty, Lady Culhaven is not a woman."

The Queen frowned at me. "Explain that opinion."

I swallowed, because I was about to endanger myself. Those who associate freely with witches are generally considered guilty of the foul heresy themselves. But there was nothing for it. "She is a vampire."

Anne's mouth formed an attractive little O. "Do you believe in such fables?"

"I do not mean that she walks only by night, has pointed teeth, and sucks the blood from the neck of her victim, Your Majesty. But she certainly has a taste *for* human blood. And she has manifested all the other aspects of being a close relative of the devil. She can cast spells. Her knowledge is vast and universal. And above all, she is indestructible."

"Oh, come now, Helier."

"You must believe me, Your Majesty," I wailed, in so far as a monster like myself can wail.

"Tell me how you know this."

I drew another long breath. "I know this because I have twice tried to kill her. And had she been a human being she would have died, twice."

"No doubt you had a reason for behaving as you did," the Queen suggested, clearly still sceptical.

"Your Majesty, I first met this creature in the German war, some twenty years ago. I was but a lad of twenty, and I thought her the most marvellous creation of the Deity."

"You fell in love with her?"

"Alas, so I did. But she was then the Princess von Hohengraffen, and I supposed her as far above me as are the stars. Imagine my consternation, but also my delight, when she invited me to her bed."

"Indeed I can," the Queen mused.

"We became lovers, and I conceived myself in paradise. But it was the reverse side of the coin. She wished the use of my strength, not the warmth of my heart. Her plan was to murder her husband and gain control of the principality. To achieve this she bound her tenants to her by sorcery and witchcraft. May God forgive me, Your Majesty, but I was forced to take part in one of these ceremonies."

"A black mass?" The Queen clapped her hands. "You must tell me of it. But later. Go on."

I sighed, but it is a fact that there are few females who are not excited by the thought of that awful overturning of the eucharist. "Even then I might not have understood her for what she was. But I refused to assist in her hellish schemes, and in my absence she caused the murder of my wife and son."

"Helier!" The Queen rested her hand on my arm. "My heart bleeds for you."

"Thus I chased her clear across Europe, and finally caught up with her only a few miles from where we now sit. I executed her, Your Majesty. But being still under the impression that she was nothing more than a witch, and being also, I have to confess, averse to the destruction of so much beauty, I elected to drown her."

"Yet you claim she still lives? The same woman?"

"All I can say is, Your Majesty, that having held her under water for several minutes, and observing her to be lifeless, I buried her, and left her. But I was assailed by some doubts and a week later, I returned to the grave and opened it up . . . and she was gone."

"You mean someone stole the body?"

20

"I do not know what happened. But she was gone."

"And this sorely concerned you? I can understand that. But the explanation is surely simple enough. Either someone did steal the body, or she was not dead in the first place. You only thought she was. And thus she dug herself out of her grave. Now, if the first explanation is true, this woman cannot be she. If the second, then I will agree she has much cause to dislike you, but yet she remains a mortal woman, and I give you my permission to execute her the moment you obtain possession of the letters. After all, to attempt to blackmail a queen is a form of treason, is it not?"

"Your Majesty," I said, "you still do not understand the truth of the matter. After the Princess's disappearance from her grave, I decided to return to Garnesey, as you know, in order that she could not find me. But find me she did, when I was recalled to the Cardinal's service. She came to me so disguised I did not recognise her, and thus she again wormed her way into my affections."

"And thus you fell in love with her all over again?" the Queen remarked, somewhat disparagingly.

"Well, yes, Your Majesty, I did," I confessed. "When she is disposed to be, the Princess von Hohengraffen can be the most irresistible of women."

"I'm sure," Anne said, more disparagingly yet. "But as she did not avenge herself on you then, why should she wish to do so now?"

"Because her vengeance was dedicated to everything that I held dear, with me only as the *pièce de résistance*. Possessing my confidence, she was able to worm her way into the bosom of my second family, and again murdered them all."

"Oh, Helier!" the Queen cried. "I am so very sorry. What a terrible life you have suffered."

"It was only after that was done that she came after me, personally."

"But you proved too strong for her"

21

"Well, as to that, Your Majesty, I overcame her in physical combat, yes, and the minions she had brought with her. In the course of the battle, which took place in this very hall, she saw that things were going against her, and fled into the kitchens. There she fell into the great fire, and was consumed."

The Queen frowned at me. "But you fear she still lives?"

"When the fire was burned down, Your Majesty, and I poked the ashes, there was neither bone nor tooth to be seen."

Once again Anne regarded me for some seconds. "If this same woman survived both a drowning and a burning alive, Helier, then she is indeed a witch."

"And thus cannot be conquered by mortal man," I pointed out.

"Well, as to that, there is generally an answer to everything. Open the door, Helier, and summon Abbé Grimaud. He will tell us what to do."

Again, I obeyed the Queen. The crowd outside the door had not diminished, and was by now in a somewhat restive mood, as these people had not yet eaten. Marguerite indeed was in a fury. But I paid no attention to her, and merely called for the priest, who hurried in, a little, grey-haired man with a drooping moustache and a shifty manner. I did not care for him, but Anne seemed pleased to see him. "Abbé Grimaud is my confessor," she explained.

I preferred not to comment about this, although the idea of this still beautiful woman, and a queen to boot, snuggled up next to this little twerp while she told him her innermost thoughts and her most private misdeeds, of both thought and act, was a disconcerting one. "We have a problem, Abbé," the Queen explained. "How does one dispose of a witch."

"A real witch, Your Majesty?"

22

"She certainly appears so."

"She must be seized, and tried, by a holy tribunal, and then burned at the stake."

"Yes, yes, but supposing there is no holy tribunal available? How may a single man cope with her?"

"He must equip himself with a holy cross, a small one will do, and hold this between himself and the witch until she surrenders, and then he should burn her alive."

"There, you see, Helier?" the Queen asked. I was speechless. "But suppose," Anne went on, "that in addition to being a witch she is also a vampire?"

"A vampire?" Abbé Grimaud fell to his knees and crossed himself. "Holy Mary, Mother of God, have mercy on our souls!"

"You would regard this as a more difficult proposition, would you?"

"Undoubtedly, Your Majesty. You cannot destroy a vampire by fire."

"Exactly the opinion of my friend here," the Queen said. "Then how would you destroy her?"

"Well, Your Majesty, it is again necessary to equip yourself with a holy cross."

"Still a small one?"

"The larger the better," the poor old fellow said reverently.

"And then?"

"The vampire must be approached during the hours of daylight, because then it sleeps. Its destroyer should equip himself with a long stake, sharpened at one end, a heavy mallet, and a sharp axe."

"Would not a sword do as well as an axe?" Anne inquired.

"Aye, well, a sword would do, Your Majesty, providing he knows the use of it."

"I think we may rely on that. And then?"

"Well, Your Majesty, the point of the stake should be placed upon the breast of the vampire, immediately above the heart, and driven into the organ with as many strokes of the mallet as may be required."

"I see," Anne observed. "And what is the vampire doing while it is thus being transfixed?"

"It will undoubtedly awake at the first blow, Your Majesty. But if the second and third blows are delivered quickly enough, it will be unable to do more than scream. I should say that there may be a great deal of blood."

"A great deal," the Queen agreed.

"But to make doubly sure that the creature is destroyed, it is then necessary to take the axe . . ."

"Or the sword," the Queen interrupted.

"Oh, indeed, Your Majesty, or the sword, and cut off the creature's head."

"When there may be more blood?"

"Only a little, Your Majesty, as the heart should have stopped beating. But the creature will undoubtedly be destroyed."

"Absolutely. There you are, Helier, what could be simpler? But there must be no stakes or swords until you have procured the letters. How may a man protect himself against the creature, Abbé, supposing he is unfortunate enough to encounter her alive and biting, as it were."

"The cross will repel her, Your Majesty. But the most absolute protection is garlic."

"And I smelt garlic as I came into your château, Helier. You must have a lot of it about."

"Your Majesty," I said. "That is the most utter clap-trap."

"Helier," she admonished me severely. "Abbé Grimaud has made a lifelong study of the unnatural."

I could well believe it. "Then all I can say is, Your Majesty, that he has been reading the wrong books. He is speaking theoretically, I am speaking from practical experience. Firstly, the Princess von Hohengraffen, or Lady Culhaven, or whatever other name she chooses to call herself by, has never been the least inhibited by the

24

sight of the holy cross, of any size. Secondly, she does not sleep during the day, but mostly during the night. She is like everyone else, when she does sleep, which is not very often."

"What have you to say to that, good Abbé?"

"She must be a very unusual vampire," the priest grumbled.

"But you still feel that driving a stake through her heart and cutting off her head will do the trick?"

"There are very few creatures which can survive both a stake driven through their heart and their head being cut off, Your Majesty."

Well, I could not deny that he might be right about that; it was persuading Richilde Bethlen, Princess von Hohengraffen, to lie down while I placed the stake, without her at the same time doing me a mortal injury, that bothered me.

"I will see that you are equipped in every possible way, Helier," the Queen assured me. "I will make a list. Garlic, mallet, stake, cross . . . you will of course provide the sword. Would you like an axe as well?"

"It pleases Your Majesty to jest at my expense?"

"Helier, I have never been more serious in my life. I want those letters. I must *have* those letters. You are the only one who can obtain them for me. It follows, therefore, that having obtained them, you are the only one who can bring them back to me. As of now, the preservation of your health is of more importance to me than my own. Do believe this."

"And if I suggest to you that it is more than likely that the Princess does *not* in fact possess the letters, but only seeks to get me into her power?"

"That is a risk we must take, Helier." Fine words. I was not aware that the Queen intended to take any risks at all. She now revealed her claws. "You will, of course, bear in mind, Helier, that this château, and everything that goes with it, was granted to you as a servant of the state. Once you cease to be a servant of the state, unless you have then been granted an honourable retirement, the château will cease to be yours. In such circumstances there would also have to be a charge of desertion. When you returned from your last mission you informed no one of it, and have thus absented yourself from your duty for five years. This could lead to a long term of imprisonment in the Bastille. Possibly for the rest of your life."

I gulped, with a terrible feeling of frustration. I, who had *lived*, where she had at best existed, and who could break her in two with a twist of my fingers, was being forced to submit to her will, even as I knew it would involve my own death. Because if there was one thing in life that was certain, it was that Richilde Bethlen would not again treat me with such contempt as to allow me ever again to come within striking distance of her. But the Queen did not only possess claws. "Whereas, when you have returned in triumph, Helier, think what you will have gained. You will have destroyed this evil creature who has made your life a misery. You will have performed a signal service for your queen, who will forever be grateful, and will shower rewards upon you. Indeed, but signify your willingness to undertake this mission for me, and I am prepared to give you an advance, as it were."

We gazed at each other, and I surrendered.

Well, what would you? I am a libidinous fellow, and it is not every day one gets together with a queen. I had had this experience before in my past, but the lady's husband being still very much alive at that time and his, and our, situations, being somewhat fluid, it had been an unfulfilling affair. Anne of Austria's husband was long dead, and her lover was a long way away.

Besides, rewards apart, she had touched a very weak point in my personality. Richilde Bethlen had made my life a hell, for twenty years. If, until today, I had not known positively that she was still alive, I had always supposed she was. That being so, I had always known, however often I had rejected the concept, that we would have to meet again one day. And *that* being so, the sooner we met the better, if I was ever going to enjoy a peaceful old age. It would have to be her or me. Then it had best be now, while I was still young enough and strong enough to have a chance of defeating her, however slim.

Besides, I had an idea. During my sojourn in England, in the course of the Civil War, I had made the acquaintance of a man called Matthew Hopkins, who was generally known as The Witchfinder–General. This villain made a living by perambulating up and down the country, seeking out anyone who might be a witch, and seeing that they were summarily dealt with. It had not taken me very long to discern that a great majority of his victims were absolutely innocent. Indeed we had fallen out somewhat violently, over his attentions to a young lady with whom I happened to be travelling. That she had eventually turned out to be at least the servant of a witch was neither here nor there. It therefore occurred to me that if I could present the man with a *real* witch, and indeed the greatest witch of this or any other century, his enthusiasm for his work would cause him to forget our past differences and join me in my mission; with a man like Hopkins at my side I might even be able to face the Witch of Hohengraffen with confidence. In any event, whether he would assist me in her demise or no, I had no doubt that his advice on how to manage the matter, based as it was on practical experience and not on books, would be of far more value than that of the Abbé Grimaud. Thus I felt I could approach my mission with some confidence.

There remained a great deal to be done. Not least with regard to Marguerite. The Queen having signified that our *tête-à-tête* was at an end, the doors were finally opened, and the hoi poloi came thronging in, starving and snarling. They fell to without invitation, Marguerite amongst them, while the Queen smiled graciously at them and drank some more wine. She then gave a pretty little yawn, and said, "I am exhausted, and will retire. Count d'Albret, you said you had a chamber for me?"

"Indeed, Your Majesty," I said.

Marguerite removed a lamb chop from between her teeth. "It has been prepared for hours, Your Majesty. I will show you to it."

"My dear Countess," the Queen said, "I would not interrupt your meal. Your husband will suffice."

Marguerite looked close to choking, but the Queen was already summoning several of her ladies. These looked disgruntled enough at having to leave their food, and they duly followed Anne and me up the stairs to the guest apartment, which Marguerite had prepared to perfection. "I trust this meets with your approval, Your Majesty," I said.

"I am sure it will do very well, Helier," she said. "Now, ladies, you may return to your meal. I am sure you are hungry."

This induced less twittering than I had expected, although one of the damsels was bold enough to ask, "But who will assist Your Majesty, Your Majesty?"

"I am sure the Count d'Albret will do very well," Anne told her, and they scuttled off.

"It must be very fine to be a queen, and a regent, and mistress of all one surveys, Your Majesty," I ventured.

"Why, so it is, to be sure. Unlace me, Helier."

This I did as rapidly as possible, as owing to the exigencies of my career I am fairly well experienced in these matters. Besides, the knowledge that I was about to possess all that *she* possessed, if only on a temporary basis, was most stimulating. I understand that to rampant youth a lady of all but fifty must appear a trifle jaded, but rampant youth is mistaken about so many aspects of life this is but an unusually glaring example. A lady in what is sometimes referred to as middle-age, who has lived and loved and lusted, and who has retained at least part of her beauty, makes your twittering virgin exactly what she is, a twittering virgin, capable only of doing, or saying, the wrong thing at the wrong time.

Besides, all queens are beautiful.

CHAPTER 2

And so, willy nilly, I set forth in search of my destiny. I anticipated a fairly brief journey, from which I would return either in triumph or in a coffin, more likely the latter. The task ahead of me seemed to be simple enough, and not a very time-consuming one: travel to England as the Queen's personal representative, hope that her authority would prevent my discovering an even more immediate acquaintance with the interior of that wooden box, discover the whereabouts of Lord Culhaven, visit him . . . and let the devil have his day. Or rather hers. A matter surely of a few weeks.

The only inconvenience seemed to be that to act out my subterfuge, I needed to go to England first, and at least pay the Prince and Princess a visit, before disappearing north of the border, instead of merely taking ship to Scotland. However, this would serve the purpose of enabling me to look up Hopkins on the way.

Marguerite was less sanguine, having had experiences similar to mine in the past and being more aware of the passage of time. "Each occasion that you have abandoned me to go on a mission for the Cardinal," she pointed out, when we were at last alone together, "it has been a matter of two years."

"You are entirely mistaken," I reminded her. "What you meant to say was, each time that you abandoned *me*."

"Now is not the time to split hairs. Tell me what you were doing, closeted with the Queen all of that time."

Well, when a woman of thirty-five years of age, a goodly number of which years have been spent in a recumbent position and not alone, has to ask a question like that, one begins to suspect her intelligence. "If I thought you were tumbling her, I would scratch out her eyes, queen or no queen," she said.

"Heaven forbid!" I said. After all, one does not want a blind queen stumbling about the place. "We were discussing affairs of state."

"So you are again employed and must go wandering off. Well, begone with you. Just remember to come back."

This was actually an easier separation than I had anticipated, in view of Marguerite's suspicious nature, and I departed d'Albret with some relief. I did not accompany the Queen to Paris, for she had brought my letters patent as her ambassador with her, she had obviously not even considered the possibility of my refusing her command. I took only Pierre with me as a servant; he was a useful man with a cudgel, although I did not see what good that would be against a vampire – possibly he could hold the stake while I wielded the mallet, supposing we ever got ourselves into that advantageous position – but a man must have a servant, or life would become simply too tedious. So off we went to Calais, from whence we hoped to make Dover in short order. And this we did, in some contrast to the last time I had attempted this crossing.

A word should be said here about the situation into which I was about to plunge. The Civil War in England had officially come to an end some years before, although no one was absolutely sure about this at that moment. In fact, what historians were to call the Second Civil War had already begun, without many people – myself in particular – being fully aware of it. The first conflict, undertaken when King Charles I had quarrelled with his Parliament on the question of taxation, had raged from 1642 to 1645, when the King's army had been routed at Naseby. I had taken part in that struggle from beginning to end, first on one side and then the other, owing to circumstances beyond my control. After Naseby, realising that the Royal cause was lost and being by then thoroughly fed-up with both the King's incompetence and his double-dealing, I had abandoned the service to return home, having the reappearance of Richilde Bethlen in my life to deal with. Others had not been so pessimistic about the Royal situation, however, least of all the King himself. He had spent the next three years attempting to regain his former prerogatives by the devious method of discerning the various points at issue between his different opponents, be they Parliamentarians, Levellers, Scots, or most important of all, Cromwell's Army, and attempting to play them off against each other until they would all turn to him as the one man who could restore the country to its former dignity.

That he had attained a measure of success may be gauged by the mere fact that he had kept this juggling act going for three years. But eventually the outcome had been the exact reverse of what he had hoped and intended. All the parties had reached the conclusion that the one man who stood in the *way* of restoring the country to its former dignity was the King himself. So they had chopped off his head. As may have been gathered, I witnessed this sad event from afar, my only feeling of compassion being for the Queen, even if I knew that she had herself contributed to her husband's downfall by her imperious arrogance.

However, a king never dies, at least to those who believe in monarchy. The day, 30 January 1649, that King Charles had been beheaded, those believers had pronounced his eldest son King, as Charles II. The Irish – who were in the main Roman Catholics and hated Parliament's religious puritanism – and the Scottish Highlanders – who were in the main Presbytarians but

32

hated the English – rose at the same time although separately, and thus, unknowingly, I was on my way to this Second Civil War. Of course I knew that the situation was very disturbed, but it seemed to me that the disturbances were all on the periphery, where they had not already been crushed. Certainly the Irish had suffered the full weight of Cromwell's anger. I had served with this strange and terrible man, briefly, and had found his mixture of domestic contentment and a religious fervour which could be demonic when aroused, too hard to stomach. Therefore it had come as no surprise to me that he should have stalked through Ireland with fire and sword, massacring the garrisons of Drogheda and Wexford, and their families, in the same manner as he had commanded all the camp-followers captured after Naseby to be slaughtered without mercy – and not all of these unfortunate ladies had been whores.

Now I understood that he was in the process of dealing in the same way with the recalcitrant Scots. As far as I was concerned, while I felt sorry for the Scots, the fact that he was out of England was all to the good; my only problem was that I was committed to visiting Scotland as well, but I intended to be there and gone before he knew anything about it, as I had no desire whatsoever to make his acquaintance again.

My arrival in Dover went according to plan, as my papers were examined and accepted, and Pierre and I were on the next coach to London. So far so good. As I have mentioned, the Queen had recommended that I should carry out the official part of my mission first, and pay a visit to the Tower of London in order to inspect the situation of the royal siblings. That done, she had envisaged that it would be a simple matter for me to disappear while seeking the whereabouts of this Lord Culhaven. I could think of nothing better than this idea, intending, as I have said, on my way north to look up Hopkins, but of course these things always seem simpler in the projection than in the commission. Having reached London, I duly presented my credentials at the Tower, but this time was met with some stony stares. "Do I not know you?" asked the Captain of the Beefeater guard.

"In which case you have the advantage of me, my good fellow," I riposted. It was of course quite likely that he had seen me before, for I am a man once seen not easily forgotten, but as he had no such remarkable physical characteristics, if I had seen *him* before it had entirely escaped my mind.

"By God!" he said. "You are the scoundrel and deserter known as Helier L'Eree. Arrest that man," he told his people.

"I would not have you make a mistake," I said, dropping my left hand to my sword hilt. "You are right in assuming that my name is Helier L'Eree, but I am better known as the Count d'Albret, and if you will look more closely at those documents, you will discover that I am an ambassador for Her Majesty the Queen Dowager of France, who is also the Regent of France, and am thus protected by diplomatic usages."

He considered this while holding my passport upside down, increasing my speculation that for all his fine uniform, he could not read. "I will have to refer the matter to my superiors," he remarked.

"Then do so. But first, give me back my passport," and I snatched it away from him. "I shall return tomorrow, and shall then require admittance, or I shall be forced to take the matter up with the French ambassador." He did some harrumphing at this, but could think of no immediate retort, and thus Pierre and I took ourselves off in search of lodgings. By now a considerable crowd had gathered. Some of these onlookers supported the captain, and wondered aloud why he did not take the two horrible Frenchmen into the Tower and keep them there. But I was surprised, and relieved, to discern that a far greater number were on our side. I was experienced enough to understand that there is an element in any society which will always oppose authority, yet it seemed to me that a lot of these people were definitely anti-Parliament, which was worth knowing.

Not that I had the least intention of becoming again embroiled in any English domestic differences. I thus looked neither to left nor right as I strode, Pierre at my heels with our satchels, to the nearest hostelry. "I will have a room for the night," I informed the publican. "And a meal, and a flagon of wine. On second thoughts, make that two flagons of wine."

"Why, sir," he said. "You may have the room, and I can even supply you with a meal, but wine, no."

"You have no wine?"

"It is forbidden, by order of Parliament, sir. Ale, now, I have a-plenty."

"Then ale it will have to be," I agreed, somewhat sadly, for having lived so much of my life in France I had become very partial to the grape. However, I sent Pierre upstairs with our belongings while I sat down to a tankard of foaming liquid, and having slaked my thirst, beckoned the landlord. "I seek information," I said. "Have you ever heard of a man named Hopkins?"

He goggled at me. "Matthew Hopkins?"

"That is the very name."

"The witch-hunter?"

"Again, the very man."

"You are a friend of Mr Hopkins?"

"By no means." I deemed this the best approach, as I was not about to tell this fellow that the last time I had encountered the foul Hopkins I had found it necessary to hit him on the head. "I but seek his whereabouts."

"No doubt you have a score to settle," the landlord suggested, adding, "Most people do."

"Aye, there you have it," I agreed.

"Well, you are too late. He is dead."

"What?"

"He died in his bed, worse luck, three years ago," the landlord said.

So there went the first lynch-pin in my plan. "Now there is a pity," I remarked.

"Good riddance," the landlord growled. "We'll have no more of his sort about. That is by order of Parliament." He served my dinner, Pierre joining me to eat our pigeon pie and roast duckling, fowl being in far more abundance in this war-torn land than beef. I fell to wondering if there was anything done, or not done, in such a supposedly free country *without* the order of Parliament.

It was while we were enjoying our meagre repast, washing it down with copious quantities of this thin drink called ale, that we were joined at table by half-a-dozen other people, who also called for ale and supper, and fell to most heartily. However, being an observant fellow, I rapidly determined that they were decidedly interested in Pierre and myself, casting us sidelong glances, and whispering to each other. Now of course this might have been because, both from our clothes and our conversation – Pierre had only a word or two of English – they could tell we were foreigners. But my experiences have been such that anyone who shows an unusual interest in me is immediately an object of suspicion, and thus I did some observing of my own. This was not an unpleasant task, for if four of the newcomers were men, two were women. One of these women was of a distinctly attractive appearance, despite the fact that the mode of dress which had become *de rigeur* in England since the triumph of Parliament was not intended to enhance feminine beauty, but quite the reverse. Your sincere Puritan felt that even to look at a woman with lascivious thoughts was as criminal as actually dragging her into bed.

But even tall hat, high collar and shapeless gown could not conceal the charms of this young woman. Of course I could not properly tell what might lie south of the collar, as it were, but I reasoned, quite illogically to be sure, that where the face was so attractive, the rest of her had to be cast in a similar mould. And the face was most certainly attractive. Indeed it was quite beautiful, with its high forehead, wide-set grey eyes, its straight nose, pert lips, and its pointed chin, while from beneath the tall hat there escaped a wisp of yellow hair. I had not seen anything so worth a second glance in a long time. What made her even more attractive was that she was clearly no less interested in me. Well, this is something I am fairly used to; ever since I was a lad women have cast me interested glances, for if no one could possibly describe me as handsome, equally it is difficult for any female with the least touch of libidinity about her not to wonder if my huge size does not extend in every direction and to every part of my body.

However, I had not expected to find myself so openly canvassed by a Puritan lady, certainly when in the presence of her menfolk. So I allowed her a somewhat nervous smile. While I am not the least averse to the average brawl, and had no doubt at all that I could deal with these fellows should they take umbrage, I did not wish to risk possible arrest for fighting. I knew the Puritans were rather severe on this kind of thing, as they were on every other form of entertainment. Imagine, therefore my consternation when, just as Pierre and I had completed our meal, the lady could be observed scribbling on a piece of paper she had taken from her reticule, and a moment later this note, suitably folded, was being passed along the table by the very men I was concerned about. It duly arrived in front of me, but I deemed it safest not to touch it, until one of the men leaned across and said, "That is for you, monseweer."

He did not appear hostile, so I picked up the paper and unfolded it. *Are you truly Helier L'Eree?* she had written. *If so, nod. And if you nod, I beg you to receive me in your chamber in one hour's time.* The note was unsigned.

Well, what would you? Is there any man with red blood in his veins who could resist such an offer? Especially a man with known libidinous tendencies such as mine? Thus before I had even wasted the time in gathering my thoughts I had nodded, and been rewarded with a quick smile. To my consternation the man sitting beside me slapped me on the shoulder. "You'll not regret it," he said.

The fact that the entire group seemed keen on the idea should have been reassuring, but no sooner had I accepted the invitation than a thousand reflections crowded into my mind. There was of course the possibility that I had stumbled across some kind of travelling brothel and was about to get the clap for my pains. Then there was the possibility that the young lady was a hired assassin – I had accumulated a good many enemies in my time. But I felt I could deal with that. Then there was the possibility that she was a Parliamentary spy, sent to discover the true reason behind my visit to England. But I felt I could deal with that as well.

The possibility that she was a young woman of sufficiently free spirit genuinely to wish to get to know a complete stranger better when in the company of five companions was of course out of the question, especially when she was being so openly encouraged by those companions.

But there remained another possibility, far more sinister than any of the above: that she was an emissary of the Witch of Hohengraffen. Or even the Witch herself. She did not look in the slightest like Richilde Bethlen, but in my experience Richilde had been adept at adopting disguises which would have fooled anyone, and had certainly fooled me on more than one occasion. Nor was it impossible that Richilde, with her supernatural powers, would have been able to discover the plans laid by the Queen and myself, and have decided to meet me halfway, as it were. But if that were the case, then why not meet her face to face right away, and settle the matter once and for all? I was of course, by this time quite full of ale, which if thin, pale stuff contained yet sufficient alcohol to heat the blood.

I thus arose, bowed to the group, and made my way to the stairs. "Is there business afoot, my lord?" inquired Pierre, following me into the chamber we had been supposed to share.

"Aye. And therefore must you take yourself and the chamber pot away until I send for you. On second thoughts, you had best bring the pot back when you have emptied it. But then conceal yourself at the end of the corridor and await my summons."

"You are not going to sleep, master?" the innocent fellow inquired.

"Not for a while, Pierre. And neither are you."

I then prepared to receive my visitor, unpacking our bags to take out the stake and the mallet, and the string of garlic we had purchased in Calais, and which I proceeded to drape around my neck, together with a silver cross. I drew my sword, sat in the one chair the room boasted, and laid it across my knees, and then waited. And sure enough, just on the hour after I had left the table, there came a quiet tap on my door.

"Enter," I commanded.

The door opened and the young woman stood there, her expression one of distaste. "What on earth is that terrible stench?" she inquired.

"It is garlic, madam," I said. "Are you not partial to garlic?"

"I enjoy it in my food," she acknowledged. "But I have never known it in a bedchamber."

"Then perhaps you should leave," I suggested.

In reply, she closed the door, but with her still on the inside. "I do believe you do not like me, Count," she remarked.

"I am a cautious man," I agreed.

She laughed. "Next thing you will be telling me you fear vampires."

I opened my mouth, and left it open, for at this moment she took off her tall hat and shook out her hair, which was of a most marvellous silky yellow, and lay straight past her shoulders. It is a fact that however beautiful a woman's face may be, it can only be enhanced by a framework of hair, and I was left quite speechless. "Am I allowed to sit?" she inquired.

I gathered my wits. "You may use the bed."

She cast me a glance, then seated herself; the springs creaked. "You are from the Queen?" she asked. Once again I was speechless for a moment. She seemed to take this as an affirmative reply. "You have arrived in the nick of time. But I do think I could have been informed of your coming. Had I not been in the crowd outside the Tower this morning, and heard your name, I would not have known you were involved at all."

"Madam," I said, once again trying to assemble my wits. "I am completely fogged. Of which queen are you speaking?"

She frowned at me. "You are not, Helier L'Eree, Count d'Albret, faithful servant of Her Majesty, Queen Henrietta Maria?"

"Ah," I said.

"Because if you are not . . ." she opened her reticule and produced a small but extremely dangerous looking pistol, which she proceeded to cock with considerable expertise, "you will have to die, here and now."

Her matter of fact way of speaking taken in conjunction with the very familiar way she was handling her weapon led me to believe that I would not be the first person she had shot. While the character of assassin went ill with her innocent face and big eyes, I had lived long enough to know that few women are as innocent as they appear to hapless males, and as for shooting people, it grows

40

easier with every occasion. "Do not let us be hasty," I suggested. "I am indeed Helier L'Eree, Count d'Albret." To my relief the pistol was lowered. "But I no longer work for Her Majesty." The pistol came up again. "I am now working for Her Majesty Queen Anne of France," I explained. "In my wallet over there are my letters patent as her personal ambassador."

"Do not move," she told me, and got up, to cross the room, open my wallet and examine my papers. Her effrontery would have been annoying in anyone less attractive. "And what is your purpose?" she asked.

"Why, to visit the Prince and Princess in the tower, and make sure they are being well looked after. The Queen of France is their aunt. Well, in-law and by marriage once removed."

"Her Majesty once warned me that you were a rogue, L'Eree," my odd visitor remarked. I understood that she was of course referring to Henrietta rather than her sister-in-law.

"Have we met?" I inquired.

"I have seen you from a distance. But I was but a young girl at the time. I doubt you noticed me."

"Ah," I said again, inhaling my garlic with a sense of relief as all my suspicions came flooding back.

"My name is Alicia Marney," she said, and paused, as if it should mean something to me. But I had never heard it before.

"I am pleased to make your acquaintance, Miss Marney . . . it *is* miss, is it not?"

"It is actually, Lady," she informed me.

"How nice. It is always a pleasure to converse with someone of equal rank."

She glared at me, and then gave a bright smile, once again seating herself upon my bed; she retained her pistol, which, if not actually pointing at me, was certainly going to discharge itself in my general direction, should she consider it necessary to pull the trigger. "Why, then,

41

Count," she said. "Shall we not also work together? We can be of mutual assistance."

"In what way."

"Well, you see," she said. "You are on a mission for the Queen Dowager of France. I am on a mission for the Queen Dowager of England. And these two queens are sisters-in-law. It is clearly the hand of fate that has cast us together so opportunely. So, I will help you to carry out your mission, and then you can help me to carry out mine."

"Your mission being?"

"You are here to ascertain that the Prince and Princess are in good health. Presumably you will be granted access to them. My problem has been how to *gain* access to them. But if I go as your companion there will be no difficulty. Do you agree?"

"So far. But what is your purpose?"

"Once we have been granted access to the children, and you have been suitably reassured, you can then help me remove them from the Tower to a place of greater safety." For the fourth time this evening this young lady had reduced me to speechlessness. "I do assure you," she said, "that Queen Anne would wish you to assist her sister-in-law in this matter."

"You have got to be stark, raving mad," I informed her.

She pouted, a pretty sight. "That is no way to address a lady, sir."

"Quite apart from the fact that Queen Anne and Queen Henrietta loathe each other, have you any idea how many guards there are in that Tower?"

"A hundred or so. But I have a plan." I raised my eyes to heaven: my entire life had drifted from catastrophe to disaster because of plans laid by ambitious women. "My friends will create a diversion," she explained. "And while this is going on, we shall escape with the children."

"May I ask how old you are, milady?"

"That is an extremely forward question, Count."

"I am an extremely forward man. Did the Queen not inform you of this also?"

"Well . . . I am twenty-three years old."

"Married?"

"I was married. My husband died fighting for the Cause."

"My heart bleeds for you. However, I happen to be approaching my fortieth birthday, and I am still alive. Therefore, you will see that I have become quite experienced. So believe me when I tell you that there is no possibility of your absurd scheme succeeding."

"Oh!" She pouted again, most attractively. "Well, I am very sorry about that, Count. I had hoped for your co-operation. As it is, I am sure you will understand that having told you our plans, I cannot possibly permit you to live." She raised her pistol.

"I take your point," I agreed. But I had anticipated our conversation reaching some such conclusion as this, and had allowed my hand to close on the hilt of my sword. Now, as she began to level her pistol, I acted with that speed which, taken in conjunction with my enormous size, is my greatest asset as a fighting man. Before she could even aim the firearm, I had stepped within reach and with a sweep of my weapon had struck the pistol from her hand.

When one is facing the possibility of immediate death it is seldom possible to treat one's antagonist with the courtesy and respect for his – or in this case her – health that one would wish. I had accepted that in order to save my life, I might have to do her a serious injury, even perhaps removing her hand. To my great relief this had not happened. The point of my sword had struck the pistol just in front of where her fingers were wrapped around its butt, and the force of the blow had been sufficient to dislodge it, leaving her with nothing more than a severe wrench. Nonetheless she gave a pretty little shriek as she fell back across the bed, and an even louder shriek when she discovered that I had joined her, straddling her thighs while I discarded my sword in favour of seizing her wrists to pin her to the mattress. "Help!" she bawled. "Rape!"

"You must not be impatient," I advised. "There are things to be done first. Excuse me a moment," and I released her to leave the bed and lock the door.

She sat up, breathing very heavily, which made her an even more attractive sight, while she blew away several strands of hair which had drifted across her face. "You are a monster," she remarked.

"So I have been told," I agreed, and sat beside her. "However, if you would think about it, you would realise that I have just saved your life, either by being shot or cut down by the Beefeaters, or by being hanged by order of Parliament."

"Beheaded," she argued. "They could not possibly hang a noblewoman."

"I doubt the actual method of execution would interest you greatly, except in passing," I pointed out.

"Yet must I carry out my instructions," she said. "Regardless of the risk."

"And I can imagine who gave you those instructions," I said. "Henrietta Maria. She has always been a trifle careless with other people's lives. So tell me, supposing your mad scheme worked, you say you intended to remove the Prince and Princess to a place of safety. I assume you mean where the Queen Mother is, in Holland. Had you given any thought as to how you were to get them there?" This question was not inspired by any backsliding upon my part as to the absurdity of her scheme, but simply to prolong our conversation. Sitting on a bed next to a beautiful woman with whom one has just been wrestling is a most pleasant pastime. However, her reply drove libidinous thoughts from my mind, at least for a few moments.

"I am not going to take them there," Alicia said. "I am going to take them to join their brother the King. In Scotland."

"Prince Charles is in Scotland?"

"The *King* is raising the entire Highlands before marching south. It is anticipated he will be in London by the spring."

There was devastating news, to be sure. But also confusing. "If the King is on his way to London," I inquired "why are you risking your pretty little neck to get the Prince and Princess out of the city? Can they not merely wait for his arrival?"

"Really, Count, the Queen did suggest that you were a man of some intelligence. Would Parliament not hold them as hostages as the King approached?"

"I see," I said. "I would still estimate that they, and you, would have a better chance of survival in the latter case. However . . ." I sighed "if you are bent on committing suicide, I do not suppose there is anything I can do to stop you. I do recommend, however, that you seize this opportunity to have a last tumble, and make us both very happy."

Alicia got off the bed. "The Queen also warned me that you are the most libidinous rascal who ever walked the face of this earth. Fie on you, sir, we are about a more serious matter than sexual satisfaction."

"Is there a more serious matter?" I asked, with genuine interest.

"Sir, you disgust me." She glanced at the pistol, lying against the far wall. "Am I allowed to retrieve my weapon?"

"Allow me to do it for you," I said, picking up my sword as I crossed the room, where I uncocked the pistol, emptied the powder on to the floor, and then removed the ball before handing it to her.

She gave what, had she not been a lady, I would have

45

described as a snort. "Do you suppose my people will let you leave this inn alive?"

"I do assure you, milady, that if they try to stop me, you will find yourself a little short of assistance tomorrow. However, it occurs to me that you and I may yet be able to come to an agreement." She raised her eyebrows to indicate that she could not herself conceive of the possibility. But I had been doing some thinking. The meaning of Richilde Bethlen's enigmatic statement was becoming clear to me. And if this woman was indeed the Queen's emissary, then she must know a great deal about the King's business. "You spoke of a diversion by your people while you and I abducted the Prince and Princess," I said. "If you have no objection, my man and I will create the diversion, while you and your people abduct the royal pair. How does that take you."

Her stare was most imperious. "May I ask what has brought about this change of mind?"

"Why, nothing, to be sure. I am merely offering such a partnership to you in return for some information."

"What information can I have that can possibly be of value to you?"

"I seek a man named Culhaven. I imagine he calls himself Lord Culhaven."

She frowned, and put the pistol into her reticule. "You know Lord Culhaven?"

"I do not think so. But I know of him, as he knows of me. I know that he is one of the King's agents in Scotland. We have some business together."

"I see," she said, thoughtfully, but also enigmatically. "Well, well." Which was more enigmatic yet. "Very good, Count. If you will assist me to get the Prince and Princess out of the Tower, I will personally escort you to his lordship. He rides with the King."

"Ah," I said. "Well, now, that would be most convenient."

"Then I shall bid you good night," she said. "I shall

46

call for you at eight o'clock tomorrow morning. Please be ready."

She really was a miss bossy-boots. However, I intended to have the last word. "There is just one formality before we can become partners," I told her.

"And what is that? Do you require money?"

"Not in the least. I require to examine you." It was her turn to be speechless. "So if you would just remove your clothing," I suggested.

She backed against the door. "Are you out of your mind?"

"So some do say," I acknowledged. "And therefore I am not a man to be crossed. Come along now, or I shall do it for you, and I may tear something. And please . . ." I held up my hand as she opened her mouth. "If you scream, I shall box your ears. A box on the ears from Helier L'Eree can do a permanent mischief."

She drew a long breath. "You intend to have your way with me? You would not dare. I am an emissary of the Queen."

I am too much of a gentleman for me to point out that I had actually all but had my way with the Queen as well. I decided instead to remind her of her situation. "This is a problem often encountered by young women who pay unaccompanied visits to men's bedrooms," I said. "As to whether I *shall* have my way with you depends upon what I find. I wish you to understand that I am undertaking this examination in no spirit of lewdity, but simply in order to ascertain that you are not a witch." This was of course not strictly true; her chances of escaping with nothing more than an examination were diminishing with every second that I looked at that heaving bosom.

"You think I am a witch?" This seemed to appall her even more than the idea of undressing before me.

"I sincerely hope you are not, but it is necessary that I find out."

"Are you then a witch-hunter?"

47

"I have some acquaintance with witch-hunting. Also with witches."

"You'll not prod me with a needle?" she requested.

"I would not dream of it. Besides, I do not have a needle. But if you do not hurry I will certainly prod you with something."

This forced her into action, as she apparently had not yet realised her danger. But her fate was now beyond recall, or at least, I supposed it was. In the course of my life I have been fortunate enough – although on more than one occasion it has been a *mis*fortune – to encounter many very beautiful women. Of them all, of course, Richilde Bethlen, Princess von Hohengraffen, was unexcelled. But then, she was not a woman, but a deathless demon cast up from hell no one could say how many eons before. Thus I may say without any reservation that Alicia Marney was the most beautiful *human* woman I had ever seen, although of course I still at that moment had some reservations about *her* humanity. But here was perfection. She was not tall, which made the splendid proportion of the body she was slowly uncovering for me the more magnificent. Her legs were long and beautifully shaped, her thighs slender. Her pubes was adorned with silky hair only fractionally darker than that on her head. This, when entirely loosed, was a golden cascade past her shoulders. Her belly was flat and her arms as perfectly shaped as her legs. Her buttocks were delicious curves, while her breasts were far larger than I had any right to expect. Her nipples were pink, and the evening being slightly chill, displayed to perfection.

I thought I might have waited all my life for this moment. And then reflected that I had had such thoughts before, and it had invariably led to my undoing. "Well?" she inquired.

She was no shrinking violet, that was certain. But her tendency to give orders and make demands was a problem I was sure could be coped with in the course of

48

time – after all, I had been coping with Marguerite for a very long time. "You must lie on the bed," I explained, needing to clear my throat before I could speak.

"Why?"

"Because I must examine you. For the witch's mark," I explained.

"But you promised not to use a needle."

"I shall not need a needle."

"You will surely not examine me while wrapped up in that evil-smelling mess."

"Why, not if it offends you," I agreed, and removed the string of garlic from around my neck. "But I would like you to touch it."

"You *do* think I am a vampire," she said, and took the string from my hand before throwing it on the floor. "Now, may I get dressed again?"

"There is still the possibility that you are a witch," I reminded her. "However, I feel sure that the examination will now be no more than a formality." She considered this, then crawled on to the bed. "Lie on your face," I commanded. This she did. I could not doubt that she was considering with great urgency how she might escape her predicament, but for the moment could clearly think of no solution. Her predicament was coming ever closer as I ran my hand over that velvet flesh, parted her buttocks to check between – often the site of the Devil's kiss and thus his mark – and stroked her legs. "You may turn over," I said.

She did so, staring at me, her beauty enhanced both by her expression and her heavy breathing. My examination had certainly not left her unmoved. But now once again it was necessary to scrutinise every inch of her flesh. It was the habit of Mr Hopkins, as I remembered too well, to probe and scratch any disturbance or even discolouration of the skin with his bodkin; a mole had always been a source of great pleasure to him. His habits had been of course both scurrilous and indecent, and decidedly

49

illegal. He sought a mark which, having presumably been implanted by the kiss of the Devil, would neither have feeling nor issue blood when pierced. As these marks are non-existent, even in the case of true witches – as I can avow from my own experiences – he had had recourse to a subterfuge worthy of the Devil himself. He would prick his first selection, as it were, severely, bringing forth both a scream of feeling and a gush of blood, and then hurry on to other parts of his victim's body, pricking away, until, at a moment carefully selected when he could tell that the unfortunate was both out of breath and no longer certain what part of her body was giving pain and what was not, he would return to his first choice. This would by now be virtually bloodless, his victim would be temporarily incapable of uttering a sound, and his witnesses – for he always insisted upon these – would be forced to agree that he had succeeded in his quest.

However, I very rapidly realised that even the foul Hopkins would have been forced to admit defeat when it came to the body of Alicia Marney. There was neither a mark nor a blemish upon than translucent white skin. And by the time I was finished, and kneeling between her legs – for it had been necessary to look into every nook and cranny to be sure – I was panting quite as heavily as she. "Well, Count," she said. "Are you satisfied?"

"Well, no, milady," I admitted. "I am satisfied that you are not a witch, but . . ."

"Then let me up. I am distinctly chilled, with nothing on."

"My dear woman," I argued, while unbuckling my belt, "If I do not have you now, I will likely suffer a mischief."

"Then send out for a whore," she recommended. "Now let me up."

"Do you suppose you can resist me?"

"I cannot prevent you raping me," she agreed, with total equanimity. "But I cannot believe you will do so."

50

"Whatever makes you think that?"

"Firstly because, although the Queen described you as a rogue, she also described you as a gentleman; secondly because I am betrothed to be married, and have sworn to remain chaste until the marriage has been consummated; thirdly because if you do rape me I will kill you if it is the last thing I ever do; and fourthly, if you rape me and I kill you, I shall never take you to Lord Culhaven, and your business, whatever it may be, will remain uncompleted."

Was ever a man more put upon? I would not like to swear, even now, which of her four reasons had the greater effect on my libidinity. It is a poor man who will not succumb to an appeal to his good manners. It is a vicious man who will use force to overcome a vow of chastity. It is a careless man who must ever be wondering when someone is going to stick a knife into his ribs. And finally, it is a poor businessman who will allow anything to come between him and the completion of his transaction. In any event, the matter was sealed by Alicia herself, who perceived that she had won the day, perhaps more conclusively than she had intended. "However," she said, "if all goes well in our enterprise, and I accomplish all of my goals, why, once I am safely wed, should you knock on my door, I may well allow you to enter."

Well, they say, a bird in the hand is worth two in the bush. But the thought of obtaining an embrace from Alicia Marney, willingly and perhaps even enthusiastically, was something worth waiting for. "I will call you early," she said again, wriggling out from beneath me and pulling on her shift.

I was awakened by Pierre knocking on the door. He, poor chap, had been forced to spend the entire night on the floor of the corridor, as he had fallen asleep before Alicia left, and I had been no longer in the mood for

51

company. "My lord," he said through the panelling in a loud whisper. "Are you all right?"

"I have never felt better," I assured him, being filled with enthusiasm for the task ahead, in the belief that every moment was now bringing me closer to my goal. "What I now require is water for washing, and breakfast for eating. Both in great quantities."

"Yes, my lord." He sounded doubtful. "Do you know what they eat for breakfast in these parts?"

"I would suggest bread, and eggs, and ale."

"Yes, my lord." His feet clumped on the stairs.

To my great delight, Alicia herself appeared shortly afterwards, and joined me for the meal, as chirpily cheerful as if we had never wrestled together, and as if we were not about to risk our lives. Within an hour we had washed ourselves, eaten, drunk and dressed, and were ready to take on the world. Which was just as well, because the world was apparently ready to take us on with equal enthusiasm. Alicia's companions had slept in various places about the inn, and were also waiting to set to. I will not bore you with their names, for none of them were of the least nobility, and, so far as I am aware, none of them had very much longer to live. But they, and we, did not know that as we sallied forth.

We had rediscussed our plans in the light of the night's events, and where before my only interest had been to save my own life I had now broadened this concept to saving Alicia's as well. This was not merely because the thought of such a gorgeous creature being cut down or strung up filled me with horror: she was my guide to this Lord Culhaven, the true object of my quest. I had therefore accepted the original idea, that she and I should gain entry to the Prince and Princess, and that her companions would start the riot which would hopefully occupy the Beefeaters while we made our escape with the royal siblings to where Pierre would be waiting with the horses. After my experiences of the previous day I had some hopes that a tumult, once commenced, would attract the interest of the mob as well, thus making our task the easier. It was a hare-brained scheme, and that *any* of us survived was simply because it never got off the ground. It was mid-morning when we again approached the Tower. Pierre had sidled off to one side with the horses, attracting some attention to be sure. Alicia's people had wandered off in the other direction, in a group. And Alicia and I approached the gate directly.

"By God," remarked the captain of the guard, the same impertinent fellow as yesterday. "I had not expected you to return, sir."

"But I always keep my word," I told him, stretching the truth slightly.

"Well, sir, I am going to keep mine," he declared. "I have a warrant for your arrest."

"Are you mad?" I inquired. "I travel under a French passport."

"It has been decided by my superiors that the fact you are now in the pay of France but increases your guilt as a deserter and an enemy of Commonwealth. You, mistress," he turned to Alicia. "You are his accomplice?"

Now was the moment for Alicia to declare that she knew nothing of me, relying on her beauty to distract the lout from the obvious fact that she *was* with me. However, this thought apparently never crossed the brave girl's mind. "His accomplice?" she demanded. "I am his wife, the Countess d'Albret."

He was not impressed. "Then you'll most likely hang beside him, my pretty," he remarked, and waved his arm. "Arrest them both."

It became obvious to me that our plan to gain access to the Tower was not going to succeed, and that we needed to concentrate upon getting out again. In this regard we had a slight advantage, as we were not yet *in*. I therefore seized the moment while the captain was waving his men forward to pick him up by arm and thigh, move forward myself, and throw him on to their advancing pikes. These they lowered in time to prevent the murder of their commander, but they were certainly checked. The crowd were greatly amused by this, and cheered loudly, but when I grasped Alicia's arm and pulled her in the direction of the horses, they became confused, some being for letting us through and others for stopping us. I drew my sword, and this persuaded most of them in our favour, for a man who measures six feet six inches tall armed with a weapon not greatly smaller and which he is clearly prepared to use, is a fearsome sight.

However, one man is severely handicapped when confronting a mob, especially when he has a woman hanging on his arm. I am not at all sure we would have escaped with our lives had not Alicia's companions realised that it was time for them to earn their keep. There now began a tremendous ruckus on the far side of the gate, punctuated by shouts of "Fight! Fight!" This interested the mob, who moved in that direction, thereby impeding the Beefeaters who were trying to force their way towards us. I was thus enabled to lift Alicia from the ground, throw her over my shoulder like a sack of coal, and in a few strides reach Pierre and the horses. We mounted, Alicia, somewhat winded, having to ride astride as in our haste she had got on the wrong saddle, and a moment later were galloping up the street, scattering the people who were hurrying to the scene of the tumult. I did not draw rein until I felt we were clear of pursuit. By then my conscience was troubling me. "What of your people?" I asked.

"They will probably be fined or put in the pillory for a night," she said. "There is no way they can be connected to us. But we have failed in our mission. We will never gain access to the Tower now."

"Then the Prince and Princess will *have* to await the coming of their brother," I said. "And it is he we must find, just as rapidly as possible."

She did not object to this.

54

It was necessary to proceed with both haste and caution. Caution was necessary because of course, while there remained a goodly number of Royalists, the fact was that the country was under the rule of the Parliament, and that we were fugitives. Haste was required to keep us ahead of any pursuers. But from my point of view, I being somewhat more experienced in these matters than either Pierre or our delightful travelling companion, it was also necessary in order that we might reach Scotland, and hopefully join up with the young King, before he was utterly shattered by Cromwell. I had little doubt that this was the likely outcome of a battle between the two forces.

Indeed, what Alicia had to tell me about events in that wild country thus far filled me with even greater foreboding. As I have recounted, Cromwell had returned from his Irish campaign in May of this year of 1650, and had immediately set off for Scotland. By then, events north of the border had already taken a turn for the worse, with the demise of the Marquis of Montrose. This man, famed in song as well as battle, was probably the most able of the Scottish generals – certainly he was the most charismatic. He had brought a mercenary force over from France in the spring, and declared for the King. This was entirely acceptable to the Scots, but being an even more pig-headed people than the English when it came to religious matters, they had been determined that their king should adhere to the Covenant which bound the Scots to uphold Presbyterianism. This commitment Montrose had refused to make, as he was not a Covenanter himself, with the result that Scot had fought Scot, Montrose had been defeated at Carbiesdale, and then captured and executed. A sad loss.

This had been at the end of April. Since then Prince Charles, or I suppose we should start calling him King Charles II, had met with the Scottish ambassadors, and pronounced himself willing to adhere to the Covenant. This might be considered a gross betrayal of the gallant Montrose, but young Charles was only ever interested in reaching the throne, and to that end would promise anyone anything and accept any implied restriction on his activities – even less than his unlamented father he was not given to such plebian behaviour as keeping his word. His acceptance of the Scottish terms had thus led him to Scotland.

Three months later Cromwell had crossed the border with an army of sixteen thousand men, for he was as determined to stamp out Presbyterianism in Scotland as he had been to stamp out Roman Catholicism in Ireland; it is doubtful that he knew Charles was in the country. Not being a religious man myself – the circumstances of my life, beginning with being born the son of a convicted witch, had been against my chances of becoming a sincere Christian, of whatever persuasion – I hope I can be excused the feeling that when Jesus Christ first preached the love of God for mankind, and hopefully, the love of mankind for each other, He would have been appalled had He known that for the rest of history these loving men would spend their time slaughtering each other in the name of whichever interpretation of His teaching they happened to believe correct.

Be that as it may, Cromwell had invaded Scotland, and the Scots had determined to stop him. To this end they had assembled a formidable army of twenty-six thousand men, commanded by no less a soldier than the Earl of Leslie. Leslie had a great reputation as a general, simply by reason of having served with the immortal Gustavus Adolphus in the Thirty Years War which had so recently been concluded. I had also learned my soldiering under Gustavus, but I had no more than a nodding acquaintance with Leslie, as even in those far-off days he had been a general, while I had never risen above the rank of captain in the Swedish army. But there you have the problem; the days when we had served with Gustavus were indeed far-off, nearly twenty years to be exact. And Leslie, a senior soldier even then, was now virtually in his dotage. Thus almost at our first stop out of London we were assailed by a ringing of the bells and cheering villagers, to inform us that there had been a great battle, at Dunbar, and that the Scots had been utterly routed. This was serious news. The question at issue was whether Charles would now change his plans, and return to Holland. From Alicia's point of view, that meant she had nowhere to go, except back to Holland herself, to the arms of her anxious fiancé; at least, I hoped he was anxious, in view of the dangers to which she was exposing herself. From my point of view, what did it mean with regard to Lord Culhaven? But Richilde's letter had stated quite definitely that he was to be found in Scotland, and this charming lady had confirmed his whereabouts. But how to find him if he was no longer with the King?

"This whole business needs consideration," Alicia said. "Fortunately, I know just the place for us to lie low for awhile until we obtain some more information and can make a decision."

"And where might such a place be?" I inquired, deciding against telling her that my decision was already made: I had to continue to Scotland, regardless of what might be happening there, as only there would I find Lord Culhaven. And Alicia had to accompany me, as she knew where his lordship was to be found.

"Why, Marney Hall, of course. It lies but a few score miles west of here.

"Marney Hall?"

"My husband's seat. Well, I suppose it is my seat now. But I have not seen it for a long time. Dear Nicholas and I were married in 1642, you see, but had only a week together, then off he went to the wars. Well, I remained at the hall for the next year, then it was attacked by Roundheads. I made my escape, and finally reached the

Queen in Holland. By then I had learned that I was a widow. And destitute, save for Her Majesty's charity. By all accounts, the hall was fired by the Roundheads."

"I have seen them at work," I muttered. "But . . ." I was totally confused and somewhat piqued. "Was this marriage consummated?"

"You do ask the most impertinent questions," she pointed out. "Of course it was consummated."

"Then you are not a virgin. And yet you resisted me the other night."

"Do you suppose that one has to be a virgin to take a vow of chastity?" she demanded.

I must confess I had never considered the matter. I felt I had been duped, and in every possible way. "If you were married eight years ago, then you were only fifteen."

"Why, yes," she agreed. "Was that not a good age to be married?"

As Marguerite le Gron had been no older when I had carried her off from Guernsey, I was in no position to argue this point, although to be sure our relationship had not been consummated for a considerable time after that. I was interested, however, to learn that my charmer had adventured on a scale only inferior to my own. I made a mental note to draw from her some more of her experiences, after we had discovered what shelter, if any, we could obtain from the ruin of her late husband's home. And at which time I intended to re-open the question of our relations.

"As we are in these parts," she told me, as we rode in a north-westerly direction, "I am most interested to discover if my father-in-law survived, as I was forced to abandon him when I fled. It was a choice of that or rape, at the very least. I would have taken him with me, but he refused to abandon his home. I do hope he died well."

The trouble with so many women is that they are always

willing to commit any mischief to avoid rape, or so they say; those prepared to die before dishonour are really a little thin on the ground. But they do exist, as this delightful creature had proved to me. However, further conversation was ended as we walked our horses up a shallow rise and looked down into the valley beyond, and the manor house. I scratched my head. "You said it had been burned, milady?"

"Well, what a remarkable thing," Alicia commented.

For the building stood solidly and foursquare, its roof intact, and a wisp of smoke arising from one of its chimney pots. About it the gardens were in order, and so appeared the farm in the distance, where some cattle could be seen grazing in a pasture, while there were horses in a corral closer to hand.

"What do you wish to do?" I asked. Obviously someone was living in the house, and doing so very prosperously. "Do you suppose it has been given to some Roundhead general?"

"That we must find out," she said, and kicked her horse forward.

The three of us descended the hill, and came across some men harvesting apples from an orchard situated beside the road. It should be recalled that Alicia was still dressed as a Puritan lady, and if my clothes were somewhat more gaudy, I was clearly a gentleman. These fellows therefore touched their hats. "What estate is this?" I inquired.

"It is the Marney estate, your worship," one of them said. At least we seemed to be in the right place.

We walked our horses up the drive to the house, and there dismounted. The door was already open, and a butler stood there.

"Do you know this man?" I asked Alicia in a low voice.

"I have never seen him before in my life," she said.

It was equally obvious that he had never seen her,

either. "Your business?" he demanded, in a rather cursory manner.

"My business, sir, is your business," Alicia snapped, mounting the steps. "What is your name?"

"Why, madam, my name is my own business," the lout declared. "It is your name that matters."

"Shall I deal with this fellow, milady?" I inquired, feeling distinctly incensed.

"Possibly. Stand aside fellow," she commanded. "I am Lady Alicia Marney."

"Begone with you," he said. "We'll have no itinerants here."

"By God," I said, my hand dropping to my sword hilt. Alicia's cheeks were pink, and I have no doubt she would have given the go ahead for a fracas had we not been arrested by a female voice, issuing from the interior of the house.

"What seems to be the problem, Roundtree?"

"Why, milady," the butler said. "There is a woman here who claims to be you."

CHAPTER 3

This sort of uncertainty can be very upsetting when one has been invited to a friend's home. I am afraid I looked at Alicia somewhat askance, but as was her wont, she looked not the least embarrassed, merely extremely annoyed. "Who is that?" she demanded of the butler, Roundtree.

"Well, madam . . ."

"Oh, let her in," the lady said.

The door was opened, and Alicia entered, myself following. Pierre had remained with the horses, but as he was now surrounded by several grooms I did not suppose he was going to be of much assistance should Alicia decide to provoke a fracas, which I felt she was quite capable of doing. Indeed, I sought to end the coming quarrel before it began by muttering in her ear, "Perhaps it would be better to seek lodgings elsewhere, milady, and conduct an investigation into this matter from afar."

"Nonsense," she declared. "This is my house, and this . . . who the devil are you?" she demanded of the residential chatelaine, who awaited us in the centre of the hall.

"Lady Alicia Marney," the woman declared.

They goggled at each other, and I goggled at them both. There could not possibly have been a stronger contrast between two women, for where Alicia Number One – as I had to consider her – was somewhat small and fair and yellow-haired, Alicia Number Two was tall and if her skin was very white her hair was black as midnight. Her features were too bold to be accounted pretty, or even very attractive, but as *she* was not wearing Puritan garb but instead a gown which would have been well received at the French court, which is to say that it sported a décolletage which all but revealed her navel, I could determine that there was nothing the matter with her figure. "You are an imposter, madam," Alicia One declared. "I will give you fifteen minutes to leave my house."

"Ha," Alicia Two commented. "On the contrary, madam, I am not going to permit you to leave this house at all, until we get to the bottom of this. Or that great lout."

Her last remark could be taken in either of two ways. Supposing she meant that I also was a prisoner, my hand dropped to my sword hilt, but then I heard a series of clicks, and realised that what I had feared had come to pass. We were in the house which, rightfully or not, was in the possession of the black-haired Alicia, and we were surrounded by her people. Quite literally, for when I turned my head I discovered there were six footmen in the hall, each armed with a pistol. "I warn you, madam," I said, with more aplomb than I actually felt, "to consider carefully what you do, before you do it. I am the Count d'Albret." I paused at this juncture, but as my name appeared to make no impression whatsoever on her, I added, "Personal ambassador for the Queen Dowager of France."

"Ha," she commented again.

"My credentials," I said, taking them from my wallet.

She came forward to scrutinise them. Alicia One was meanwhile becoming more and more impatient as well as irritated. "Who the devil *are* you?" she demanded again. "You!" She pointed at Roundtree. "Who is this woman? And who are you, come to think of it. I do not recall your face."

Roundtree looked at his mistress, who had finished reading my papers. "I would tell her, Roundtree," Alicia Two said.

"This is the Lady Alicia Marney, madam," Roundtree said. "And I am her butler. It is not surprising that you do not recall my face, because I have never seen you before in my life."

Having thus been returned to square one, as it were, Alicia One looked on the verge of an explosion.

"Count d'Albret," Alicia Two mused. "And what brings you so far into the centre of England, milord?"

"Well, to say truth, we are on our way to join King Charles in Scotland," I explained. Alicia One stamped her foot in dismay.

"I see," said Alicia Two. "You mean that your Queen Dowager has sent you as her ambassador to King Charles?"

"In a manner of speaking, yes," I agreed.

Alicia One stamped her foot again, this time in despair. "God save me from fools," she cried.

I felt this was being unnecessarily brusque, but Alicia Two appeared to agree with her namesake. "He does seem a rather oafish fellow," she agreed. "Well, Count, I doubt you will have any further use for this document." Saying which she tore it in two pieces and threw it on the floor. I was so utterly taken aback by this cavalier treatment of the Queen's warrant that I was momentarily speechless. "I also do not think that you will have any further use for your sword, Count," Alicia Two said. "Would you kindly remove it?"

"If you do that, you are a dead man," Alicia One snapped.

"If he does not do it he will be an even deader man," Alicia Two pointed out.

I decided that hers was probably the more accurate prognostication, in view of the array of pistols directed at my back. I hated being separated from my sword, which I had made into the most feared weapon in Europe. But of that fact this woman was clearly unaware, and in my years of derring-do I had discovered that it is always better to surrender, when there is a prospect of being able to resume hostilities in a more favourable climate, than needlessly to die in defence of a principal. Equally, of course, this woman would be quite unaware that I could be quite as deadly *without* a sword, when given the opportunity. Thus I lifted my baldric over my head, and Roundtree hurried forward to relieve me of it.

"Thank you," Alicia Two said. "Roundtree, put that in a safe place. Then I wish you to send a messenger to Captain Ferrers, who commands the garrison in Leicester, and inform him that I have gained possession of two Royalist spies, who are in urgent need of hanging. I should be obliged if he would come and collect them, as soon as is convenient." Roundtree hurried from the hall. "Now," Alicia Two said, "come in and sit down and we will discuss the situation. In there."

She appeared totally in command. Well, so she was, with six armed footmen at my back. However, we were still a good way from Leicester, and I could not see the Roundheads arriving much before the next morning, so I reckoned we had some time to consider our position, and even make some plans. My biggest fear was that Alicia One might decide to take what might be termed executive action on her own – so far as I knew she still had her pistol in her reticule, which no one had thought to remove as yet. However, for the moment she also seemed prepared to wait, contenting herself with remarking, as she accompanied me into the reception room, "You have ruined us, you great lout."

"On the contrary, milady, if we are ruined, it was your doing for bringing us here in the first place." She gave one of her snorts.

"You may sit down," Alicia Two said kindly. I cast a glance over my shoulder, but the six footmen were still with us. So I sat down on a settee, and gestured

64

Alicia One to sit beside me. This she did, after a brief hesitation. Alicia Two sat opposite us. "So you are Lady Alicia Marney" she said. "How quaint."

Alicia One stared at her in amazement. "You mean you admit you know who I am?"

"Well," Alicia Two said. "I am prepared to believe you, as I can see no reason for you to claim the name if it is not your own. Besides, you resemble a portrait which used to hang over the fireplace."

Our heads turned together, and Alicia Two smiled. "Oh, I had it burned. I could not possibly live with you overseeing my every move, milady. However, I have always felt that you and I would meet, one day."

"Then who are you?" Alicia One inquired for the third time, and clearly still keeping her temper under control with a great effort.

"I am your husband's widow," Alicia Two explained.

"My husband's . . .?"

"You see, milady," Alicia Two said, "your flight was a trifle precipitate."

"My husband was killed . . ."

"He was *reported* killed, my lady, and on receipt of that report, you fled the country." She shook her head. "A true wife would have at least remained here long enough to receive her husband's body, and give him a Christian burial." Alicia One bit her lip. "However," Alicia Two went on, "you chose not to do this. As it happens, your husband was not killed. He was brought back here, grievously wounded, and it was my pleasure, as well as my duty, to nurse him back to health."

"Your duty? Where did you spring from?"

"My name is Abigail Smith, milady, and I am the daughter of Parson Smith, of the next parish."

"Smith!" Alicia snapped.

"Of the next parish. What would you? Sir Nicholas was badly wounded, and there were no women left in the house. As I say, I considered it my duty. And of course, there was old Sir Nicholas to be cared for as well; he was quite distraught at the injury done to his son, and the manner in which his daughter-in-law had abandoned him. I found both the gentlemen very pleasant company, so much so that they soon gave me the run of the place. I became their housekeeper. It was then that I decided to get rid of those of your people who had remained, and replace them with people I could trust. In any event, your people were all staunch supporters of the King, and I could not possibly continue to employ them. I am a sworn supporter of Parliament, and loathe and abhor the King, and all he stands for."

"You bitch!" Alicia commented.

"I am a possessive bitch, milady. But I kept your husband alive for several months, during which we received a report of your death."

"That is not possible. I am alive."

"Temporarily," Abigail assured her. "Who can say whence such reports arrive? Those were troubled times, milady."

"You mean you invented the report!"

"Sir Nicholas certainly believed it. And it was never denied. So we considered it best that he and I should marry, in order to regularise my presence in the house. It would not do for a parson's daughter to be accused of fornication."

"Bigamist!"

"We also decided," Abigail continued, with perfect composure, "that I should adopt your name, again in order to avoid gossip. In those troubled times, milady, nobody knew the truth of anything, and that Sir Nicholas again had a wife named Alicia seemed to satisfy everyone. Especially the Roundheads, with whom I made our peace. Thus I have enjoyed being Lady Marney now for nigh on seven years. My husband, or should I say *our* husband, sadly died six years ago. But then, he had served his purpose, would you not agree?"

"You killed him?"

"He had never fully recovered from his wounds, alas. When the pain became too great . . . well, he was happier dead."

"And his father?"

"Sadly, the death of his son proved too much for his frail health and great age. He ran quite out of breath."

Alicia bounced to her feet, and faced the footmen. "You can stand there, and listen to this tale, of lies and lechery, bigamy and murder?"

They gazed at her, impassively.

"My people are dependent upon me for their livelihoods, milady," Abigail explained.

"And do you not suppose I shall tell the truth to this Roundhead captain, when he arrives?" Alicia inquired.

I sighed. I might have been guilty of revealing our plans to our captor, but Alicia was now putting her in the way of a very great temptation. To which she obviously intended to succumb. "The question you should ask yourself, milady," Abigail suggested, "is whether *you* will be here when he arrives. I am sure you would choose to escape, were it possible. Sadly, so many people think they can escape imprisonment when it is *not* possible. Still, we must make it look right for the good captain. Jonathan, take milady upstairs and lock her in the Blue Room until I have found some proper clothing for an escaping spy to wear. And Jonathan, if she attempts to resist you, you have my permission to have your way with her. There is no need to be gentle about it."

Alicia gave her a glare which should have shrivelled her ovaries. "You . . ."

"Bitch was the word you chose, milady. Be a good girl and go with Jonathan, else I shall have him discipline you here, in front of all of us. I am sure you would find that most humiliating."

Alicia turned her gaze on me, and I gave her what I hoped was a reassuring smile. When she stood up, I did

67

also, but Abigail waved her arm. "Not you, Count. I wish to speak with you, privately." I sat down again, and we watched Alicia leave, most reluctantly, impelled on her way by the foul Jonathan, who was looking most anticipatory. "Now tell me, Count . . . are you really a count?"

"Of course I am. But you are not really a lady."

She frowned at me, and decided to take it as a jest. "What do you do with Lady Marney?"

"We are travelling companions, as I told you. We both seek the King."

"That is not true, Count. I cannot believe a lady like Alicia Marney would willingly travel in the company of a man, without even a maidservant."

"Ah," I explained. "Our travelling arrangements were forced upon us by circumstances."

"You mean you are fugitives. I suspected this from the beginning. Well, remember that a squadron of Ironsides will soon be on its way here, and will place you under arrest. There can be only one end to that game: the noose."

"I shudder to contemplate it," I assured her. "But are you not going to shoot me first, with Lady Marney, escaping?"

"I think that would be rather a waste," she remarked. "Would you not rather live, and prosper?"

I decided against telling her that I was already prospering very well on my estate in Normandy. My business was to arrange matters so that I regained that contented existence. "Who would not?" I asked. "What must I do?"

"Please me," she suggested, without even a flush. I sighed. But there it is. Few women have been able to pass me by, even if it has been their intention to do me a mischief. "In the first instance," she went on, "by telling me your mission. I want the truth, mind."

"And you shall have it," I agreed. "Lady Marney and I were sent to kidnap the young Prince and Princess from

68

the Tower and convey them to their brother in Scotland."
I could see nothing wrong in telling her that piece of truth,
as sadly, I felt obliged to do *her* a mischief just as soon as
it became profitable.

"Kidnap the Prince and Princess from the Tower?
There is a hare-brained scheme."

"Absolutely. It failed, and we were lucky to escape
with our lives. Thus we determined that our only course
was to seek the King ourselves as rapidly as possible. Unfortunately, Lady Marney, finding herself in this
neighbourhood, decided to pay her old home a visit."

"Unfortunate indeed, for her. But most fortunate for
me, as I shall now be rid of the last person who could
possibly denounce me. Except for you, of course. But I
wonder if, with dear Alicia truly dead, your denunciation
would carry any weight? After all, you are a foreigner
. . . you *are* French?"

"As a matter of fact, no, Miss Abigail. I am a
Garneseyman."

"Garnesey!" she cried. "Good heavens. I had an uncle
who lived in Garnesey. My mother's sister's husband. He
was rector of Torteval Parish."

"Not Master Grimalle?" I cried in turn.

"That is the very man. You will not claim that you
know him?"

"Why, he brought me up, after my mother had died
. . . somewhat suddenly." I did not think this woman
should know that I was the son of a witch. "And you
mean that Mistress Grimalle was your aunt?"

"Indeed. And you say she brought you up as her own?
Why, what a small world it is, to be sure."

"Yes," I agreed, my resolution hardening with every
second. For the truth of the matter was that although
Mistress Grimalle had indeed had charge of my upbring-
ing, it had certainly not been as her own. Through the
dozen years I had lived in her house she had treated me
as a servant and worse, and it had been her incessant

lambastings, delivered with either a broom handle or
her tongue, that had finally driven me to abscond, and
launch myself upon that ocean of adventure which has
been my life.

Now, although that life has had its share of both
triumphs and tragedies, it is not an experience I would
have missed. It has brought me both wealth and the
intimate acquaintance of some of the most lovely women
of my time, and therefore it may be felt that I should
acknowledge a debt of gratitude to Mistress Grimalle.
Without her inadvertent urging I might still have been
digging graves in the Torteval cemetery. But when I had
fled I had been aware only of a deep-seated resentment
towards the creature, and this resentment had become
more and more deep-seated whenever my life had taken a
downwards spiral, which had been often enough. I would
not say that I hated the woman; we only truly hate those
we fear, and thus my strongest emotions were directed
towards the Witch of Hohengraffen. But I most certainly
disliked her intensely. It was no difficult matter to decide
that I disliked her niece in equal proportion.

"Why," I said, "that makes us almost first cousins."

"But not truly so," Abigail pointed out, clearly not
wishing to allow any considerations of incest to interfere
with what she anticipated might be an enjoyable night.
"There is no blood between us."

"To be sure," I agreed. "But there are some politics."

"Nothing that cannot be sorted out amicably, I am sure.
You are a Garneseyman. Did not Garnesey declare for
Parliament?"

"So I believe. I was not there at the time."

"But I would say you have no strong adherence to
the monarchy. Come now, Count: you are a mercenary.
Admit it."

"I will admit that I like to be paid for what I do," I
conceded.

"Quite. Now, I could do with a steward here on

70

Marney, a man with a strong right arm and a knowledge of business. Am I not looking at such a man?" She went on as I did not argue. "The pay would be handsome, and of course there would be fringe benefits." She gave what I presume she imagined to be a coy smile. "Or even permanent ones, if I find you suitable."

The problem with people born and brought up in the country parishes is that their horizons are limited. Did this beldam seriously suppose that she could offer me anything worth one-tenth of my French estates? Or that she could hope to match the favour of a Queen – or perhaps, more correctly, that her *dis*favour could possibly be as unpleasant as that of a Queen? But there were still those six confounded pistols, and the villain Roundtree had removed my sword. Besides, I was both hungry and thirsty, and there was Alicia to be rescued. "I shall certainly put your offer under consideration, Mistress Marney," I said.

"Excellent. Shall we dine?"

"There remains the matter of the Roundhead cavalry," I said, as we delved into our rabbit stew. "Will they not be here tomorrow morning?"

"Not before noon, to be sure," she promised me.

"By which time Lady Marney will be dead."

"Absolutely. Well, she will only be a nuisance if she is still alive."

"Oh, quite. However, will they not be interested in me?"

"I am sure they will. But if I tell them you are my steward, and that the other villain mentioned in my message has escaped, they will be content. Of course, if you are *not* my steward, you will have to be the other villain. They are very heavy on Cavaliers in this part of the country."

"As they should be," I agreed. "However, my mind is already made up. I should very much like to be your steward, for a season." I am not a man for telling lies,

71

except where unavoidable, and the length of a season is surely open to individual interpretation.

"Then I am pleased," she said, and raised her goblet to me. "Most pleased."

I raised mine in turn. "It is my pleasure, mistress. Now there are two things I would ask of you."

"Yes?"

"Firstly, the whereabouts and health of my servant, Pierre."

"The French lout? My people are entertaining him."

"He is not hurt?"

"I should not think so. He seems a simple soul. You had another question?"

"It is more a request. How do you intend to dispose of Lady Marney?"

"Well, I suppose it would be most appropriate to shoot her in the back. That is what normally happens to people trying to escape."

"Unfortunately, it is not conclusive. I have known fellows live for years with a bullet in the back. I assume she is in an upper chamber?"

"The very uppermost."

"Then surely it would be most convenient for her to fall from her window, while attempting to reach the leads. Your house is four stories high. She would certainly break her neck falling from such a height."

"Why, that is a capital idea," Abigail cried. And then frowned. "I had supposed she was a friend of yours."

"Heaven forbid," I protested. "If she were a friend, could I thus agree to her death? No, no, she was placed in command of this venture by the Queen Mother," I did not consider it necessary to specify which Queen Mother I had in mind, "and has treated me like dirt since its commencement. Me! A count! Treated like dirt?" I am no mean Thespian myself when pushed.

"My dear Count, my heart bleeds for you. By the way, do you have a Christian name?"

72

"Helier."

"Helier. How quaint. Very well, Helier, we shall throw her from her window. If she does not die the first time, well, we can always take her up and throw her out again. It will be most exciting sport."

"Absolutely," I agreed enthusiastically. "However, there is a request I would make before we actually start throwing."

"Another one?"

"I have not actually requested anything yet," I pointed out. "Only recommended."

"Well, then, request."

"That I should have the privilege of doing the throwing."

"You must hate this woman very much."

"I do," I said fervently. "I do. You have no idea how badly she has treated me."

"Very well, then, you may do the throwing."

"And, ah . . . before then . . ."

"Helier," Abigail said severely. "You lust after this woman."

"Well," I protested. "She is quite attractive, would you not say? And I am a randy fellow. I confess it freely. And if she is going to die anyway . . ."

Abigail lacked the wit to realise I was actually speaking of her. "You are a sinner and a fornicator," she said, more severely yet. I hung my head in shame. "I should chastise you," Abigail said. How like her aunt she was, to be sure. "Indeed," she announced. "I shall."

I raised my eyebrows. She was certainly in no condition to go on eating, from the quality of her breathing or the rich colour in her cheeks. Indeed, had she clearly not been both young and healthy, I would have said she was close to a seizure. "Right now," she said. "You will accompany me to my chamber." She rose, signalling her ever present footmen as she did so.

"Dear Abigail," I said, "nothing would give me greater

73

pleasure than to be chastised by you. But surely not before these louts? How could I ever be your steward and command authority over them once they have seen me so put upon?"

"Hm," she said. "Dickon, you will keep your men in the corridor, but be sure you attend me on the instant should I cry out."

"Immediately, mistress," Dickon said.

From here on it was necessary to play by ear, as it were. My first disappointment was the impression that Abigail's bedchamber, although most luxuriously appointed – and gaining in splendour, so far as I was concerned, from having no doubt been Alicia's bedchamber some years before – was entirely lacking in weapons of any sort. However, it is an ill wind that blows no good, as they say. I duly dropped my breeches, as commanded by my mistress, who laid on with a stinging cane on several occasions, before she dropped her weapon in turn and threw both arms round my thighs to bury her face in my nether regions, having turned me round as she did so to gain possession of the object she had really been seeking from the beginning.

With my bottom smarting, it was the greatest temptation to strangle her there and then, but truth to tell her activities were not altogether distasteful, and I submitted to them, until she released me, leapt to her feet, bared her breasts with a violent tug on her bodice which did the material no good at all, and cried "Take me, Helier! Take me! I am thine!"

Well, what would you? It may be considered a most ungentlemanly act for me to tumble a lady upon whose execution I had resolved, but making her totally pleased with me, and therefore trusting in me, was a necessary part of my plan. Besides, she had confessed to the most black-hearted villainy, including the murder of her husband and father-in-law, and she certainly intended the murder of Alicia. In fact, I was doing her a great kindness by allowing her one last happy memory of life on earth. I did hesitate for a moment, but that was to ascertain that her shriek was not going to bring her six footmen, with their pistols, into our midst. However, they did not appear, leading me to believe that she had used those words and that tone before to some other happy fellow, and so I fell to.

Abigail was quite consumed with passion. I swear I could have done anything to her and she would not have protested; I suspect she had been a long time without, or certainly without anyone of my stature. And I will confess that when I had stripped her of her clothing, quite ruining it in the process, and was kneeling between her handsome legs while she, eyes tight closed, gave herself over to paroxysm after paroxysm of pleasure, it was again a great temptation to wrap my hands round her throat and end the matter there and then. However, there were still the six pistols in the corridor, and I still did not know where Alicia was incarcerated, or where my sword was concealed.

Abigail's eyes opened. "Helier, that was magnificent," she said. "I can see that you are going to be of great value to me in the management of my estate, not to mention my personal affairs. Now tell me true, do you still think you can ram her ladyship before we dispose of her?"

"I would certainly like to try. Ramming her is a dream I have long considered."

She gave me a tweak, which caused me no great discomfort as for the moment I was very loose. "You are a rogue," she declared. "An utter rogue. But it will be sport watching you try. Will she squeal, do you suppose?"

"Undoubtedly," I agreed. "Shall we set about it?"

Abigail got out of bed, and, a brief inspection of her clothing revealing that she would need a seamstress before any of her garments would again be wearable, she settled for an undressing robe. "For when you have had your way with her ladyship," she told me, "I shall expect you to retire with me. So that," she added as she watched me pull on my breeches, "there is absolutely no necessity for you to dress yourself any more completely than that. Especially in view of your next appointment."

"A man should always be fully and properly dressed," I told her. "Even if he is going to his own hanging." I opened the door. "Do we really need these fellows dogging our every footstep?"

"Can I really trust you, Helier, dear Helier?"

"To the death," I promised her, sticking to my policy of absolute truthfulness.

She thus dismissed the footmen, and then proceeded to rummage in a wardrobe which, surprisingly, still contained her husband's clothes. "He was a small fellow," she explained. "And thus his clothes will fit milady. It will be rather amusing, do you not think, for her to die in her husband's clothes?"

"Very droll," I agreed, and tucked a pair of boots and some hose under my arm, while Abigail selected drawers and breeches and shirt.

"I don't think we need bother about vest or coat," she said. "She is unlikely to feel cold where she is going."

Thus laden, we ascended the stairs to the uppermost floor, me wearing only my breeches. Abigail opened the door of one of the garret chambers, and blinked in the candlelight, for it was now quite late and dark outside. I was distressed by what I saw, for it appeared that Alicia had indeed determined that her only salvation lay in herself. She had thus, at some stage while I was occupied with Abigail, produced her pistol with the intention, no doubt, of overawing the fellow Jonathan. But he had clearly been too quick for her, and had taken his mistress's admonition to heart. The pistol lay on the dressing table, unfired I estimated as there was an absence of any burnt powder smell.

Alicia lay in a bundle on the bed, quite naked, with

several bruises evident on that pale skin. This naturally caused me to place Jonathan in the same class as his mistress, especially when I considered that he had forced his way where I had been barred. "The woman was armed, milady," he now explained. "But I saw to it."

"And gave her a sound tossing, eh?" Abigail said. "Good fellow. Now come along, milady. Here is another forceful fellow eager to breach your defences."

Alicia had not stirred at our entry, being it seemed anxious to shut herself off from this suddenly obnoxious world in which she found herself, but this threat caused her to raise her head. When she discovered it was me, she lowered it again to the pillow, without a sound. I could hardly regard this as a compliment, but reflected that she must be feeling pretty fed-up with life, while not actually being fed-up at all, for there was no evidence that she had been offered anything to eat during the several hours that Abigail and I had been chatting, and dining, and tumbling. "She treats you with contempt, Helier," Abigail remarked. "So do you set to."

"In a moment," I said. "First, let us take a look at this drop."

"Very well," she agreed. "Open the window, Jonathan."

The villain obeyed. In truth, the aperture was not very large, and I had some difficulty in getting my shoulders through, but when I succeeded I could see that it was a good forty feet to the cobbled yard below. Much of course would depend on how anyone falling from this height landed, but I had no doubt that she would be terribly shook up, while if she were to land on her head the matter would be beyond dispute. "What do you reckon?" I asked Abigail, as I pulled myself back into the chamber.

She obligingly inserted her own shoulders into the window and leaned out. "I would say that is far enough," she said.

"I still think we should test the drop," I said, and

gathered up her ankles into my arms, thus lifting her entire body from the floor. She gave a little shriek, more of surprise than alarm, which became a much louder shriek – entirely of alarm – as I thrust her legs forward. She shot out of the window, her cry wailing on the wind. Then it was silenced; even from our height we heard the *crump* as she struck bottom.

My action certainly stirred both Jonathan and Alicia. Alicia sat up, and Jonathan gave a startled exclamation and reached for his pistol. But I was there before him, seizing his wrist in such a grip that the weapon fell to the floor. Alicia meanwhile was out of bed and bending over to peer through the window, a most attractive sight. "My God," she remarked. "You have killed her." For the first time in our brief relationship I thought I detected a note of admiration in her voice.

By now there was considerable agitation from within the house, Abigail's scream having been heard far and wide – I would not be surprised if they caught it in Leicester. But all the movement was towards the yard and the body of their late mistress. "Are your clothes wearable?" I asked Alicia.

"They have been torn to shreds."

"Then dress yourself in these men's garments. They are your husband's, and I am told will fit you. Now you, friend Jonathan," I said. "Do you wish to follow your mistress into flight?"

He goggled at me in terror. "That he is certainly going to do," Alicia vowed as she dragged on her husband's clothes.

Well, she had every reason to bear the fellow a grudge, but I needed certain things from him first. "You hear," I said. "Thus, if you wish me to intercede with Lady Marney on your behalf you must tell me what I wish to know."

His head jerked up and down as if someone was pulling a string attached to his hair. "Helier," Alicia said, earnestly. "That man is guilty of rape and must suffer for it."

"Everything comes to he who waits," I promised her. "Now, Jonathan, my sword. Where is it?"

"In . . . in milady's chamber," he gasped.

Well, really! I had been within a few feet of it all the time, and had not thought to look. "Show me," I said.

"What of all these people?" Alicia inquired, again looking out of the window. She was now fully dressed. Man's clothing certainly suited her very well just as they fitted her very well, save for a slight tightness across the chest. "They are carrying that harlot inside."

"Then they will continue to be preoccupied for a little while yet," I pointed out. "Besides, I must dress myself, and arm myself." We left the chamber, I carrying Jonathan's pistol in one hand, while I kept the other on his shoulder, and Alicia following, she also having armed herself, with her own weapon. Jonathan, at my command, carried the candle.

From below us there was a tremendous hubbub, but no one had as yet sought to come upstairs to ascertain from where Abigail had fallen, or indeed, whether she had been pushed. This led me to believe that she was not actually dead, and that they were trying to resuscitate her. I determined to leave a decision on that until later, and having gained milady's bedchamber, I finished dressing myself, and took my sword from the wardrobe, while Jonathan cowered against the wall and Alicia did some investigating, with a most practised air. "Helier," she accused. "You tumbled her!"

"Ah," I said. "It was necessary, you see, my dearest, in order to gain access to you."

She glared at me, and then changed the subject. "I am so hungry." I assumed she was referring to food, and had this confirmed by her next. "And thirsty," she added. "That lout . . ." she pointed at the shivering Jonathan, "would give me nothing."

Well, of course, he had certainly given her *something*, but I could see she was not in the mood for syllogisms. I had by now finished dressing myself, and with my trusty sword at my side felt ready to face the world and certainly a bunch of disorganised servants. "Then let us find you something to eat," I decided. "And my faithful Pierre, before we leave this place."

"And what about him?" She continued to regard her assaulter.

"He will, first of all, tend to our creature comforts," I told her, and him, and forced him to go in front of us as we cautiously negotiated the stairs. The noise beneath us continued unabated, and it appeared that the entire household, some twenty persons of both sexes, were accumulated in the kitchens, into which they had carried their mistress's body. As I had suspected, Abigail had not died from her fall, but she was such a mangled mess that it was obvious she had not long to live. Her people, had wrapped her body in blankets and were trying to force various liquids down her throat: their knowledge of medicine was clearly limited. So upset were they that our appearance hardly distracted them, save for Pierre, who sprang up from his knees beside the unhappy woman. "Master!" he cried. "Thank the Lord you are safe. But this poor woman . . ."

"What on earth is the matter with her?" I asked.

"Fell, she did, from an upstairs window," said Roundtree the butler. "But how . . ." then he frowned at me, realising that not only was I fully armed, but that I was accompanied by the real Lady Marney, wearing male attire, as well as a very frightened looking Jonathan. "We are betrayed," he bawled. "Murder! Rape! Arson! Treason!"

Presumably these were all the capital crimes he could remember at that moment, but it is remarkable that only one of them was unapplicable, looked at from various points of view . . . at that moment. Naturally Alicia and I replied vigorously. I whipped my sword from its scabbard and advanced most menacingly, while Alicia levelled her pistol. This caused the servants to scatter, although they were a stout crew, and several waited to pick up various pistols or cudgels they had left lying around the place. However, although they outnumbered us by four to one, they were really in an inferior position. In the first place, eight of their number were females, and Alicia was more than a match for *them*. In the second, it is generally conceded that I am worth six men in any set-to. And in the third place, one of their number, Pierre, promptly defected to the right side – looked at from our point of view – and on one of his recent hosts levelling a pistol at me, caught him such a buffet on the side of the head as to strike him senseless to the floor.

While this was going on Alicia had discharged her pistol, causing a good deal of alarm although no one was actually hit, but she had immediately possessed herself of another of the loaded weapons that were lying about and fired that one as well; this ball struck one of the serving maids in the general area of her legs – it was difficult to be certain because of her skirts. In any event there was a great deal of blood, a great deal more screaming, and a general withdrawal of the distaff side towards safer territory, ie, the pantries. I meanwhile was advancing towards the remaining footmen behind my drawn sword. Only one of these had actually managed to arm himself, and he discharged his weapon in my general direction, but the operative word was general, and the bullet merely smashed into the wall behind me. He then hurled the pistol at me, but I swept it aside with my blade and pinked him most severely in the shoulder. He fled howling and carried most of his friends with him.

However, before I had the time to savour my admittedly easy victory, I was assailed at once by a shout from Alicia and a buffet on the back of the head. This quite made me stagger, and as I turned, I was struck again.

81

My assailant was Roundtree the butler, who had more courage than sense, and was attempting to belabour me with a stout broomstick. I gave a roar of pain and anger, and swept my sword across with sufficient force to slice the stick in two. Then I was disturbed by another shout, and turned to see Alicia wrestling with the foul Jonathan, who had plucked a burning brand from the fire and was intending to set me alight with it. This development naturally drew me away from Roundtree, but Pierre was in front of me, dealing the fellow a severe blow on the side of the head so that he tumbled right over a chair and fell to the floor, while the burning wood flew from his hand and ignited one of the drapes by the window. This window was open, it being a warm night, and through it there was issuing a brisk breeze, with the result that the curtains burst into flames.

This in turn excited the fleeing men, who conceived that if they kept going in their original direction, towards the cellars, they might be trapped by the blaze. So they promptly turned and ran back the other way, virtually bowling us over in their anxiety to be away. I could of course have laid about me with my sword, but that would have been murder, and however much of a score I had had to settle with Abigail and Jonathan, I did not know what crimes these fellows were guilty of, or if any of them deserved death. Thus I suffered them to bundle past us, but the delay involved was critical, as by the time the last of them had fled the kitchen the whole exterior wall was burning merrily, and the heat was intense. "My house!" Alicia shouted in a fury.

"We must get out," I told her, and stooped beside Abigail, seeking some sign of life. But there was none, and from the amount of blood around her head – her face was quite disfigured – it was obvious that if she had survived her fall it could only have been for a few seconds. I therefore made the sign of the cross to help her soul on its way, downwards I suspect, and then abandoned her to the flames.

"I must have food," Alicia declared, and headed for the pantries. When she opened these doors, naturally the women came flooding out, screaming fit to raise the dead as they saw the flames, before following the menservants out into the night.

In their charge they knocked Alicia over, so I pulled her to her feet. "We must get out of here," I repeated.

"Not without food." I had already had several occasions on which to observe that she was a most determined young woman – others might have used the word stubborn – and so I realised that there was going to be no extricating her, except by bodily force, until she had eaten. Thus I decided to assist her, dashed into the pantry, seized a half-consumed leg of mutton, a loaf of bread and two bottles of wine, and returned to her side. "Now will you get out," I begged. We ran through the door, and only just in time, for the flames had by now reached the ceiling, and it came crashing down only seconds after we had left. We tumbled on to the grass, listening to all manner of booms and crashes behind us, and then sat up to watch the flames climbing the stairwell to ignite the upper floors. "Oh, my home, my home," Alicia groaned, sitting on the grass and gnawing her leg of lamb between gulps at one of the bottles of wine, the cork of which had become dislodged in the tumult. I naturally took her distress with a grain of salt, as so far as she had previously been aware, the house had anyway been destroyed by the Roundheads several years ago.

"It burns well," Pierre remarked. He had opened the second bottle, and had equipped himself with two more.

"That house was in the Marney family for five hundred years," Alicia moaned, tearing off chunks of bread.

"Yes," I pointed out, "but you have only been a member of the family for eight years, and then briefly."

"That has nothing to do with it. Shit! This bottle is empty. Pierre give me yours." Pierre yielded his bottle somewhat reluctantly, and, coming to the conclusion that I was being left out, I took a swig myself before passing it to milady; I must say, it made the evening much brighter, although possibly this was the result of the flames, which had now reached the upper storey, and were gushing from that very window from which Abigail had made her last flight. "I am the last Marney," Alicia sobbed, taking a swig.

"Well," I said, deciding to resume command before my little army became incapable of further movement, for Pierre had opened another bottle, "I have no doubt that, in view of your enormous services to His Majesty's cause, the King will finance the rebuilding of your home just as soon as he regains his throne. And as I am sure he cannot do that until we regain *him*, I suggest we make a move in that direction."

Somewhat reluctantly they got to their feet, and I headed them towards the stables, brilliantly illuminated by the leaping flames. Where the various retainers of the late Abigail had got to I had no idea, but I presumed they were all still in full flight. I have always been an optimistic fellow. We saddled our horses, mounted, and walked them out of the stableyard. By now the drive immediately in front of the house was a dangerous place, as burning pieces of timber were crashing down every moment, not to mention chimney pots; the roof was clearly about to give way. We thus turned our horses through the paddock, making for the orchard, and were proceeding in good order when there came a shout, "There go the scoundrels!" followed by a loud explosion, which my practised ear immediately recognised to be that of a blunderbus.

The possession by our enemies of so formidable a weapon was disturbing, even if this first discharge had failed to hit anything, probably from having been fired

84

at too great a range. But it had been fired from in front of us, and behind us the house continued to burn away and collapse in parts. There was only one way to go. I drew my sword. "We must charge those people," I said. "Do you stay close behind me."

Because of course my two companions were now quite unarmed. They were also more than half drunk. However, possibly because of that, they wheeled into line behind me without argument, whereupon I kicked my steed in the ribs and urged it forward. We went from the walk to the trot to the canter to the gallop in very rapid succession. Now I could see before us quite a crowd, illuminated by the leaping flames behind us, and I realised that the servants must have been reinforced by various yokels drawn to the fire. How I wished I was riding my great warhorse Hannibal, who had carried me the length and breadth of Germany in triumph, but Hannibal had long been drawn to his ancestors, and I had only this hired nag. However he did well enough, even when realising, as did I, that we were opposed by a variety of weapons, including pitchforks, but only the one blunderbus, which the lout who had fired at us was still in the process of reloading. But the pitchforks were fearsome enough. I rode straight at them, steam rising from my horse's nostrils, evaded their thrusts easily enough and cut one of the would-be pikemen down with a sweep of my sword while listening to a cry of pain and alarm from behind me. In the second row some bold varlet attempted to grasp my bridle, and I struck him with the hilt of my sword and probably broke his jaw, from the crunch, while swinging at another rascal who was attempting the same game on my other side. He fell away from me in a spurt of blood, and I was through, looking over my shoulder as I careered along the road. To my relief, there were still two mounted horses behind me, but to my dismay I saw that both riders were reeling in the saddle, although I reflected that this might only be the results of the alcohol.

It was necessary to get beyond the reach of the recharged blunderbuss before I dared draw rein and let them catch me up. "I am hit," Alicia said, quietly enough, and forthwith tumbled from the saddle.

I dismounted immediately, and knelt beside her, aware that Pierre had also fallen from his seat. But I was far more concerned about this beautiful woman. She gave a little cry as I fumbled about her clothing in the darkness. There was certainly some blood. But the wound itself, when I found it by pulling down her breeches, was not severe. She had been gashed in the thigh by one of the pitchfork points, which had torn her pants as well as her flesh, but not deeply, although I could see it would be painful. She was also losing blood, so I tore my own shirt into strips to make a bandage. "Oh, Helier," she said. "Am I going to die? I should hate to die, when there is so much to be done."

"You shall not die," I promised her. "Unless infection sets in."

"Infection." She shuddered. "That was a pitchfork."

Thus it could hardly have been very clean.

"I shall cure you," I said, and proceeded to apply my lips to the wound, sucking out the blood. I may say that I had been taught this medical remedy by none other than the Witch of Hohengraffen herself, during one of those periods when we had been working in harness in preference to attempting to destroy each other. The Witch, to be sure, being also a vampire, had sucked the blood from wounds in order to swallow it. But at the same time she had convinced me, in a most empirical sense, that human saliva, provided it is itself healthy, is a very good antidote to any other poisons that may be lying about. Or even inhuman saliva. I did not of course swallow Alicia's blood, having only limited unnatural tendencies myself, but she seemed grateful for my ministations, and made little gurgling sounds, so that the whole thing was a most enjoyable process, culminating, as it did, in my wrapping the strips of shirt-bandage round and round her delicious thigh, a process which had I not been a gentleman and she wounded, might well have over-ridden all of her objections to my sexual ambitions. This task completed, I left her to adjust her own breeches while I at last attended to poor Pierre. He had actually received a slash from a billhook or scythe, and was in considerably worse condition. I decided against sucking the blood from his wound however, having had my fill of this for one evening, and so bound him up, completing the ruin of my shirt, whereupon we resumed our interrupted journey to the north, and the King.

CHAPTER 4

Our journey, as may be supposed, was a long and arduous one. Obviously it was in our interest to press on just as rapidly as we could. In addition to the pursuit from London, supposing this was being continued, we could not doubt that the Roundheads from Leicester, following a chat with Abigail's servants, would also be hot on our trail and from a much closer starting point, while the charges against us would now include every one of the villain Roundtree's original assessment: treason, rape, murder *and* arson, even if, looked at in the cold light of day and regarding Abigail's sad demise as a well-merited execution, we were actually guilty of none of them. After all, we were on the side of the rightful king, Abigail had invited me to her bed – nay, she had insisted upon it – and it had not been us set fire to the drapes. But I doubted any Roundhead judge would see it that way, even supposing we were ever taken before a judge and not summarily hanged by the troopers.

Sadly, haste was out of the question with two invalids. Alicia's wound, as I have suggested, was more painful and annoying than dangerous, but she was in too much discomfort to sit a saddle for very long, and it was necessary for me to redress the wound whenever we halted. This was of course a pleasure, and I took care to suck it clean at every opportunity, while she sighed, and stroked my head and declared what a good fellow I was, rather as if I were a large dog. But if I ever allowed my lips to drift from her wound round the softness of her thigh towards that tangled undergrowth I longed to penetrate, the stroke immediately became a slap. Of course I could have taken her by force, but I was reluctant to let so simple a matter as a tumble interfere with our by now intimate friendship, especially when I still had no doubt that she would be mine, eventually, and sooner than later. And when she, as an acquaintance of Lord Culhaven, remained so important to my mission.

Sadly, Pierre was in a far more serious condition, and it was only four days after leaving Marney Hall that I realised there was nothing more I could do for him. His very presence became offensive, as gangrene had set in with its resultant unspeakable odour. This was an experience I had undergone myself, following the Battle of Breitenfeld, and as is well known, once gangrene appears one's life expectancy can be counted in hours rather than days. Certainly I had been deposited with those other poor souls whose imminent demise had been equally anticipated. I had been rescued, by the Witch of Hohengraffen, who at that time had had an urgent reason for keeping me alive, and she had restored me to health by using to the fullest extent her knowledge of the Black Art. Sadly, I had no such knowledge with which to treat Pierre. And yet I could not just watch him die.

It should be understood that in our dangerous situation I had deemed it unwise to stay on the roads or to approach any human habitations. We had kept to the heaths and the woods. This had also had a profound effect upon our diet, as I had been forced to carry out a series of raids upon isolated farmhouses, seeking chickens and ducks, and more than once encountering irate farmers armed with blunderbusses. Fortunately, none of them was a good shot. More important, as it had been necessary to avoid Roundhead patrols and encampments, of which there appeared to be an inordinate number, I had found it impossible to trace a direct line from where we had been, somewhat west of Leicester, to the Scottish border.

Indeed, willy-nilly, I had found myself inclining ever more to the west, until it seemed to me that we would most likely wind up in Wales.

But Pierre was my most serious problem. On our fourth afternoon after leaving Marney, during which our progress had been mainly lateral, the good servant had simply fallen from his saddle into the bracken. "I very much fear," I told my charmer "that he is not long for this world, unless I can obtain help."

"And how do you propose to do that?" she inquired.

"You recall that church steeple we saw in a valley this morning?" I said. "Where there is a church there is a village, and where there is a village there may well be a medical man. Or at least, knowledge of one."

"You propose to ride into a Roundhead village?"

"Well, as to that, milady, we do not know that it is a Roundhead village. Indeed, as I recall affairs a few years ago, the west was pretty solidly for the King."

"Times change," she grumbled. "And so do loyalties."

"Yet must I try, milady. I cannot abandon a faithful servant to die a horrible death."

She sighed. "So be it. And what of me?"

"You will remain here, milady, with Pierre, and await my return."

"And if you do not return?"

"I would not even consider such a situation, if I were you," I recommended. Because obviously, if I did not return, she would be up a most unpleasant creek with nothing even resembling a paddle.

I left her with all three of our pistols, but considered it best that I should take my sword, which she was not strong enough to use anyway, and my dagger.

"Take care, dear Helier," she said.

"I intend to. However, the best laid plans of men can go astray. I do not suppose you would care to

90

give me something to remember you by? Or indeed, receive something from me to remember *me* by, in the years to come?"

"Now, Helier," she said reproachfully. "You know that cannot be."

"But surely, as you were raped by the foul Jonathan, your oath is no longer valid?"

"Being raped by Jonathan has nothing to do with it," she argued. "That was forced upon me. But you are a gentleman, Helier, who I know would never force a woman."

Sadly, she was absolutely right. I *had* never forced a woman. I will be honest and confess that I had begun what might be called my amatorial life by determining to force Marguerite, but had been prevented from doing so for various reasons. Since then, however many women I had bedded, the boot had always been on the other foot, so to speak. Yet in this instance I could not help but wonder if she was actually extending an invitation. However, I felt it necessary to stick to my principles, for as regards this woman I wanted more than one tumble, as it were. So I grumbled, "God spare me from faithful women," and rode off.

Getting back to the village was simple enough, and as it was now dusk, even someone of my bulk did not attract very much attention. However, it was necessary for me to enter the inn to gain the information I sought, and that did arouse a certain amount of interest. "I seek a surgeon," I explained.

"Ah, well, and what would ye be wanting with a surgeon?" the landlord asked, at the same time giving a quick nod to one of his customers.

I turned round to survey the room, and saw this fellow sidling for the door. "Hold there," I recommended. "If anyone attempts to leave this inn I shall spit him like a chicken."

The fellow promptly sat down again, while I received

91

a thumping blow on the back of the head. This did me no great harm, as I was wearing my hat, but it sadly dissipated my feather, and quite aroused my ire. I turned round again, seized the landlord – for it was he who had struck me, with some kind of mallet – by the throat, and bounced him up and down several times. When he had run out of breath I set him on his legs again. "A surgeon," I repeated. "And be quick about it, or he will have two patients to attend to."

The landlord got his breath back. "At the end of the street. Dr Brewin. He is the man you want."

"Thank you," I said courteously. "Now, fill me a jug of ale and tell me why you took so instant a dislike to me." I surveyed the other customers as I spoke.

The landlord obeyed. "There was a cavalry patrol here, your honour, saying that they sought a most vicious highwayman, who murders defenceless women, after having had his way with them, and burns down their houses."

I drank deeply, as I had a severe thirst, and besides, this was the first alcohol to pass my lips in four days. "And what made you suppose I might be this fellow?" I asked.

"Well, your honour, they spoke of a giant, seven feet tall."

"There was a reward," muttered one of the customers.

"Well, well," I said. "But you can see that I am not seven feet tall. Indeed, I am some inches short of that. So obviously you have made a mistake."

"Well, your honour . . ." he rolled his eyes. And truth to tell, as he was not very many inches taller than five feet, from his point of view I must have looked even bigger than I am.

In any event, now that I had obtained the information I wanted, it was necessary to do something about him, and his friends. "This is excellent beer, landlord," I said. "Do you have a good stock of it?"

"Oh, indeed, your honour. Indeed."

"But it is not all in this taproom, I will swear?"

"No, no, your honour. It is in the cellar beneath."

"And how is this cellar reached?"

"Through this trap here," the simple fellow explained.

I peered over the counter. "You would never get a barrel of beer through that hole."

"No, no, your honour. This trap is for me to gain access. There is another, double trap, in the yard, with a ramp leading to the same cellar, through which the barrels are rolled, either up or down."

"Exactly as I had supposed would be the case," I remarked. "Well, now, landlord, I suggest that you open that trap, and go down the ladder, and make sure no one is tampering with your beer."

"Your honour?" He goggled at me in confusion.

"Nay," I said, drawing my sword and presenting its tip to his throat. "I insist upon it." Thus constrained, he opened the trap. "And do you good fellows descend with him," I told the customers, moving towards them behind my blade.

They obeyed me rapidly enough, whereupon I slammed the trap on them, pushed what might be called an active barrel of beer across it, and ran into the yard. And just in time, too, for the landlord was about to emerge from the larger trap. "You are too impatient," I told him, pushing him back down the shute, and barring this trap by thrusting several pieces of stout timber through the grab-handles.

I returned inside the inn, again in the nick of time, because a large female had appeared, somewhat querulously seeking the whereabouts of her husband. It was the work of a moment to move the cask of beer, open the hatch, and drop her down amidst the men, whether more to her discomfort or theirs was difficult to determine, as the noise was confused. I then considered it necessary to search the remainder of the house, and discovered four other females, two children, and a scullery boy. These also I required to descend into the cellar, whereupon I replaced the barrel of beer over the trap, and took my leave.

I understood of course that my advantage would be a short-lived one. I had to make haste, but I did manage to discourage two would-be tapsters I met on the street just outside the inn, by telling them that the landlord had been taken ill, and that plague was suspected. I was, I assured them, on my way to fetch the doctor now. They beat a hasty retreat, obviously to arouse their neighbours, but I reckoned I had gained a few more minutes. They would be afraid to enter the inn, however much noise the landlord and his friends might be making in the cellar, until they could be assured by the doctor that he did *not* have the plague, and I intended to have first call on that worthy's services.

I mounted my horse and rode to the end of the street where, reassuringly, there was a building more substantial than the others, outside of which there hung a shingle, advertising the skill of Dr Roderick Brewin. I tethered my horse and rapped on the door, and was rewarded by the opening of a window above my head. "Who is there?" asked a woman.

I liked the sound of her voice. "I need the doctor, most urgently. A man is in danger of his life," I told her.

"Wait there." I stamped up and down, somewhat impatiently, for now there was a considerable hubbub arising from up the road. But a few minutes later the door was unbarred and opened. "You are hurt?" inquired the woman, looking me up and down. She carried a candle, which she held above her head the better to see me, and which was all I had to go by in discerning her appearance. The delay had been caused by her feeling the necessity to dress herself, in a manner of speaking. She had obviously retired to bed early, and thus wore a cloak over her nightgown. This totally concealed her figure, but she had splendid features, crisp and strong, and a mass of auburn hair, loose on her shoulders. This last gave me pause for consideration. The Witch of Hohengraffen had also sported red-brown hair, when in the mood. Equally, she had also appeared from time to time with yellow tresses, and obviously I could not go through life suspecting every woman I encountered of being the Witch in disguise, however salutary some of my earlier experiences. Besides, this woman's hair was curly, and Richilde Bethlen's had been straight.

Additionally, although this may be hard to credit, at that moment I had more important things on my mind than even a handsome woman. "The doctor," I said.

"He is not here."

"Damnation. Then I must be away."

"Wait!" She looked past me at the flickering lights up the street. "Are you the cause of that rumpus? Or the effect?"

"I fear the cause."

"But you are hurt?"

"No, no. A friend of mine."

"Then bring him in."

"He is not here. And you said your husband was away."

"Not my husband, my brother." We gazed at each other, my attention for the first time being distracted by her femininity, which, as my eyes grew accustomed to the gloom, I was discerning to be considerable. "I also have a knowledge of medicine," she explained. "Gleaned from watching my brother at work. I may be able to help your friend."

"Unfortunately he is some distance away."

"Then give me time to dress properly, and I will accompany you."

"You? A woman? This is a cutting business."

"Do you suppose I am afraid of the sight of blood,

sir?" she demanded. "I have assisted my brother at more than one operation."

"And you will ride, alone, into the night with a strange man?"

She gave a rather attractive little toss of her head. "Faith, sir, it is obvious that you are a gentleman."

This was really getting too much. Was there no woman could discern the devil that lurked in my breast? I was in a quandary, and took refuge in trivia. "That mob will be upon us long before you can get dressed."

She nodded. "So do you leave. Wait for me in the copse behind the church."

"You? Or the mob?"

She tossed her head again. "If you do not trust me, sir, then no doubt your friend is a dead man."

"I will wait in the copse," I agreed, and mounted.

It was a trying period, for soon enough the mob had become sufficiently curious to break into the inn, and then to flood down the street to the doctor's house. My new friend, if she was my friend, had deemed it necessary to await this event, but apparently told them I had ridden off in the opposite direction, so away they went again, now seeking horses and arms. I had to wait another half-an-hour before I heard hooves approaching. Throughout my wait I had kept my sword drawn. Now I presented it. "Identify yourself."

"I am Felicity Brewin," she said. "Does that make you any the wiser?" It was difficult to make her out in the darkness, but the voice was the same.

"Are you sure you know what you are about?" I asked.

"Medically, yes. And in that respect, I can admit to no politics. However, I assume you are he being sought by the Roundheads."

"It seems that I am wanted for rape, treason, murder and arson. Does that not disturb you?"

"There were also some minor matters mentioned, such as theft, disturbing the peace and grievous bodily harm."

"The story of my life," I admitted. "If you ride with me you will certainly be similarly attainted."

"I am acting as a doctor," she repeated. "Is it your intention to spend the night in this copse?" I kicked my horse and led her towards the distant wood. But being a woman, she was curious. "Is this sick friend of yours also a criminal?"

"Oh, indeed he is. And she also."

That made her think a bit. "Your wife accompanies you?" she asked at last, whether in relief or disappointment it was difficult to be sure.

"I have no wife," I reassured her.

She made no comment to that, and rode in silence for a while, before remarking, "But you are Cavaliers."

"What makes you say that?"

"Firstly because you are fugitives, secondly because the Roundheads charged you with treason above all else, which nowadays simply means any opposition to Parliament, and thirdly, because you do not look the least like a Puritan. Nor, if you are travelling with an itinerant woman, can you possibly be one."

"I do beg of you not to refer to Lady Marney as an itinerant woman," I said. "At least in her hearing. She is about the least itinerant woman I have ever known."

"Lady Marney," she said thoughtfully.

"Do you know the name?"

"I may have heard it."

"Because you are a Royalist yourself?"

"Me, sir?"

I smiled at her. "I estimate you to be a Royalist. Firstly because you refer to our enemies as Roundheads, which you would not do if you were one of them; secondly, because you are riding with me, knowing me to be a Cavalier . . ."

"I have told you," she interrupted, "a doctor can have no politics."

"And thirdly," I went on, "because you neither look nor act like a Puritan yourself, or you would not be taking a moonlight ride alone with a villain like myself. Or are doctors not allowed to be afraid of rape, either?"

She shot me a glance and then looked in front of her, and we rode the rest of the way in silence.

I was somewhat disturbed, on approaching our primitive encampment, to discover no sign of life. Then one of the horses whinnied, and I realised that they had merely been moved, while Alicia had gathered some branches to conceal herself and Pierre.

Now she asked, "Is that you, Helier?"

"It is I, and I have brought a surgeon with me."

"Thank God for that." She stood up, peering into the gloom as Felicity Brewin dismounted. "This is a doctor? Helier, you have been up to your tricks again."

"Are you sure this is not your wife?" Felicity asked.

"Sadly, yes. This young woman claims to possess medical knowledge, milady. And she is the best I could procure at short notice."

"I would request you, sir," Felicity said, "to remember that you did not 'procure' me, as you put it. I am here of my own free will."

I perceived that I might be in for a difficult time. "Will you not look at your patient?" I inquired.

"I will need a light."

I found my tinder box and a lantern I had pilfered, amongst other things, on our journey, and soon had a glow, by the light of which Felicity bent over poor Pierre, who was groaning most horribly. "My God," she said, opening his shirt. "This should have been attended to days ago."

"I did the best I could," I explained.

"I cannot save him," she said. "To cut out the infected flesh would be to expose his vitals."

"Is there nothing you can do?"

"I can ease his last hours. Because there are only hours left to him." She went to her horse, and from her saddle-bag brought a bottle of some noxious smelling liquid.

"Do you mean to poison him?" Alicia inquired. She had clearly taken a strong dislike to our medical friend.

"In effect," Felicity said, without rancour. "This drug will put him to sleep for several hours. My brother uses it when he needs to operate. In the normal course of events, the patient will wake up, eventually, with little ill effects. But this poor fellow will simply not wake up." Alicia hugged herself. "Well?" Felicity asked. "The decision must be yours . . . good heavens, I do not even know your name."

"It is Helier L'Eree," I told her, deeming it best to keep things as simple as possible. But what a decision to have to make. "We cannot remain here until he dies," I said.

"I understand this. Once he is unconscious, if you will assist me, I will take him back to my brother's house. There he will die in peace, and I will arrange for a Christian burial. I can do nothing more than that."

"I think that is uncommonly generous of you," I said.

She gave a brief smile, the first time I had seen her teeth, which were white and even. "I will require payment."

"Absolutely," I agreed. "But as you are here, milady is also requiring attention."

"Milady, is it?" Felicity remarked.

"I'll not have that witch touch me," Alicia declared. "Why do you not examine *her* for the Devil's mark, Helier?"

"Are you then a witch hunter?" Felicity inquired.

"I have been all things in my time," I told her. "And

shall be again. However, right now, I wish you to examine milady."

"But she does not wish to be examined."

"Her wishes do not enter into it."

"Helier!" Alicia brought up her pistol. "If she attempts to lay a finger on me, I will shoot you both."

"With one bullet, my poppet? Now consider the situation. Supposing you did manage to shoot us both. What then? You are a wounded wanted criminal. Would you have any hope of reaching Scotland without me?" The pistol sagged as she realised her helplessness. "There is also the point that, despite my ministrations, without expert aid you might yourself develop gangrene. Can you consider winding up in such a state as poor Pierre? Think of the smell. It would be most unladylike."

She surrendered and lay back with a sigh.

"Where is this wound?" Felicity inquired.

"On her right thigh."

"And you have tended it?"

"As best I have been able." She made no comment, although her expression spoke volumes. "Did you expect me to let her bleed to death?" I inquired.

"Bring the light," she said, and released Alicia's breeches. "Hm," she commented, as she unfastened the bandage. "This is quite clean. I suspect you found this more congenial work than caring for yonder poor fellow."

"I am an unmitigated rogue," I confessed.

"All the evidence points that way," she agreed, and applied a fresh bandage to Alicia's thigh. "Of course, compared with the man's injury, this is the merest scratch. Continue as you have done, and she should survive. Now, it is getting late. Help me with this fellow." Pierre was by now quite unconscious, so we tied him to the back of his horse, while Alicia dressed herself, and then also mounted. "Must she come too?" Felicity asked.

"I am not remaining here alone any longer," Alicia declared. "Besides, you do not know him as well as I do. Left to himself, he would have your skirts about your ears before you could draw breath. Or has he already done this?"

"Unlike some," Felicity said coldly, "I am a respectable woman."

"She is right," I agreed, seeking to prevent the simmering quarrel from erupting. "Once we have delivered Pierre we must be on our way."

"To Scotland," Felicity remembered.

"Helier," Alicia said, "you simply must overcome this habit of sharing our plans with every female you encounter."

"Had Master L'Eree not told me his intentions, I would not have come," Felicity pointed out, deliberately refraining, I estimated, from adding, "milady". We rode back towards the village, but had just topped the rise overlooking the houses when we saw a huge glow in the distance. "It seems that wherever you visit is followed by a fire," Felicity remarked.

"It is not the inn," I observed. "Worse luck."

"No, it is at the other end of the village," she agreed. "It is . . . my God! My house!"

"Did you leave your dinner cooking?" Alicia inquired, politely.

Felicity shot her a glance, then kicked her horse. But I caught her bridle. "What do you intend?"

"Why, to get down there, and see what can be saved."

"Listen," I told her. On the breeze we could hear a kind of baying. "That is a mob," I said, "surrounding your house. They have fired it because they have found out, or decided, that you must have given me assistance. Go down there, and you will be torn to pieces. Or at least, hanged."

"Those people are my neighbours!"

"Unfortunately, I gave them some cause to dislike me. They also identified me as the wanted man. If you are considered my friend or accomplice, well . . ."

"What evil day brought you to my door?" she muttered. "What's to be done? I am homeless. My brother is homeless."

"Have you no relatives at all?"

"I have an aunt over in Dormintsley. That is a dozen miles away."

"Then at least let us escort you there."

"It is not in your direction."

"Nonetheless, it is the least we can do."

"It is far more than we need to do," Alicia said. "Pay the woman what you owe her, and let us be on our way."

"I will see her to her aunt's home," I declared. "Would you have me play the villain?"

"Ha!" she commented.

"You are most generous, sir," Felicity said. "But what of your friend? I am afraid my aunt would scarce welcome me if I visited her with a corpse."

I nodded. "Are you certain he will not regain consciousness?"

"Quite certain. I gave him an extra large dose to *be* sure."

"Well, then, here on the greensward is as good a resting place as any." I took poor Pierre from the saddle, and indeed he was scarce breathing at all, and then stertorously. I laid him on the ground in the shelter of a bush, and covered him with a horse blanket.

"The foxes will get at him, just the same," Alicia pointed out.

"And if we bury him, will not the worms get at him even quicker?" I asked. "Let us be on our way."

"Will you not say a prayer over him?" Felicity inquired.

"I know nothing of prayers," I confessed.

"Truly, you are a strange fellow." She herself knelt beside Pierre and uttered a prayer, following which we mounted and rode into the night. But, in the oddest fashion, I conceived that I had made a friend. It was,

102

indeed, one of the most fateful meetings of my life, although I then had no means of knowing this.

It is one of the peculiarities of humanity that our emotions can be most perversely directed. Felicity Brewin was actually a far more attractive personality than Alicia Marney, and not so very inferior in terms of looks. Yet did I remain totally besotted with Alicia, my sole amatory ambition being to hold her naked in my arms. Well, it must be admitted that I had a great deal to remember in that direction.

When we arrived at the village of Dormintsley, which lay almost due west of where we had left poor Pierre, it was almost dawn. Felicity invited us in, to spend the day and a night if we chose, but I actually had the poor sense to refuse, despite my observation that the house of her aunt was a very large and imposing building, standing in its own grounds outside the village proper. "But if you could sell us some food and wine," I suggested, "we would be most grateful."

"You mean you do not wish my aunt to see you?" Felicity said sadly. "I do assure you that she is as staunch a Royalist as yourself. But perhaps you are wise. Wait here. I shall return in half-an-hour." Fortunately, Alicia had other ideas.

It was now all but dawn, and we had been riding for four days without the slightest degree of comfort. "I think we should take advantage of Miss Brewin's kind offer," she said. "Be sure the entire countryside will be alive with Roundheads looking for us, and thus to travel in daylight will be a most hazardous business. If we could remain here in safety until dusk . . ."

"Of course," Felicity said.

"And perhaps have the use of a bath?"

"Of course."

"And then, a soft bed?"

"Certainly," Felicity agreed. "How many beds?"

"Why two, of course. And two rooms. Do you take us for man and wife?"

"In faith, milady, I do not know what to take you for," Felicity confessed. "But you will be welcome, I am sure. Just permit me to go in first and acquaint my aunt with the situation." She walked her horse down the slope.

"If she betrays us, we are lost," I remarked.

"She will not betray us," Alicia asserted confidently. "She is too much in awe of us. Besides, she has taken a great fancy to you, Helier. You will not pretend you have not noticed this?" As a matter of fact, I had not till that moment. "Just remember to behave yourself," Alicia said severely.

Something to think about. But before I could do so, Felicity returned and told us that her aunt would be pleased to receive us. Mistress Brewin was a maiden lady, who had inherited both her house and her fortune from another aunt, who had, no doubt with reason, by-passed the father of Felicity and her brother. She was a formidable woman, although she was both small and elderly. "You'd serve the King," she remarked, giving a loud sniff. "God bless him. And a right royal layabout he is too, God bless him. Milady, your appearance is a disgrace to your sex." It was difficult to be certain whether she was referring to Alicia's male attire or the fact that it was torn in several places, most of them revealing.

"I do assure you, Mistress Brewin, that I am in this condition through no fault of my own," Alicia protested.

"And travelling with but a single companion! Male! And clearly a lout!"

"I beg your pardon," I said, bristling. "I am the Count d'Albret."

"A wanted murderer, rapist and arsonist," she declared. "Oh, the Roundheads have been here from Leicester. And a Frenchman?" Clearly the ultimate crime.

I looked at Felicity for assistance, suspecting that I

should be the loser in a bout of verbal fisticuffs with this dragon. "I do assure you, Auntie, that any crime the Count may have committed was in the Cause of the King," she declared.

"The King!" Miss Brewin remarked again, disparagingly.

"You spoke of a bath," Alicia said, determined to change the subject.

"Indeed, the maids are drawing one now. And for you, Count d'Albret?"

"I think that would be very acceptable," I said. "If it were also possible to obtain something to eat . . ."

"Of course," she agreed.

Alicia opted to have her bath first. "And find her something decent to wear," Miss Brewin bawled after her niece.

I was escorted to the kitchen, where there was good bread and cheese and beer waiting for me, while more water was brought to the boil. One of the male servants escorted me to a bedchamber and filled a large tin tub. "Does your worship require assistance?" he asked.

"I can manage, thank you."

"I will see what can be done about your worship's clothes," he said, scooping them up, somewhat disdainfully, and leaving the room.

I must say that few things in life feel better than a hot bath after one has spent several days in the open. I soaped myself most thoroughly, and leaned back, feeling relaxation spreading through my muscles . . . and heard my door opening, and then closing again, very softly. Equally must I say that there are few situations in which a man is at more disadvantage than when sitting naked in a bath, especially when he has inadvertently left his sword lying across a bed which is several feet away. However, I had no doubt that the intruder had to be one of only two people, and as the chances that it was Alicia were several hundred to one . . . I opened my eyes. "You have me at a disadvantage, Miss Brewin," I said. "And I fear you will be embarrassed."

"Do you not suppose I have seen naked men before?" she inquired. I did not doubt she had. But clearly none to match me, if her pink cheeks and rather heavy breathing were anything to go by.

"In your capacity as your brother's assistant, of course," I added. "However, would I not be right in assuming that in every case those fellows were either dead, dying, or quite beyond the proper use of their bodily functions? Whereas, I, as you can see, am in full possession of mine." And I stood up to illustrate my point.

If I had anticipated that my hostess would beat a hasty retreat, I was entirely mistaken, although she did lean her back against the door. "You did not tell me you were a count," she remarked.

This was the first occasion on which I had really had the leisure to study her, and why not, as she was very obviously studying *me*, possibly with some anatomical treatise in mind. Of course, she held a great advantage as I was naked. I could not say that she was fully dressed, as I now observed that she had discarded her riding habit and was wearing some kind of loose gown. Her feet were bare, suggesting, to a born optimist like myself, that there might be very little underneath the gown itself. Save flesh, of course, and I could quickly determined that there was an abundance of that. Felicity Brewin could not be expected to match Alicia Marney in voluptuousness – few women could – but she was taller, and more strongly built, had long legs, and a sufficiently well developed bust. These observations, as I applied a towel to various parts of myself, naturally had an effect. Obviously I had to suppose I was having a similar effect upon her, but it is always difficult to be sure with women. "My title was bestowed upon me by the French, for services to them during the German war," I explained.

106

"Ah," she said. "Well, milord, if everything is to your satisfaction . . ."

I allowed the towel to drop to the floor. "Everything is not to my satisfaction. I have no clothes."

"Well, milord, they were sorely in need of a wash. I will have them brought up to you the moment they are dry."

"And until then?"

"Why . . . I am sure you must be exhausted. Why do you not lie down and have a rest? I believe that is what Lady Marney is doing."

"And what will you be doing?" I asked, moving towards her.

"I also have had a sleepless night, milord . . ."

"And therefore need to lie down as well, I'll be bound." I had now got up to her, and gently untied the bow at the neck of the garment.

"Milord," she protested. "Does not your mistress sleep but a wall away?"

"Lady Marney is not, and never has been, my mistress," I assured her, at the same time sliding her gown past her shoulders. I was relieved to discover that my earlier judgement had been entirely correct and that she was lacking nothing that might gladden a man's heart.

"A man and a woman, travelling alone together . . ."

"Did you not suppose I am a gentleman?" I asked, gently caressing her breast, circling the nipple with my finger, which caused it to harden. She shivered, I presume with pleasure, as she made no effort to resist me.

"Well, of course," she said. "But . . ."

"Lady Marney is engaged to be married, to a gentleman of King Charles's court," I explained, "and is utterly faithful to him." I bent my head to bestow a tender kiss on the portion of her anatomy I had just been stroking.

Felicity gave a great sigh. "Then I am mistaken, and apologise."

"But at the same time," I said, "I hope you will

understand the torment I have undergone, spending all day and all night in close proximity to so much beauty and yet being unable to touch any of it."

This was actually a tactical error, but even as I spoke I had eased the gown past her thighs, from whence it slipped to the floor about her ankles, further convincing me that she was a total delight. "And so you must launch yourself at the first female you encounter?" she said.

I knelt to kiss her pubes. "Quite the contrary. Had you not come in just now, I would never have touched you, either. And were you to assure me that you are a virgin, I swear I would not touch you now." I looked up at her as I spoke.

She had rested her hands on my head. "What would you, milord?" she said. "I grew to womanhood during a war."

I stood up, and lifted her on to the bed.

"I wish you could stay longer," Felicity said.

It was evening, and my clothes had been washed and dried.

"I must go," I said. Because Alicia, outfitted in clothes belonging to the elder Miss Brewin, a trifle old-fashioned to be sure but not the less becoming for that, was waiting.

So was Miss Brewin, equipped with a bag which contained a side of smoked gammon, a recently cooked chicken, and a large cheese, together with half-a-dozen bottles of wine. "How much do I owe you?" I asked. Not that I had much money left.

"I have not added it up. When next you are in this district, if you will call upon me, I will present my account."

Well, as I have indicated, the size and appearance of her house certainly suggested wealth. But still . . . "I am most grateful, ma'am," I said. "And be sure that I *will* visit you again, God willing." Or more appropriately,

108

the Devil. "Are you sure you will be all right?" I asked Felicity. "What of your brother?"

"He will know to come here, when he returns," she said. "So fare thee well," and she bestowed upon me a warm but entirely chaste kiss, in view of the presence of her aunt and Alicia, at the same time pressing a purse of coin into my hand, as she had readily perceived my destitution. This was embarrassing, especially in view of our tumble, but beggars cannot be choosers.

"And not a word for me," Alicia remarked, as we walked our horses out of the yard and into the night. "Helier, I will wager that you could have had that wench by snapping your fingers."

"Let's be off," I said. And so once again we rode north.

Having had a continual sequence of alarums and excursions to get this far, we had to anticipate a similar series of unfortunate adventures in the future. However, fortune now turned in our favour. We made good time, and thanks to Miss Brewin's gift of sustenance did not need to approach a village until we were well clear of the district where we were wanted. Then we were really in the north-west, where the King had always had his best support. As we approached the Scottish border and crossed it, we found the inhabitants even more welcoming than in the south. Soon we were even being given directions as to where and how to find the King. Most of these were inaccurate.

The fact is that this new King Charles was not an improvement on his unlamented father when it came to steadfast behaviour and keeping oaths. He was a good deal inferior when it came to personal morals, his father's having been impeccable. The easiest way to discover the whereabouts of the son was to follow a well-laid trail of pregnant women.

It may be recalled that the gallant Montrose, in the

spring, had landed in Scotland as a kind of advance guard, intending to raise the country for the King. He had indeed been invited to do so by the Scots. They wanted a king, but he had to be a king who entirely conformed to their religious ideas, and that meant accepting the Covenant. In the first instance, therefore, they had demanded of Montrose that, in the name of the King, he renounce all his previous religious affiliations and take the oath. Montrose was an honourable man who was not about to change his religious stance to gain a political advantage, and Charles had expressly declared that he would not accept the Covenant. The result of all this was that the Scots had warred on the gallant Earl, and as they were able to bring vastly superior forces into the field, defeated him, captured him, and hanged him. A tragically unfitting end for a great and gallant soldier.

Possibly, as he mounted the gallows, Montrose may have reflected that this King's father had similarly sacrificed *his* best soldier, the Earl of Strafford, back in 1641. Charles, realising that he would not get the throne without accepting the Scottish terms, and counting the throne as far more important than personal honour, had taken the oath to the Covenant virtually at the moment he had learned of Montrose's death. All forgiven, he had landed in Scotland in June, only shortly before I had landed in England, and had been making a nuisance of himself ever since.

The Scots had got their Covenanting King. They rapidly had been forced to realise that they had taken on a very poor bargain indeed. The King had been allowed nine thousand pounds a month for the sustenance of himself and his court, a very large sum of money. Unfortunately, it was not half large enough for Charles, who spent it all in a week. They had expected that the King, having taken the oath, would be a true Covenanter, and thus abjure women, except in wedlock, and drink only whisky in small quantities.

110

Unfortunately, Charles was not married. Instead they discovered that his 'court' was awash with French wine and French whores, cunningly disguised as members of the nobility.

These antics had caused a great deal of unease. But they now discovered that they had accumulated a far worse evil than a dissolute spendthrift king: their acceptance of him had aroused Cromwell. Again as I have mentioned, the great soldier had marched north almost as soon as he had got back from Ireland. The Scots had opposed *their* best soldier, David Leslie, to the Ironsides, but Leslie, however famous in his youth, was now an old man, and after much manoeuvering had been roundly thrashed.

During this manoeuvering, King Charles had appeared in the Scottish army, his wine and women with him, apparently eager to display his military talents, but Leslie had soon sent him off, as he *had* no military talents. The King therefore had to oversee the battle from afar, and, one gathers, was by no means overcome with grief at the total destruction of the Covenanting army, conceiving that he now had the opportunity to assert himself, and his prerogatives.

He had thus sought to escape back to the Highlands, with a few of his most intimate cronies, and on the pretence of going hawking had made off. He had soon been recaptured, but the situation had now assumed all the characteristics of a farce. The Scots had made a great business of having gained a king. Were they now to send him packing? Or perhaps emulate the English and cut off his head? But even if the Scots did not have a total aversion to such goings-on, Charles was guilty of no crime save that of lascivious living, which has been the prerogatives of kings since time began. They also had the problem that they were now entirely regarded as enemies by Cromwell, who was busily securing the Lowlands for Parliament, and who was totally opposed to Presbyterianism and the Covenant. Thus Charles had to be forgiven for his misdemeanours, and indeed, when we crossed the border, preparations were already in hand for his coronation.

Alicia and I arrived in Scotland in early December. As I have mentioned, we were welcomed by the people, once it was known we were fugitives from Parliament, because they were all in the same boat themselves. Only shortly before our arrival there had been an uprising in favour of the King, led by the Earl of Ross. Like Leslie, Ross had been rapidly defeated, his troops dispersed, and now Cromwell's troopers were ranging far and wide, hanging and burning, cropping and beating, people they apparently regarded as being somewhat lower than the beasts in the field.

Well, to be sure, the condition of the average Scot leaves a great deal to be desired. The country was in the hands of a small but very authoritarian aristocracy. In the Highlands, indeed, such was the activity of this aristocracy that each clan was hardly more than that, a vast family. But at least in the Highlands the *laird*, or clan chieftain, fared very little better than the cousins who supported him. In the south however the *lairds*, not claiming relationship to their tenants except in a few instances, lived very well in great houses while their people, certainly in December, shivered in draughty and ill-protected hovels and ate a curious brown gruel which they called porridge. My instincts were to apply to the great houses for food and shelter, but Alicia was against this, arguing that we did not know which of the local aristocracy had medized, as it were, and were supporting Cromwell. Thus we took our places amidst the common folk, being well received, as I have said, once we let slip we were seeking to join the King. That my charmer was right to be cautious was revealed on more than one occasion, as we were forced to leave several overnight lodgings in a hurry on being warned that troopers were approaching.

It is my considered opinion that December is no time to be in Scotland, although of course a great many people, the Scottish nation no less, are forced to experience this misfortune every year. In my youth I had campaigned in central Germany, in winter, and found it most unpleasant – it seldom snows in my native Garnesey and so I had had no experience of it. But in Germany it had been, on the whole, a dry, crisp cold. In the Lowlands of Scotland it was a wet, sodden cold. Certainly it snowed from time to time, but then the snow would melt, and the entire country would turn into a vast bog, with every river overflowing its banks, so that progress was slow and difficult. Our only saving grace was that it was even more slow and difficult for those who would pursue us; they seldom kept at it for very long. And yet, we were happy. Or certainly I was. Two people cannot travel together, alone for the greater part of each day, without discovering an enormous degree of intimacy, and ours was compounded daily. Alicia's wound required regular attention. This was always a pleasure, and I swear for her also – it was equally frustrating for me, for although my immediate carnal needs had been well taken care of by Felicity, whom I remembered fondly, my set-to with her had but whetted my appetite for a similar experience with my beautiful companion.

As it happened, my treatment proved entirely efficacious, and by the time we reached Scotland Alicia was perfectly healthy again, with just a jagged brown scar on the white of her thigh. However, this did not mean an end to our physical intimacy. We found it necessary to assume the role of man and wife, for the Scots are a terribly prudish people. This meant that our bed – such as it was, for more often than not we had nothing more than a heap of straw and a blanket on the mud earth of a wattle hut – had to be shared lest our good hosts became suspicious. But by then I was the sole of propriety. Besides, because of the cold we never took any of our clothes off except when entirely alone, by some bubbling brook, where we could have a bath. This was hardly less frustrating, for Alicia had no objection to my seeing her in the nude, as long as I did not seek to take advantage of the situation. I cannot say how many times I was tempted almost beyond the bounds of reason. But I reflected that every day took us closer to our goals. Or at least, my goal – I had no idea what hers actually was. I knew I had to complete my mission, for my own sake no less than the Queen's, and I was determined to make Alicia mine at the end of it, supposing I survived. As for what Marguerite might make of it, she would have to accept the situation.

Thus we made our way north, avoiding Roundhead patrols, while the country began to rise, and the lochs grew grander and darker, and the rain teemed down. One day as we rode along, drenched to the skin, we rounded an outcrop of rock and found ourselves confronted by a dozen men. They were armed with muskets, which were obviously useless in this weather, and somewhat short swords with a basket hilt. These, from my knowledge of the weapons of all countries, I recognised to be claymores, as carried by the Highland Scots. But even had they been unarmed I would have known they were Highlanders, for unlike those people to the south they did not wear trousers – which the Scots call trews – but rather the kilt, which revealed a good deal of knobbly red knees. Over their shoulders were slung plaids, all of the same design, in which red and black predominated. These matched their bonnets. "I think we have arrived," I told Alicia, who was loosening her pistols in her saddle holster, although these weapons also would be useless in the wet.

"And where might ye be going?" asked the leader of this somewhat uncouth-looking group.

114

"We seek the King," I answered.

"Sassenachs, by God!" muttered another man.

"And Roundhead spies, nay doot," said a third. "We'd best have at them. I'll take the woman."

"You are welcome to do so, of course," I said, resting my hand on the hilt of my sword. "But it may cost you a few lives."

By now their leader had taken in the situation. Both Alicia's and my clothes had suffered severely in our journey; my breeches were torn in several places, as were her skirts; our boots were sadly scuffed, and my feather had never recovered from the attentions of the innkeeper's mallet. However, he could have no doubt that he was looking at a fighting man, nor could he fail to observe that the one part of my equipment which was totally untarnished was the great sword that hung at my side – this was due to the care with which I polished it and honed the blade every night, no matter where we might be. "Ye're for the King, ye say?" he remarked.

"We have ridden the length of England to serve His Majesty," I assured him. "And knocked a few Roundheads on the head while doing so."

"Well, then, welcome, stranger. Ye'll take a wee dram. Hector MacGregor's the name."

"Helier L'Eree," I said, dismounting to clasp his hand, "and this is Lady Alicia Marney."

The Highlanders were by now very interested indeed in Alicia's femininity, which was naturally accentuated when she dismounted as she had been riding astride. Their gazes were most appreciative, not to say lascivious, and I suspected I was going to have my work cut out. But first, the wee dram. We retired to a cavern, where the Scots had made their camp. "On patrol we are," Sergeant MacGregor informed us, while he gave us each a cup of golden-brown liquid, and saying something which sounded like "Slanverjar," swallowed his share at a gulp.

I nearly choked on mine, but Alicia, clearly having tasted whisky before, downed hers without a blink. "The King," I said, when I had got my breath back. "Where might we find His Majesty?"

"Why, he's at Stirling, so I believe," MacGregor said. "Waiting to be crowned. Did ye not know this?"

"As a matter of fact, no," I confessed. "But we must be there for his crowning."

"Aye, well, 'tis not so far," MacGregor said. "Ye'll need a guide."

"I am sure you can provide one," I suggested.

"Oh, aye, that I can. But it'll be expensive, ye ken. Have ye money?"

"Virtually none. But we are on the King's business."

"Aye, well, perhaps ye'll sign a paper, so that ma man can have his payment."

"Willingly," I agreed.

And so, as the Highlanders were more attracted by the prospect of money than even Alicia's charms, we completed our journey.

CHAPTER 5

It took us a further five days to reach Stirling, and we arrived in the town where the King held court on 30 December, to find everything a-bustle, for two reasons. The first was that the King was due to be crowned on the first day of the New Year, and great preparations were in hand. The second was that news had just come in of the royal rising in the south-west of Scotland, which had been dealt with most firmly by Cromwell. Indeed, on it being discovered whence we came, we were led in the first instance, without even being granted an opportunity to eat or change our clothes, before the Provost-Marshal that we might make a full report. "You have passed through that country and seen and heard nothing of importance?" this fellow asked suspiciously.

"We found it necessary to mind our own business and keep away from the public eye," I pointed out.

"I would have you know that I am Lady Alicia Marney," Alicia said, very importantly, "and this is the Count d'Albret. We require a bath, and a change of clothes."

"And food," I added. "And wine."

He glowered at us, but was interrupted by the appearance of a young man, who gave a whoop of joy and folded Alicia in his arms. "Alicia, my dearest!" he squealed – there is no other way possible to describe his tone. "My darling girl!"

Alicia looked at me over his shoulder, her eyes, the only part of her I could see, redolent of apology. "Why,

117

Rupert!" she said, apparently equally delighted. "I had no idea you were in Scotland."

"I am with the King. But to have you here!" the young man said, holding her at arms' length. "But . . . such clothes!"

"It has been a long journey," she explained. "And an eventful one. Rupert, I would have you meet the Count d'Albret, my travelling companion. Count, this is my future husband, Sir Rupert Norton."

Sir Rupert Norton turned to look at me. Undoubtedly he did not like what he saw. But the feeling was mutual. I had been prepared to dislike this fellow from the moment I had first heard of him, entirely due to the invisible barrier he presented between me and the object of my lust. Now I beheld the most foppish looking fellow one could imagine, with a little moustache and a preening manner. No doubt he was handsome enough if one likes pretty boys, but my tastes were all in the other direction. And when I considered that this typical example of a courtier had prevented me from achieving my currently greatest ambition, I felt quite out of sorts. As was he, as his imagination began to work overtime. "Your travelling companion?" he inquired, attempting to get some depths into his tone. "But there were others, of course?"

"Not one," his fiancée assured him. "The gallant Count has escorted me all the way from London, protecting my virtue most assiduously."

As this was not quite true, it was evident that Alicia enjoyed teasing her future husband. Well, there was no doubt that she was a tease. But he seemed even less amused, at the same time disconcerted by my size and demeanour. "My gratitude, sir," he said, "for guarding my fiancée over so long a period. No doubt we will speak again. Come, Alicia."

I decided against reminding her of our bargain at that moment. I was here, and I did not doubt that Lord

Culhaven was here as well. That being so, I would find him.

My first business, as far as I was concerned, was to locate myself something to eat. Stirling is quite a large town, situated on the right bank of the River Forth, across which there is a solid stone bridge. The streets and houses climb steeply up a hillside overlooking the river until they reach the shelter of the castle, an imposing pile. This castle had played an important part in history even before King Charles graced it with his presence. It was here, in 1307, that Sir William Wallace defeated an English army attempting to cross the bridge, and it was from here, seven years later, that the immortal Bruce did cross the bridge to do battle at Bannockburn, just over two miles to the south, and secure that Scottish independence which was to be lost again by the amalgamation of the two crowns in 1603.

At this moment, however, history was of less importance to me than the condition of my stomach, which was rumbling fiercely. I thus made my way to the nearest inn, but I had not got very far in the direction of relieving my discomfort when I was approached by an equerry. "Are you he who calls himself the Count d'Albret?" he inquired.

"I do not call myself anything, young fellow," I told him. "I *am* the Count d'Albret."

"His Majesty wishes a word with you," this fellow announced.

I had made my wishes known to the landlord of the inn, and he was just producing the joint of lamb I had ordered. I was thus not inclined to be interrupted. "His Majesty will have to wait," I said, finishing my pot of ale and summoning another. I was in fact relieved to discover that ale was actually available in this benighted place, and that I was not going to have to exist on a diet of whisky.

"His Majesty waits on no man," the youth informed me.

"Ha ha," I laughed. "He has waited on me before, I do assure you."

He departed, discomfited, but returned only fifteen minutes later accompanied by a file of musketeers. "Now, sir," he said.

I had actually managed to swallow a few mouthfulls of food, and to drink another pint of ale, and was thus feeling considerably more amenable. Besides, it was no part of my plan to fight with these people, certainly until I had located Lord Culhaven. Thus I wiped my mouth and accompanied them back out into the snow, and up the last steep street into the castle. A few minutes later I was bowing before the King. "Well, well," he remarked. "L'Eree? I thought you were dead."

The Prince, or, I suppose, I *should* now start calling him the King, and I were old acquaintances. I had first met him in 1642, when I had been sent by Richelieu to persuade the Queen, his mother, to flee England. Without going into the barrel of worms which had thereby been opened, I can say that I had liked him on sight. He had then been eleven years old. Later we had both fought for his father, and I had been forced to modify my opinion somewhat, as I came to know him better, but I always remembered that he was an unfortunate with the most pitiable ancestry one could imagine. Of course, my own mother was burned as a witch, and no one has ever identified my father, but a glance at me will surely convince anyone that he had to have been large, and bold, and determined. Poor Charles had for a mother, Queen Henrietta Maria, a princess of a house – that of Valois – which was well known to number a madman in its ranks every two or three generations; a father, King Charles I, who was quite incapable of keeping his word and had died for his double-dealing; a grandfather, King James I of England and VI of Scotland, who had been a man of decidedly irregular tastes; mostly frowned upon by polite society; a great-grandmother, known as Mary Queen of Scots, who was not averse to murder; a great-grandfather, Henry Darnley, who was an imbecile from another house, and who was one of the people his wife, the aforesaid Mary, had had murdered; and a great-great-grandfather, King James V of Scotland, who had died in battle against his own subjects.

An ancestral background like this is a heavy burden for a young man to carry. Like most people, I was thoroughly relieved that he had turned out to be an amiable and quite shrewd fellow, even if he was totally devoid of any talent save that of getting in and out of ladies' beds with great dexterity. It seemed, however, that he remembered me just as well. "I have heard it said that you were captured at Naseby," he remarked.

"Sadly, sire."

"And sentenced to death by Cromwell."

"Ill gratitude, to be sure, sire, as I once saved his life."

"But . . . you'll permit me, Count . . . in my experience, those sentenced to death by Cromwell are usually dead. Or at least transported to the Barbados. Yet here you stand before me, as *large* as ever before in my life."

"I was fortunate, sire." I saw no reason to acquaint him with the various agencies, whether human or superhuman, which had come, for even more various reasons, to my aid.

"'Tis a pity you did not see fit to communicate with us, Count," the King remarked. "My poor mother, for one, was sorely distressed at the thought of your demise."

I was forced to wonder just how much this rascal knew of the relationship between his mother and myself. But it was not my place to enlighten him on that score, either. "I had urgent personal reasons for retiring, Your Majesty," I said.

121

"Yet here you are again," he pointed out.

"Well, sire, when I heard that you had taken up arms in defence of your inheritance, what else could I do?"

He studied me for some moments. "You are a rogue, Count. But this is well-known. What of Lady Marney?"

It was clearly a time for decision. But, if Alicia's reputation was in any event tarnished by her adventure with me, I could not see that I could do her much harm. In any event, I could certainly not do myself much harm in the eyes of such a lecher as the King. "I will not deny, sire," I said, "that milady played an important part in my decision."

"Then you are doubly a rogue," Charles pointed out, "as the lady is bespoken; you could at least have waited until she was actually married. However, you are here, and right glad am I to see you. You understand that it is my intention to undertake an invasion of England, with a view to regaining all of my prerogatives?"

I did not know that. Nor did I see that he stood the least chance of success, for Cromwell had defeated far better generals than himself. However, as even less did I see that this disastrous ambition concerned me, I contented myself with saying, "And why should you not, sire? I will wish you every success in your venture."

"Nay," he said. "You will wish *yourself* every success in *our* venture, my lord Count."

"Eh?" I inquired, with a sad lack of decorum.

"You are my champion," the King said. "It has long been my opinion that had my father followed his instincts rather than the prejudices of his courtiers, and made you commander of his armies instead of my cousin Rupert, we might well have won the war."

"Your Majesty flatters me," I mumbled, while trying to think.

"Sadly, thanks to the contumacy of these Scottish *lairds*," the Prince continued, in a low voice, for although there was no one close the room was still filled with men,

"I also cannot give you command of my army at this time. However, you will be my chief of staff, and I shall follow your instructions in all things."

I was here faced with a considerable difficulty. Having declared that I had hurried to Scotland to serve this lad, I could not now either claim that I had been but escorting Lady Marney, or that I was pursuing a private business matter. Besides, that private matter had not yet developed to any extent. But the concept of again going to war on behalf of a mishmash of half-formed ideas that was the Stuart monarchy, and against such a man as Oliver Cromwell, was distressing, to say the least. The King, watching the expressions flitting across my face, entirely misinterpreted them. "Capital!" he declared. "And to begin with, you shall be my champion the day after tomorrow, when I am crowned. But first, you must find some better clothes than those rags. And then, why, we shall celebrate the New Year. I am told the Scots do this with style."

This was actually one of the few absolutely true statements Charles Stuart ever made. It appeared that even the Covenanters, grim-faced men never far separated from the Bible to which they referred at the slightest excuse, somewhat relaxed their strict morals on this frankly barbaric occasion. I found myself, dressed in some new clothes, seated in a vast hall in the castle. At the top table was Charles and his lords, and ladies. Amongst them, I observed Alicia Marney, wearing a new gown which seemed all plunging décolletage, and with her hair dressed, so that she was the most entrancing of sights . . . but seated beside her was the dreadful Rupert, all smiles to suggest that he had not been about to wait on his wedding night to discover her charms. Well, this was obviously to the good, from my point of view, but I could not help but experience a distinct pang of jealousy that he should have had so much while I had had so little. As yet, I was determined.

Meanwhile, there was much to be done, in the eating and drinking line. The drinking came first, in the form of innumerable wee drams of whisky. These were tossed off in a single gulp by my neighbours, and I could not do less than follow their examples. But as I was less used to the fearsome liquid I soon found the room going round and round my head, and began to understand that when the Scots said they went to war beneath the fiery cross they were thinking less of a burning piece of wood than of being totally inebriated. However, the universal drunkenness served a purpose, in preparing us for the meal, which was quite the most revolting repast I had ever encountered. In Garnesey we live mostly off fish, of both the shell and the spine variety, caught in our own ample waters. In Normandy I had, for the past five years, enjoyed all the delicacies of French *cuisine*, and this had perhaps spoiled my palate. As a soldier I was of course prepared to take the tough with the tender, as I had had to do on my journey north from London. But this revolting mess, which turned out to be some kind of sausage enclosed in a sheep's bladder, would have been unacceptable had I not been quite drunk.

Actually, it was quite tasty once in the mouth, and I fell to most heartily, while matching those around me in getting more and more drunk as rapidly as possible. Soon we all left our seats and were dancing about the place to the accompaniment of what I shall have to call music but which was actually a weird sound emanating from the instruments being manipulated by the pipers scattered about the hall. These also seemed to have an intimate acquaintance with sheeps' bladders. It was while disporting myself with my companions, a large number of whom were kilted and therefore barelegged, suggesting all manner of irregular goings-on in the course of time, that I suddenly found myself cavorting with none other than Alicia. If she had been worth a second glance at a distance she was worth several more close to, her cheeks pink with the whisky, her hair loose, and her breasts equally so, bouncing up and down and in and out of her décolletage. "My dear girl!" I cried. "You have not forgotten your promise to me?"

So far as I was aware she had not yet married the foul Rupert – there had simply not been time. But she had other things on her mind. "I never forget a promise, Helier," she told me, and held my hand to lead me up to the top table, to the left of where the King was seated. "I would have you meet Lord Culhaven."

Obviously, being drunk has its disadvantages, in that one's reactions are not as quick as they should be. Thus I merely goggled at the object of my quest, having forgotten all about him in my recent revels. On the other hand, he also goggled at me. I fancy he had more reason, in view of my size. I beheld a somewhat small man, considerably older than I had anticipated, who wore a moustache and a little van Dyke, and looked every inch a courtier. There was certainly nothing the least sinister about him. Nor, for that matter, was there anything sufficiently masculine about him for him in any way to attract the Witch of Hohengraffen – at least as I remembered her.

He was seated away from the table, and taking no part in the festivities, although he was watching them with some interest. "Count d'Albret claims to have business with you, milord," Alicia explained.

"Business?" He waggled his eyebrows. "Why, sir, have we met?"

"We have not, milord," I said. "And what I have to say to you requires privacy." I looked at Alicia as I spoke.

"Well!" she remarked, clearly in a huff, and stalked off.

"You have offended that lady, sir," Culhaven declared,

and then frowned at me all over again. "By God, are you not the fellow who brought her up from London? The court is agog with it."

"I was coming this way in any event, milord," I explained. "To see you."

"Me? Whatever for?"

I was beginning to wonder if Anne of Austria had not sent me upon some wild goose chase. But I persevered. "If we may speak in private . . . Have you not heard my name?"

"Can't say that I have."

This confounded me even more, as Richilde had instructed me in the first instance to report to this man. "Well, then," I said. "Privacy."

"Business, is it?"

"It is to do with your good wife."

He blinked at me, and then, without another word, rose from his chair, turned and walked from the hall. As he had not specifically forbidden me to follow, I did so, at the same time drawing deep breaths in an attempt to clear my brain of the alcoholic fumes which were swirling about in there.

Culhaven led me along a corridor, up a flight of steps, along another corridor, and then down another flight of steps. By now even the sounds of revelry had faded behind us, and although there were torches flaring in the sconces on the walls, I loosened my sword in my scabbard, just in case this fellow was less witless than he appeared. And so it proved, for when he opened a door at the end of this interminable corridor, to admit me into a bedchamber, which presumably was his own, he turned quite suddenly, now as sober as if he had never had a drink. "Close the door," he said.

I did so, while inspecting the chamber, which was quite large, and which, most disturbingly, contained an inner door, presently shut. But as the bed was in this room, I naturally wondered what might lie behind the inner door, and wondered even more when I heard movement behind it. Instantly I whipped my sword from my scabbard. "Whatever are you doing?" Culhaven inquired.

"Show me who, or what, is behind that door."

"It is no concern of yours."

"Everything to do with you, milord, is a concern of mine. Open the door, or I shall break it down. If I do that, I will not answer for the life of whoever is behind it."

He looked me up and down, then decided I was not a man to be trifled with. Muttering under his breath, he unlocked the door, to reveal an inner chamber, sparsely furnished, out of which there now sprang a young woman, quite comely in a plump sort of fashion, instantly discernible as she was stark naked. To her looks she now added a pretty line in supplication, throwing herself into my arms and saying, "Save me, sir, I beg of you, from this monster."

"Why, so I shall," I agreed, grasping her to hold her up, an agreeable task.

"Sir, be careful," Culhaven warned. "You know not what you do."

"On the contrary, milord," I retorted. "What matters here is what you *intend* to do with this young lady." He was, after all, the purported husband of the Witch of Hohengraffen.

"Fie on you, man," he snapped. "It is a private matter."

"Then it must become public," I informed him.

He glared at me, then shrugged. "Since you are determined to play the dolt, the wench is for the King."

"The King?" I asked.

"The King?" the girl cried, wriggling from my grasp.

"Aye, there you have it. The lad does like the ladies, even when they are not ladies. It is my duty to produce them."

"You are the King's procurer?" I was more astonished than ever.

"And why not? Someone has to be."

"The King!" the girl breathed, stepping away from me. After all, I was only a count, and she did not even know that.

"You will understand that this is a private matter, as I have said," Culhaven said. "His Majesty would be highly displeased were anyone to learn of it."

"Absolutely. I quite understand," I agreed.

"The King!" the girl said again, eyes shining.

"Aye, but he is not ready for you yet," Culhaven told her. "He is still welcoming the New Year. So get back in your room and await my summons."

"Of course, milord." She cast me a glance as if to indicate her displeasure at my being there at all, and scuttled back into the inner room.

Culhaven closed and locked the door behind her, then turned to me, and without any further preamble, said, "You are from the Queen Dowager of France?" A sudden arrival at the nitty-gritty.

"I am."

"There are some letters Her Majesty would purchase from my wife."

"That is exactly it."

"And you are the envoy?" He looked me up and down. "I had expected a woman."

It became obvious that there was a great deal I needed to know about this man's relationship with the Witch; it was certainly not as close as it should have been, if she had neglected to inform him of the terms on which she had insisted. But equally obviously I had to feel my way very carefully, as I did not wish to scare him off and perhaps lose him as a guide. "I am Queen Anne's most trusted servant," I explained.

"Ah." He went to a side table and filled two goblets with wine, I was relieved to see, rather than whisky.

"You know my instructions?" I asked.

He gave me one of the goblets, then sat down, waving

me to the other chair in the room. "You were to contact me, and I was to take you to my wife."

"Precisely. When can we leave?"

"Not until this campaign is fought."

"What did you say?"

"I am close to His Majesty, as you can see. And so are you, I gather. You are also a wanted man by the Parliamentarians, I understand. Lady Marney has told me this." Again suggesting, as he must have inquired of her, that he was not quite the dimwit he had first appeared. "For us to desert the King now would be to damn us in every direction. Besides, the army will protect us as we move south."

"Your wife is not in Scotland?"

"I am not going to tell you where my wife is. I shall take you to her."

"When this campaign is completed. Do you seriously suppose it will be successful?"

"Do you? I have heard it said that you are a soldier of experience."

"That is why I expect it to fail."

"We shall have to wait and see."

"For how long? I was given to understand that our business was a matter of some urgency."

"Bah!" He refilled his goblet. "Everything is a matter of urgency, to the ladies."

I digested this; it was still difficult to decide whether this man was, at best, a dupe of the Witch, or whether he was very deep indeed. If he was employed by the King to provide nubile young women for the royal bed, I was inclined to the latter. Either way, I simply had to find out, in order to assess the odds ranged against me. "May I ask, milord, how long you have been married to Lady Culhaven?"

"That is a damned impertinent question," he said. "Is my wife known to you, sir?"

"As a matter of fact, yes."

"What did you say, sir?"

"I first met your wife very nearly twenty years ago, milord."

For a second time he goggled at me, then gave a brief laugh. "That is quite impossible. Twenty years ago my wife would have been a babe in arms."

"Ah," I said. So Richilde was up to her old tricks again. "Then I am clearly mistaken. It must have been her mother I met. The Princess von Hohengraffen?"

"Why, that is absolutely true," he said. "You knew my wife's mother? Well, well. What a coincidence. Richilde has often spoken to me of her. Was she as beautiful as they say?"

"She was the most beautiful woman I ever saw," I told him. "But is not her daughter also very lovely?"

"She is superb," he said, fervently.

"May I ask how you met?"

"Why, it was by chance. I was in Holland, with His Majesty, and I encountered the young lady. Her mother's sad death – you know she was murdered?"

"No, I did not," I replied. I did not consider my last attempt to rid the world of the Witch as anything less than justifiable homicide . . . which in any event had been unsuccessful.

"Done to death by some monstrous villain," Culhaven said, again refilling his goblet; it seemed remarkable that while the whisky he must have drunk with his dinner had not appeared to have any effect, the wine he was now consuming was very rapidly making him drunk. "Thus, as I say, poor Richilde was left to make her way as best she could. Imagine, the heiress of a German principality reduced to such straits. I fell in love with her at first sight."

"Was she already in possession of these letters which belong to my mistress?" I asked.

"I do not know. I did not pry. I do not pry now. I only know that my wife possesses something which is of value

130

to the Queen Dowager, and wishes to dispose of them. Is there anything wrong with that?" The wine had now reached the stage of making him belligerent.

"Why, nothing in the least," I assured him, certain now that he was in total ignorance of the true situation. As for whether or not he would prove to be an enemy, that would depend upon how enamoured he was of his "young" wife – which at the moment seemed to be considerably. But he did not know enough to be *already* an enemy, and that was important. "So long as you are sure that your lady wife will not grow tired of waiting for me and sell the letters elsewhere."

"My wife follows my lead in all things," he assured me, which was just about as fatuous a statement as anyone could make, with regard to the Witch of Hohengraffen. As it appeared to be all I was going to get out of him at the moment, I merely bowed, bade him good night, and retired to my lonely couch.

I was one of the few wholly sober members of the party that next day to accompany Charles to Scone, where he was to be crowned. It seems that all Scottish monarchs require to be crowned in this little village, even though the Stone of Destiny, or Stone of Scone, as it is sometimes known, above which they need to sit, had been removed to England by Edward I in 1296 and never returned. We were thus faced with a journey of some thirty miles, as Scone lies immediately northeast of the town of Perth. We departed early, a great cavalcade of men and horses, women and dogs, all wearing our finest but also wrapped up in furs as it was distinctly cold. Thankfully the snow had ceased, although there was a lot of it about.

I spotted Alicia, but she was riding in the midst of her future husband and his friends, and quite failed to notice my wave; she was obviously still annoyed about my treatment of her last night. In any event, as I was required to ride at the King's shoulder, being his champion, I could not have joined her even had she smiled at me. It was, indeed, an odd occasion. Having reached our destination, Charles first of all knelt, and on his knees swore to maintain the Covenant, to embrace Presbyterianism, and to establish it throughout his dominions as soon as he had recovered them. This act of abnegation completed, the Duke of Argyll placed the crown upon the new King's head – not without a censorious glance at me, standing close by, as a champion should. Argyll, it should be understood, was the most covenanting of the Covenanters, and had played a leading part in the downfall of Montrose, who he had always hated.

As if all of this was not humiliating enough, the new King now had to endure a sermon from the minister, Douglas. This turned out rather to be a lecture on the ills that had befallen both him and his people through the apostacy of the new King's father and grandfather, not to mention his grandmother, for Mary Queen of Scots had been a profound Roman Catholic. There was also a stern reminder that he was king only through the will of his people, a suggestion that what the people had given they could also take away again. This of course totally negated the entire concept of a coronation as an annointing and assumption of the sceptre, which by its very nature conveyed the rights of kingship for life and even beyond. In fact the entire event was a total farce, for Argyll, who appeared to dominate the proceedings, was only enabled to do so by his strength in the west of the country, and as Alicia and I were able to tell everyone, that strength no longer existed, thanks to the rout of Ross. Thus almost as soon as the ceremony was over, Charles turned his back upon the once foremost duke, and indicated that he preferred the company of Hamilton, who was for the monarchy, first last and in the centre. He was further strengthened by the enormous enthusiasm of the people, undoubtedly taken in by his handsome face and engaging manners, while of course every woman in

Scotland was at this time very anxious to have a royal bastard to be the support of her declining years,

From this motley, I am happy to exclude Lady Marney, or Lady Norton, as she became the day after the coronation. This was possibly because she was already acquainted with the habits of the King. But this event, her marriage, so full of promise for my future, loomed less large than it should have done, because I was suddenly a very busy man as Charles, having been crowned, was suddenly a very busy king. "Our first, our only, objective," he told his assembled lords and generals, "must be the defeat of Cromwell and the restoration of the monarchy in England." He looked around our faces, seeking disagreement. We all managed to look as positive as possible, even if I am sure there was not one of us who did not feel sure that, quite apart from defeating Cromwell, the concept of inflicting Presbyterianism upon the English could only lead to disaster. "To this end," Charles announced, "I have invited General Leslie to join us with his people."

At this, naturally, Sir Thomas Middleton, who was presently in command of the royal forces, cleared his throat most loudly. He had not been pleased to see me, but at least I was a personal aide, as it were. Leslie was his superior.

Charles smiled at him. "Why, Sir Thomas," he said. "You and General Leslie will share the command."

At this, Argyll joined in the throat-clearing. I was inclined to join *him*, as I had never heard of so disastrous a practice. It had very nearly brought the ancient Romans to catastrophe, and their consuls had at least commanded singly, albeit on alternative days. The King was not unaware that not everyone was happy with his dispositions, and that evening he confided as much to me in the privacy of his bedchamber. "What am I to do, L'Eree?" he asked. "I need men, and men of quality. Leslie has those. I know he is too old to command, but

133

he will not accept an inferior position. War, as they say, is an option of difficulties."

"Absolutely, Your Majesty," I said. "But the difficulties can be reduced as much as possible."

He shot me a glance. "Tell me how, I beg of you."

"Well, sire, with the best will in the world, you will never have men of sufficient quality to stand against the Ironsides on an open field. This was surely proven at Naseby, and again at Dunbar. And in fact, it has been proven a hundred times in history, that when the Scots assault any disciplined English army, they are beaten. What is the most famous battle in Scottish history?"

"Why, Bannockburn, I suppose."

"Which was fought entirely on the defensive by the Bruce. This must be your plan. Concentrate your forces, choose a defensible position, and make Cromwell come to you."

"And suppose he does not?"

"Well, sire, in the first place, you will have lost nothing. But he will come to you, as until you are destroyed Parliament is an usurping government. And you will aid his decision, by loosing your Highlanders against his communications."

"Will they come to my standard?"

"Have they not already done so, sire? Raise the Fiery Cross again, and call them out in their thousands."

This he did, summoning every man able to bear arms to come to the support of their lawful, and now crowned, king. Leslie, arriving a few days later with the remnants of his army, could not dispute that this was an essential course of action, but to my distress, immediately began to speak of taking the offensive once all the clans were raised, and this despite the savage beating he had recently suffered. Even more to my distress, the King seemed eager to listen to him. My only hope was that Cromwell would attack us before we had begun any movement south. But although he had to know what we

134

were doing, as Parliamentary spies were everywhere, he made no move. Indeed, at the beginning of May we received the remarkable information that the great man had put various of his troops into garrisons throughout the Lowlands, and had himself left Scotland for his home. As may be imagined, this put paid to any hope of my persuading the King to remain on the defensive. "The man is afraid of us," Charles declared.

I couldn't believe that. And in fact, it was later learned that Cromwell had been taken ill, hence his departure. But as he was unlikely to die of his malady, we could also be sure that he would again be in the field before long. The question was, where would *we* be at that moment?

It may be accepted that these were very trying times for me. Queen Anne had insisted that regaining the letters was a matter which required the utmost haste, and yet, having left Normandy in September, here I was six months and more later hardly any closer to the completion of my mission. And I was dealing with two women, each of whom was as proud and impatient as the other. Thus I had no means of knowing whether the Queen would by now have written me off and, as she had threatened, sequestered my estates, or equally, whether the Witch would have grown tired of waiting, and published the letters, to bring down the French monarchy and accomplish my own ruin at the same time.

I made a point of visiting Culhaven every evening. He was seldom to be found during the day, and I assumed he was out and about on the King's business, as when I called he always had a nubile young woman awaiting the King's summons. He assured me that he had written to his wife and received in reply assurances from her that she looked forward to receiving me after the campaign. I found no reason no disbelieve him, as I knew that the Witch possessed the patience of the Devil – as indeed she was one of his daughters. And now that Culhaven would have told her that I was with him, I could imagine her rubbing her hands and laying all manner of unpleasant plans for me. I could even imagine her praying to her lord and master to make sure I survived the coming campaign, which was in fact a somewhat reassuring thought.

Meanwhile men continued to join the colours, which had been officially erected at Stirling. By the end of June we numbered some twenty thousand . . . I would hesitate to call them soldiers, as the most part entirely lacked any discipline, or concept of it. But they were at least armed, and used to fighting. I would have attempted to instil some notion of proper soldiering into them, but was forbidden by Leslie. "Ye'll never discipline a Highlander," he told me. "Ye can only turn him loose at the right moment, like a mad dog, and hope for the best."

Not very sanguine words from one's commander-in-chief!

But now I was entirely distracted, by a visit from Alicia.

I had seen little of her since the coronation. She had been married the next day, and Rupert had carried her off to some remote area so that they might honeymoon. However much I had disliked this general idea, I had had to accept it and had, in fact, endeavoured to put her entirely from my mind. Although I knew that she and her husband had returned to join the King at Easter, as I never mingled in the court circles I had not seen her, nor made any attempt to do so, not wishing to reawaken my passion, especially with the campaign clearly so close upon us. Imagine my surprise then when one morning in June there came a knock on my door, and on my servant opening it – I had accumulated a hardy Scotsman named Murdoch, to whose bare legs I had even managed to become accustomed – there was Alicia, looking as cool and delicious in a muslin gown as I had ever seen her.

"A lady," Murdoch said, rolling his eyes. I was already on my feet.

"Who would speak with the Count alone," Alicia announced.

There was nothing for it, nor, now that I was actually face to face with her again, would I have had it any different. "You'll leave us, Murdoch," I said.

Some more eye-rolling, but he obeyed me, and Alicia entered and closed the door. "You have been avoiding me," she declared.

"Well, as to that, I have been busy, on the King's business. Equally as to that, should I not avoid another man's wife?"

She took off her hat, and the room became filled with the scent of her perfume. "That hardly goes well with your reputation, Helier. Or your known desires, as expressed to me."

"Well, milady, if my reputation is as widely known as you say, then you are doing *your* reputation no good at all by visiting me like this."

She sat down, in my one chair. "My reputation is already ruined, by adventuring with you in the first place."

"I am sorry to hear that. You mean your husband does not believe your vow of chastity?"

"My husband is an oaf."

"Well, that was obvious at a glance. Yet you persisted in marrying him?"

"Well, what would you? I am absolutely penniless. Or was. Even more so now that my home has been destroyed. Rupert is very wealthy, and will be even more so when his father dies."

"But you have no intention of being faithful to him, any longer?"

"We have made our mutual position clear. He has . . . other interests, anyway,"

"Your honeymoon must have been amusing."

"As a matter of fact, it was. And by no means chaste, I can assure you. Even if much of what he desired, and I accepted, was illegal. That is what has given me the freedom I wished, and now possess. Sodomy is a hanging offence."

"Good God!" I sat on the bed.

"Does that thought not increase your desire for me, Helier?" she asked in the most dulcet of tones.

Now here I must confess myself an utter villain, because it did. Not that it was a pleasure I had ever indulged in myself. This may seem a remarkable confession from one of the great roués of history, but it had simply never occurred to me to attempt it, possibly through lack of imagination. But the fact is that when one has a woman on her knees, there is another, far simpler, more attractive, and entirely natural orifice at one's disposal, and this had always been enough for me. But it was the *thought* of someone so mishandling that delicious body . . . even if it had apparently been with her consent. "I was sure it would," she remarked, having been watching my expression. "So you see, I may now do as I wish, and may spend whatever I wish, too. In return, Rupert may do whatever *he* wishes."

"A perfect marriage," I suggested.

"Why, yes," she agreed. "Are you not going to kiss me?"

Certainly I was, and at the same time slipped my hand inside the bodice of her gown: I had been waiting a long time to get my hands on those most prominent aspects of her personality. Nor was I disappointed. They were everything a woman's breasts should be, large, yet round and firm, with entrancingly hard nipples . . . "You are going to tear the material," she pointed out. "Would it not be simpler if I removed the gown?"

I agreed with her, still not fully able to believe my good fortune. Thus I helped her disrobe, with as much delicacy as I could. I remembered what she looked like, of course;

hers was not the sort of figure a man ever forgets. But to be able again to stroke that velvet flesh, and this time to hold it against me while I kissed every part of her that I could reach, was one of the most memorable events of my life. "And what of you, dear Helier?" she said. "Shall I not be your valet?" This also was entirely agreeable.

Thus we came together at last, with so much fervour that I began to believe that our period of trial had been as frustrating for her as it had been for me. But she proved herself a vigorous and enthusiastic lover, not to mention experienced, although this was to be expected in a widow who had now remarried. I could only conclude that the dreadful Rupert must be several kinds of a fool. We kissed and nuzzled and sucked and stroked, without any haste to complete the matter, as we presumed the entire night was ours. Indeed my head was between her legs when this delightful episode was suddenly terminated, by a banging on the door from Murdoch, who informed me that an equerry from the King was below. I was forced to abandon Alicia's lilywhite thighs, drag on a pair of breeches, and hurry down the stairs, where I found a young fellow whose face was every bit a white as Alicia's nether regions. "Haste, Count, haste," he shouted. "To the King! Cromwell approaches."

These are the sort of words which can abate the sexual ardour of even a roué like myself. I ran back up the stairs, bestowed a hasty kiss upon Alicia's lips, and finished dressing, with some assistance from Murdoch, when he could stop rolling his eyes at my naked companion. "But what is to become of me?" she inquired.

"Get yourself dressed, and return to your husband. I will let you know when the crisis is past," I promised her. And with that left her, to hurry to the castle. On the battlements I found the entire royal party, including even Culhaven, staring most anxiously to the south, whence there were indeed a great number of flaring torches to be discerned.

"Count!" Charles was in a state of high excitement. "You told me Cromwell was ill."

"I told you nothing of the sort, sire," I pointed out. "I was with you when the report arrived. And are you sure he is there now?"

"Of course we are sure, Garneseyman," Leslie snapped. "That disposition bears all the hallmarks of the lord general."

"Well, then," I replied. "We could ask for nothing more. He has come to us, as we always wished."

In this, I was, of course, using the term 'we' loosely, as I was about the only one of the King's captains who sought a defensive battle. "We are outnumbered," Middleton said.

"But we hold the ground," I argued. "He needs to cross the river to reach us."

"Bah!" Leslie said. "He will have siege artillery. We have none of it. He will merely sit over there and blow us to pieces."

"He may blow the castle to pieces, General. But that is not to say we need be in it. If we dispose our people properly, there is no reason we should not escape severe casualties. And at the end of the day, he must still come to us."

"The Highlanders will never sit out a bombardment," Middleton asserted. "It is not in their nature. They need to attack."

I was aghast. "You cannot mean to lead your people across the river? That would be to throw away our every advantage."

"It is the only way we can win," he insisted.

I turned to the King. "You said you would take my advice in these matters, sire."

Charles was chewing his moustaches. "Yet is Sir Thomas right about the Highlanders, l'Eree."

"I agree that to attempt to cross the river in the face of Cromwell's Ironsides, and his artillery, would be a mistake," Leslie said. "But I also agree that our people will never stand on the defensive. Thus we must choose a course which involves neither disadvantage." We all looked at him, no doubt equally expecting him to produced a large rabbit from his hat. "We must retreat," he explained. "And seek a better ground."

"Retreat?" I demanded. "And will the Highlanders retreat, or will they just go home?"

"They will retreat, and stay with us, if they are promised a fight at the end of it," Leslie asserted. "Besides, if we retreat towards Perth, ever further into the Highlands, we will attract yet more recruits, while Cromwell's line of communications will be stretched ever further."

"Capital!" Charles exclaimed. "Now, Count, surely even you must agree that is a most military diagnosis."

I would have felt more sanguine had I not felt that Leslie's over-riding determination was to avoid battle at all costs. But I realised there was nothing for it: I was the only member of the King's staff who wished to remain in Stirling with the enemy immediately across the river. "As you say, sire," I therefore agreed.

"Then let us make haste," the King said. "Haste, haste."

Instantly all was bustle. The people of Stirling bustled as busily as anyone. A good number of them were uncertain whether or not to remain and hope that Cromwell did not hand the town over to the sack, an even larger number of them were owed money, in varying sums, by the Cavaliers, not to mention the Highlanders, who were never keen on parting with coin. Indeed, on returning to my lodgings, where I found Alicia gone and Murdoch asleep in my bed, I had no sooner turned him out and commanded him to pack up our scanty belongings, when I was visited by my landlady, a very stout Scotswoman with gnarled hands but a sharp mind. "There's the rent," she said. "And sundry other items. That'll be two pounds sterling. And four shillings for the woman."

"Woman?" I demanded. "You brought me no woman."

"Aye, that I did not. But ye brought your own. I've eyes in me head. So you pays your four shillings. Do you think I'm running a bawdy house?"

The question seemed open to debate. But it was all irrelevant, anyway. "Well, my good woman," I said. "I will have to give you an IOU."

"What's that?"

"An acknowldgement of my debt, and a promise to pay it when next we meet."

"When will that be?"

"Put your trust in the Lord," I recommended.

"I'll have none of that," she declared. "Ye are a Papist scoundrel. I could tell it at a glance."

"Madam," I protested. "You do me a grave injustice. I am as big a heathen as any man."

"Rascal!" she bawled. "Jaimie! Ian! Moultrie! There's a wretch here will not pay his rent." The stairs became filled with three large young men.

"Madam," I said. "Do you not trust your fellow man?"

"I'll not trust you, for a start."

"Well, then, I have some information for you. My man and I are about to descend those stairs and leave your premises. If anyone attempts to stop us, I will break his head. I hope you understand me. And you," I said to the waiting louts. Sadly, they did not heed my warning, having no concept of the force with which they were dealing. Thus heads were broken, and some bannisters as well, not to mention sundry items of furniture. But then Murdoch and I were on the street, and hurrying for the stable to fetch our horses. Naturally there was a great to-do behind us, and shouts for the constables, but as every other landlady in the town was also shouting for the constables, and the streets were crowded with armed

142

men and anxious young women, there was no one to attend to us, and soon enough we were mounted and leaving the town.

I rode up to where Leslie was directing the assembly of what pieces of ordinance we possessed. "What of the bridge, my lord?" I asked.

"What *of* the bridge, Count?"

"Well, it is the only means of crossing the river, certainly at this point. Were it not there, Cromwell would be forced to march west for some distance to find a ford, certainly for his artillery."

"Are you suggesting we break down the bridge, Count?"

"That seems to me to be an admirable plan, milord."

"My dear Count, we are fighting for these people, not to destroy their property."

I perceived that this campaign was likely to be even less successful than I had feared. "Then at least the bridge should be held, as long as possible, so as to slow the enemy's advance, milord. Have I your permission to call for volunteers?"

"Harrumph!" he commented. "Ye may call, Count. But I doubt ye'll raise many."

I thought differently, but no sooner had I turned my horse towards the mass of men marching out of the town than I encountered the King. "Where are you going, L'Eree?" he asked me, jovially. I am bound to say that the prospect of total disaster invariably brought out the best in him. "Looking for Lady Norton, eh? I know you for a rogue. Well, she has already left. You'll find her in Perth."

"Actually, sire, I seek volunteers, for a forlorn hope."

"Forlorn hope? What do you propose to do?"

"I am going to hold the bridge, sire, to gain time for the army to reach Perth and put itself into a proper state to fight a battle."

"Hold the bridge? Cromwell will merely blast you with his artillery."

143

"He will still need to cross the bridge, sire."

"And blast the town too," Charles added. "No, no, L'Eree, it will not do. There is only the one bridge. Cromwell will need time to cross it with all his people, not to mention his guns. That will give us time to reach Perth and put ourselves in order. But if we defend the bridge, why, he will force his way across eventually, and then he will treat Stirling as a town which has defied him. There will be a sack, and no quarter, and no love either for the King who so sacrificed his people."

He was of course absolutely right, as he saw it, and I could see little point in again reminding him that there was an alternative – to call a halt to this frantic rout, assemble his men, place himself at their head, and engage Cromwell in a battle to the death here and now. If he intended to wear the Crown of England, such a battle would have to be fought, eventually, and I did not suppose we would ever have a better position than this.

But there it was. I wheeled my horse and rode at his side, to safety rather than glory.

As we thought. We were to be sorely mistaken. What none of us, myself included, had taken into consideration was that we were opposing our puny wits to the greatest general of the century. That I did not realise this was because I had begun my military career with Gustavus Adolphus, and had reckoned there had been no greater soldier since Alexander. But Cromwell was a colossus. Thus, we arrived in Perth in good order, imagining ourselves to be at least twenty-four hours away from any enemy – the more sanguine amongst us considered it to be twice that. Our men pitched camp, while their officers went off in search of quarters, our intention being to arrange our people in order of battle the next morning. I have to confess that I went off in search of Alicia, with whom I had some considerable unfinished business.

Various inquiries led me to the lodging secured by the Nortons, but when I knocked on the door of the bedroom they had been allotted – there was nothing more than this, the arrival of the Royalist Army having severely overcrowded the town – it was opened by the dreadful Rupert himself, clad only in a nightshirt, which was a most unprepossessing, and – having regard to what Alicia had told me of him – somewhat unnerving apparition.

"Why, Count," he observed. "Can I do something for you?"

"Ah . . . I doubt it," I said. "I will return at a more suitable moment."

"You will do no such thing," Alicia remarked, from inside the room. "Come in, Count."

I looked at Rupert, and Rupert looked at me, then he shrugged and stepped aside. I entered the room, and gazed at my beloved. Sitting up in bed and lacking even a nightshirt, she was a most inviting sight, with the covers folded across her waist. But not in the presence of her husband. "I have called at an inopportune time," I suggested.

"Indeed, sir, only in that I had expected you sooner. Leave us," she commanded the unfortunate Rupert.

"In my shirt?" he protested.

"Oh, put on your breeches, then," she conceded.

This he did, as well as his hose and boots, watched the while by his wife and her lover. Alicia seemed not the least put out by this manoeuvering, but I was acutely embarrassed, and breathed a great sigh of relief when the door at last closed on the poor fellow. "I do believe you are a gentleman, Helier," Alicia remarked.

"Never," I said. "But I am a man."

She laughed. "Touché. Are you not going to come to me?" As she spoke, she threw off the covers, and became more attractive yet. I undressed as hastily as I might, but was yet disappointed with the end result. Alicia, as was her wont, took it all in her stride, as it were. "You have

145

allowed that oaf to put you off," she remarked. "But no matter. We will soon have you stiff as a rod. Helier, dear Helier, come and kiss me."

This I did, folding all of that soft beauty in my arms, and being immediately informed that I was suffering no permanent malady. "Now," she said, "I would like you to resume exactly where you left off, yesterday. That should do the trick."

I have no doubt at all that she was right, in principle. Sadly, no sooner had I rolled her on her face and turned my attention to those magnificent buttocks than we were assailed by a banging on the door. "Godsblood but I shall have his balls for dinner," Alicia bawled, rising to her knees in a fine frenzy of outraged womanhood.

I reckoned I might well be facing an equally fine frenzy of outraged manhood – supposing Rupert had managed to find some guts from somewhere – and prudently drew my sword before opening the door. Having seized the coverlet to wrap around my waist, I had left Alicia a bit short of protection, but she did not appear concerned about this.

However, I was not faced by a deprived and out-raged Rupert, but by the same beastly equerry who had interrupted my meal on my first arrival in Stirling. "Haste, Count, haste!" this fellow bawled. "The enemy are upon us."

CHAPTER 6

I really thought that the fellow was demented, until I heard the sound of rolling gunfire. This convinced me that by some miracle Cromwell had managed to perform a two or three day march in twelve hours and that I needed to be up and doing. I thus snatched up my clothes while the equerry no doubt enjoyed the view of Alicia Norton rising to stand on the bed wearing only her best birthday suit. "Helier," she protested. "You cannot leave me so."

"I must," I told her. "But do not fear, I shall be back." I preferred not to indicate when this might happen, but I fear Alicia suspected it might be a lengthy interval, for she threw herself down again with such force that the mattress burst and the room became filled with feathers. I left hastily, having no wish to choke to death. "How did you know where to find me?" I asked the equerry, as he assisted me to dress on the stairs.

"Why, Count," he said, "the entire town knew where to find you." I felt this was a double-edged remark, but there was no time to pursue the matter further, as we tumbled out into the street and the tumult. This was considerably greater than that in Stirling, as firstly, the good people of Perth – and this included the Army – had not had the slightest apprehension that they were about to be attacked, and secondly because, even more distressing to the faint-hearted, they were being attacked from the wrong side – the east instead of the south-west.

In fact, it had been no miracle, but merely far-sighted generalship. Even before he had moved against our position in Stirling, Cromwell, anticipating that we would make a stand in so well defensible a position, as all the rules of military common-sense dictated, had sent Colonel Lambert with a picked force eastward into Fife. His orders were to ferry his men across the Firth of Tay and come in upon us from the rear. This Lambert, a most skilful soldier, had done, but as we had abandoned Stirling, he came upon us much sooner than either he or we expected. Nonetheless, although he had to realise that Cromwell was still some distance away, he immediately commenced hostilities. With startling results. The Royalist Army can best be described as uneasy after its hasty departure from Stirling. Now it rapidly entered a mood of flat panic. Men ran every which way, women screamed, dogs barked, officers galloped to and fro, and muskets and pistols were discharged without the slightest idea of at whom they might be aimed. It did not seem to occur to anyone that we had to outnumber our assailants, possibly by more than two to one, and that we had the time to beat them – with a total restoration of morale – and still form up to face Cromwell whenever he arrived.

I endeavoured to suggest this to the King, when I finally found him, but Leslie and Middleton would have nothing of it. "We must evacuate the city," the old man declared. "Lest we be caught between two armies." One would have supposed that Cromwell was already firing upon us from the west.

"However," Middleton went on, "as you are so anxious to fight, Count, we give you permission to cover our retreat."

Clearly all considerations of exposing the good people of Perth to a sack were now subjected to the urgent necessity of escaping. But I was perfectly happy to undertake the duties of a rearguard. It took me some time to find sufficient men for my purpose, but fortunately the King had brought with him from the continent a regiment of musketeers, recruited from French and Dutch soldiers of fortune, both disciplined and warlike. To them I was able to add a regiment of Leslie's Scots, again, disciplined troops, and these I led out of the town, leaving the tumult behind us. It was now dusk, and of course Lambert – I did not yet actually know the name of the Roundhead commander – had no intention of attacking us in the dark. He knew he would do sufficient damage to our dispositions by a few well-aimed shots from the one battery of artillery he possessed, and deemed it best to await both dawn and the hopeful appearance of the main Parliamentarian body on the far side of the town. But as we did not know this, we were forced to stand to all night, with scarce a bite to eat and only whisky to drink when the sun finally turned up.

We then discovered that we were opposed by some three thousand men, which but confirmed my opinion that we could have won an easy victory had we immediately attacked with all our force. However, I now commanded a mere fifteen hundred, and we did not possess any artillery, as all of that had accompanied the army in its mad flight. "Your orders, Count?" inquired Colonel Lemaitre, who commanded the Continental regulars.

"We must occupy them as long as we can," I told him. "Have you a reliable junior officer?"

"I have several, Your Excellency," said Colonel Stewart, commanding the Scots; he was no relation to the King, no doubt fortunately.

"Then despatch one, with half-a-dozen men, to the west of the town, there to oversee the western approaches, with orders to report to us the moment Cromwell's banners are sighted."

"And the rest of us?"

"We remain here."

Which we did, as the sun rose to bring every promise of a fine day. We were chilled from the night, but the whisky was warming, and I reckoned that the enemy commander, being a Puritan, would be lacking the sustenance of strong drink. He did, however, have those cannon, and I was forced to tell my people to lie down as best they were able to avoid the round shot which came ploughing through the heather towards us. This went on for some hours, while the morning became hot. By then I had sent a detachment back into the town to find us some food, and this expedition had been quite successful, there being a good deal of looting going on in any event. With our bellies full and our brains suitably inflamed, we began to regard the morning with some satisfaction, when, without warning, the Parliamentary force rose up and dashed at us.

In the light of after events I am convinced that this advance was made at a time estimated by Lambert to coincide with the arrival of Cromwell's army, which must have involved a nice bit of calculation as to speed of march, etcetera. However, we had no time to consider other possibilities as the Roundheads came rushing down on us, and we discovered that perhaps a third of their number were the dreaded Ironside cavalry. We gave them a volley, but there was no time to reload, and it became push of pike and thrust of sword in one of the fiercest melées of my life. We gave as good as we received, however, and had the great satisfaction of driving them off. But clearly they were but regrouping for another charge, and when I looked around me and saw how many good fellows had fallen I realised that we had done all that could be asked of us: the fact that at least an equal number of Roundheads lay scattered around the field was neither here nor there, as they had begun with the advantage in numbers anyway. My decision to command a retreat was made the easier to take by the return of our cornet and his men to say that the enemy were in sight on the road from Stirling. "Then we must go," I told Lemaitre and Stewart, and we commanded our men to withdraw, but in good order.

Of course our intention was perceived by Lambert,

and he promptly charged us again, but this was a far less desperate affair; not only did they now have a healthy respect for our abilities, but they also knew that Cromwell was coming up. Even so, as we withdrew to the north, our position was a precarious one. Fortunately Cromwell apparently could not believe that the King had again abandoned a good defensive position, and was preoccupied with the idea of driving the non-existant Royalists out of Perth. Not until the banners of the Commonwealth were flying above the city did he send his cavalry after us. The fact that we could see those banners indicates that we had not got very far, because most of my people were on foot. Thus we had to stand and fight yet again, on two occasions, receiving the charges of the Ironsides with musketry and pikes. Fortunately, this time the Roundheads did not possess any artillery, yet it was a bloody business. Although I kept my people well in hand, and we eventually reached country so broken that the cavalry had to retire, when we came to count heads we reckoned that we were some eight hundred men short of our original numbers. Again, the fact that we reckoned we had downed at least as many of the enemy was scant satisfaction, because once again we were on the run.

And we had a ways to go yet, because the King and his army had fled up Glen Almond and not stopped until they were on the banks of Loch Tay. Truth to say, they were easy enough to follow, from the amount of discarded material, and even more, from the numbers of stragglers we picked up as we went along. A large number of these were women, camp followers who had decided to continue following rather than risk being taken by Cromwell's men, less in fear of their virtues – such as these were – than their lives. It was two days later that I came to the King.

As was to be expected, he was in a thoroughly depressed frame of mind. As were his generals. It seemed to me that were a single man to enter the encampment shouting, "Cromwell is coming," the entire Royalist Army would melt away overnight; a large proportion was doing that anyway. In all the circumstances, I considered this a wise course. But of course I could not just melt away. I went to see Culhaven.

"This is a pretty mess," he remarked. He seemed more depressed than anyone, but I had observed that his moods were more at the mercy of the weather than most men's. Today was bright and hot, and he looked thoroughly enervated. Equally, he was, as usual, alone in his tent. This was another aspect of his personality which was unusual. He was, it appeared, a peer of the realm, he possessed a large estate somewhere in the country, he was a close confidante of the King – although in no very reputable circumstances – and yet he did not appear to have any servants, although he was always immaculately turned out.

Unfortunately, I had been so busy since the occasion of our first visit that I had not had the time to consider his peculiarities very closely. However, I was aware that out on this desolate heath he could have very little to do in the way of procuring young girls for the Royal bed. "Do you not consider that we have done our duty by the King?" I asked him. "He is faced with one of two alternatives: either to spend the rest of his life skulking here in the Highlands, or take himself back to Holland just as rapidly as possible and forget about his dreams of sitting on a throne in Whitehall. Either way, we can do nothing to help him, and I have my mission to complete."

"Hm," he said. "Hm. It would be a perilous journey, without the army."

"It could hardly be more perilous than with *this* army," I pointed out. "However, if you are not prepared to risk it, tell me where I can find your good lady, and I will go to see her by myself."

"No, no," he said. "I am to bring you to her."

No doubt to plunge a dagger into my back at the appropriate moment, I reflected. "Well, then," I said. "Tell me when we leave."

"I will have to consider the matter," he said. "I will let you know."

I could see that he intended to remain with the King; no doubt he had his own canoe to paddle. But I was becoming quite desperate. I thought I might relieve my feelings by seeking out Alicia, but she was not in the camp, and no one knew where either she or her husband was. Truth to say, no one knew where anyone was, or was doing, or intending to do. Thus it was that I decided to take the bull by the horns, or at least the King by the ears. I attended him where he sat on a stone looking out at the waters of the loch, a dismal figure, but hardly more so than the lords who were grouped behind him, muttering amongst themselves. I stood beside Charles, and he raised his head. "A sorry business, eh, Count?"

"The fortunes of war, sire," I said. "They go up, and they go down. But they more usually go up when one assails them with vigour and confidence, and above all, energy."

"You mean I should have stood and fought at Stirling. I can see that now. I have made a sorry hash of things through not listening to you." He sighed. "As I promised to do."

"Sire, looking backwards is a total waste of time, except for the purpose of moving forward with more confidence. Suppose we take a larger view of the situation, pretend we are some enormous bird flying over this sorry land, perceiving everything that lies beneath us. What do we see? I will tell you. Firstly, a messenger galloping south from Perth, to inform Parliament that the King's army is totally routed, disorganised, dissolved, indeed, and that they may sleep easy in their beds as it is just a matter now of scouring the Highlands until Charles Stuart is captured and brought to them in chains."

Charles shuddered. "Is it your intention to cheer me up, Count?"

"You have not let me finish my bird's eye view, sire. We are now flying over Perth, and there below us is the Roundhead Army, a large, well-disciplined and apparently invincible body of men. However, it is also a body of men which has marched a considerable distance in the past week; it is tired, and needs rest and replenishment before it is decided what next to do with it. It will remain at Perth for several days yet, I would say."

Charles gave another shudder. "And then come after me."

"Very probably. Now let us wing our way to the west and south. There we see half a dozen small, scattered Roundhead garrisons, concerned only with keeping down a populace crushed by the rout of Ross. These men will not move without orders from Cromwell."

"My poor people," Charles groaned.

"South of them, in England, there are more scattered garrisons. But all of these will be receiving, from Cromwell's messengers, the news of the dissolution of your forces. They will, in a manner of speaking, roll over and go back to sleep. While the people they rule will mutter to themselves, can it be true that the King, this youthful hero upon whose shoulders rest all our hopes to be rid of these cursed Puritans who make our lives a misery, has given up the quest for his crown? He must know that he has but to appear in our midst and as one man we will draw our swords and follow him to victory?"

Suddenly the King frowned, as he began to catch my drift.

"And finally, sire, we swoop low over Loch Tay. There we see the remnants of an army, a fine army, but one which, as Cromwell will be claiming, is on the point of dissolution. Indeed, it is already dissolving. But can it not be reassembled, very shortly, and given a purpose? You

154

came here, sire, to regain your throne. By that, I mean the throne of England. Who is the one man that can stop you? Cromwell. But Cromwell is resting, away in the east, deeming you no longer a threat. Moving swiftly down the west side of the country, this army of yours could be in London before Cromwell knows that you have left this stone."

"By God," the King said. "By God. But . . . have we the men?"

"Will we not gain men as we march south? From the west country certainly. And then England. Have you not many supporters in England, just waiting for you to come to them? That is how it appeared to me as I travelled through the country." If he did not have the support of a majority of Englishmen, then he was bound to fail in any event, no matter even if he defeated and killed Cromwell personally. But I thought it best not to mention this.

"By God!" the King cried, rising. "You are right, Count." He turned to his lords. "Gentlemen," he cried. "Gather round." This they did. "I have been considering our situation," the King said. "And it seems to me that we need to take a positive step. Gentlemen, raise the fiery cross and recall the clans. We are marching south."

"For what purpose, sire?" Leslie inquired. "Ross has nothing to offer us."

"To invade England."

That left them speechless. "You cannot invade England with Cromwell sitting on your flank, sire," Middleton protested.

"That is where I intend to leave him," Charles declared. "By the time he discovers what we are about, we shall be across the border."

"He will carry fire and sword the length and breadth of Scotland," Leslie said.

"I doubt that, general. His business will be to follow us. Were I to come to Westminster while he dallied up here would be to lose his head."

155

I reflected that if the King did come to Westminster in one piece, Cromwell's head would be rolling in any event, but again opted to hold my tongue. I had set things moving, and that was all I intended to do. "It is a crazy scheme," Argyll said. "I'll have none of it."

"Just what do you mean by that, my lord Duke?" Charles inquired.

Argyll went very red in the face and cleared his throat. "I mean, sire, that if you persist in this unwise course, I will beg your permission to withdraw to my estates and remain there."

"He is setting up to be a traitor," Hamilton declared.

"Why, sir . . ." Argyll's hand dropped to his sword hilt.

"Gentlemen," the King said. "There'll be no quarrelling. You have my permission, my lord Duke, to withdraw to your estates, as you have requested. You also have my permission to remain there, until I send for you again."

Argyll glared at him, realising that he had been banished from the Court. Then he bowed, and marched off. "He should be hanged, before he commits a mischief," Hamilton growled.

"He can do us no harm, now," Charles asserted. "Providing he rides west, which is where his lands are. Now, gentlemen, haste, haste."

The response to his enthusiasm was equally enthusiastic, and off we went, horse, foot, and what guns we still possessed. Sadly, with us went the Church Commissioners, and they were to be the ruination of our cause. That they accepted me was simply because the King would have it so, but they rejected a large number of men who came forward to offer us their swords, on the grounds that these volunteers had not taken the Covenant. This was not immediately serious, in Scotland, but now we were marching with great haste, quite unrestrained by any Roundheads. They preferred to remain inside their various fortresses when they saw the horde of kilted, bonneted, claymore-wielding and whisky-drinking Highlanders flooding past their doors. Thus we were across the border in a week.

In this time I saw nothing of Alicia, although I did understand that the Nortons had rejoined the army, and not even much of Culhaven, who seemed pleased that I had arranged for the entire army to escort us to the south. I was too busy riding with the advance guard, haranguing the populace in every town we came to, recruiting wherever possible, and seeking information regarding what the Roundhead forces, and more particularly Cromwell, might be doing. The recruits I despatched back to the main body, not really concerned with how they might be assimilated into the army. For the rest, I sent my scouts ranging far and wide, and was rewarded by their return with a Roundhead captain, captured while attempting to reconnoitre *us*. He proved a mine of information. From him I learned that Cromwell was indeed pursuing us, having left General Monk in command in Scotland, and that he had sent Lambert with three thousand cavalry to catch us up and harry us to a halt until the main body could come up. As we had neither seen nor heard anything of Lambert, I considered that we still had the advantage of time and distance, at least in that direction.

I was more concerned about what might lie ahead, for the captain informed me that Cromwell had sent a messenger galloping from Perth, not only with the information regarding his own dispositions – which was how the captain knew of them – but to command General Harrison, in Newcastle with a sizeable force, to make a junction with Lambert at Warrington, and fall upon the flank of the Royal army. They appear to have had designs of forcing a battle on Knutsford Heath. This did not seem to me to be a very bad idea, as a victory would greatly improve morale, but our morale was actually high, and I realised that our prime objective must still be to get between the various Parliamentary armies and London. The slightest delay could be hazardous to our cause. I therefore myself escorted the prisoner back to the army, and the King. I pointed to the map. "The enemy hope to concentrate here, sire. But we are already *here*, close to the Mersey. Once we are across the river, they will bay helplessly at our heels."

"Hm," Charles commented. "Hm."

"It seems we are more running away from them than carrying out a campaign," Leslie grumbled.

"We are pursuing a strategic objective, General," I reminded him. "That of gaining, and taking, and holding, London before Cromwell can catch up with us. Any unnecessary delay is a negation of that policy."

"Hm," the King said. "Hm. But have we really the time to get across the river before they catch up to us?"

"Well, as to that, sire, a well-placed rearguard would see to our safety. I would be happy to command it."

He shook his head. "Not you, Count. You have done enough in that regard. I prefer you out in front. My lord of Derby, you will see to our rear."

This to the Earl of Derby, who had become an adherent since we had crossed the border. He was surrounded by several English noblemen, such as Lord Widdrington and Sir Thomas Tyldesley, and these nodded their heads most eagerly at the honour thus conveyed upon them. I was not happy with this arrangement, but I could not overrule the King. And all went well in the immediate future, as we crossed the river without a sight of the enemy, and made our way south, and so came to Worcester.

This was the greatest moment of our *chevauchée*, so far. The people of Worcester naturally had had some warning of our coming, and thus sufficient time to decide whose side they were on. Now they turned out in their thousands to welcome us. The mayor and all the corporation were eager to read addresses of welcome, the young men and women cheering us and throwing garlands in the air. Best of all, the Lord Lieutenant of the County was awaiting us with the news that he had several thousand men under arms, ready to join with us on our march to London. One would have supposed we had just gained a great victory over the Roundheads, instead of having spent the past fortnight running before them as fast as we could. The King was clearly gratified. He was, after all, still a youth of but nineteen, and his head was therefore easily turned by physical adulation. "We are most pleased with your resolution in our favour," he declared, when he dismounted at the steps to the Town Hall. "And do graciously accept your professions of loyalty, especially in respect of the regiments you have raised for our service."

But immediately the dreadful Douglas spoke up. "Your Majesty must take care that you are not led astray by infidel enthusiasm, sire," he said. "These men who would fight for you, have they taken the Covenant?"

The King looked at his lords, askance. "Well, no, sire," General Massey said. "There is no such thing in England."

"Then they cannot serve Your Majesty," Douglas declared.

There was a moment of silent consternation. But this was too much. "Sire," I protested. "Will you then refuse the aid of every man in England? The people over whom you would reign?"

Douglas pointed, face crimson with fury. "That creature must go," he bellowed. "You have taken a solemn oath to uphold the Covenant, sire, yet you admit this self-confessed heathen to your very bosom?"

The King looked suitably embarrassed, but at the same time revealed a spark of character which could only have been inherited from his great-great-great-great-grandfather, King Henry VIII – there was no one of comparable stature in his ancestry between. "My dear Reverend," he said, "you have no need to remind me of my oath, for I recall it as well as you. It was to establish Presbyterianism throughout my dominions, once I had regained them. Now, sir, let us not place the cart before the horse. I have not yet regained my dominions. Nor am I likely to, without the aid of stout fellows like Count d'Albret, or such brave men as are now eager to muster beneath my banner. You'll leave the conduct of military matters to myself and my officers, if you please."

The parson withdrew in some discomfort. Actually, I doubt that Henry VIII would have been so polite.

Sadly the King, although lacking neither courage nor resolution, suffered greatly from indolence. He had now marched long and hard, as had we all, for a fortnight. Thus he felt that he needed some respite, and where better than in a town which had welcomed him with such open arms? As was ever the case where Charles was concerned, some arms were more open, and more attractive, than others. But he could also advance a sound reason for remaining in Worcester a few days; the countryside was declaring for him, and he issued a proclamation that all men capable of bearing arms, between the ages of sixteen and sixty, were to muster beneath his standard, at Worcester, on 29 August. I was not at all happy with this. Charles reckoned he would then command a force of some hundred thousand men. I reckoned he might well be right, but they would not be soldiers.

However, the King considered that he had yet another solid advantage: the Earl of Derby and some two thousand men were still covering our rear, between us and any Roundhead force of any size, and no untoward report had reached us from this rearguard. "Therefore they can hardly have been approached by any enemy," the King said gaily. "You worry too much, Count. Now, I tell you what you do: go and find that lovely Lady Norton, and give her a good tossing. That will relieve your spirit."

I conceded that he could be right, but I am happy to say that I placed considerations of duty first, and went in search of Lord Culhaven instead. He was, as usual, alone in his quarters. Indeed, had I spared the time to think of it, he was an increasingly unusual fellow, for one of his rank. Apart from not having any servants he equally seemed to lack friends, besides from the King himself, with whom he was quite familiar. But there again he was unusual, as except when carrying out his duties, he was never to be seen in any female company, or any male either, or at least such as might have interested Rupert Norton. "Well, milord," I said. "We have come halfway down the length of England, and we have placed the King in as strong a position as he is ever likely to achieve. Surely we are in some proximity to your good lady?"

"Your constant wish to desert the King is unseemly, Count," he admonished.

"I am here on a mission, not to serve the King," I reminded him. "When can we leave?"

He considered. "What is your estimate of the situation?"

"As I have said. The King will never be stronger. When all his people come in, he will march on London. I do not believe we can help him further."

"And Cromwell?"

"We have given him the slip. Listen, if you are bothered about sacrificing your interest with the King, surely this business with your wife cannot now take more than a few days? I am sure he will not miss you for that time, and you will be able to catch him up in time for his triumphal entry into London." Supposing that ever happens, I reflected.

Culhaven considered some more, then said, "Very

well. We leave tomorrow." I was so astonished I did not immediately reply. "Do you not like that idea?" he inquired.

I regained my wits. "Tomorrow will suit me perfectly, milord," I said.

"At dusk. Meet me at the bridge."

He was referring to that across the River Severn, which runs hard by the town, and indeed, at certain times of the year, through it. "I shall," I assured him.

I felt a great weight lifting from my mind, while my conscience was absolutely clear. I had given my all for the King. It was thanks to me he was here now, and tomorrow his ranks would be swelled by all the thousands of men who we were assured were hastening to his banner. There would be nothing left for him to do but march on London, overturn Parliament, and assume his reign. I could not help him there, and unlike Culhaven, I neither sought nor expected any rewards for my services. But I would be riding to death or glory.

In such circumstances, I regarded myself as worthy of some entertainment, and determined to obey the King's command.

Locating the Nortons was not a great problem, as both Alicia's beauty and Rupert's proclivities were well known, thus I rapidly made my way to the inn where they were quartered. I may say that Worcester was by now even more crowded than Perth or Stirling had been, and it was clear to me that we could expect very little privacy in which to complete our business, a matter which was now almost consuming my mind, not to mention other important parts of my body. I have no doubt that Alicia felt the same, and besides, she was a woman who did not bear grudges. "Well," she remarked, when I appeared at her door. "I had supposed you had forgotten all about me."

"I am a soldier, my pet," I reminded her. "And have been soldiering. But you have never been far from my thoughts." I looked past her into the very small space behind her, and realised that it had once been a reasonably-sized room but had been made into two by the simple procedure of hanging a curtain down the middle – indeed, I could hear voices from beyond this primitive partition. "Does your husband enjoy himself?" I inquired, as Rupert was not to be seen.

"My husband is out," she informed me. "And thus you find me alone."

"Unfortunately not," I pointed out. "What's happening behind there?"

"Faith, I do not know. The landlord would allow us nothing more than this."

"Do you know those people?"

"We have not been introduced. But does it matter? There is a bed, and I have missed you sorely. Missed you! I have not yet had you." I refrained from pointing out that the situation was entirely of her creation. But I did point out that making love in the company of others, to all intents and purposes, was not my idea of amusement. "Well, then, no doubt you have a more private place of your own," she said, somewhat coldly.

"Indeed I do. Will you accompany me?"

"Allow me to get dressed." Thus proving that she wanted me as badly as I wanted her; our exact relationship could be determined later. She added nothing more than a gown and a cloak, as it was a fine summer's evening, but looked somewhat askance as I led her out of the town and across the bridge I hoped to be crossing again on the morrow. Beyond were nothing but rolling fields. "Where are you taking me?" she demanded.

"Somewhere private," I replied. "That copse over there will do."

"You mean to have me on the ground?"

"I think that is a delightful idea. But I will not require you to get earth in your privies. I have a cloak, and so do you."

"You mistake me for some village wench, I do declare," she grumbled.

"Quite the contrary, my dearest girl. I regard you as the most beautiful of women, and I am afire to have my way with you."

This naturally entirely mollified her, but she looked around herself somewhat suspiciously. "I have never done it in the open air."

"It is the best way," I assured here. "A true return to nature while doing the most natural thing in the world."

"What would you have me do?"

I spread my cloak upon the grass. "I would have you undress, and recline upon my cloak."

"You mean, take my clothes off?"

"You have done that before, for me."

"But not for such a purpose in the open air."

"You will find it a delightful experience to be caressed by the breeze. As well as by me, of course."

She took off her cloak and spread it beside mine, then untied her bodice. "You mean, everything? Will you do the same?"

"Of course." Thus we uncovered our respective charms. Modesty bids me make it clear that I was considerably the gainer. I had of course seen Alicia several times before in the altogether, but to my surprise I found that my prognostications, meant entirely to allay her fears, were equally entirely correct. Beautiful as she had always been, even in the confines of a bedchamber, she was quite glorious when seen in the rays of the drooping sun, with the slight breeze rippling through her hair, and her body a great glow of femininity.

I made her kneel, and kneeling myself, against her, took her in my arms for a long, slow kiss, while my hands slid up and down her flanks and made free with her buttocks. "Oh, Helier," she breathed. "Do you remember what we were doing when we were interrupted?"

"How could I ever forget, my darling."

"Then shall we not resume from there? I was so enjoying it."

"So was I. But remember, I pray you, that it can be for a limited period only, or I shall be spent."

"And can you not manage it twice?"

"Given time. I am no longer in my first youth."

"But we have all the time in the world, have we not?"

Actually, there is no man, or woman, who *ever* has all the time in the world, but I could not help reflecting that we certainly had all evening and then all night, and if tomorrow I was setting off to joust with the greatest of demons, this might well be my very last opportunity to enjoy this glorious woman. It is, of course, odd that our prognostications never turn out exactly as we suppose, but then, that is what makes life exciting. Anyway, the long and the short of it was that I allowed her the fullest advantage, enjoying the delicious sensation of being possessed by those cherry-red lips, while I did the best I could at the other end. I was not unrewarded, I am certain, although one never can be sure with women who can sigh and moan in the greatest apparent orgasm while actually planning the menu for tomorrow's lunch.

The result may be imagined, and I was left temporarily bereft. Greatly to Alicia's delight, I may say, as she continued to suppose the night was yet young, and so turned right-side up to kiss and cuddle and fondle, while making appreciative noises as I began to respond far sooner than I had supposed possible. Sadly, from these delicious activities we were aroused by the sound of hooves. I sat up. Alicia endeavoured to pull me down again. "They can be of no interest to us, my darling," she said.

However, I could now tell that there were several hooves, and all galloping as if the devil himself was after them. From a Royalist point of view and Richilde Bethlen being a female, there was only one devil loose in England. I had to be interested. I freed myself from Alicia's arms and dragged on my breeches. "Helier!" Alicia made an abortive grab at me and missed. "If you desert me now I shall never speak to you again."

"Give me but a moment, my pet," I begged, and stepped from the trees, to see a dozen horseman charging towards me. I waved my arms, and they drew to a halt, peering at me in consternation.

"It is Count d'Albret," their leader said.

"My Lord of Derby," I acknowledged.

"What are you doing, man, standing around in your breeches?" the Earl demanded.

"What are *you* doing, my lord, in the vicinity of Worcester when you should be commanding our rearguard?"

"Rearguard" he snorted. "Rearguard! It is no more. Routed! We have been routed."

I reflected that it is scarcely the duty of the commander of a body of troops personally to bring the news of his defeat, but this was the material with which we had to fight. "And Cromwell, milord?" I asked. "Is there news of Cromwell?"

"Cromwell!" Derby flung out his arm, pointing to the north-east. "Why, sir, he is there! Not a day's march away." And with that he and his companions galloped off again.

Obviously I had to follow. I dashed back into my copse and snatched on my clothes. "Helier!" Alicia said. She was again kneeling, a pretty sight, but I did not suppose she was in a supplicatory mood.

"You heard!"

"Of course I did. But Cromwell is at least a day's march away. And you have not yet accomplished your purpose. Did not Drake finish his game of bowls even when learning of the approach of the Armada?"

Fully dressed, I stooped to kiss her forehead. "Drake, my sweet, was playing a game which did not demand the entire concentration of heart and mind to carry to a successful conclusion. I fear I would be no more use to you than a bent reed. To say truth, I *am* a bent reed at this moment."

"Shit on it," she said. "Oh, shit on it. What am I to do? I am on fire!"

I refrained from suggesting the obvious, being a gentleman. "My advice to you is to get dressed, return to Worcester, and seek out your husband. Then take yourselves away, before the battle."

Her mouth made an O. "There will be a battle?"

"If Cromwell is but a march away, there will be a battle. You may depend upon it."

"But Helier, at least wait for me to dress."

"I cannot, my pet. Duty calls." In fact, as my body was hardly less afire than hers, I feared that if I remained with her I would succumb to the desire to stay right where we were, and this I could not risk, for a multitude of reasons, so off I strode, followed by her curses.

As I was on foot, and Derby and his companions had been mounted, they had a considerable start, and by the time I regained the town the tocsin was sounding and people were rushing about in every direction. Much as I was inclined to seek out Culhaven immediately, my years of service to the Stuarts – most of it unwilling – called upon me to seek the King first. I found him in his nightshirt, surrounded by his hardly better equipped lords, listening to Derby with open mouths and shivering limbs, while a pretty little miss – presumably procured by Culhaven – cowered in the bed behind the King. "L'Eree!" Charles shouted as I entered. "Thank God you are here. What's to be done? We have been outmanoeuvered."

"We must flee," Derby was insisting. "To the southwest. There was always your father's strongest support."

167

"May I ask, sire, if anyone knows the exact where-abouts of the Roundhead army?" I inquired.

Everyone looked at Derby. "They are there!" Again he flung out his arm. "Not two marches away."

Two was somewhat longer than his original estimate. But not long enough. "Have you any idea of his numbers, my lord?"

"Oh . . . thirty thousand, at the least."

There was a moment's silence. "Did you say *thirty* thousand, my lord?" Leslie asked.

"At the least. I saw them, man. Three great bodies, at least ten thousand each. And a third were cavalry."

So, while the King had been taking his ease here in Worcester, Cromwell, with his customary energy, had been raising all England. "How many men do we muster, General Massey?" the King asked.

"With the recruits that have come in, approximately twelve thousand men, sire."

"Twelve thousand, sir? I was promised eight times that number."

"Only twelve thousand are under arms, sire," Massey said.

"Then that is it," Leslie declared. "We must avoid battle."

"We must go to the south-west," Derby said again. "There we will gain recruits."

The King sighed. "Is there an alternative?"

He was looking at me. "There is no alternative, sire," I said. "Other than to stand and fight."

"What? What did you say?" Leslie protested.

"Your Majesty," I said. "We have again a strong pos-ition. Cromwell must needs cross the river to reach us."

"He outnumbers us by more than two to one," Middleton argued.

"That may be, general, but our strength is doubled by our position. Do but let us be resolute, and we may yet gain the day. And, sire, think what a check

168

to Cromwell's career of victory will mean. Why, his reputation will collapse, and with it, the Parliamentary cause."

"By God!" the King said. "You are right, Count. We will fight." His generals looked most unhappy. "And I will lead you. With Count d'Albret at my side."

It was my turn to look unhappy. Having again set events in motion, it had been my idea to take myself and Culhaven off, long before the first shots were fired. But now I was again hoist by my own petard. So I smiled, and said, "I shall be there, sire."

There was a great deal to be done, and thus I abandoned any idea of again seeking Alicia. I did seek Culhaven, to inform him that I was committed to remaining and fighting with the King. I had expected him to be pleased at this, but again to my surprise he seemed greatly put out. "When, then, can we leave?" he demanded.

"After the battle," I promised him, mystified at this role-reversal we had undergone.

"Hm," he said. "Hm."

I had not the time to consider the implications of his *volte-face*; my duty called me to arranging the King's dispositions. These in part had to depend upon Cromwell's dispositions, naturally, and so the next day the King and I, with his various commanders, climbed to the top of the spire of Worcester Cathedral, the highest vantage point available, and looked out to the north-east. We did not have long to wait before the Parliamentary banners were sighted. But our enemies had barely hove into view before they pitched their camps, although their cavalry patrols came down to look at us from close range, most insolently.

A word here needs to be said about our position. The City of Worcester is actually protected by two rivers, the Severn, which runs down from north to south, and the Teme, which crosses the Severn, immediately south of

169

the town. These rivers provided considerable obstacles to any attacking force, hence my confidence. I was not overly concerned when, during the course of this day, I saw one large body of Roundheads moving to the south; Cromwell would know as well as anyone that if the King did decide to withdraw, it would be to the south-west and the support he would hope to find there. We observed this movement – which was commanded by my old foe Lambert – but resisted any temptation to counter-attack, our forces being too small. For the next twenty-four hours we stood to our arms, awaiting Cromwell's move, but none came. I realised, of course, what he was waiting for. "Tomorrow is 3 September, sire," I told the King. "The anniversary of his victory at Dunbar. It is then he will make his move."

However, while it was in a sense reassuring that Cromwell was, for all his religious ranting, as superstitious as any other man, and was thus as predictable as any other man, it was still necessary to brace ourselves. On the next morning, as I had prophesied, the second of the three Roundhead battles, this one commanded by Fleetwood, commenced to cross the Teme, and we had to react. Charles, who had spent the entire previous twenty-four hours perched on his cathedral spire watching the enemy manoeuvres, insisted upon leading the counter-attack himself. He mounted, I mounted, we all mounted, and led our more experienced troops against the enemy. They had established a formidable bridgehead, and it was a fierce tussle. I was delighted, and perhaps saddened, to witness the courage with which the boy King fought, when his position was hopeless. This was because, for all the King's courage, and the military experience and skill of men like Leslie and Middleton, and, dare I say it, myself, too many of our men were mere militia, as I had feared . . . and we were confronted by the foremost soldier of his age. Thus while we tackled Fleetwood, with considerable success, and

170

gained a local victory, Lambert, seeing us preoccupied, crossed the Teme. Far worse, Cromwell, with his third battle, forced the Severn on our left.

It was thus necessary to abandon our victorious assault on Fleetwood, and withdraw to the city. I was still not without hope, for taking a city is a hazardous affair. Sadly, it had been necessary to use our best troops in the attack upon Fleetwood. Those we had left behind were mere farmhands called from the plough hardly a week earlier, given a musket or a pike, and told to fight for the King. They were not the men to resist the Ironsides. I could tell at a glance that the battle was lost. Our people were running every which way, the Roundheads were already ranging the streets of Worcester, and there was no position at which we could even attempt to rally our people. This placed me in a considerable quandary. I was well mounted, and the temptation to abandon the field myself was strong – I had never intended to take any part in this war. But I was forced to reflect that to flee Worcester without Culhaven was a total waste of time. I was also placed in the difficult position of having advised the King to stand here, rather than run away yet again. Therefore I was responsible for his person. I am not an entirely dishonourable fellow.

Yet I had my mission to accomplish. And I also had Alicia on my mind, as the thought of that delectable white body in the hands of rampant soldiery was most distressing. Reconciling all of these different points of view when in the middle of a battle was exceedingly difficult. In the first instance, I led the King and his staff in a mad dash back to the city, where some of our people, the Scottish cavalry, were making a determined stand against the enemy. "Here I stay," Charles declared. "I shall die, sword in hand. They will not cut off my head, as they did my father's."

"Defend yourself as long as possible, sire," I advised, and took myself into the city itself. Here the streets were thronged, with fleeing soldiers, shrieking women, wailing children, barking dogs, and neighing horses. Through this mob I forced my way towards the dwelling of Lord Culhaven, and found him already mounted, looking irritated but not in the least afraid.

"By God, L'Eree," he remarked when he saw my huge form approaching, "but the King has got himself into a pretty pickle. We must leave immediately."

I was sufficiently surprised to see Culhaven up and about at such an hour, even if it was dusk. But I was also relieved. "I agree with you," I said. "But we must take the King with us."

"Whatever for?"

"Because he is the King, whom you have been serving faithfully for the past year."

"Well, I can tell you that his star is set, as I ascertained some time ago."

"I will not leave without him," I said. "He is on the western outskirts of the town. Go to him, and await me there."

"And where are you off to?" he demanded.

"I shall return in a little while," I assured him, and rode on.

Finding Alicia was no more difficult, for she and Rupert were also busily loading a pack horse with their belongings, and mounting themselves, trying to hold off a crowd of rascals, of both sexes, who were clutching at their goods and their mounts, and indeed themselves. "Helier!" Alicia screamed, as she saw me. "Help us, for the love of God!"

I used the flat of my sword to beat my way through the mob, and seized her bridle. "Whoever attempts to stop this lady is a dead man," I bellowed. I have a loud voice, and the crowd fell silent, at least for the moment. "Or woman," I added for good measure.

"By God, Count, but it is good to see you," Rupert said, his voice high with excitement.

172

"It will look better out of town," I told him, and led them back through the streets.

Culhaven had already joined the King, who was accompanied by a considerable body of gentlemen and their servants, as well as the Scottish cavalry. Of his generals there was not one to be seen, but from the tumult all around us I had to suppose that these gentlemen were doing their best. "I shall not flee, L'Eree," Charles declared. "Not when my people are dying all around me."

"You have a duty, sire," I told him, "to preserve yourself for a better day."

His people clearly agreed with me, but I had already determined that we would do better without them; the Roundheads were more likely to go seeking a large than a small body of men.

"Do you cover our retreat," I told the horsemen. "We shall wait for you in the copse beyond the bridge."

I was of course being a villain in so deceiving them, but there was nothing for it, if we were to escape. So away we rode.

CHAPTER 7

When we were finally free of the cavalry, we discovered that we mustered a party of about sixty men, and one woman, Alicia. On the advice of one of the King's servants, a man named Francis Yates, we made first of all for a house called Whiteladies, situated in the village of Boscobel, which belonged to a Roman Catholic family named Giffard. Here we were assured of a welcome, and received one, for Yates was the brother-in-law of one of the Giffard servants, George Penderel. Indeed it was Penderel who answered our banging on the door. He was astounded to find himself in the presence of the King, and terrified to be told that the battle had been lost. But he admitted us, and roused the family as well as the other servants. There was a great to-do, as may be imagined, for the Giffards had been keeping a very low profile so as not to be persecuted by the Puritans, who hated all Catholics. Now they could not but fear that our tracks would be followed come daylight, when they would find themselves in the deepest of trouble should the King be discovered in their house. They were good enough to feed us with what they had – simple bread and cheese although there was some drinkable sack to go with it – while they determined what must be done.

In this regard the Giffards themselves were all of a twitter, and the management of the matter was deputed to the Penderels, who seemed made of much sterner stuff. "Clearly Your Majesty must escape this place, as rapidly as possible," declared William Penderel, the father, and the family butler.

"Indeed," Charles agreed. "But where can I go? The whole countryside will be looking out for me."

"You must be disguised, sire." This seemed an admirable plan, the more so as we were all by now quite full of sack. Thus the business was approached in a somewhat light-hearted manner. Charles submitted to having his hair cut, by Lord Wilmot, until he became a Roundhead himself. While this was going on, Alicia and myself rubbed his hands and face with soot from the fireplace, to make him look like any gardener. Then he was stripped and re-dressed, in the coarsest clothes the servants could supply; his own clothes were buried in the back garden. It was even determined to change his shoes, but none could be found to fit his rather large feet, so that holes had to be cut for his toes.

When all this was completed he looked as rustic as anyone could wish, save for his hair, which had been so badly managed by Wilmot that it made him resemble a lunatic; Richard Penderel got to work with the scissors and managed to improve it somewhat. Charles himself took all this in good part, but when he spoke we realised that we could not make the King into a farm labourer simply by changing his clothes. This was even more evident when he started to move about. "We will secrete you on the estate while you take lessons, sire," William Penderel suggested. "At least until the hue and cry has passed on."

It had now come on to rain, and Charles was clearly unhappy about his immediate fate, but it had to be better than being captured by the Roundheads. "You'll come with me, L'Eree," he said.

"I doubt that would be wise, sire," I said, as I watched the rain pounding on the window-panes. "You are thoroughly well disguised. But I am impossible to disguise, and my presence could be the ruination of our cause.

I will come to you as soon as I am able." That is, I reckoned, whenever the rain stopped.

So he departed, muttering, with Richard Penderel, into the downpour. In truth I was again presented with a considerable quandary. As were we all. It was obvious to everyone that Charles' only hope of escape was to travel with as few companions as possible, suitably disguised. That left the rest of his party somewhat out on a limb, as it were. In fact, quite a few of those who had fled Worcester with him had already departed again, anxious to put as many miles as possible between themselves and any pursuit. Rupert and Alicia were naturally as anxious as anyone else, and Alicia was quite put out at the amount of time I was spending with the King rather than attending to her. She was, of course, considerably put out about other aspects of our relationship as well, but there was nothing I could do about that with her husband ever at her side, wringing his hands in terror, and with the house so crowded with people rushing to and fro, weeping and wailing.

I was also concerned about Culhaven, who had certainly been with us when we had fled Worcester, and when we had arrived at Whiteladies, but who I had not seen since. Indeed, I went hunting for him, but he was nowhere to be found. I could not believe that he had taken himself off without me, as he had seemed to accept that it was his business to conduct me to his wife, and I became quite alarmed that some mischief had befallen him. It was while I was standing in an upstairs passageway of this house, wondering if there was any place I could have overlooked in my search, that I was discovered by Alicia, who even had Rupert in tow. "Helier," Alicia said in her usual brusque fashion. "What are we to do?"

"I suspect that your best course is to take horse and ride like the devil," I recommended. "Back to Scotland would probably be safest. The King's cause is most certainly lost."

"While you do what?" she inquired.

"I am considering that very matter."

"Then you must come with us."

I looked at Rupert, and he looked at me, at the same time giving a nervous grin. I could not be sure whether he had thoughts of three in a bed, or whether he was merely afraid of his wife. Or both. "I cannot. I must find Lord Culhaven."

"That odd fellow?"

"As you know, I have business with him."

"Helier," Alicia said with great patience. "Would you put business above your life?"

"This business *is* my life," I pointed out. That gave her something to think about.

Meanwhile, the night was now well-advanced. The King had been removed by the Penderels to some remote part of the estate, and most of our party had taken themselves off. We were, in fact, down to Alicia and Rupert, and myself. And presumably Culhaven. "What are your plans, Count L'Eree?" inquired Squire Giffard, clearly anxious to be rid of us as well. "I suspect the Roundheads will be here by dawn. They must not find you on the premises."

"I assure you that I have no desire to be on the premises, squire," I replied. "But I cannot leave without Lord Culhaven, and he has taken himself off somewhere."

"Hm," the squire commented, and went to consult with his wife.

Alicia had been consulting with Rupert, and now she returned to me. "We will remain at your side, Helier," she said.

"Now you are putting your carnal desires above *your* life," I pointed out.

"Well, I will not deny our unfulfilled relationship has played a part in my decision," she admitted. "But far more important, if I am to travel alone around this country, again a fugitive, I would feel far safer with you than with my husband."

"But he has also decided to remain with me," I suggested.

"Oh, indeed. Poor chap, he would be quite helpless on his own. He knows nothing of fighting. Now, Helier, while I appreciate that you feel you must wait for Culhaven to turn up, it seems to me that just sitting around here is going to be very tiresome. Have you noticed how many bedrooms there are in this house? And at least half of them are vacant."

To say truth, exhausted as I was, the prospect of sharing a bed with Alicia was extremely attractive. Having come so close on so many occasions I was determined that the next time there was going to be no unnecessary foreplay to put our union at risk. But there remained problems. "What of Rupert?"

She shrugged. "I have told him I wish to lie with you. Well, he no longer has any wish to lie with *me*. So . . ."

She took my hand and drew me to the stairs, when, as usual, we were interrupted by one of the servants posted outside the house calling out, "Who comes?"

It clearly was not yet the Ironsides, for there was no sound of horses' hooves or jingling of harness.

And now the intruder replied, "Lord Culhaven, you fool."

"Thank God for that," I said, and ran to the door as Culhaven came in. "Where in the name of God have you been?" I demanded.

He looked somewhat taken aback at my form of address, presumably, I supposed, at the brusque tone of my voice. But he answered quietly enough, "I have been reconnoitering."

"But . . ." I peered at him as he came into the light. "You are wounded." In fact he was soaked to the skin by the rain, but there could be no question that the water was mixed with blood.

178

"No, no," he declared. The man had clearly lost his senses.

"You are covered in blood," I pointed out.

He looked down at himself; there were great splodges of blood on his coat and vest, and down his breeches. "I was attacked," he said. "By a wolf or some such animal. It sprang upon me unawares, and was against me when I ran it through."

I regarded him for several seconds, taking into consideration the fact that his sword hilt was as clean and bright as it had ever been. No doubt he had wiped it clean. But yet . . . Alicia apparently felt the same way, as she remained present. Now she plucked my sleeve. "Helier," she whispered. "I do not like that fellow. Do we really have to take him with us?"

"You have got hold of the wrong end of the stick," I pointed out. "He is going to take *me* with *him*. If you wish to come along, no doubt you are welcome, but I must warn you that it may be a dangerous journey. Anyway, I thought he was a friend of yours?"

She shuddered. "Not a friend. Never a friend. I knew of him, and his odd reputation."

"Yet the King certainly trusts him."

"The King has some very odd friends," she said, somewhat enigmatically.

Lord Culhaven had been waiting on the result of our muttered conversation with some impatience, but now we were invaded by the family and their servants, news of his return having spread upstairs. "Milord," declared Squire Giffard. "You are covered in blood." And we had to go through the whole rigmarole again. From which the important point emerged that Lord Culhaven had seen or heard nothing of any Roundheads during his 'reconnaissance', of which I was beginning to have some doubts. "Then now is the time for you to be on your way," declared the squire. "While the coast is clear."

"And what of the King?"

"He is securely hidden," Giffard assured us. "And he has many friends in this district. We shall smuggle him out."

"Well then," I said, "let's be on our way. The sooner we reach your good lady, Culhaven, the better."

Alicia immediately bridled. "Good lady?" she demanded. "You are on your way to see a woman?"

I decided this was not the time to debate that assumption.

"I have business with Lady Culhaven, yes," I said.

"*Well*!" she commented.

"So, are you coming or not?"

"*Well!*" she repeated, even more vehemently.

"We are certainly coming with you until we are clear of the Roundheads," Rupert declared. "Haste, haste, let us make haste."

"But his lordship has had nothing to eat," cried Mrs Giffard. "We cannot send him forth without sustenance."

"I assure you, madam, I am not in the least hungry," Culhaven said gallantly. "I also think that we should be away."

Sadly, as he spoke, a servant ran into the room. "Roundheads!" he shouted. "Roundheads are coming!"

And indeed, now we *could* hear hooves and the jingle of harnesses; we had been so pre-occupied with Lord Culhaven's adventures they had got virtually to the front door before being detected. And Culhaven's adventures had been supposed to include a reconnaissance. There was no time to resolve that conundrum, for all was a-scatter hither and yon. "There is no time for you to escape now," Squire Giffard said. "You must hide."

"Where?" Alicia demanded, ever practical.

"The priest's hole," declared Mrs Giffard.

Her husband looked doubtful. "All four of them?"

"One could go up the chimney," William Penderel suggested. "So long as we remember not to light a fire."

180

"I should think so too," Alicia remarked. "Well, I am for the priest's hole. Lead me to it. Helier, you'll accompany me."

The Giffards looked surprised that she should choose me in front of her husband. But they had a more realistic reason for opposing her idea. "That huge man will never fit in there," Mrs Giffard explained.

"How big is it?" Alicia inquired.

"Why, big enough for a priest. That is why it is called a priest's hole. It was created during the destruction of the monasteries in the last century. But most households only have one priest, you see. And they are usually small. Certainly not outsize."

"Are you telling us there is only room for one person in this hole?"

"Well, two at a pinch, providing neither is very large. You, milady, and Lord Culhaven, would fit in there very well."

This was the first time I had ever seen Culhaven looking the least bit animated. "I think that is an excellent idea," he declared.

"Well, I do not," Alicia riposted. "With respect, milord, but no one is shutting me up in what is virtually a coffin with you."

"Then what is to be done?"

"Where are you secreting Count d'Albret?"

"As Penderel has suggested," Squire Giffard repeated, "he will have to climb the main chimney. It is quite simple to do, and when eight feet up, he will discover an aperture, into which he may insert himself, and remain in perfect safety until the Roundheads have gone."

"How big is this aperture?" Alicia asked.

"Big enough even for the Count, certainly. It is a good space."

"Then I shall climb into it, with the Count."

"But, my lady . . ." Giffard looked at his wife, askance.

She looked at Rupert, askance. Then they all looked at Penderel, askance.

"Milady," the butler said, "think of the soot," preferring not to touch on the subject which was obviously concerning everyone else – the fact that if she carried out her plan Alicia would necessarily be pressed tightly against me for the duration of the Roundhead visit.

"I shall be brave," Alicia said, bravely. "If the Count is going up, then so shall I."

They all looked at Rupert again. "Do you suppose," Rupert asked, "that Lord Culhaven and I could squeeze into this priest's hole of yours?" Lord Culhaven looked even more pleased.

It was decided that I should go up the chimney first. Fortunately, the month being September, the fire had not been lit for some months, and so both hearth and chimney were quite cool. By the same token, however, the chimney had not been swept in that time, it apparently being the Giffards' habit to have this done just before the onset of winter. Wherever I put my hand it came away covered in black muck, and my hand was the least of it, as it was necessary to brace my back against one side of the chimney while using my boots on the other. In this way I dislodged a great deal of the stuff, and poor Penderel, peering into the hearth to see how I was getting on, got an eyefull. However, I reached the aperture without difficulty. This went into the chimney some three feet, and was some seven feet tall; it resembled a sentry box let into the stone. Thus I could stand upright . . . and that was about it. But now I was about to be joined by Alicia.

This proved quite a difficult matter, as women's clothes do not lend themselves to climbing up the interior of chimneys, or the exterior either, I fancy. Thus it was that Penderel and Giffard had to push her from underneath, a task I am sure they found enjoyable even if sooty, while I reached down as best I was able from my perch to grasp her hands and lift her up into my arms. There was nowhere else for her to go.

"Oh, Helier," she said. "I feel so safe."

I did not altogether share her confidence, as I had no idea how long we might be required to remain in this uncomfortable if, intensely intimate, position. But in fact it was not very much later – during which brief interval Alicia made our position far worse by unfastening my breeches and putting her soot-covered hands inside, not entirely for warmth – that there came a banging on the door, which was immediately opened by William Penderel. Squire Giffard and his wife had meanwhile waited in the drawing room, and it was into this room that Penderel showed the Roundhead captain. Thus Alicia and I could hear every word that was said. "By God but it is wet out there," the captain declared. "Have you ale?"

"Ale for the captain, William," Giffard commanded.

"And for my men," the captain added. "Now, squire, you were visited last night by a good number of people. Don't trouble to deny it. The tracks of their horses are everywhere."

"I shall not deny it, sir," Giffard said. "We were visited, as you say, by some three-score men."

"Were you aware that they were Royalist fugitives, from the Battle of Worcester?"

"They told me so themselves," Giffard admitted.

"And so you gave them shelter."

"I sent them on their way, you mean. If I had given them shelter, would they not still be here?"

While the captain was digesting this, Penderel apparently returned with the ale. The captain, having no doubt drunk deeply, sat down, with a sigh, in one of the armchairs before the fire. "I am cold and wet," he declared. "I'll have a fire."

Alicia's hands closed with alarming strength, which, as she had them both wrapped around one of the most sensitive parts of a man's body, caused me considerable pain, and I am afraid some soot got dislodged. Fortunately, the captain did not notice it, but yet was our situation alarming enough. "Fire?" inquired Squire Giffard. "We never have fires in September."

"You'll have one tonight," the captain declared.

"There is no wood," Mrs Giffard pointed out.

"Then fetch some. You . . ." this was clearly addressed to Penderel, "fetch some wood."

"It is stored outside. It will be wet, your honour," Penderel protested.

"But it will burn, will it not?"

"Well . . . there will be a deal of smoke."

"What care I for a little smoke? Fetch the wood, man, or I will have your ears."

"Helier . . ." Alicia whispered.

"Hush," I told her, trying to think.

Penderel no doubt retreated, because the captain took up his interrogation. "Did these people you sent away know anything of the King?"

"They did not speak of him," Squire Giffard said.

"Are you sure? Are you sure he was not of their party? There are those, prisoners we took after the battle, who declare that the King rode to the west."

"If he was amongst the fugitives we saw, he did not declare himself."

"Hm," the captain commented. "Then what of a fellow named Helier L'Eree, who calls himself the Count d'Albret?"

"C-c-count d-d-d'Albret?" Squire Giffard asked, definitely agitated.

"You can hardly have overlooked him," the captain said. "He is an outsize fellow, several inches taller than six feet, and built to match."

"There was one such large man with the fugitives," Mrs Giffard said, coming to the aid of her husband.

"Then where is he now?"

"He went off with them."

"I hope you are telling the truth, mistress," the captain said. "This L'Eree is a known wizard, an associate of devils and vampires, and a traitor to boot. He is the lord general's most bitter enemy, and there is a reward of five hundred pounds for his head."

"Five hundred pounds, did you say?" Squire Giffard asked.

I would have given a great deal to see his expression as he uttered the words, but I had problems closer to hand, as Alicia gave me another squeeze. "Are you really a wizard, Helier?" she whispered.

"Sssh," I begged, trying to determine which of them was likely to betray me first.

"Well, wizard or no, he has gone," Mrs Giffard declared, before her husband could come to a decision. Clearly she was a woman of good character.

"Then tell me this, do you have a large and fierce dog on the premises?"

"We have dogs, hounds for hunting," the Squire said. "They are not particularly large, or fierce. And they are locked up when not after the fox."

"Then you should look to yourselves. There is undoubtedly some such ferocious animal loose in these parts."

"Mercy me," Mrs Giffard cried. "That is exactly what Lord Culhaven said."

"Lord Culhaven?" inquired the captain. "Lord Culhaven is here?"

Now it was the turn of the squire to come to the aid of his wife. "He was here," he explained. "But he has also left."

"But before he did," Mrs Giffard put in, "he told us that he had had an encounter with a ferocious beast, which he slew."

"Oh, yes? When did he make this claim, mistress?"

"Oh, heavens, it was some hours ago. Why, is it important?"

"It is simply that, on our way here, mistress, we came

across the body of a young woman. She had been most cruelly done to death, by some ferocious beast. Why, mistress, her entire throat had been torn out."

"May the Lord have mercy on us," Mrs Giffard cried.

Alicia took her hands out of my breeches. She was trembling. "Nor did it seem to us that she had died very long before we found her; parts of her body were still warm," the Captain said. "Thus, you see, if Lord Culhaven did indeed kill the beast, he must still be in this neighbourhood. Perhaps in this very house."

"You are welcome to search the house," Squire Giffard said. "But you will find nothing. Lord Culhaven was here, not more than an hour ago. But he stopped only for a glass of wine before hurrying on."

"He also stopped long enough to tell you about this wolf, or whatever?"

"Why, yes, so he did. It had been quite an experience for him."

"But he did not mention finding the slaughtered girl?"

"No, he did not."

"Well, I think we will just search the house, as you have invited us to do so." The captain went off, shouting orders, and all around us became one vast bustle. But he was soon back again. "Ah, fellow," he said, apparently addressing Penderel. "That took you a considerable time."

"There was no wood cut to size, your honour," Penderel explained.

"Well, get to it." Penderel started laying the wood.

"Helier?" Alicia whispered. "What are we going to do?"

"Get warm," I whispered back, fastening my breeches, while I tried to plan. I knew I could drop down the chimney and dispose of the Roundhead captain, and perhaps even fight my way through his troopers, although that was a debatable point. But there was no point in my leaving Whiteladies without Culhaven, and there was no way that I could hope to fight my way out of here and, at the same time, find the priest's hole and get him out of there. So I had no choice but to go up, if it came to flames, reflecting that as Alicia was on the outside it was her bottom that was going to be the warmest, a thought which was no doubt occurring to her at the same time, for she was wriggling quite desperately.

However, the Giffards were doing their best to save us. "Lord, lord," Mrs Giffard declared. "Look at the time. It is gone midnight. And it is still pouring. Will you not have a bed till dawn, Captain?"

"I did not come here to sleep, mistress. Fellow, have you never lit a fire before?" Penderel was clearly making a deliberate mess of it.

"Then how about some food?" Squire Giffard asked. "You must be famished, man, having fought a battle and then ridden so far."

"Aye, well, I'd not say no to some food."

"'Tis only bread and cheese, I am afraid," Mistress Giffard said. "But there is more ale. So if you'll step into the dining room, Captain . . ."

"You can bring the food to me here, mistress," the captain said. "I'm after getting warm. But you can feed my men as well. For God's sake, man," he bawled, presumably at Penderel. "That's enough kindling. Strike the tinder."

Alicia and I listened to the scraping of the metal, and I hugged her tightly to stop her from crying out. I can only imagine the looks that were exchanged between the Giffards and Penderel as the spark ignited the kindling and the first whiff of smoke came up the chimney. The wood may have been wet but the kindling was dry, and before Alicia or I could draw breath there was a roaring sound which quite drowned out the voices beneath us, and a good deal of both smoke and heat came up the chimney, causing us both to choke and gasp. "Helier!" Alicia cried.

"Hang on to me," I instructed her, and, pushing myself out of the aperture, commenced to climb. This involved the same process as before, back against one wall of the chimney, boots against the other. True, I was weighted down by Alicia's arms round my waist – she had tucked her fingers into my belt in the small of my back – but then I was driven upwards by the heat and the smoke, and covered a considerable distance in a matter of seconds. Now we were above the immediate heat of the fire, but yet the smoke swirled about us, and had there not been a considerable draught coming in from the pot on the roof I do not doubt we would have suffocated in very short order. However, we reached the next floor fairly quickly, as I could tell from our own chimney being joined by another, perfectly cold. There was no time for finesse, and drawing my dagger I hacked at the stonework, very soon opening an aperture into this first floor fireplace, into which Alicia crawled with the utmost gratitude, to fall upon the floor and draw enormous breaths.

I followed her example in every way. A considerable amount of smoke got into the room from the hole in the chimney-breast, but it did not appear as if anyone had heard the noise of my hammering through. The room had been thoroughly searched by the Roundheads, as there were drawers and clothes and bedclothes scattered in every direction. From which it will be gathered that we were in a bedchamber, and if the clothes had been thrown on the floor, the mattress did not seem to have been slit open. This was rapidly observed by Alicia, who crawled towards it and then on to it. "Helier," she said. "Oh, Helier. Are you really a wizard?"

I really could not wait any longer, and so crawled behind her, and joined her. "Oh, Helier," she said. "You have saved my life." I decided against pointing out that I had been saving my own life, and that she had just been a hanger-on, so to speak. "Not for the first time," she added. Well, that was true enough.

"I think fate has always intended us for each other," she murmured, taking me in her arms. "I have never had sex with a wizard, before." There seemed a good deal of truth in that statement as well, and I was actually intending to delve into her various undergarments, dislodging in the process an enormous amount of soot, when I fell fast asleep.

Well, what would you? I had not slept now for some forty-eight hours, and it had been a most enervating period. One does not get sexually aroused, be interrupted, spend several hours arranging for a battle to be fought, fight the battle, ride for one's life, assist a king to safety, then be roasted in a chimney, without feeling a trifle weary at the end of it. Unless, presumably, one *is* a wizard. And I, sadly, am not. The fact that I was allowed to fall asleep, and stay asleep, for several hours, indicates that Alicia was no less weary than myself, and thus we snuggled against each other until we were somewhat suddenly awakened by William Penderel. "By all the saints, milord," he said. "We have been seeking you everywhere. It was even supposed that you had gone up in smoke." There was still a little hanging about.

I sat up, and realised it was daylight. "What time is it?"

"Past six, milord."

"Good heavens!" I leapt out of bed, discovered that I was still wearing sword and boots – I *must* have been tired – and even my hat.

Behind me, Alicia stretched. "Oh, Helier," she murmured. "Dear Helier. Come back to bed." Then she opened her eyes and discovered Penderel, and sat up herself with a pretty little shriek. "What is happening?"

"Why, milady, at the moment, nothing," the stout fellow replied, perhaps enigmatically.

I had moved to the window, cautiously, but could

see nothing other than a light mist. "Where are the Roundheads?" I inquired.

"Why, milord, they have taken themselves off."

"Then we must do the same," I determined. "Are Lord Culhaven and Sir Rupert up?"

"I believe so, milord. But . . ."

A formidable word, 'but'. "Yes?" I inquired.

"The Roundheads have taken all our horses. All our stock, indeed."

"Shit!" Alicia commented.

I was inclined to agree. Without horses one's mobility is sadly reduced. But she of course was not thinking about horses.

We went downstairs, to a new crisis. "'Tis poor Rupert, dear boy," Culhaven explained. "He has been taken poorly. I suspect it is being confined for several hours in that ghastly priest's hole."

Culhaven himself looked in the most perfect health, better indeed than I had known him; no doubt being confined in a small space reminded him of various episodes in his past. But Rupert was undoubtedly in a bad way, his skin pale, his breathing mottled, his whole attitude one of total confusion. Well, it may be asked, so what's new? But clearly he was too weak to travel, even on horseback, much less on foot. Alicia was all the solicitous wife. "My dearest love," she said, hugging him to her bosom. "Whatever can the matter be?"

"I do not know," the poor fellow muttered. "I fell fast asleep in that hole, and when I awoke, I was so weak. So very weak."

"He had the most terrible dreams," Culhaven explained. "Crying out he was, so that I had to hold his mouth so as not to alarm the Roundheads."

"He has caught a fever," Mrs Giffard decided.

Alicia was still hugging and kissing him, but now she frowned. "He has been bitten by some insect," she declared. "See, there are the marks."

We all bent over the unhappy fellow, and sure enough, there were two small punctures in his neck. "Now that is very strange," remarked Mrs Giffard. "I have never seen anything like that before."

"They were made by a bat, I would say, ma'am," Penderel suggested.

"A bat? In the priest's hole?" the good woman cried, and looked at Culhaven.

"Indeed, there was more than one," Culhaven said. "I was quite afraid."

"But they did not trouble you," Giffard observed.

"Not so far as I am aware. But then, I didn't know they had troubled poor Rupert."

"He must be put to bed," Mrs Giffard said. "There is no question of his being allowed to travel."

"But the Roundheads . . ." Alicia protested.

"Will not return here now. They have searched the place most thoroughly." Mrs Giffard signalled the servants to take Rupert upstairs, and Alicia, after a glance at me, followed.

Lord Culhaven would have gone also, but I checked him. "I think it is necessary for you and I to have a little chat, milord," I said.

"Oh, indeed," he agreed. "We must leave this place just as rapidly as possible. My wife is waiting for you."

"I am sure she is," I said, ushering him into the downstairs parlour and closing the door. "And now I understand why you call her your wife, just as I am now discerning all the falsehoods you have told me over the past few months."

He bristled. "Are you accusing me of being a liar, sir?"

"Milord, I am accusing you of being a liar, a murderer, a criminal in every sense, and a vampire. Not to mention being a blackguard." He goggled at me in consternation. "So," I continued, "would you care to challenge me to a duel, secure in your supernatural power? I should be

191

delighted to accomodate you. You see, my lord, I have been around a very long time. Not so long as you, to be sure. How old would you estimate you are?"

"Well," he said, "eight or nine hundred years, give or take a century. I do not keep a diary, you know."

"You would need a large one, to be sure. I can only claim to forty, sadly. But a good portion of these have been spent in the company of your wife, and her mother, which is one and the same thing, is it not?" I smiled at him. "Now, my lord, should you challenge me, you should understand that I know one or two things about your breed, having associated with them for so long. I know, for instance, that you are a creature of the night. Thus, while you are not entirely bereft of strength during daylight, you are not at your best, shall we say. So you see you would not stand very much chance against me, here and now. But I take leave to doubt that you would have very much chance against me, even in darkness. Because, for example, I keep always on my person, this." And from my pocket I took my silver cross. He blanched. And I smiled again. "I also know that you cannot be killed by ordinary methods. However, should we come to blows, I will tell you what I intend to do. I shall lay you out unconscious, with a blow from my fist. I do assure you that I can do this. Then I shall take that poker over there which you see with the tongs, and I shall drive it through your heart. Then I shall cut off your head. And then, do you know what else I am going to do? Just in case I have made some kind of mistake and you manage to put yourself together again? I am going to pull out all of your teeth."

If he had blanched before, he now looked positively ill. "I do hope we understand each other, milord," I said. "I am telling you these things because while I know you dare not attempt to assault me until bidden to do so by your wife, I simply cannot have our travelling companions subjected to nips in the night, and I would take it most ill should the Lady Alicia be nipped in any shape or form by anyone save myself. Do you follow me?" His head jerked up and down as he nodded. "Very good," I said. "Now, it appears that it will be at least twenty-four hours before Rupert recovers sufficiently from your attentions for us to take our leave. I am sure that, what with that poor young woman and now Rupert himself, you are feeling quite sated. Therefore I strongly recommend that you retire to some dark hole, hang yourself upside down or whatever position you find most comfortable, and sleep off your excesses. Be sure I will call you before we leave."

He scuttled off, leaving me greatly relieved that things were out in the open between us. I still was not sure whether or not I could defeat Richilde Bethlen, but I was sure that I could deal with that misplaced bat, when the appropriate moment arose.

Meanwhile, there were things to be done. I went first of all to the chamber in which Rupert had been laid. Around the bed were not only Squire and Mrs Giffard, and a cluster of servants, but also Alicia. "He is so weak, I fear he is dying," she said dolefully.

"Quite the contrary," I told her. "Your husband will recover, and be ready to leave by tomorrow morning."

"Are you now a surgeon as well as a wizard?" she demanded.

"I am a man who has seen many such injuries," I said. "Now, Squire, as you say, the Roundheads have passed on. Have you thought to recover the King?"

He clapped his hand to his forehead. "My God! With so much going on he had quite slipped my mind."

"I will see to it, sir," William Penderel said, and hurried off.

"Are you really a wizard, Count?" asked Mrs Giffard. definitely interested.

"I assure you, madam, that I am as normal as the next man. I would be quite willing for you to examine me."

She was a comely female, and not all that old. "Ooh,"

193

she commented, blushing most prettily and looking at her husband.

The Squire had his mind on more mundane, if also more dangerous, matters. "Is there really a price of five hundred pounds on your head, Count? Why, man, that is a fortune."

"It is not a fortune that I recommend anyone attempt to collect," I told him. "And now, if I could have a bath," I suggested.

"Oh, really, Helier," Alicia complained. "At a time like this you can only think of a bath?"

"Have you looked in the mirror recently, milady?" I inquired.

As it happened, she had not, and now that she did, she received quite a shock. For of course her face and hair were still thick with soot. As were mine, as well as various other parts of my body. We were hurried away to tubs, sadly in different parts of the house, but I did not doubt that we would soon get back together. I therefore retired to bed in one of the other empty bedrooms in this vast pile. The one we had used during the night was quite uninhabitable, not only from soot, but from smoke damage and the draught caused by the hole I had hacked in the chimney. I was awakened, as I had expected, by the arrival of Alicia, this being in the middle of the afternoon. "Helier!" she cried, ascertaining that I was naked by the simple procedure of lifting the sheet and peering beneath. "Are you really *not* a wizard?"

I assume she was confused by the fact that my appurtenance was in proportion to the rest of me – this does not always obtain with large men, or, indeed, vice versa with small men. "I do assure you that I am utterly human," I replied.

Whereupon she crawled into bed beside me, saying happily, "At last!"

And so, after so many misadventures, we consummated

our love. Except of course that love had nothing whatsoever to do with it. But the fact is, that not even lust was entirely satisfied. Perhaps we were still both exhausted. Perhaps it was that we had postponed the event for too long. Certainly we both had a great deal on our minds. On roughly the same subject. "Helier," Alicia said, squirming on my stomach. "You have made me the happiest of women."

I felt that she was but paying me a compliment, yet I had to reply in kind. "As you have made me the happiest of men," I assured her.

"Now, let us talk about this fellow Culhaven. And his wife."

"She is purely a business acquaintance, at this time," I assured her. "I have been sent by Her Majesty the Queen Dowager of France to purchase something that Lady Culhaven possesses. There is nothing more to it than that."

"Then why have you not completed your business and returned to France, instead of persisting on living as dangerously as is possible?"

"Simply because, as I am sure I have told you, I do not know where Lady Culhaven is to be found. I am relying upon Lord Culhaven to take me to her."

"Lord Culhaven," she snorted. "He is a charlatan."

"I would not dismiss him so easily," I recommended. "I agree that he is not all he seems . . ."

"He is a pervert."

"Would you say so?"

"I know so. How do you think Rupert got into this state?"

"Well . . ." I did not wish to frighten her by informing her that we were travelling in the company of a vampire.

"It is because he and Culhaven spent the entire night making love," Alicia asserted. "You saw the mark on Rupert's neck?"

195

"Yes, I did."

"That is a love bite."

"Is it really?"

"Have you never bitten a woman, Helier?"

"I don't think so."

"Fie on you. That is the sign of true love. But you have never bitten me," she reflected, somewhat sadly.

"It is not what I do," I explained. "And I think you are mistaken about Lord Culhaven. He is married to a most beautiful woman."

"With whom you have had your way, I have no doubt," she complained, bouncing up and down on my nether regions to leave me in no doubt as to her displeasure.

"I knew her in my youth," I admitted.

"Ha! In any event, being married to a beautiful woman is no guarantee of a man's orthodoxy. Is not Rupert married to a most beautiful woman?"

"That is true," I agreed, although to compare Alicia's pale prettiness with Richilde's glowing loveliness was like comparing the moon with the sun at noon. "Well, then, if you are right, we should make a jolly party."

"Do you not think it would be best for you and I just to ride away and let them get on with it?" she asked. "Oh, I understand that Queen Anne would be upset, but it is just a business matter, as you keep telling me. And I know that Queen Henrietta Maria would willingly again give you employment."

"And my estates in France? And my wife?"

"Your what?" This time she bounced right up, nearly doing me an injury with her knees, as indeed, she may have intended. "You have a wife?"

"Very much so. She has been my wife for twenty years." Well, that was stretching the point a little, as in addition to not actually being married, Marguerite and I had only taken up regular co-habiting some six years previously. But I reflected that I *would* have married her, twenty years previously, had circumstances been

196

appropriate . . . and had she been willing. Which she most certainly would not.

"Well, really!" Alicia complained.

"You have a husband," I pointed out.

"That is not at all the same thing," she argued.

I could not actually follow her reasoning, but decided against pressing the point. "Well, my dear girl, let us consider the situation. Your husband is unwell. My wife is a very long way away. And you are lying naked in my arms. I think we should use the situation to our best advantage."

And I gave her another tumble. This one was far more enjoyable than the first, as we were both more aroused. But no sooner was I spent than she returned to the subject of the immediate future. "But you will still not give up this 'business' venture of yours?"

"That is correct."

"Men! I know what you are at. You wish to see this old mistress again. No doubt you wish to tumble her as well."

"I do not think it will come to that," I promised her. "But I do wish to see her again, yes. I believe it may be for the last time. Do you still wish to accompany me?"

"Indeed, I do."

"Very well. I hope you do not regret it. But I will make you a promise: should we survive our coming adventure, I will take you back to d'Albret with me."

"What, to live with your wife?"

"Why not? I think you both would have a great deal in common."

Further speculation was ended by a considerable to-do from downstairs: when Willam Penderel had gone out to fetch back his son and the King from their concealment, he had found they were not there. This aroused the entire household, everyone being very concerned that Charles had gone and got himself caught. It may be imagined that we were a distinctly sober party that evening, with poor Rupert still not recovered his strength, and all of us wondering what might have become of the King. At least I was reassured to observe that Culhaven showed no inclination to disobey me and leave the house. Mrs Giffard was concerned that he did not appear to eat very much, but I knew that his kind take enough at one sucking, as it were, to sustain them for several following days.

As there was nothing for it, other than abandon Rupert – and to say truth I was inclining in this direction – than to wait until the next day, I retired to bed with Alicia, the good Giffards having long since given up any attempt to make moral sense out of our relationship. Thoroughly sated, I was sleeping heavily when as usual I was awakened by a great deal of noise from below: the King had returned.

He had had considerable adventures, which he proceeded to recount to us in some detail: so far as I could gather his attempts to escape had been a total disaster. Alarmed by the sound of the Roundheads arriving at Whiteladies, he and Richard Penderel had determined to make themselves scarce, and walked to a house known as Hobbal Grange, where the King was passed off as a carpenter. He now had the idea of crossing the Severn and getting into Wales, but had fallen foul of a miller who had chased them off. This was a typical example of the mishaps of this peculiar adventure, for the miller was actually a Royalist who was concealing some other fugitives from Worcester, and got it into his head that Charles and Penderel were Parliamentarian spies!

Running away from the miller, Charles and Penderel had eventually made the house of a Mr Wolfe, who was also a Royalist. The town in which Wolfe lived, Madeley, was full of Roundheads, and so, after lying concealed during the day, it was determined that his best course

198

was to return to Boscobel and Whiteladies. So here he was, in a truly wretched condition, for apart from being soaked to the skin and half-starved, the King's feet were so swollen from the ill-fitting shoes that he could scarce walk. We were back to square one, as it were. Myself more than anyone else. "I'll not set off again without L'Eree," the King declared.

It was time for a decision. It is invariably regarded as reprehensible to refuse to serve one's king; in fact, in many cases it may be called treason. However, while I found some things to admire about this hapless young man, principally his physical courage, I knew him for what he was, a human being with scarcely any redeeming features whatsoever, except that courage. I did not then believe that he would ever become King of England in fact as opposed to name. And I was quite certain that if he did, it would not be to the benefit of the country. I had no wish to see him captured by the Roundheads, exhibited as a peepshow in London, and then, no doubt, have his head chopped off like his father. But even less than that did I have any wish to be at his side when this unfortunate fate overtook him. Besides, I had matters of my own to attend to. I reflected that in that direction, to take him with me – as opposed to my going with him – would be to expose him to the venom of the Witch of Hohengraffen, which could hardly be expected to prolong his activities, except perhaps as a vampire, and I was sure the people of England would not want that.

So once again I dissembled, which is, after all, just another word for lying. "Sire," I said. "I am sure you understand that I would willingly die for you. However, it is my duty, as it is the duty of all of us, to keep you alive. Now, sire, that can only be done by getting you out of England, and in this regard I strongly recommend that you find your way, with the aid of your friends, to Bristol, from whence you may board a ship for Holland. But, sire," I hurried on as he would have spoken, "it

199

would be the most absurd of follies for me to accompany you. I am known to the Roundheads, and my great size makes me impossible to disguise. What is more, there is now a price on my head."

"Indeed?" inquired the King. "How much?"

"Five hundred pounds."

"Why, they are only offering a thousand for me," the King complained.

"I am afraid that Cromwell regards me as a most bitter enemy," I said. "So you see, sire, that while you might escape notice, I would very rapidly attract the attention of anyone interested in becoming wealthy overnight."

"Yes," Charles agreed, sadly. "Yes, I can see that." He looked around our faces. "Then what is to be done?"

"I will organise it, sire," said William Penderel. "I know of a family named Lane, who are loyal supporters of Your Majesty, and whose business takes them into Bristol often enough. If you were to travel as their servant . . ."

Charles sighed, and then gave one of his charming smiles. "Needs must when the devil drives, eh? But you, L'Eree? What will become of you? As you say, you are easily distinguishable, and now that there is a price on our head . . ."

"Do not fear for me, sire," I said. "Lord Culhaven has a plan."

CHAPTER 8

"Do I have a plan?" Culhaven asked anxiously, when he got me to one side.

"If you do not," I told him, "you had better think of one very quickly, milord, or this entire venture is going to turn out badly, and," I added for good measure, "you will have failed your wife."

That made him blanch even more than the cross in my pocket. "But if the entire country is full of Roundheads . . .?"

"Tell me this: how far are we from Lady Culhaven at this moment? I know we are close, as it was to this neighbourhood you wished to come with the army."

He chewed his lip for several seconds before daring to answer. "My seat is in Wales. Lady Culhaven awaits us there."

"Why, that is just across the border," I cried.

"It is considerably further than that," he said. "And through some pretty rugged country. How may we get there without horses? Especially if you intend to drag that young woman along."

"Do you not wish to drag her along? Or are you only interested in male blood? What of all those girls you procured for the King's bed? Are you going to pretend you never nipped any of them? Or indeed, all of them, once the King had finished with them?"

"Women lack the body," he pointed out.

"You obviously haven't looked very closely at Lady Norton, recently," I said. "And you are not going to tell me that Richilde does not like female blood. I have seen her at work."

"Why, of course, you are absolutely right," Culhaven said. "I had forgotten that. Are you saying you mean to offer the girl to Richilde?"

"We shall have to wait and see," I told him. "I cannot offer Richilde anything until we get to her. We will have to look at a map, and see what can be done."

Squire Giffard had a map of the area, and indeed of the land for some distance around, including well into Wales. "Now, milord, show me," I said to Culhaven, "exactly where your wife is situated."

"Do you take me for a fool, Count?" he inquired. "I was not born yesterday."

"I appreciate that, milord," I agreed. "But I must have some idea of how far we have to travel."

"Well . . ." he went into another lip-chewing exercise. "My seat is right in the middle of that lot." He thumped a group of hills, not very far from the border, indeed, but I could tell at a glance that it was, as he had claimed, pretty inhospitable country. Well, that figured, where Richilde Bethlen was concerned. "But only I can take you there," Culhaven said.

"Well, of course," I conceded, reflecting that for a man who claimed to have been around for several centuries he was indeed a fool. The whereabouts of his castle would be sufficiently well-known for me to find it, without him, once I had got within fifty miles of it. However, when I studied the map, I found myself agreeing with Culhaven. We had in front of us a most arduous journey, through country which seemed totally uninhabited and which went up and down in a series of mountains and valleys. To attempt such a journey on foot, carrying an invalid and a woman with us, seemed impossible. And then, returning to the map, and understanding that we would have to risk capture by stealing horses if we were going to achieve our objective, I saw a name I recognised. "Dormintsley!" I said. "Why, it is only ten miles from here. And in the right direction."

"What is important about Dormintsley?" Culhaven asked.

"Why, simply that I have friends there, who will provide us with horses."

Culhaven frowned. "You have friends in Dormintsley?"

"Indeed, very good friends."

"Hm," he remarked.

"Why? Do you know the area?"

"Not at all," he assured me.

"We will leave immediately," I decided.

That was of course easier said than done. We had first of all to see off the King, and then to resurrect poor Rupert, who was not at all happy at the idea of walking ten miles. Alicia was even less pleased when she was told our destination. "Back to that woman?" she demanded. "That doxy of yours? I'll not have it."

"Then you and Rupert had best remain here," I told her. "You would undoubtedly be better off."

"Would you desert me to be taken by the Roundheads, and raped and murdered?" she cried.

I sighed. I must be honest here, and confess that my feelings regarding Alicia were more ambivalent than they should have been in a gentleman. I had, for a long time, sought possession of that delicious body. This I had now achieved. But even before that culmination of what might be called my short-term quest, I had been considering her as a useful tool for conbating what lay ahead. When in the mood for sex, Richilde Bethlen would take man or woman with equal abandon, or both together. However, she most certainly did have an eye for beauty and virility, in either sex, and Alicia possessed both of those assets in abundance. Of course I had no intention of sacrificing my charmer, except in so far as I had no idea whether or not

203

I was also sacrificing myself, but if Alicia could be used to attract and therefore distract Richilde it might be a great aid to both our survivals. "Then," I said, "as you are determined to accompany me, let us have no more argument."

We invigorated Rupert as much as we could by giving him a glass of wine and a hearty breakfast, and then the four of us set off. It was now just dawn, and we were perhaps an hour behind the King and his companion, they having shared our breakfast before leaving. The rain had stopped for a few hours, but no sooner had we left Boscabel than it began again, in a steady, miserable drizzle, which in addition to being wet, had the serious drawback of limiting visibility. Thus it was that, trudging along the road which led in the general direction of Dormintsley, we nearly encountered a Roundhead patrol. It was Culhaven, with the unusually sharp hearing of his kind, who first heard the jingle of their harnesses coming through the rain mist. "Horses!" he snapped.

"Quick, into the ditch," I commanded, and swept Alicia from her feet.

The ditch, sadly, was full of extremely cold and muddy water, and I had to hold her mouth to stifle her shriek of dismay. Then it was a matter of pressing ourselves against the bank, only our heads exposed, while the troop of cavalry walked by above us.

"I will swear I heard a splash," said the cornet.

"Several splashes, your honour," suggested his trumpeter.

I loosened my sword in its scabbard, but we were saved by the sergeant. "Ducks!"

"Are you sure, sergeant?" inquired the cornet.

"It certainly weren't the King," the sergeant said. "Whoever heard of a king hiding in a ditch of water."

Thus reassured, the cornet led his men on, while I reflected that our journey was going to be even more difficult if the Roundheads were still scouring the country in such force, looking for Charles. In fact, as I later learned, they all but caught him, as he had not gone very far in the other direction, and was forced to spend the entire day hiding in the hollow interior of an oak-tree while the troopers hunted all around him. But escape he did, with the consequences that are well known. Meanwhile, I had problems of my own. "Helier," Alicia complained. "I am soaked through."

I gave her my hand to pull her back on to the road, the Roundheads having faded into the mist. "We are all soaked through, my pet."

"I shall catch my death of cold."

"Then the sooner we reach Dormintsley the better," I told her, and we set off again, now proceeding with an enormous squelch, for water was spurting out of my boots with every step. It was a most tedious journey. We had to stop from time to time to allow Rupert and Culhaven to rest – the one still suffering from his "love-bite" and the other not at his strongest during the daylight hours. There was a village before we reached our destination, but I deemed it best not to enter, as there could well be a Roundhead patrol about. In any event, we would have had to explain our wet and muddy clothing, which clearly could only have been accumulated through hiding in a water-filled ditch. People who hide in water-filled ditches, especially where there has recently been a battle and one side has lost, are by definition fugitives.

So we had to tramp through the fields and the woods, becoming even more water- and mud-stained. As a result of all this it was mid-afternoon before we sighted Dormintsley church steeple. By then we were all pretty exhausted, for although Mistress Giffard had provided us with a sack containing some bread, a cheese, and a bottle of wine, that had long been consumed. The food had suffered somewhat from immersion in dirty water – while the long walk had left even me tired. It may therefore be imagined with what relief I led my little band up the drive to Dormintsley Manor.

My only fear was that the Brewins might no longer be in residence, for situations can change very rapidly in the middle of a civil war, but to my enormous relief the butler was the same fellow I remembered. He goggled at me, because he clearly also remembered *me*. "Count d'Albret?" he asked.

"The very man. You remember Lady Marney?" He did some more goggling. "Actually, she is Lady Norton now," I explained.

"For God's sake, man," Alicia said. "Let us in. Cannot you see that we are half-starved? And very wet?"

Hurriedly he opened the door wide, and we stamped into the hall, shedding mud and water. "Harrison?" asked a female voice, and I beheld my fondest recent memory standing at the break of the great staircase. She wore a housegown and her hair was concealed beneath a cap. In other words, she was totally unequipped for receiving company, as she herself understood, especially when the quality of the company registered. "Oh, good lord!" she cried. "Count d'Albret!"

"I hope we are welcome, Miss Brewin," I said. "Our situation is a trifle desperate."

She looked from me to Alicia, then to Rupert, and then to Culhaven, a slight frown crossing her features. Then she descended the stairs. "Are you pursued?"

"Not at this moment," I assured her. "But we are definitely sought."

"What we need are horses," Rupert said. "And something to eat."

"And hot baths and dry clothes," Alicia said.

Felicity looked at Culhaven, as if expecting a request from him, but he merely shrugged. "Some relief from this light, perhaps," he suggested.

That made her raise her eyebrows, as thanks to the low clouds and the rain there was actually very little light, especially in the house. Then she turned back to me. "And you, Count?"

"I would second all of those requests, Miss Brewin."

"Once you called me Felicity," she said, and smiled. "We must see what can be done."

We were led off to various parts of the house, which I remembered very well, and soon I was installed in a steaming tub. As I had hoped and anticipated, I had not been there very long when I heard the bedroom door open. "I cannot tell you how I have looked forward to this reunion," I remarked.

"Is that so?" the man asked. "Have we ever met?"

My head jerked round, and I instinctively reached for a weapon, but with my usual carelessness I had left my sword lying across the bed. However, I was somewhat relieved to recognise the intruder's features, even if, as he had intimated, we had never met. "Dr Brewin!"

"Roderick Brewin, at your service. And you are Count d'Albret." He pulled up a chair and sat beside the tub. "My sister speaks highly of you."

"Then I thank your sister. She was of great assistance to me when last I passed this way."

"Assistance which caused the destruction of my house."

"Believe me, doctor, I regret that most bitterly. I can only hope to repay you. And your sister. Indeed, I owe her, or your aunt, more than just gratitude. Unfortunately, as of this moment I am destitute. But I intend to settle the debt just as soon as I am able."

"I am sure you do. Would I be correct in estimating that you are now on your way from the field at Worcester?"

"Sadly, yes."

"Do you know anything of the King?"

"I am happy to say that he escaped with us, but we deemed it best to separate. I would hope that he is in safety, by now." Actually, as I later learned, at that moment poor Charles was still concealed in his oak tree.

207

"And your plans?"

"Are to reach the Welsh mountains."

"With Lord Culhaven"

"That is correct. He and I have some business."

Roderick Brewin considered me for some seconds, then rose and walked to the bed, where he drew my sword. I could not help but regard this action with some concern. "Have I offended you, sir?"

"It is the company you keep that offends me, Count," Brewin said, facing me, the drawn sword still in his hand.

"You mean that Culhaven is known to you?"

"In a manner of speaking. I suspect him of being a murderer, or worse."

"Absolutely," I agreed.

"What did you say?"

"That I entirely agree with your suspicions. Whose murder did you have in mind?"

"That of a patient of mine. A young fellow, who died quite horribly."

I frowned. "When was this?"

"Oh, a year ago or more."

"I see. Would you tell me the facts of the case?"

"So that you can compare notes with his lordship?"

"Well, then, let *me* tell *you* the facts of the case. Your patient was found with his throat torn out and nearly all the blood drained from his body. Am I correct?" He stared at me in consternation. "So at least tell me what made you suspect Culhaven." I asked.

"Simply that he was seen, shortly after I estimated the time the crime had been committed, with heavily bloodstained clothing. The person who saw him had no idea that my client had been killed, and was indeed concerned about Culhaven. But his lordship explained that he had been attacked by a savage beast, and the blood had been incurred when he had defended himself. By the time the body was found, Culhaven had taken himself back into his Welsh mountains."

I got out of the bath, which was cooling somewhat, and dried myself, watched all the time by Brewin and my sword. "But he was known here," I said. "Or you would not have suspected him."

"He has passed through the village often enough, down to about a year ago. The time of the murder, indeed. On his way to and from his Welsh castle. There is quite a good road for most of the way."

I began to dress, keeping a watchful eye on the doctor, to be sure. "Have you ever seen his wife?"

"Well, not really. She has accompanied him in the past."

"Tell me what she looked like."

"I'm afraid I do not know that. Her face was always veiled."

"Ah. And when last did they pass through here?"

"Well, as I have said, it was a matter of a year ago. Just after the death of that boy. Which is suspicious in itself."

"But you did not consider Lord Culhaven guilty of that crime simply because of his story and the fact that he then ceased using this road?"

"Well, no. There were other factors."

"Tell me."

This time he did not demur. "The attack was made by no wild animal I had ever seen before. Or any tame one, either. I would swear that he had been killed by another human, who had used teeth and nails as his weapons."

"Another human, you say? I think you are being optimistic. But you never brought charges against his lordship?"

"Well . . . consider the situation. The country remained in a turmoil. He was a lord, who it was said, was well regarded by Parliament. I am a humble country doctor. And I had no proof. Only my instincts."

"Then can you charge him now?"

"It is even less possible than before, as I no longer

possess a shred of evidence. However, I do not intend to permit him to lodge beneath my roof. Or my aunt's roof, for that matter. And that prohibition extends to his friends. Indeed, were you not a friend of Felicity, I would hand you all over to the Roundheads. They are not far."

"I see," I said. "Well, then, I will have to convince you that his lordship and I are not friends."

"You travel with him."

"I have business with him, as I have told you. Or rather, with his wife. I must tell you, Dr Brewin, that these two are vampires."

"What did you say?" He sat on the bed, obviously without intending to.

"That they are vampires."

"Good God! Do you believe in such rubbish?"

"One should always be careful not to dismiss what one may consider rubbish, without having experienced enough to be certain of that fact," I told him. "Especially when in the medical profession. You yourself have just told me that you suspect your late patient had actually been attacked by a human agency, in fact Culhaven, in a most unnatural manner."

"My God!" Brewin looked absolutely shattered.

"Only, you see, it was actually an *un*human agency."

"But . . . a vampire? Here in this house? Will the creature not destroy us all?"

"No, no," I said, as reassuringly as I could. "He is carrying out a mission for his wife, who, I may say, is far more formidable than he. His mission is to take me to her."

"Why, if you are not one of them yourself?"

"Simply because I am the man she hates more than anyone else on earth. She thinks she is luring me to her by the offer of a business deal. Once I am in her presence, she means to kill me."

"You can just say that? And go?"

210

"Well, I have every intention of disposing of her in turn. Hopefully, first. And her husband."

"You think you can cope with a vampire? Two vampires?"

"I have had some experience at it."

"And your other two travelling companions?"

"They know nothing of the situation. Nor should they. They have elected to travel under my protection."

"You call taking them into the lair of a vampire, protection?"

"It's that or being hanged by the Roundheads. Now, sir, I have told you my secret. I am troubling you only because, if we are to reach Castle Culhaven, we need horses. But there are also some items of equipment with which you may be able to provide me. I lost all my gear at Worcester."

Brewin had by now laid down my sword, he was in such a state of agitation. I thus picked it up and restored it to its scabbard, and hung my baldrick around my shoulders. This stirred him. "I cannot have that thing in my house. You say that he will not attack you, because he is commanded not to do so by his wife. And you may be right that he will not attack Sir Rupert and Lady Norton, as they are travelling with you. But what of my aunt? What of my sister?"

"Actually, at this moment Lord Culhaven seems to be somewhat sated with female blood."

"Ha! Then what of me?"

"Dr Brewin, I will give you my word that you are in no danger. Lord Culhaven understands that I am aware of his proclivities, and in fact I have warned him off, you might say. I will do so again before nightfall. He never has any desires during the day."

Brewin did not really seem reassured, but he was in a quandary, poor fellow. If Culhaven really was a vampire, and as I was very obviously really Helier L'Eree, the largest as well as the most feared swordsman in Europe, and we were in cahoots, as it were, at least in the short term, he lacked the strength to turn us out. Even if he produced pistols and blunderbusses, he could not expect firearms to have much effect on a vampire. Thus he no doubt determined to possess himself in patience, only asking me, "You swear that you will execute this evil thing, as soon as you have accomplished your purpose?"

"By all that I hold holy," I promised him.

Which, as I did not hold very much holy, was not as convincing as it sounded. But poor Brewin did not know this.

It was now possible to do some organising of our situation. Old Miss Brewin was delighted to greet me again. "My dear, dear Count," she said, clearly having taken a great fancy to me.

"I am ashamed, Mistress Brewin," I confessed. "I had promised to pay you all I owed you when next we met. But here I am again, again a fugitive, and again destitute, and begging of your charity."

"My dear Count," she said. "The sight of you is repayment enough." This made me slightly uneasy. I am never one to turn away from a lady, but this one was old enough to be my grandmother! "You shall have all you require," she assured me. "And again, payment may be deferred. Now tell me, Count," she said, lowering her voice and casting a glance across the room. "Is that not Lord Culhaven?"

I began to feel even more uneasy, as the very last thing I desired was to have to take any more of this household, and especially the distaff side, into my confidence. "Why, so it is. Have you not been introduced? But surely you must have met before, as I understood that he used to be a regular visitor to your village."

"We have just been introduced; we had never met before today," Miss Brewin told me. "But I have heard of him."

212

"Have you now? In what connection?"

"Why, simply that he is an odd fellow, who lives in a lonely castle in Gwynedd, together with his so-beautiful wife."

"Well, mistress," I said. "What is so odd about that? Were I so fortunate as to be blessed with a so-beautiful wife, I should think it entirely natural to lock myself up in some remote castle. So long as she was there as well, of course."

She giggled girlishly, but could not resist casting a quick glance at Alicia. Clearly she was confounded at my travelling with a woman she could not doubt was my mistress, but with her husband in tow. Miss Brewin, of course, was not used to the carryings-on of polite society, where such a situation would have raised no eyebrows at all.

I conceived that that problem, at the least, was solved.

I had sufficient others, for as the Good Book says, as ye sew so shall ye reap. I assumed that the sole reason Felicity had not paid me a visit during my ablutions was that her brother had got there before her. Certainly when we all gathered for a pre-supper aperitif she cast me the most longing glances, and at last seized the opportunity to find herself beside me when I moved to one of the great bay windows to look out at the rain. "You surely do not plan to go out into that?" she remarked.

"I would prefer not to. Do you suppose your aunt would grant us beds for the night?"

"I have no doubt of it."

"She is a most kind old lady."

"She is that," Felicity agreed. "Do you know, I doubted that you would ever return?"

"I always knew that I would."

She gazed at me. I may say that she presented a most attractive sight. This was actually the first time I had beheld Felicity Brewin dressed as a lady, in all the

213

splendour of deep-blue gown, which perfectly set off her splendid auburn hair, with plunging décolletage, jewellery and perfume. And now, a becoming blush to her cheeks. "That pleases me, Count," she said. "But do you travel everywhere with that woman?"

"Lady Norton? Why, she is a fugitive, as am I."

"You were both fugitives, together, when last we met," she pointed out. Medical people have an eye for these kind of details.

"That is absolutely true," I agreed. "But it is pure coincidence. We both serve the King, thus we were both at Worcester, and thus we are both again fleeing for our lives. In any event, on this occasion her husband is with her."

"An insipid sort of chap," Felicity commented.

"Absolutely. Nonetheless, he is her husband, and a most jealous fellow, I can assure you."

"So you do not still spend a portion of each day sucking her thigh?"

"Decidedly not." I hoped she would not inquire too closely into any other parts of Alicia's body I had recently sucked.

"Hm," she remarked. "As for your other travelling companion, well . . ."

Oh, no, I thought, not again. "I know absolutely nothing of him," I said. "Save that he too served the King, and thus he, too, is a fugitive. He has, in fact, promised us asylum in his castle in Wales until we can find a ship to take us to Holland."

By this time I was telling so many lies to so many people on so many subjects I was sometimes uncertain myself what was the truth. "Did you know that my brother suspects him of being a criminal?" she asked.

"A murderer. And an abductor of young girls. Not to mention boys." She raised her eyebrows. "He told me of his suspicions," I said. "I can only say that I have managed to allay them. Lord Culhaven was, and indeed

214

is, an intimate of King Charles. One can hardly suspect such a man of committing murder. Except in defence of the King, of course. While as for abducting young girls, well, this is entirely possible, given the character of the King. I will not venture an opinion as to the boys."

"He still gives me the shivers," she said. "However, Helier, now that you have returned to me, and are, as you claim, unencumbered . . . I should like to pay you a visit, tonight."

"I can think of nothing I would enjoy more," I said, truthfully enough. Although immediately I could see difficulties ahead. "But suppose your brother were to discover us?"

Roderick Brewin was not, of course, the difficulty I actually had in mind. "He will not," she promised.

"Then I shall look forward to your visit," I said.

It was necessary to make some arrangements. The Brewin women were of course delighted to have our party spend the night. Roderick was not so happy, certainly as regards Culhaven, but there was nothing he could do about it when confronted by such a domineering aunt, not to mention a forceful sister. My only remaining task was therefore to have a word with Alicia before we retired. But in fact it was Alicia who decided to have a word with me, just before we were called in to supper. Alicia, I may say, was wearing clothes borrowed from Felicity, as her own were ruined beyond repair – but that did not apparently make her any more friendly towards the young woman. "I saw you tit-a-titting with that female," she said.

"Well, she is our hostess. Would you have me be rude to her?"

"I will not have her in your bed."

"Oh, good heavens!" I said. "Nothing could be further from my thoughts. I am quite done up. Exhausted! I can hardly raise my finger, much less anything else."

"I am sure you will feel better after a meal and a glass or two of wine," she said. "I will join you at midnight."

"I beg of you, my sweet," I said. "Stay in your own bed and have a good night's rest. You may not realise it, but you are clearly as exhausted as I. And tomorrow is going to be a very long and difficult journey. You will need all your strength."

She was still considering this when the gong sounded. It was in truth a rather odd meal, all the conversation being carried on by Miss Brewin, Felicity, and myself. Roderick spent the time staring at Culhaven, who as was his habit, ate sparingly and drank little. Rupert was apologetically overcome by a series of yawns, and Alicia was clearly brooding. I fancy we were all relieved when, the meal over, I suggested that we have an early night, in view of our journey tomorrow. I bade my two hostesses goodnight, thanked them again for their hospitality, and retired to my chamber. I promptly fell into a deep sleep, to be awakened as my door opened.

It was, as I had anticipated, Felicity, as I discerned from her voice, for the room was dark. "Helier?" she whispered.

"Here," I told her.

She came to the bed, a shimmer of white in the gloom. Standing above me, she let her nightgown slip past her shoulders to the floor, and crawled into bed beside me.

"Oh, Helier," she breathed. "Do you know, I feared this moment would never come?"

I kissed her mouth, her nose, her chin, her cheeks, her eyes, her forehead and her hair. I could reach no more of her at that moment, as she was lying half across me, but I could stroke her buttocks. She may not have been as beautiful to look at as Alicia, but somehow she was infinitely more attractive to touch. "I had supposed you would be married by now," I chided.

"Never."

216

"But you have yourself admitted you did not expect me to return."

"I was prepared for a lonely life."

I began to feel distinctly uneasy all over again. It may be difficult for any of my readers, who may not have the facility for attracting women, to believe, but it is possible to be encumbered by just too many of the delightful creatures. "That is absolute nonsense," I told her. "You are a lovely woman, born to be a wife and mother. I can never be your husband, as I already have a wife. What is more, it is extremely unlikely that you and I will ever meet again, after tomorrow, as I am engaged upon a most perilous mission, so . . ."

In saying this I naturally made a mistake. The fact is that however many years I have enjoyed tumbling my various charmers, I had never really got around to understanding any of them. "You mean your business with Lord Culhaven?" she asked, stroking my face with her hair as she was stroking my nether region with her other hirsute attribute. "I will come with you, and help you combat him. And his wife."

"My dear girl," I protested. "That is quite out of the question. Why . . ."

"Oh, Helier," she gasped. "Now, now, now!"

Carrying on a serious conversation in these circumstances is next to impossible, and then I was left gasping in turn. We thus lay silent, nuzzling each other, while we both got our breaths back. But before we did so, the door opened again.

Felicity's head jerked up as she heard the handle turn, but I hugged it back down again, intimating that it were safest she neither moved nor spoke. I dropped my right hand over the side of the bed in search of my sword. Then the intruder spoke. "Are you awake, Helier?"

Calamity! Here was I expecting my visitor to be a relatively simple problem, such as a thief or even a murderer . . . and it was Alicia, disobedient as ever! Once again Felicity would have moved, but I merely pushed her further down beneath the covers, which, fortunately, we had pulled over ourselves following our tumble. I then gave one or two convincing snores.

"Helier!" Alicia closed the door. "Wake up! Have you no candle?"

I gave a few more grunts. "What?" I muttered. "What, what, what?"

Alicia had reached the bedside, but of course in the darkness she could not tell there was anyone more than me in the bed. "Good God, woman," I said. "I told you I needed my sleep. As do you."

"I could not sleep," she said. "Besides, Rupert wished me to leave."

"Eh?" I sat up.

"I think he is expecting another visit from Culhaven," she complained. "He is quite madly in love."

"With Culhaven!" Oh, the rogue, I thought. By God, I will have his teeth out for this. "You must return immediately."

"Oh, really, Helier! I really have not the slightest interest in what they get up to together. I wish to spend the rest of the night here with you." Saying which she lifted the sheet and crawled into bed, on the far side from Felicity. I could think of nothing better to do than kick her back out, but this would have caused an immediate crisis, and I was still hoping to avert that.

I held her close, and kissed her forehead. "And right glad am I to have you here, my dearest girl. But I am afraid I shall be absolutely useless to you as a lover. Never have I been so exhausted."

"Oh, Helier, I shall soon restore you. Why . . ." Her hand slid across my thigh, and I realised that the crisis was upon us. It was, after all, only a matter of seconds since my tumble with Felicity. "Why," Alicia said again,

218

and then sat up. "You foul wretch. You have attended to yourself."

"Well," I said weakly.

But now there was someone sitting up on the other side as well. "He did not," Felicity said.

"You!" Alicia cried.

"And who else did you expect it to be?" Felicity demanded. "Unlike your husband, as it appears, Count d'Albret is a man of the most orthodox tastes."

"Whore!" Alicia screamed.

"Adulteress!" Felicity retorted.

Following which they fell to. Now, it may be supposed that the spectacle of two most attractive women wrestling naked would be most stimulating for any watching man, and this may well be true. But I was not watching them. I could not even see them as more than two shadowy figures. And I was not in the position of a spectator; rather was I the ring. Within seconds of their grappling I had received knees in various most painful parts of my lower abdomen, which in fact caused me to lose all possible interest in sexual matters, at least temporarily. Thus I gave a roar myself, and sat up, throwing an arm round each pair of delightful thighs, and while they jointly squealed their alarm, got out of bed. Now they were striking at me as much as at themselves, so, having gained the ascendancy, as it were, I dropped them both to the floor.

I have no doubt that the noise aroused the household, or at least, that part of it which remained capable of arousal, but no one came to investigate, no doubt wisely. While Felicity and Alicia were gasping for breath, I located my tinderbox and lit a candle, with which I was able to survey the scene. Both the women were looking somewhat wild, with their hair scattered across their faces, and several contusions upon their bodies. But both remained intensely attractive. "Helier!" Alicia said. "You have betrayed me."

"I never swore any fealty to you, my pet," I pointed out.

She blew hair from across her nose and glared at Felicity. "And you prefer this wretched creature to me?"

"I consider that we owe this charming young lady far more than can be repaid by only an hour in bed."

Felicity now also did some blowing away of hair, following which she got up, and got back into bed, sitting up with the covers arranged across her thighs. Alicia stared at her in amazement. "Are you out of your mind?" she demanded. "Leave this room this instant."

"As Count d'Albret has just reminded you," Felicity said, with total composure. "He owes me much more than a single tumble."

"Why . . ." Alicia looked fit to burst. She turned to me. "Helier! Send that woman away."

"I cannot do that, my pet," I said. "It happens to be her bed, in her room, in her house."

"*Well!*" Alicia marched to the door, realised she was naked, marched back to the bed to pick up her discarded undressing-robe, and put it on. She glared at Felicity a last time, and marched back to the door. "We shall speak of this in the morning," she said, and banged the door behind her, causing the house to shake some more.

"There will have to be a great deal of speaking about things in the morning," Felicity said. "But there are still a few hours remaining. Will you not come back to me?"

This I was perfectly willing to do, my nether regions having somewhat recovered from being knelt on, while my memory of the two delicious creatures fighting was now having a delayed reaction. But I had no sooner folded Felicity once more in my arms than we were disturbed by a most unearthly shriek. I was out of bed in an instant. Felicity sat up. "That can only be Lady Norton discovering her husband in bed with Lord Culhaven. Poor woman, she is having a disturbed night."

I pulled on my breeches. "That was not the shriek of

a woman either shocked or offended. It was a scream of mortal terror." I drew my sword.

"But what . . .?"

I fumbled in my clothing and found my cross. "Will you assist me?"

"Of course." She leapt out of bed and pulled on her nightdress.

"Have you any garlic in your kitchen?"

"I should think so. There nearly always is a string in the house."

"Go down and fetch it, and then come to me at Sir Rupert's room."

"But . . . what will you be doing?"

"Waiting for you," I assured her. "Haste, now."

She hurried down the stairs, while I made my way along the upper gallery. I was in a state of some agitation, equally cursing myself as a fool for having believed that Culhaven had been sufficiently afraid of me to obey me. I was also concerned that if he had put himself beyond the pale, as it were, I had lost my guide, my mission would be a failure, with the twin results that Richilde would continue her evil career, and her pursuit of me, and that Anne of Austria would doubtless strip me of my estates. Yet I could not have Alicia mangled by a vampire!

In fact she had not been, although my heart did a somersault as I saw her lying stretched on the floor of the gallery outside the door of the room she had shared with her husband. I knelt beside her, but there was no blood to be seen, as I would have expected had Culhaven assaulted her. On the other hand she was definitely unconscious. Indeed she lay so still that I had to put my head to her heart to make sure she was breathing.

"What has happened?" I had been joined by both Brewin, and his aunt. Miss Brewin had equipped herself with a blunderbus. From above us I could hear the servants calling to each other, also asking what had happened.

"I very much fear that Culhaven has disobeyed me," I said.

"My God! Where is he?" Roderick asked.

"That I am about to find out. But I am acting on the assumption that he is still inside that room."

"May I ask what we are talking about?" Miss Brewin inquired. "That is Sir Rupert's room. And that is Sir Rupert's wife, is it not?"

"Yes. I will explain later. But you would do us all a great favour, Miss Brewin, if you would go upstairs and calm your servants. Under no circumstances must any of them be allowed on this floor."

She looked as if she would have argued – after all, it was her house – but then contented herself with asking. "And that poor woman?"

"Has fainted, and I think she may have struck her head when falling. She is in no danger. Please do as I ask."

"Well . . ." While she hesitated, Felicity reappeared, carrying her string of garlic. "Felicity," the old lady said. "Where is your robe? You are quite indecent."

"This is an urgent matter, Aunt," Felicity protested.

"Please do as I ask, Miss Brewin," I said.

Muttering, she went off. I then turned my attention to Alicia, lifting her to remove her some distance along the corridor. By now she was recovering consciousness, all fluttering eyelids and heaving bosom. "Helier," she said. "My God, Helier . . ."

"Tell me what happened?"

She looked past me at the Brewin siblings.

"You must brace yourself for a shock, Felicity," I warned.

She glanced at her brother. "I already know of it," Roderick said. "The Count told me."

"Tell us what happened," I asked Alicia again.

"I opened the door," she said. "There was a candle

in the room, and by its light I saw Rupert and Lord Culhaven. They were both naked, and Culhaven was bending over Rupert, his back to me. Well, I had expected something like that. But then I realised that Rupert was lying absolutely still. And then Culhaven, having heard the door open, turned towards me, and I saw blood, nothing but blood, dripping from his mouth and rolling down his shoulders. While his teeth . . ." She looked about to faint again.

"Whatever can it be?" Felicity asked.

Roderick looked at me, and I took the plunge. "It is simply that Lord Culhaven is a vampire," I explained.

"A *what*? Your friend?"

"My travelling companion," I reminded her, and hurried on before she could have hysterics. "Alicia, would you say that Rupert was dead?"

"He looked dead. My God, he *is* dead." She sat up. "Killed by that fiend! That monster! Helier . . ."

I nodded, even as I sighed. But there was no way I could continue if all my companions were going to be at the mercy of Culhaven. "Rupert will be avenged," I promised her. "Tell me, what did Culhaven say, or do, when he saw you in the doorway?"

"I don't know if he identified me. In any event, I fainted."

"And were not attacked in turn by the creature?" Brewin asked suspiciously.

"Lord Culhaven has very definite tastes in blood," I pointed out. "However, he must be dealt with. Did you make up that list of items I required, doctor?"

"You mean the mallet and stake and hammer and nails? Yes."

"Would you fetch them? Now ladies, I wish you each to equip yourselves with a cross, which you will hold in front of yourselves at all times."

"Where am I to find a cross?" Alicia demanded.

"I have more than one," Felicity said, and hurried off.

"Oh, Helier," Alicia said. "Do you really suppose Rupert is dead? I was terribly fond of him, you know."

I reflected that she could have fooled me, but pressed her hand. "He will be avenged," I said again.

"It is not that," she said. "It is the marriage contract."

"What marriage contract?"

"The one between Rupert and me, signed at the insistence of his father."

"Was his father with the army?"

"No, no," she said. "His father is dead. But before he died, he wrote into his Will, that any woman Rupert married, and the heirs of her body, could only inherit the family fortune, in the unhappy event of Rupert's death, if she had shared bed and board with her husband for a year and a day. I suppose he knew of Rupert's proclivities, and did not wish to risk someone marrying him for his money and leaving the moment she discovered what those proclivities were."

"Hm," I said. "What dashed bad luck."

"So if he is dead . . ." She gazed at me with enormous eyes.

"Then you are a pauper. We shall have to see what can be done. But first, we must deal with Culhaven."

She frowned. "What of your business with him?"

"What indeed. But he can no longer be permitted to foul the air. He is our first priority."

I thought it best not to tell her that if Culhaven had been giving Rupert love-bites on a regular basis, then he too was undoubtedly contaminated with the dread disease of vampirism, which these creatures transmit to their victims at every opportunity. To be sure, it normally takes several impregnations, as it were, but Culhaven had clearly enjoyed more than one go at Rupert, always using the more traditional method of sucking the blood rather than tearing out the throat of his victim, as he had practised when hungry. But this was in itself sinister, as the more violent method at least ends the business there and then, whereas this nipping and sipping suggested that he was indeed seeking to discover a companion through eternity.

Felicity and Roderick returned with the items of equipment I had requested. Each of the women and also Roderick equipped themselves with a cross, while I, using the hammer and nails, arranged the garlic in a wreath around the bedroom door.

Needless to say, the noise of hammering brought Miss Brewin back into our midst, at least figuratively. "What are you doing down there?" she called from the head of the servants staircase.

Behind her there was a great deal of anxious twittering.

"Do not fret yourself, Auntie," Felicity called back. "All is well." Presumably, in these circumstances, it is permissible to lie.

"Now, then," I said. "Is everyone ready?" They nodded together, faces pale but determined. "Very good." I drew my sword, took my cross in the other hand, leaving the mallet and stake on the floor for the time being, and with a single kick knocked down the door.

I leapt into the chamber, sword thrust forward, cross held high, ready to defend myself to the utmost against the creature. But the room was empty, certainly at first glance, save for the body of Rupert Norton, lying on his back on the bed. As two candles burned, I could tell there was not even a great deal of blood. But presumably Culhaven had drunk all of that. "Where is it?" Roderick asked at my shoulder, determined no longer to grant the creature the least semblance of humanity.

"That is the question. Stay here," I told the women, who were peering past me with the invariable curiosity of their sex. I stepped further into the room, and slowly advanced to the bed, looking left to right and even above my head, for if he really had some affinity with a bat, Culhaven could well have been against the ceiling. But

225

he was not, and then I saw that one of the windows was open, which, although there was no wind, just the steady downpour, explained the amount of air in the room. "The bat has flown," I said, and went to the aperture. In fact he would not have needed to fly. There was both a drainpipe and a good deal of strong ivy clinging to the wall beneath the window, and he could have descended without the least difficulty. "Quick, the stables."

I closed the window and ran back for the door, and the others followed me. I checked only long enough to close and lock the bedroom door; I wanted no one entering that room without me.

Then we tumbled down the stairs and out of the side door. Roderick and I easily outstripped the ladies at this, and reached the stables ahead of them. But we already knew we were too late. The horses were in a state of great agitation, neighing and leaping about in their stalls, and in the doorway we found the body of a groom, a mass of blood from his severed throat. Culhaven had clearly been in a hurry, or perhaps he had had enough to eat and drink from poor Rupert. "What's to be done?" Roderick asked.

"I am afraid there is nothing that can be done about him, now. But we have a most unhappy duty to perform."

He frowned at me. "You mean . . ."

"We must at least make sure." I led him back to the house and the two women.

"Alicia," I said. "I want you to be very brave. There is something that Roderick and I must do. I do not wish you to be present, unless you insist upon it, but I must tell you what needs to be done. I intend to cut off Rupert's head."

"His head? How awful! But why?"

"Simply because we must be certain that he is dead."

"You mean he may be alive? Oh, I must go to him."

She turned to run for the house, and I caught her arm.

"If he appears to be alive, Alicia, it will be because he is a vampire."

Her mouth made a huge O. "My Rupert?"

"I am afraid so. These creatures contaminate those on whom they feed."

She gulped, and accompanied us back to the house. By now the servants had refused to remain closeted in their attic any longer, and were swarming all over the place, while Miss Brewin was highly agitated. It was all I could do to calm them, and tell them that Dr Brewin and I had some surgery to perform upon Rupert. "Then you will need hot water and towels," the good lady said efficiently.

"No, no," I said. "Not now. Afterwards, no doubt."

She looked puzzled, but as her nephew and niece seemed to understand, subsided. We gave strict instructions to the servants not to come up to the family floor, and then returned to the dreadful bedroom. "I really do think it would be best for you ladies to remain out here," I said.

"I must be present," Alicia said. "He is my husband."

"I have assisted at many an operation," Felicity reminded me.

I hesitated a last time, then shrugged, and opened the door. I was as usual prepared for anything, and carried my sword in one hand and my cross in the other. But the room was as we had left it, and Rupert still lay on his back on the bed, looking positively peaceful. "Oh, my poor darling," Alicia said. I wondered if she had ever called him that during their brief married life.

I remained alert. As it was not yet morning, had Rupert become a full-fledged vampire he should have been up and biting. Therefore it was obvious that Culhaven's venom had not yet taken full control of his body. This posed something of an ethical question: was he at this moment more vampire or more human, and if the latter, did I have any justification for killing him?

But then I reflected that, as he was utterly besotted with his lover, if I let him remain alive, they would probably get together again at some time, with all manner of unpleasant results.

Thus I hardened my heart, and stood above the poor fellow. I laid my sword on the bed beside him, and beckoned Brewin. "Will you do it, or shall I?" he asked. He was not lacking in courage. "It is my house."

"It is my responsibility," I said, and took the stake from his hand, as well as the mallet.

As I rested the pointed end on Rupert's breast, he opened his eyes, and then his mouth. This was a great relief to me, as both from his expression and his suddenly elongated fangs I could feel certain I was not killing an innocent man. However, his sudden awakening had entirely the reverse effect upon Alicia, who uttered a piercing scream. "He's alive!" she shrieked. "Oh, my darling Rupert!"

She ran forward, clearly wishing to embrace him. "Grab her," I shouted, and Felicity threw both arms round her waist.

"Let me go, you whore!" Alicia shouted. "And you, if you touch him . . ."

"I do assure you that he is not really alive," I said, and, having assured myself that Felicity would prevent her from interfering – Felicity was both bigger and stronger – swung my mallet. And just in time, for the creature that had been Rupert was beginning to twitch.

I swung with all my considerable strength, with the result that the stake was driven right through Rupert's breast, through the mattress beneath him, through the bedboard beneath that, and just about disappeared. There was a fountain of blood – Culhaven had clearly been interrupted by Alicia before he had completed his meal. Then Rupert subsided. However, I was not going to neglect any of the essentials that had been recommended by L'Abbé Grimaud, and so I dropped the mallet, picked up my sword, and with a single swing decapitated the corpse, to the accompaniment of another shriek from Alicia.

"Thank God for that," Roderick said. "I shall dispose of the corpse. But you, Count, what will you do now? Go after Culhaven?" It was obvious this was what he wanted me to do.

I sighed. "I would if I could, doctor. But he has undoubtedly taken himself off to his Welsh castle. And I have no idea where it is. My mission has come to a dead end."

"But I know where the castle is," Roderick said.

CHAPTER 9

"Are you serious?" I cried. "How can you know that?"

"Simply that after the death of that boy, last year, I tracked Culhaven to the village which stands at the foot of the castle." He flushed. "I attempted to gain admittance to the castle itself, with a view to interviewing him, but I was refused by some ill-favoured major-domo, and I had not the means to force an entry. So I returned here."

"But Lord Culhaven, or really, Lady Culhaven, will know that you called, and are therefore familiar with her lair?"

"Well . . . yes. But she only knows me as an itinerant country doctor. When I called I had no idea that she was a vampire. I find it difficult to credit now."

"Did you actually see her?"

"Only from a distance, but I certainly gained the impression that she is very beautiful."

"She is that," I agreed. "And also quite exceptionally intelligent. Thus she will learn all about you when her husband gets home this time. Therefore we must make haste, in order to arrive there as soon as possible after him. I am sorry, doctor, but I must ask you to revisit that place, at least as far as the village, to show me the way."

"I will certainly come with you," Roderick agreed. "And if you can find your way into the castle, I will accompany you there also. My only wish is to bring that thing to justice."

"I also will come with you," Felicity said.

"No, no," I protested. "That is quite impossible."

"I am my brother's assistant," she pointed out. "Where he goes, I go."

I looked at Brewin. "Well, now that you have shown us how to deal with these creatures . . ." he said.

"We have not dealt with any of them yet," I pointed out. "Only a half-formed one."

"Surely the others are merely matters of degree."

"If she is accompanying you, then so am I," Alicia declared.

"You have to be out of your mind," I protested.

"Helier, do you realise that with Rupert dead, you are my only hope of salvation?"

I had no idea what she meant by that, and at that moment had no desire to find out. My only instinct was towards haste, and I remembered some of my earlier thoughts. If Alicia was determined upon such a self-destructive course, she might provide us all with a useful diversion. Yet did I have to make one last appeal to reason, principally with the thought of Felicity at the mercy of Richilde Bethlen in mind. "I would have you understand," I said, "that the creature with whom I have to deal is as inhumanly evil, relative to Lord Culhaven, as a tiger is to a pussy cat. Anyone who accompanies me is at severe risk of his or her life."

"But you believe you can deal with her, Helier," Felicity pointed out. "Or you would not be assaulting her citadel at all." I had no immediate answer to that, and she was triumphant. "So, let us sally forth, and do battle with the devil, and emerge victorious," she said.

I felt that to argue further would be pointless, and besides, I really did need all the help I could get. To begin with, leaving Dormintsley was not all that easy: there was Rupert to be disposed of. Miss Brewin and the servants felt that this should be done in the presence of a priest; my companions and I demurred, being of the

231

opinion that this business had absolutely nothing to do with Christianity. We prevailed, but there was even more of a to-do when Rupert was laid out, as a corpse with a stake driven right through its body is always certain to arouse interest amongst the hoi poloi. Miss Brewin, indeed, now went to the other extreme, and wanted to refuse poor Rupert a last resting place on any soil that belonged to her.

She was in turn persuaded by her niece and nephew, and Rupert was finally interred, but everyone was extremely agitated. "This tale will spread all over the village in twelve hours," Roderick told me.

"We will be gone by then."

"But some of us will hopefully be coming back."

"Any of us who come back, friend Roddy," I told him, "will give not a tinker's damn for village gossip. We will have looked upon the dark side of the moon and lived to tell the tale."

I do not know whether this reassured him or not, but we then got our expedition together. I wished everyone armed with silver crosses and strings of garlic, with stakes and mallets. It would have been pointless equipping the ladies with swords, but I saw that they each had a brace of pistols.

By the time all this equipping had been completed it was mid-morning, and it was decided, logically enough, that we should have a hearty breakfast before setting off. There was no point in worrying about the amount of time we were wasting. No matter how hard we tried Culhaven would certainly be at his home before us, and Richilde would be alerted as to my presence. But she was expecting me anyway, and equally that I knew who and what she was, and would undoubtedly have equipped myself to cope with her. It remained to be seen how she intended to cope with me.

Thus I was as prepared as anyone to eat a hearty

meal. Sadly, we had not yet completed our repast when a servant came hurrying in to say that there was a troop of Roundhead cavalry at the end of the lane, and approaching the house. There was no time to determine whether this was an ill chance or whether they had been directed after the Nortons, Culhaven or myself by someone in Boscabel. It was a matter of swallowing our last mouthful, draining our wine goblets, and leaping into our saddles. Then we were galloping away to the west. "They will undoubtedly follow," Roderick opined.

"Hopefully, not for a few hours," I said.

Out of Dormintsley we followed a good road leading west, always with the Welsh mountains looming before us. We made, I fancy, a pretty prospect, for both ladies wore attractive habits – courtesy of Felicity. Hers was in deep blue, clearly her favourite colour, and Alicia's was in pale green, which well set-off her pale complexion and yellow hair. Sadly, this attractive picture was soon diminished by a return of the rain, which settled into a steady downpour. We were all equipped with cloaks to protect our finery, but despite these were soon soaked to the skin. "Oh, really, Helier," Alicia complained. "Surely we should stop to shelter until this storm is past?"

"And let the Roundheads catch up with us?"

"I cannot believe the Roundheads will follow in such weather."

"Oh, they will," I assured her. "There is five hundred pounds on my head."

"Five hundred pounds?" she cried. "Well, really! You might have told us that before."

"I thought you knew. You were in my arms when that Roundhead captain told the Giffards." Clearly she had been thinking of other things, at the time.

"Ha!" she snorted. "Well! And what am I valued at, may I ask?"

"I do not believe you have been valued at anything, my pet."

"Well" she declared again, obviously grossly insulted.

The storm lasted the better part of the day, and by the end of it we were in Wales, although still some distance from the mountains. "We should reach the castle tomorrow night," Roderick said. "If we maintain this pace."

That idea did not entirely suit me. If I knew that Richilde, being a spawn of the devil in addition to her other inherent vices, cared nothing whether it was night or day, I had the evidence of my own observation that Culhaven dwindled somewhat in daylight. This weakness might well affect any other servants Richilde might be currently employing. Thus to arrive at the castle as night was falling could not possibly be to our advantage, whereas to arrive as day was breaking could not possibly be to our *dis*advantage. When we came upon a village, therefore, I decided that we could all do with a square meal and a good night's sleep.

This certainly pleased the ladies, but now a new crisis arose, as we discovered there were only two rooms available. "I think it were best, as we have all manner of trials ahead of us tomorrow and will need all of our strength," I told them, "that you two ladies should share one room, and Roderick and I will share the other."

"Under no circumstances am I sharing a bed with that harlot," Alicia announced.

"Listen," Felicity told her, "I wouldn't take a bite out of you if you were the last corpse left on earth."

"Well, really," Alicia remarked. It occurred to me that she hadn't actually been thinking of bites, at least of the blood-sucking variety.

As usual, I endeavoured to keep the peace. "My pet," I said as winningly as I could, "you cannot expect Dr Brewin to share a bed with his own sister?"

"Why not?" she demanded. "I am sure they have indulged before."

"I am going to slap her face," Felicity decided.

"Ladies, ladies," I begged. "It really will not do to attract attention to ourselves." As if we had not already done that. "Now, Alicia, if you really do not wish to share a bed with Felicity, will you not consider sharing one with Dr Brewin?"

"Eh?" the doctor demanded.

"Well!" Alicia commented, and looked Roderick up and down. He was not as well made as me, that was evident, on the other hand, having maintained her chastity for so long to honour her husband, and having discovered that it had all been a waste of time, she had some interest in making up for lost opportunities.

"Just for the one night," I pointed out.

Roderick was by now looking Alicia up and down in turn, and as I have intimated, there are few more pleasant occupations.

"I might consider it," he said at last.

"Well!" she remarked again. "Do I not have a say in this?"

"Of course you do, my pet. It is bed with Roderick or a nest of straw in the stable."

"Well!" she said a third time.

That settled, we ate and drank as much as we could, following which I was able to have a chat with the landlord. "Lord Culhaven," he said. "Oh, aye, he was through here this morning."

"You know him?"

"Of course. He comes here regular enough. Friend of his, are you?"

"A business acquaintance."

"Oh, aye," he commented again.

"I think you should explain that remark," I suggested.

"There are dark things said about that castle of his."

"Tell me."

He glanced left and right, as if afraid of being overheard, although there was no one else in the taproom at the time: Roderick and Alicia were investigating their bedchamber, and, I imagined, getting to know one another, and Felicity was waiting in our chamber. "There's talk of young folk being kidnapped, never to be seen again. And of weird noises coming from the castle, screams and the like. And of the stream which runs by and forms the moat sometimes being red with blood."

All this sounded likely enough. "You have seen and heard these things yourself?" I asked.

"No, fear, squire. I don't go near Culhaven."

"But there is a village at the foot of the castle, is there not?"

"Dead souls," he muttered. "Dead souls."

I was not sure whether he meant they were already dead, or whether they were doomed. However, as he was clearly operating solely on hearsay, I did not press the matter; I prefer to deal in facts. "If you know this," I said, "then all the neighbourhood must know it."

"Oh, aye," he agreed.

"But nothing has been done about it?"

"Well, squire, what would you? Lord Culhaven is a lord, and lord of the manor about his castle, too. We are but simple folk. And then there has been all the upheaval caused by the war, with no proper magistrates . . . I did hear say that the major-general in Shrewsbury was interesting himself in what has been happening, but you see, he fled with the approach of the Royal army." He is no doubt back in the city by now, I thought. Could it be possible that the troop of Ironsides behind us was actually seeking Culhaven rather than me? But that was surely wishful thinking.

I joined Felicity, who was, as always, pleased to welcome me. But she was not quite as sanguine as she endeavoured

236

to appear when in the company of her brother or Alicia, although her concerns were of an absurd nature, considering what the morrow might bring. "Oh, Helier," she sighed when we had both got our breaths back. "What is to become of us?"

"I am afraid I can offer no definite opinion on that, my sweet," I told her. "I still think it would be far better for you to remain here, and let your brother and I assault the citadel and come back to you. If we do not come back, then you at least will still be alive to return to your aunt. As for the Roundheads, they have no business with you."

"Oh, tush, Helier," she said. "I am not concerned about either the Roundheads or tomorrow. I know you will triumph, because you have always triumphed. I am concerned with what happens after."

"It never pays to look too far ahead," I suggested. "Let's reach tomorrow night, first."

"But I must look beyond that. I love you. I adore you. I fell in love with you at first sight. I shall always adore you."

Words such as these cannot help but warm the cockles of a man's heart, and various other parts of his body as well. Thus it became necessary to do some more panting. But I fear that I was less successful on this occasion. This was not only because I had not properly recharged my weapon, but because I could not help but recall that only three other women in my life had ever so addressed me. One was the Witch of Hohengraffen herself, who had only turned against me when she had discovered that I, having learned the truth about her, could not reciprocate. The other two had been the faithful companions of my youth, Jeanne the Frenchwoman, and Helga the German. Helga I had married, as she had been the most loving and faithful woman I had ever known. And both had been most cruelly done to death by the very Witch who tomorrow I must beard in her den. Was this lovely girl to be a third victim? "Helier?" she asked, rising on her elbow. "I have displeased you."

"Of course you have not," I said. "You have flattered me enormously. But . . ."

"Are you really married to a woman in France?"

"Ah . . . as a matter of fact, no. We live together as man and wife, but it is not a legal matter."

"Ah," she commented, thoughtfully. "Then what of Lady Norton?"

"I will have to do something about her."

"Do you really believe her when she claims she has not a friend in the world save yourself?"

"I very much fear she is telling the truth. Although she may be making one now, hopefully."

"Roderick? My God! I could never have such a creature as a sister-in-law. Unless, of course, I was married myself." She moved her nipple up and down my arm to leave me in no doubt she would make a good wife.

"Listen," I told her. "All of these fantasies are splendid, and most exciting. But I can contemplate no future at all until I have dealt with the Witch of Hohengraffen. Again I can but ask you to remain here and await the outcome of that fracas."

"How can I? When the only two men I have ever loved are seeking the creature? If I cannot live at your side, Helier, I shall die at it." Women can be very perverse. But also charming.

Eventually, after another hearty meal and a good deal of ale, we slept soundly. At least I did, as thus did Felicity also. I am not in a position to answer for Alicia and Roderick, save to observe that they both looked somewhat frazzled in the morning. Roderick, of course, had led a sheltered life regarding women like Alicia. And Alicia had not encountered too many men who had led a sheltered life. Therefore they had both undoubtedly had a great deal to teach each other. However, as regards

238

days to go witch-hunting and vampire-chasing, we could not have asked for a better. The sun shone, what clouds there were flittered gently across the blue sky, there was little wind, and it was perfectly warm. And there was no sign of any Roundheads.

"Where do you go now, squire?" asked the landlord, as Roderick settled our account; I had no money whatsoever.

"Castle Culhaven."

"May God have mercy on your soul," the poor fellow said.

"I am sure He will," Felicity retorted calmly.

We mounted and rode off. For the rest of the morning we made our way through slowly rising but attractive country, following a well-used and thus well-rutted road. Eventually we topped a hill from whence we could look both forward and back. Forward the road descended into a deep, wooded valley, through which there hurried a brook large enough almost to be called a river. On the far side the ground commenced to rise again, quite sharply, into a series of peaked hills. Beyond we could see mountains of perhaps three thousand feet. "We do not have to go up there, I hope," Alicia remarked.

"No," Roderick told her. "Look there." He pointed, and we squinted into the afternoon sunlight. At the top of one of the closer hills, overlooking the valley, but half hidden by the shadow of the higher peaks beyond, we made out the walls and turrets of a castle.

"Oooh!" Alicia squealed and clutched Roderick's arm. I reflected, with some relief, that before last night she would have clutched mine.

"Is that our destination?" Felicity asked, quietly. Her brother nodded.

I, meanwhile, had been inspecting our situation. To our left was open country. To our right was another valley, from which there issued a thin plume of smoke, suggesting human habitation. While behind us . . . I strained my eyes, and was sure I could discern, albeit at a considerable distance, a body of horsemen. They looked about to commence a campaign, for they were accompanied by a supply wagon and even, I was sure, a field piece. But they were at least a march behind us, and in addition, flattering though the concept might be, I could not see the Parliamentarians sending artillery to deal with Helier L'Eree. Which re-aroused all those interesting possibilities I had earlier dismissed as wishful thinking. "How far do we have to go?" I asked Roderick.

"It is about ten miles across the valley."

"And the village?"

"Lies beyond those trees."

I studied the lie of the land before us, which we could see quite clearly as it was now all below us. It looked devoid of humanity. "This has got to be the loneliest place in England," Felicity said, and hugged herself.

"Save that we happen to be in Wales," Roderick said, with an attempt at humour. Neither of them had troubled to look back, and they were therefore unaware of the Roundheads.

"We will camp down by that stream for tonight," I decided.

"There!" Felicity demanded. "Sleep out on a wind-swept heath?"

"There is no wind," I pointed out.

It was of course a matter of bivouacing, and we could feel at least relieved that it was not raining, although I could make out clouds again gathering over the hills to suggest that our respite might not be for very long. But the site was good, the water rushing by provided us with everything we needed, and we had still sufficient food to have a hearty meal. "What will we eat tomorrow?" Alicia asked.

"No doubt Lady Culhaven will provide something," I said. "Now, tonight there is to be no messing about. I

240

intend to leave here before dawn to arrive at the castle at sun up."

Even Alicia was no longer in the mood for argument, or amatory dalliance, and indeed the two women worked quite well together in preparing our meal. While they were doing this, Roderick drew me aside. "What is your plan?" he asked.

"I am afraid I have none, save to gain entrance, and confront the Witch."

He considered this for some moments. "You mean, destroy her?"

"If that is possible, yes."

"Right away?"

"As soon as is possible, certainly." I had not confided to him the whole truth about my mission, but while my instincts were commanding me to attack Richilde the moment I saw her, I supposed I would have to go through the rigmarole of requesting the Queen's love letters.

"Will she not have servants?"

"Undoubtedly."

"Who may well also be vampires"

"I would say that is very likely."

"Then are not the odds too heavy?"

"Looked at in a superficial light, yes. But there are certain factors in our favour."

"You mean that we know who and what she is? I do not think that is a very great advantage."

"It is nonetheless an advantage. Because you must keep this always in mind, Roderick: the Witch will not seem in the least unhuman, or frightening, when you first meet her. Indeed, she will probably appear as the most beautiful and desirable woman you have ever seen." Roderick could not resist a glance along the river bank to where Alicia had removed her boots and stockings and was washing her feet in the rushing water. "You want to keep *her* image ever in mind," I recommended. "As something pure and noble."

Obviously, describing Alicia Norton as pure and noble was stretching the bow a bit, but compared with Richilde Bethlen it was not an entirely inept consideration. "There is, however, a far more important factor working in our favour," I went on. "My personal knowledge of Richilde Bethlen. She has the mentality of a cat, which is combined with her conception of her own immortality. She will wish to play with me before she executes me. Even more, she will wish to play with the rest of you, before she bares her claws and her teeth."

"This is something to reassure me?" Roderick inquired. "You are exposing my sister and the woman I love to such a creature?"

This last was news to me. But it was certainly good news. "While she plays, we have the more time to encompass her own destruction," I explained. And the Roundheads have more time to arrive, I reflected. "Providing only that we remember always what she is and what she intends. As for the ladies, if you can persuade them to remain here, or better yet, to return to Dormintsley, I should be more than happy."

I knew of course that he was unlikely to succeed. And he did not. In fact, I do not even know if he tried. I personally slept soundly. I might have been waiting all of my life for this moment. Tomorrow I would rid myself of this horrendous succubus who had been hanging around my neck now for twenty years, or I would die. My only concern was for Felicity. She snuggled close to me in her blanket, but knew better than to importune. I could do nothing more than squeeze her hand.

I was awake well before the appointed hour. It was still very dark, the more so because the sky was obliterated by heavy cloud: we had had our brief spell of fine weather. I washed myself, and listened. There was a wind soughing down from the mountains, and I was sure it was carrying sound with it, but I could not be sure what it was. Nor did I really wish to find out. I regard myself as being as bold as the next man, but I would be lying were I not to confess that I was apprehensive of the coming day. I had faced death on innumerable occasions. When standing shoulder to shoulder with one's comrades in battle, one draw's strength from their courage and experience; here my companions would be drawing their strength from me – they had nothing to offer me in return. But then it was true that I had faced Richilde Bethlen in mortal combat twice before in my life, alone and unaided, and each time I had triumphed. Or had I merely survived? She would know all of my tricks now. True, I knew all of hers, or I thought I did. But did I?

I heard movement behind me, and saw my companions stirring. We ate the last of our supper and drank the last of the wine. "Now listen to me very carefully," I said. "Stow your garlic and your crosses in your saddlebags; we will not be allowed entry if they suspect how well we are equipped. But keep the bags always at your side, ready to protect yourselves at all times. Leave the talking to me. And obey me without question or hesitation, no matter what I command you to do."

I had expected some objection from Alicia to this assumption of total command, but there was none. We mounted and walked our horses along the river bank, in single file. All our pistols were primed, and I assumed Roderick's sword was as loose in his scabbard as was mine. But I knew this affair was not going to be settled by swords and pistols. We had not gone very far when the trees thickened, and we were in the wood. The sky was just beginning to lighten, but very little of the dawn got into this dark and dismal place. Even our horses seemed affected, and had constantly to be urged forward. I did not look back at my companions; I assumed they were still following.

Then the trees thinned again, and we saw houses, or at least, huts. The scene reminded me of some of the ghastly remains I had come across in Germany during the devastation of the Thirty Years War, for there was neither paint nor glass to be seen, merely walls and turf roofs. A dog barked, and then another, and some people emerged. "Do not stop," I said over my shoulder.

The people glowered at us, and we ignored them. "Whence come you?" someone shouted.

I saw no reason why we should not terrify them before they terrified us. "The dark side of the moon," I replied.

That gave themselves something to think about, and before they could regain their wits we were outside of the village and facing the hillside, up which the road continued to lead. "Have them!" someone shouted.

Alicia gave a little shriek of alarm, and looking back, I saw several dark figures running at her, she being the last in our cavalcade. I wheeled my horse, drawing and cocking one of my pistols at the same time. Roderick and Felicity also turned their mounts, although obviously with no clear idea of what they should do. But I never hesitated, and as the lead man reached up for Alicia, while she endeavoured to spur her mount to get away, I levelled my pistol and shot him in the chest. He gave a great cry and tumbled backwards, and his companions checked. "Ride," I told Alicia. "All of you, ride."

While I spoke I holstered my smoking pistol, and drew my sword, advancing my horse towards the villagers at a walk. They gazed at the huge blade, gleaming in the first light, then turned and ran, leaving their companion moaning and writhing on the ground. I wheeled my horse and rejoined the others, who waited at the foot of the ascent. "Will they not be waiting for us when we return?" Felicity asked.

"When we return," I told her, "*if* we return, I don't think a pack of peasants is going to stop us."

We began the ascent. On one side the drop was sheer, and

soon became precipitous, as we climbed. On the other was the craggy side of the cliff. But above that loomed the walls of the castle, and I could not doubt that we were being overlooked; the sound of the pistol shot had echoed upwards. To add to the general unpleasantness of our situation, the long threatening rain now began again, accompanied by several flashes of lightning and peals of thunder. This set our horses to prancing, which was not at all comfortable on the somewhat narrow roadway. I therefore dismounted, and my companions followed my example. We then led our horses upwards, the roadway stretching for another quarter of a mile while it wound round the hillside. By now it was broad daylight, but the sun was invisible behind the rainclouds.

At last we came upon the castle itself. This was situated on the far side of a deep ravine cut into the hillside; below us, at a distance of some hundred feet, was the same rushing stream beside which we had camped for the night. The only way across this ravine was by the drawbridge which faced us, presently raised. To either side of this massive piece of wood were stone walls pierced with loopholes, while above our heads was a crenellated battlement. There was no sign of life. "How do we get in?" Felicity asked.

"We shout," I suggested, and cupped my hands around my mouth while taking a deep breath. "Hullo!" I bellowed.

The sound echoed upwards even more loudly than the pistol shot or the last rumble of thunder. And the reply was immediate, confirming my conviction that we had been overlooked since leaving the village. "Is that you, L'Eree?" My companions gasped at the liquid gold of the voice. Richilde did not appear to be shouting, but the sound drifted around us like the sweetest of music. "Take off your hat," she recommended, "that I may look upon your face and be sure that it is truly you."

I obeyed. "I assume you are expecting me?" I asked.

"Of course. And how sweet of you to bring some friends with you. Bulstrode has told me of them." I might have known someone like Culhaven would have a Christian name like Bulstrode!

But now the drawbridge was slowly coming down towards us. "She does not *sound* like a witch," Felicity remarked.

"Or a vampire," Alicia put in.

"Well, remember that she is, and the most black-hearted creature who ever walked this earth," I told them. But I could see that they were already half-seduced by those dulcet tones.

The drawbridge thudded into the earth before us, and beyond it the portcullis began to raise. I drew a deep breath and led my horse across the wood, my companions tramping behind me. We passed beneath the teeth of the portcullis, and found ourselves in a small court, open to the sky, and thus the rain, which continued to teem sullenly down. Behind us the portcullis descended a good deal faster than it had gone up, and the drawbridge began to creak upwards.

My companions were looking around themselves with interest mingled with apprehension, but there was nothing to be seen save bare stone walls. Then, on the far side of the courtyard, a gate opened. We led our horses through, and found ourselves in a much larger courtyard. Now we could determine more of the lay-out of the castle. To our right were the stables – in which there were several horses, remarkably quiet – and behind and above them were presumably servants' quarters; to our left there was what again was obviously a barracks; both of these were silent and despite the gloom of the day we could see no sign of light or life. But in front of us was the knights' hall, reached by a flight of wide stone steps, and at the top of the steps the great double doors stood open to reveal a perfect cavern of light. "Leave your horses," Richilde's voice said. She was clearly using some kind of speaking trumpet which amplified her voice, while in no way interfering with its beauty. "My people will see to them. Now come to me, L'Eree. And bring your friends."

"What people?" Felicity asked, instinctively speaking in a whisper.

"I am quite sure they are about. Bring your saddle-bags," I said in a low voice, and slung mine over my shoulder. Then I mounted the steps, and stood in the doorway of the hall. This was empty, of people, but was furnished as I would have expected, with a huge table and several chairs at the far end, while to the right a staircase mounted against the wall.

"My home, L'Eree," Richilde said. "At least for a season."

I looked left and right, but could not find her. "Do you mean for a year, Richilde?" I asked. "Or ten years? Or a hundred?"

"I could never spend a hundred years in this gloomy place, L'Eree," Richilde said, and this time her voice lacked the additional depths given by amplification. I looked up the stairs, as did my companions, and saw her standing there.

How adequately to describe the Princess von Hohengraf-fen, or Lady Culhaven, or any of the dozens of other names she had used in her time? When first I had beheld her, it had been in the midst of the sack of Magdeburg in 1631, one of the most horrendous events in history, and I, may God forgive me, had been one of the sacking scoundrels. Thus when I had discovered a mere chit of a girl, as I thought, hiding from the rampant soldiery, it had seemed the most natural thing in the world for me to appropriate her as my own, at least for a tumble. I had been quite unaware of the force with which I had been contending. Even when, as happened fairly shortly, I realised that far from my appropriating her, she had appropriated me, having immediately discerned that a man of my build and aggressive habits could be a boon to a lonely devil, I had not found any reason to terminate our relationship. Indeed, as she had sought to bind me to her by every art known to woman, I had revelled in it. It was only as I had slowly uncovered the beauty and discovered what lay beneath that I had sought to flee her, and earned her enmity. Yet even so, I had been so bewitched by her beauty that, as I had confessed to Queen Anne, I had been quite unable to deal with her properly, and thus had permitted her to reappear in my life more than once, with horrifying results.

And now here she was again, and for the last time, as it had to be, for one or the other of us. I caught my breath. Magdeburg, it should be remembered, was twenty years in the past. Yet here was the same chit of a girl slowly moving towards me, the same somewhat pert face with its wide red lips and pointed chin, its slightly upturned nose and high forehead, the whole shrouded in that flowing auburn hair I remembered so well, a thick strand of which lay in front of her shoulder. Here was beauty, but yet, only beauty. It was not until she had completed her descent to within a few steps of the floor that I saw the real Richilde. The splendour which transcended humanity lay in her eyes, deep, deep green, stretching forever into her skull and beyond, a succession of priceless emeralds, set one behind the other. This morning the emeralds were molten, soft, welcoming. I had seen them hard as flint, and sparkling with demonic rage; I could not doubt that I would see them in that state again, soon enough. For the rest she wore a deep blue gown, modestly high-necked, although the swell of her bodice reminded me of all the treasures that lay there concealed. The gown did not quite reach the floor, and as she came down the stairs we could see her neat little shoes uncovered, and above them, her ankles. No doubt my companions were surprised to discern that she wore no stockings. I could have told them that our hostess wore no underwear at all.

Even without that knowledge, however, my companions were struck dumb. Alicia had every reason to consider herself a beautiful woman, but even she could tell she was in the presence of one far superior to herself. Had they both been asleep, now, she might have compared. But there was no woman who ever lived could give out quite the *glow* of Richilde Bethlen, when she wished to. Felicity, not herself a beauty although an extremely attractive woman, was perhaps less affected, although she was also clearly overwhelmed.

While Roderick . . . poor Roderick, as I had feared, was on the verge of falling in love at first sight. Well, had I not done the same, once, and suffered for it?

"Won't you introduce me, L'Eree?" Richilde asked. She had stopped on the bottom step.

Before I could speak, Alicia had stepped forward. "Lady Alicia Norton, your highness." She actually gave a little curtsey.

"Ah," Richilde said, and looked at Felicity.

"Felicity Brewin, ma'am."

"Ah," Richilde said again, and looked at Roderick.

"Dr Roderick Brewin, milady. I visited your castle once before."

"Of course you did," Richilde said. "Dear Bulstrode has told me all about you. All of you. He found your husband, Lady Norton, such a pleasant companion."

"He sucked his blood!" Alicia declared.

"Well, of course, my dear. What else would you expect him to do? Do you know, I think I am going to suck yours. I think you will be very tasty."

Alicia looked at me in consternation.

I had been considering our situation. At the moment, there were four of us to just the Witch. I could not doubt she had help at hand, or she would never have admitted us in the first place. But a great deal would depend upon whether or not her help was human. I needed that information, and so I asked, "Do I then gather that Lord Culhaven got home safely?"

"Oh, indeed, dear Bulstrode got home yesterday. What a tale he had to tell. But I'm afraid he is not very happy with the way you have been treating him, Helier."

"Yes. Well, like most of us, he brings his troubles upon himself. Now, there was a matter of some letters I was to purchase from you."

"But you have already done that, Helier, by coming to me," Richilde said. "They are in my bedchamber. Would you care to come with me and examine them, to make sure they are the genuine article?"

"We shall all come with you," I decided. "On our own terms. Roderick! Ladies!" As I spoke I threw my saddlebag on the floor, and from it whipped my cross and my string of garlic, as well as the mallet and hammer and stake.

Sadly, my companions were less eager to act. "You cannot seriously mean to harm this lady," Roderick protested.

"For God's sake!" I shouted. "Is that not why we are here?"

"He means to drive that stake through my body," Richilde remarked, showing not the least fear of my various accessories. "Can you permit such a crime, Dr Brewin?"

I was advancing to the foot of the stairs, but Roderick placed himself in front of me. "Helier, I beg of you," he said. "Do not let us do anything rash. I am sure this good lady has an explanation for everything."

"Well said, sir," Richilde agreed. "I can see that you and I are going to be the best of friends."

"Roderick," I said. "I feared this would happen. And I must say that I consider you a most shallow fellow, to be taken in by a beautiful face and a handsome figure."

"Well!" Richilde remarked. "Handsome?"

"Well!" Alicia protested. "Shallow fellow? You are speaking of my betrothed."

Her romance was progressing at a breakneck speed. But I was now thoroughly angry. "Then you had best call him aside," I told her, "for I swear, Roderick, if you attempt to stop me dealing with this foul creature, I shall cut you down." And I drew my sword.

Roderick stared at me, then looked at the Witch, then at Alicia. He knew he stood no chance against me. But now the one person he had neglected to look at took up his cause. "Helier!" Felicity cried. "You cannot mean to harm my own brother!"

I looked at her in consternation. "You have got yourself in a bit of a bother, Helier," Richilde said.

"I have come here to destroy you, Richilde," I said. "And so help me God, I intend to do that, even if I have to slay my own friends to do so." Saying which I moved with that tremendous speed I always have in reserve, and was at Roderick before he knew what was upon him. I seized him by the shoulder and sent him sprawling on the floor, while I dashed at the stairs, sword in my right hand, mallet and stake, cross and string of garlic in my left. I must have presented a pretty fearful sight, for Richilde took several quick steps back up the stairs, but I was halted by an explosion. Someone had fired a pistol at me. Fortunately, she had missed, but I still checked, and turned to see which of my mistresses could have been so misguided.

To my disgust I saw that it was Felicity, aghast at the sight of her brother so upset, for he had struck the floor so hard he had lost consciousness. She regretted what she had done, of course. "Helier!" she cried. "Forgive me. But . . . Roderick is my brother. Helier! Let us fly this place."

"It amazes me why all of these women fall for you, Helier," Richilde said, having regained her composure.

251

"But we have played the game long enough. He is yours. But do not kill him."

I turned even further, and saw, coming through the doorway at the far end of the hall, a good dozen powerful looking but singularly ill-favoured men. I could tell at a glance that these were not vampires: they looked extraordinarily human – and extraordinarily vicious, too. I also saw that they were armed merely with clubs, no doubt as previously instructed by their mistress, although four of them were carrying a box, but what it contained I could not tell. I was determined not to allow them to distract me from my purpose. I had no doubt that I could deal with them after I had settled with Richilde, supposing, indeed, they hung about after the demise of their mistress. I therefore again ran at the stairs, and had the satisfaction of seeing Richilde definitely alarmed, her teeth bared as she retreated up to the first landing. But then I was distracted by a most piteous howl from behind me, and turning again, saw that one of her henchmen had seized Alicia, and forced her to her knees, while he had drawn a knife from his belt. "Surrender, or I will cut her throat," he threatened.

"Helier! Save me!" Alicia screamed.

I could see no reason why I should. And there remained Felicity, standing there with a smoking pistol in her hand. But there was another in her belt. "Shoot the wretch!" I commanded.

Felicity certainly intended to obey me. She dropped the first pistol and drew the second, but in such haste that she released the trigger before she knew what she was about, and the ball smashed harmlessly into the ceiling. This left me in a considerable predicament. My support, such as it had turned out to be, had been utterly destroyed. Roderick still lay unconscious on the floor, Felicity was disarmed, and Alicia was in the hands of this lout, who had been reinforced by two of his fellows to hold her arms and render her quite helpless. While Richilde had gone to ground in the room opening off the landing, the door of which was closed.

The temptation to assault it was tremendous, but I could not doubt that Alicia would then die, and even if I had gone off the boil regarding her I remained a gentleman. Besides, I still had some hopes of regaining the upper hand in the course of time, knowing Richilde's propensity for toying with her victims before actually destroying them. Thus I descended the stairs. "Throw your sword on the floor," said the fellow who was holding the knife to Alicia's throat; she was by now all but swooning with terror.

I obeyed, and my great weapon clattered to the stone. "Do not suppose him any the less dangerous because he lacks a weapon," Richilde advised; she had re-emerged on to the landing above me. "You know what to do." The four men carrying the box placed it on the floor, opened it, and from it took a considerable length of iron chain. "You see, Helier," Richilde said, returning down the steps. "I remember how, six years ago, you popped the ropes with which I bound you, as if they had been string. But I do not believe that even you are capable of bursting iron links."

I had to admit that she was probably right. And that, in fact, I had been totally outmanoeuvered. Not by Richilde, there was the damning part. Had my companions followed my lead without hesitation, as they had sworn to do, we would by now have had the Witch at our mercy. But her very appearance had suborned them as easily and as quickly as she had suborned too many others. It was scant consolation for me to recall, again, that she had had a similar effect upon me when first we had met. But now all my hopes had come tumbling to the ground, and I could only await whatever fate her devilish mind had concocted for me to suffer. Again, it was even less consolation for me to reflect that those companions who had so let me down would suffer equally.

So why not die in one last mighty upheaval, pitting my bare hands against these louts? I had fought at such odds, successfully, in the past. But then I had had the power of surprise on my side. This was lacking here. One of my enemies had picked up my sword, another had relieved Roderick of his pistols, and these were presented to my breast while I was being bound with the chains.

Richilde, meanwhile, was inspecting her catch, one could say. She stood first of all above Roderick, who was just sitting up, rubbing his chin, as it had been that portion of his anatomy which had most forcefully come into contact with the stone floor.

"Is he badly hurt?" Felicity asked, taking a step forward, and checking as the Witch looked at her.

"I do not think he is hurt at all," Richilde said, and daintily extended her right foot to push Roderick over. He fell on to his back again, this time banging his head. He looked up at the apparition rising above him, for Richilde was now standing by his head. "I think he may prove to be an amusing fellow." Saying which she lifted her right leg again, and this time placed the shoe on Roderick's stomach, easing herself forward to transfer all of her weight onto that leg.

Roderick instinctively tried to grasp Richilde's skirt, but she stooped slightly to give him a resounding slap across the face. He gasped and fell down again. "You have hurt him!" Felicity cried, this time running forward, only to have her arms seized by two of Richilde's people, who brought her to a halt, panting.

"Why," Richilde said. "So I have." There was blood dribbling down Roderick's chin from where her blow had cut his lip. Now she daintily raised her skirts to her knees, knelt beside him, and proceeded to kiss him on the mouth. He made no effort to resist her. Well, no doubt he found it pleasant enough. Only we could see that she was actually licking the blood from his lip and swallowing it.

254

"Vampire!" Felicity cried, somewhat late in the day, to be sure.

Richilde straightened. "Why, yes," she said. "I have the taste. But you . . ." she stepped up to the girl, who was still held immobile by the two men, took her chin between thumb and forefinger, and turned it to and fro. "A pretty child," she remarked at large. "Yes. I think I know what I shall do with you. Put her in the yellow room," she commanded. "But remember . . ." she held up her finger, "no one is to touch her, until I say so."

"You cannot do this," Felicity shrieked feebly, as she was dragged from the hall.

Alicia continued to be struck dumb by the horror into which she had so carelessly strayed. It was now her turn to be inspected by our captor. The knife had at least been removed from her throat, but her arms were still gripped by two of Richilde's people. "Now, you," Richilde said. "You will be worth having." She did not waste her time on Alicia's face, but instead dug her fingers into the bodice of her habit to rip it open and expose her breasts. "Oh, indeed. There is a wealth of rich red blood in there. Put her in the red chamber, and secure her."

The two men dragged Alicia to the stairs, and forced her up them. "The man?" asked another of the Witch's henchmen. He was referring to Roderick.

"Throw him in the dungeon. Lord Culhaven may wish to have him, when he wakes up."

"And this one?" He gave a tug on the chain securing my arms.

"Bring *him* to my chamber," she said. "We have much to talk about, Count d'Albret and I."

CHAPTER 10

I realised that I was probably in the most dangerous situation of my life. In fact, we all were. As I had anticipated, and relied upon, the Witch certainly intended to enjoy herself at our expense before destroying us . . . but it was difficult for me to determine how I was going to take advantage of any delay in our demise. There was no hope of my bursting these chains. There was no possibility of my obtaining a weapon. And the Witch had a lot more support than I had estimated. Thus I could do nothing more than allow the men to push and pull me up the stairs and into Richilde's bedchamber. It was a large room decorated in glowing purple drapes, as one might have expected in view of the personality who slept here.

"On the bed," Richilde commanded, and I was laid on the sweet-scented sheets beneath the huge tester, while more chains were produced and my arms and legs were secured to the four posts, leaving me absolutely helpless. "You make me think of Prometheus," Richilde smiled. "Thank you, Giles, that will be all for the moment. I wish you to inform Blacking that there will be a Mass tonight, and that he is to bring his people up."

"A Mass!" The villain Giles' eyes gleamed. "I shall prepare it."

He hurried off, closing the door behind him. I was alone with my bitterest enemy, who was also the most beautiful and alluring creature – I use the word advisedly – I had ever known.

Perhaps Richilde was similarly affected, for she stood at the foot of the bed for several seconds, gazing at me. At last she said, "Do you know, Helier, that you have changed very little in twenty years. A bit of weight, perhaps."

"And you have not changed at all, from the day of our first meeting."

"Why, Helier, what a nice thing for you to say. I really am pleased to see you again. I have so looked forward to it. And now you are here. We are going to have such fun together."

"Before you kill me."

"Well, I am afraid that will be necessary. Not only do I hate you for destroying so many of my ambitions, but if I do not kill you I suspect you are going to keep on trying to kill *me*. One day you may just work out how to do it. But I shall endeavour to make even your death enjoyable, at least for me. But first . . . " she went to a bureau against the wall, and from one of the drawers took a sharp-bladed knife. I caught my breath as she came back to the bed, but convinced myself that she could hardly mean to kill me so easily – although I did not exclude mutilation, of one sort or another . . . and neither sort appealed to me or my prospects. This fear was enhanced when she sat beside me and began cutting away my clothing, while she smiled at me: she could see the sweat on my forehead. "Oh, I am not going to harm you, now, Helier," she said. "I am going to *love* you. Because I have looked forward to this also, you know."

"I am not sure that in my present frame of mind I would be much good to you," I confessed.

She continued to smile as she snipped away. "I am sure we will be able to find something to do."

And in fact she was perfectly right. The nearness of her, the glorious scent of her, the brushing of her hair across my now naked chest, was a most powerful stimulant. I tried to resist her by distraction. "As I am surely entirely

257

in your power, and doomed to die in any event, will you not tell me the truth of it?" I asked.

"The truth of what?" She completed the destruction of my shirt, and gave my chest a little rub of satisfaction.

"Confess to me what you really are. When first we met, you told me you were the natural daughter of Bethlen Gabor, Prince of Transylvania, and that you inherited your lust for blood from your mother, who was incestually conceived and therefore cursed. Do you expect me still to believe that?"

"It was a pretty tale, was it not?" She turned her attention to my boots, slicing at the leather so that she could draw them from my feet without having to release the chains round my ankles. "But it was my mother gave me the gift of eternal life, even if I was born long before Gabor ever saw this earth."

"I did not know that vampires could give birth."

"There are many things you do not know, L'Eree."

My feet were bare.

"And Culhaven?"

"A wandering spirit, like myself. But a useful servant. Although he has his weaknesses."

She commenced work on my breeches, handling the knife with such exquisite care that only her fingers ever touched my flesh.

"So I have noticed," I said. "But he is also a vampire. I have seen him at work. However, I wish you would explain it to me. Both you, and Culhaven, do not in the least conform to the popular understanding of such creatures."

"Such creatures," she remarked, contemptuously, sliding the knife down the entire right side of my pants to split them in two. "Popular understanding is nothing more than a collection of legends, created partly to give people some hope, but mostly to inspire them with fear. Thus we are reputed to be capable of movement only by night, but of transporting ourselves into all manner of shapes,

258

principally that of the bat, of course." She began work on my left pants leg. "We are supposed to be able raise storms, and mists. These concepts are all very flattering, but they are sadly untrue, and ridiculous. What your popular understanding is incapable of comprehending is that there are certain 'creatures' as you call us, who live off human blood. It is as simple as that."

"And this gives you immortality?"

"Certainly. And logically. By constantly renewing our blood with the blood of others, preferably young and strong people, we equally renew our life force, time and again. Night by night, when it is possible. We prefer the night, as a rule, because then we can more easily accomplish our purpose, undetected. Only some of us, such as dear Bulstrode, are actually debilitated by light. Then this business of crosses, and garlic! I gather you had some success by opposing these trifles to the poor fellow. I assure you they mean nothing to me. But it is entirely natural that vampires, like humans, vary in their personality and their strengths. I merely happen to be one of the strongest."

"I never doubted it," I agreed, as, my breeches now lying in strips away from my legs, she turned her attention to my drawers. "And your relations with the King? First Culhaven would not leave him, keeping me waiting for this meeting. Then he could not get away soon enough."

"The King," she sneered. "A paltry fellow. Having seen so many revolutions come and go in the course of my lives, I know that this Parliamentary success is but a passing fancy of the English people. They will have a king back soon enough. Sooner than later. Thus I supposed I could be of some service to this lad, in return for a grant of lands here in Wales. I sent Bulstrode to him, and the terms were agreed. This boy would sup with the devil to regain his throne. Thus I told Bulstrode to support him in every way, and I had no doubt that he would prosper,

259

if Helier L'Eree were also at his side. But you see, I was mistaken. This lad is doomed to failure, even with your support. To do him justice, the moment Bulstrode realised the cause was lost he determined to abandon the King, and bring you to me."

"But the failure of the King's cause was at least partly due to me," I pointed out.

"Oh, absolutely. Even you have been a disappointment to me."

"May I ask how you intend to kill me? Will you suck my blood?"

"Do you know, I have considered that. You understand that were I to do so, I could transform you into a vampire as well, and thus implant the seeds of immortality within you. But I cannot quite convince myself that would be a wise thing to do. The thought of a Helier L'Eree, filled with evil, rampaging through the centuries, is somewhat unnerving. No, I think you will have to die a human death. However, I do not have to make a decision now. I have those other three delicious toys to play with first." Removing my drawers was a matter of only a few passes with the knife. "Oh, Helier," she said. "What memories that sight brings back to me." She rose, and began to undress herself.

I still wished to resist her, although I knew that was going to be next to impossible. On the other hand, I might yet put her off. "So tell me this," I said, watching her gown sliding past her hips to the floor; as I had estimated, she wore nothing underneath. "Are you truly immortal?"

She made a moue, standing above me, and the sight of the naked Richilde Bethlen, Princess von Hohengraffen, was suffcent to drive any further thoughts of resistance from my mind. "In the normal course of events," she said.

"You will not even die if a stake is driven through your heart?"

She laughed, one of the most delightful of sounds. "Oh, that would probably cause my death, Helier. But not because of the stake being driven through my heart. I would die from loss of blood. Once I removed the stake, and had replenished my blood supply, then I would survive. As I live by renewing my blood, I can *only* die from loss of blood. All of my blood."

"But whoever drove the stake through your heart, would he not also cut off your head, so that you would lack the motive power to remove the stake?"

"How knowledgeable you are, Helier. But you are never going to be in a position to use that stake of yours, or those brought by your friends. Or cut off my head. Now . . . I think you need to have your appetite whetted. I know I do. Don't go away," she smiled, and went to the end of the room, where there was a pair of double doors. These she threw open, to reveal beyond what she had earlier described as the red room, in that the drapes and carpets in here were all in crimson. The blaze appeared as the veritable entrance to hell.

Which perhaps it was, for against the far wall opposite me, and secured to it, was Alicia. She was naked, and her arms were outstretched and strapped to brackets set in the stone. Her legs were free, and she was able to stand, but she remained able to do nothing more than kick, and even this did not seem to interest her at the moment. But when she saw me she let out a shriek. "Helier! Save me!"

"He is in no condition to do so," Richilde pointed out, going up to her. "Now, my dear, I have chosen you as my mid-morning snack."

Alicia's head jerked, and she gave another terrifying scream, then seemed to pull herself together. "Listen," she said. "Your highness, your grace, whoever you are . . . spare me, and I can make you rich."

"What an exciting thought," Richilde said, going right up to her.

"Listen," Alicia said. "That man, L'Eree, is worth five

hundred pounds to the Roundheads. They are out there looking for him now. You could send a messenger to tell them that you have him. Five hundred pounds, your highness."

"I think you need to pick your friends more carefully, Helier," Richilde remarked. "But that was always your weakness."

"Five hundred pounds!" Alicia shrieked. "If you will let Dr Brewin and myself go."

"My dear girl, what on earth am I going to do with five hundred pounds, when I have all the riches of the world at my fingertips? And what of Dr Brewin's sister? Are you going to ask for her as well?"

"Oh, you can have *her*," Alicia said contemptuously. "She is of no use to anyone. Save him." She jerked her head in my direction.

"But she is of use to *me*," Richilde pointed out. "Although not in the way you might think. As for you . . . you are far too delicious-looking a nibble for me to let you go without at least sampling you. Now, hold your breath."

Alicia gave another frantic shriek, and an equally frantic kick, but that was apparently what Richilde wanted her to do, for she caught the leg as it flailed through the air, and held it extended. Alicia tried to kick with her other leg, but of course this left her suspended only by her wrists, with the consequent risk of dislocating her shoulders, so she very rapidly dropped it to the ground again. While Richilde, now holding the ankle, in a grip so strong that Alicia appeared unable to do more than jerk, bent her head over the big toe, and made a quick movement with her mouth. Once again Alicia's scream bade fare to lift the roof, but Richilde continued to ignore her while she appeared to be sucking the toe. From my position I could not clearly see what she was doing, but I could guess, and my suspicions were confirmed when she raised her head to let me see the blood dribbling from the

262

corners of her mouth, a sight no less terrifying because I had seen it before – and from that same mouth.

Alicia had by now stopped screaming, and was instead staring at her toe in horror: the digit had turned quite white. "It will refill itself," Richilde assured her, and turned her attention to me, but not, as she had intimated, to suck my *blood*.

For the rest of that never-to-be-forgotten day, Alicia and I, alternately, were at the mercy of the vampire. At some time I was fed, by some ill-favoured female, and Alicia also, as Richilde was in no hurry to suck her victim dry. Indeed, at that time she took very little of Alicia's blood which was not very reassuring, as it occurred to me that she was in the process of transforming Alicia into one of her own kind, as Culhaven had done with Rupert. For myself, by dusk I was exhausted, and in a most peculiar frame of mind. To be the victim of a beautiful woman, over a period of several hours, when she is in an entirely amatory frame of mind, cannot be other than a pleasure for any man with red blood in his veins. Yet was I terribly aware that she had every intention, when she was sated, of emptying these veins, if not necessarily with her own teeth. This awareness ruins one's objectivity. But wrack my brain as I might, I could see no way out of my, and indeed, our, predicament. Alicia of course I had to count as already lost, but I still felt some necessity to aid Roderick and Felicity, if I could, no matter how they had let me down. Meanwhile, throughout the castle there was a growing amount of stealthy noise. Richilde's creatures were preparing for the Mass. At which, who was going to be the victim? I could no longer doubt that.

It was dusk when she aroused me, accompanied by half-a-dozen of her henchmen, and I was not at all sure that these were human; in any event, at their head was Bulstrode Culhaven himself, looking totally refreshed and full of energy. I had to presume that he had been visiting

263

poor Roderick. "Well, Count," he remarked. "Now our situation has changed somewhat, has it not?"

"Temporarily, I am sure, my dear Bulstrode," I suggested.

He gave a sinister smile. "Oh, yes, indeed, temporarily."

I now observed that he, and his people, and indeed, Richilde herself, wore but a single garment, a flowing black robe caught at the waist with a cord. This I remembered from the last time Richilde had forced me to attend one of her Masses, so many years ago. They also had a robe for me, but just to make sure that I behaved myself, Culhaven presented a pistol at my head on one side, while one of his people did the same at the other. Richilde stood at the foot of the bed with a long, slim-bladed knife in her hand, while the rest of the people released my chains. "I do beg of you to be sensible, Helier," she said. "I have no wish to kill you now, but I shall if you make the slightest untoward movement."

Again I could see no alternative to accepting the inevitable, on the grounds that my situation could only improve – it could not possibly grow worse. At least I would be out of this bed. I was released, set on my feet, and draped in my black robe. My hands were manacled together again, behind my back, leaving me just as helpless as before. "Now come," Richilde said.

"What about Lady Norton?" I asked. "Doesn't she get to take part in the fun?"

"I think she needs to rest," Richilde said. "She has had a tiring day."

From the landing I looked down at a transformed knights' hall, in that a dais had been erected at one end. On this dais there was both a high-backed chair and a long table, covered with a black cloth. In front of the dais were gathered some forty people, men, women and children, and even babes at the breast, all wearing the black robes, all gazing most expectantly at the stairs and ourselves. Clearly the entire village had been assembled here. "Welcome, my people," Richilde said, her voice drifting over them. "Welcome to my castle. I have much to offer you, tonight." She lowered her voice. "Go down, L'Eree," she commanded.

I descended the stairs, watched by the throng. But there was no spark of friendship or sympathy there; they remembered me from this morning. Richilde followed me, with her men; I realised that Culhaven had not followed us out of the room, and understood why. There had to be another, secret way down from Richilde's bedchamber, and a Black Mass has to have a devil!

When we reached the floor I was marched up to the dais, and made to kneel beside it, two guards ever at my back. The worshippers stared at me, hostility evident in their eyes. But then their attention was drawn to the back of the hall, where, as I had expected, Culhaven had re-appeared. He was now naked, save for an enormous goat's-head mask which rested on his shoulders and completely obscured his own features, but which added a good foot to his height. That his body, and certainly his appurtenances, did not in any way match up to his head did not dismay the onlookers, who gave a great moan of approbation as he slowly came forward, mounted the dais from the rear, and seated himself upon the chair. Richilde took her place at his side, while the great fire was stoked up to cause an immense heat to permeate the hall.

When she was sure her devil was comfortably seated, Richilde clapped her hands. Immediately two of her people came forward from the side of the hall, carrying between them a huge wooden cross. This they hurled to the floor at the foot of the steps. Richilde then clapped her hands again, and the congregation rose, to come forward, one after the other, man, woman and child, and relieve themselves upon the Christian symbol. Quite apart from the obscenity of the ritual, it was also awesome, for the entire misdeed was carried out in total silence, the only sounds being the roaring of the fire and the scraping of the acolytes' feet.

And the sound of their breathing, to be sure, for they knew this was but the preliminary to the main event of the evening. When the last child had returned to its place, Richilde looked at me. No doubt she was remembering that it was my refusal so to abase myself that had caused the original breach between us, and I wondered if she would now attempt to force me to comply with her wishes. But she apparently thought better of that idea, and instead clapped her hands again.

This brought two more of her henchmen from a side door, dragging between them Felicity. She was naked, as was to be expected, but yet did not appear to have been harmed in any way. apart from a few bruises. Although she was clearly very frightened she yet had her wits about her, sufficiently so to take in her surroundings, and then to observe myself, on the far side of the platform from her. Her eyes widened at the sight of me, but unlike Alicia, she did not immediately cry out. My heart bled for her, as I had no doubt that she was about to be sacrificed . . . and there was nothing that I could do to help her, much less myself. Thus I watched as she was dragged to the dais and up the steps, making no attempt to resist her captors but yet being most brutally manhandled by them. She only attempted to fight them when they forced her to lie on the table, on her belly, as she then for the first time grasped that something at least very unpleasant was about to happen to her. But now two other of Richilde's people came forward to assist, and Felicity was helpless, her wrists and ankles being bound to the four uprights of the table, so that she was as spreadeagled as I had been earlier on Richilde's bed, only the other way up.

Now she was definitely terrified, her head moving to and fro, but she had been placed with her feet towards me, so that she could no longer see me. Obviously she understood that calling upon me for help was a waste of time. Richilde stepped forward, eyes gleaming with anticipated pleasure.

Felicity's first duty was to act as an altar. A lighted candle was placed between her buttocks, and upon the curving flesh Richilde broke into pieces several old and gnarled turnips and other roots. Then again the congregation came forward, to be given something to drink from a silver cup – again remembering that earlier Mass, I suspected it was *aqua vitae*, to inflame their senses – then with their teeth and lips each took a piece of the crumbled root from Felicity's trembling back. The brave girl preserved her silence throughout this ordeal, but I knew that tears of shame and terror were dribbling down her cheeks beside her hair to fall to the wooden floor of the dais.

It took well over an hour for everyone to celebrate the Mass. By then the candle had burned down so far as to scorch Felicity's flesh, not to mention coating it with hot wax, and then at last she did utter a moan of pain. But her ordeal was not yet completed, as Richilde summoned up the biggest and most masculine of her followers, to take possession of my charmer in the most vicious and obscene manner, driving himself into her with great triumphant thrusts. Now Felicity cried out, in both shame and agony. The fellow spent and withdrawn, Richilde stepped forward again, and another of her acolytes presented her with a wooden box. This box she now opened and held up for all to see, myself included. It contained a doll, the model of a man, dressed in the height of fashion, with flowing black hair and an incipient moustache, for he was clearly very young.

I knew at once who it was intended to be. And again my memory went back to that terrible night at Hohengraffen in 1632, when Richilde had produced a model of the great

Swedish king, Gustavus Adolphus, and had sacrificed a woman over the box, and prophesied that where her blood fell, there would the King suffer his death wounds. As had indeed happened. There could be no doubt that she intended the same for Charles Stuart, as she now made plain. She advanced to the edge of the dais, the box held above her head, while the folds of her black robe fell away from her shoulders and thighs to leave that unforgettable beauty exposed. "Behold!" she cried. "The body of a traitor. This man promised us much, and has failed us in everything. Now he cowers, a beaten fugitive. We have placed our trust in a man of no account. He must die, as we must pray to our master the Devil that in his place there shall arise a man greater than he."

The throng moaned their approval, and Felicity writhed ineffectually. Richilde returned behind the sacrificial alter, and placed the box on the floor, beneath Felicity's throat. For a moment the two women stared at each other, faces almost touching, then Richilde straightened again, and picked up her long-bladed knife. "Now!" she shrieked. "By the powers vested in me by my immortal ancestors, by the . . ."

The castle was shaken by a bugle blast from beyond the drawbridge. Every head turned, even Richilde's, as well as Felicity's, while Bulstrode stood up in consternation.

"Who is that?" Richilde demanded. "Giles!"

Her principal henchman hurried from the hall, while the rest of us waited with bated breath. I had a pretty good idea who it had to be, and reflected, better late than never. The exchange was clearly heard, for the doors to the courtyard were opened. "Who comes here?" Giles demanded.

"Open in the name of the Parliament of England," came the challenge.

"Who do you seek?"

"I am here to serve a warrant for the arrest of the foul

traitor and murderer Bulstrode, Lord Culhaven, and his equally guilty wife, Richilde, Lady Culhaven."

Bulstrode tore off his mask and threw it to the floor; he was shaking with terror. "What will we do?"

"Be quiet!" Richilde snapped, and herself strode from the hall, followed by most of her people. I was on my feet as well, straining at my chains, but there was no way I could free myself.

"Helier!" Felicity gasped. "Oh, Helier. How I have failed you."

This was scarcely the time for recriminations. I was more interested in what might be happening at the gate. Our visitor was making another pronouncement. "Open these gates, or I shall blow them down."

"Cannon!" someone shrieked. "They have a cannon."

I realised that Richilde, demon though she might be, was singularly lacking in military ability. She had summoned her every last tenant to the Mass, leaving the approaches to her castle so unguarded that the Roundheads had been able to drag their cannon up that twisting roadway, unheard and unheeded. "Captain," Richilde called, using her most dulcet tones. "I am sure there is some mistake."

"Is your name Richilde Bethlen, Lady Culhaven?" the captain demanded.

"Why, yes, to be sure. I am Lady Culhaven. And my husband and I have always been most faithful supporters of Parliament."

"We have evidence to the contrary, milady. We have witnesses to prove that Lord Culhaven was an intimate of the so-called King, Charles II. We have letters written in your hand pledging support for the King in return for grants of land and amnesties for various crimes. We have depositions regarding those crimes. We also have witnesses to confirm that you have given shelter to the wanted traitor Helier l'Eree, also known as Count d'Albret."

"L'Eree!" Richilde said. "Yes, indeed, Captain. The wretch is here. I will turn him over to you, if you leave us in peace."

"It matters naught whether you surrender him, or not, milady," the Roundhead said. "My orders, given me by General Cromwell himself, are to destroy this castle and arrest everyone in it. I will give you half-an-hour to come out and surrender, and then I shall open fire."

"And if we surrender?" Richilde asked. "Will we then be spared?"

"Then you will be hanged in a decent manner, together with your accomplices. After due process of law." There was a brief silence, and I could imagine Richilde considering the pros and cons of the situation. To be hanged would cost her nothing save some discomfort and humiliation – certainly not her life. But that would not apply to her people. However, the captain was not yet done. "There are also charges of witchcraft and vampirism to be brought against you, milady, and these may well result in a different form of execution. However, we will have to leave that to the courts."

"I will see you in hell," Richilde told him, still speaking quietly. A moment later she was back in the hall, followed by her people, most of whom were looking terrified.

"They will destroy our houses," wailed one of the women.

"I would say they have already done that," Richilde told her, brutally. "There is a great glow in the valley."

"What is to become of us," wailed another. The children began to cry.

"Oh, get them out of here. Blacking, we must prepare a defence."

The lout – it was he who had sodomised Felicity – twisted his hat in his hands. "We cannot defend the castle against a cannon, milady."

"Nonsense. Let them batter down the outer gate. Once they have done that, there is still no way they can get

270

the cannon across the ravine to assault the keep, without block and pulley. That will prove impossible, if we resist them."

"They will send for additional help, milady."

"Are you suggesting you surrender? They'll hang you all."

Blacking grinned. "There's the secret way out, milady. We could be away."

"They'll still come behind you, and hunt you down like the rats you are," Richilde told him.

Blacking continued to smile, but now it was a sinister smile. "They won't come behind us, milady, because it's you they really want. And him. And him!" He pointed at Culhaven, then at me. "So, we'll just leave you here, and take ourselves off."

"You wouldn't dare abandon me," Richilde snapped.

"What are you going to do, darling? Tell them Round-heads all our crimes? Crimes you drove us to? Oh, they'll be interested in that." He looked left and right, at the now eager faces. "You with me?"

"Yes," they declared to a man, and a woman, and a child.

"Bastards!" Richilde shouted. "Bulstrode . . ."

Before Culhaven could react – not that I could imagine what he might do, as I had never come across any human being, much less a vampire, more averse to physical combat – one of the men had dealt him a buffet on the side of the head which stretched him senseless on the floor. "Bulstrode!" Richilde screamed.

Then she gazed at the men coming towards her, ropes in their hands. For a moment she clearly considered fighting them, and with her razor sharp teeth she would certainly have done some damage. But she decided against it, as she no doubt realised that they knew enough about her to destroy her, if pushed far enough. So she submitted to being forced to sit in one of the highbacked chairs, and be thoroughly trussed up with ropes. The half-conscious Bulstrode, who was groaning most horribly, was similarly tied, and then Blacking gave her a mocking bow. "Work yourself out of this one, milady, and I truly will believe you are a witch."

His people disappeared through the door at the back of the hall, not without a good deal of cursing and swearing. Some of them waited long enough to slap Richilde's face or pull her hair, and when they were finished, Giles himself actually slit her shoulder open with his knife, a wide and deep gash, causing rich red blood to course down the white skin, and proving that he knew her better than most. "You'd best hope the Roundheads get here before you bleed to death," he sneered.

Richilde said not a word, but her eyes spoke volumes, and I would not have liked to be any of those people at who she stared so viciously: they were certainly doomed to have nightmares for the rest of their lives.

But then they were gone, although we could hear them for some time, as they descended into the bowels of the hillside. The last sound had only just died when outside the front gate the cannon roared, to the accompaniment of the sound of shattering wood.

"Well, Princess," I remarked. "At least you must now have some idea how my old comrade Jeanne felt, when you abandoned her, just like this, to face the German witchhunter Carpzov."

Richilde glanced at me, her face again serene, although there were discolourations where she had been hit, and blood continued to seep from her wound and dribble down her arm. By her own confession, she was dying, unless tended. The cannon roared again, and some more wood splintered. Richilde's lip curled. "Do you think that pack of curs can defeat me, L'Eree? I will show you." She bent her head. By twisting her neck so that it seemed it would break she could just reach the topmost rope, which was draped over her shoulder before being

272

secured to the back of the chair. This rope she sucked between her teeth and began to bite.

"Helier!" Felicity whispered.

"Ssssh," I told her. I was utterly fascinated. Here was beauty, however awful, fighting for its life. I could not do other than wish her well.

I watched the teeth chewing away, while she panted, and sweat rolled out of her hair. But then the rope fell loose. It was the work of only a few minutes after that to unravel the entire web in which she had been cocooned. She stood up, free, and as terrible as at any time in her life, because her entire body swelled with anger and outrage, while still blood dribbled down her arm. A few seconds more and Culhaven was also freed, clearly still somewhat dazed and confused. But then, he had always been somewhat confused. "Now we must away," she said.

"What of them?" he asked.

"I am sure the Roundheads will think of something to do with them. They will certainly delay any pursuit while they consider the matter. So you see, Helier, it will be *your* opportunity to consider how Jeanne must have felt, as she watched her fate approaching while unable to do anything about it."

"We could take the good doctor with us," Culhaven said, somewhat wistfully.

"We can take no one with us," Richilde told him. "Now, away with you and get dressed. I must see to this scratch." There was another roar, and another resounding crash; the castle shook. Culhaven gave a squeak of fear and hurried up the stairs. Richilde stood before me. "You are a pitiful sight, Helier," she remarked. "Prometheus, indeed. You make me think more of a legend there is in Paris, of a hunchback who rang the bells of Notre Dame Cathedral, and who had to be bound with chains because of his excesses."

"Why do you not kill me now, Princess?" I asked, my mood as savage as my situation.

"I do regret not being able to do that, but as I have explained, your presence will delay our pursuit. Besides, I am sure the Roundheads will do it for me," she said. "I may even overlook your hanging, from a suitable distance." She went up the stairs herself.

"Helier," Felicity panted, straining with desperate urgency against her bonds. "What are we to do?"

I wished I had an answer. It occurred to me that I might do as well as Richilde, and thus I knelt beside the tormented woman and buried my head in her flesh as I attempted to gnaw her bonds away, but I had barely started when Richilde was back, fully dressed in a dark green riding habit, and armed and accoutred, as it were. She had apparently dressed her wound and staunched the bleeding, for there was no sign of it, although blood trickled from her lips to suggest that she had paused for a last replenishing snack at the expense of Alicia. Culhaven, also dressed for travelling, was at her back. "Now what are you up to?" Richilde demanded. "You are really a joke, L'Eree. But I doubt your teeth are as sharp as mine. I will wish you and your friends *adieu*. No doubt, should any of you escape the hangman, we will meet again." She went to the door leading to the secret passage, where Culhaven already waited. "Oh, by the way, the letters are in my room. I have bound them up and addressed them to General Cromwell. No doubt he will enjoy them."

The door closed behind them. At that very moment there was another ear-shattering explosion, which again caused the castle to shudder, but this came from *inside* the walls rather than out, although things were obviously happening there as well. There came cheers from the far side of the ravine, which indicated that the drawbridge had finally been shattered, although the Roundheads had yet to cross the crevasse and get past the portcullis before they could reach us. "Helier," Felicity said. "Oh, Helier! Is there any hope?"

"There is always hope," I assured her, although truth to tell, it was difficult to decide what we were to hope for, as my teeth had made not the slightest impression upon her bonds, nor were they likely to, so far as I could see. And now, while we were assailed on the one side by the chattering of the Roundheads as they reloaded their cannon, apparently determined to see what effect roundshot would have on the iron portcullis, we were at the same time assailed on the other side by a kind of roaring shriek of anger.

I turned my head in consternation, wondering if Richilde had loosed some kind of wild beast to add to my torment, and saw the wildest beast of all, Richilde herself, re-emerging from the secret passageway, Culhaven as ever at her heels. Her husband indeed looked quite shattered, but she was herself a seethe of anger . . . with just a tinge of despair. "The wretches!" she declared. "The foul emanations from the pit of hell."

"Trouble, Princess?" I inquired.

She glared at me. "They have closed the door at the foot of the stairs, and fired the charge on the far side. And that creature . . ." she bent upon poor Culhaven the most contemptible stare, "lacks the strength to clear it."

"You need to pick your husbands more carefully, Princess," I suggested, recalling that the Prince von Hohengraffen had been a pretty poor specimen as well.

She stared at me, the anger slowly leaving her eyes. I stared back. I knew what she had to be thinking. And I knew too that if I were right, then Fate had after all only been playing with me, and had now delivered her into my hands. If I had the wit to keep her there. "L'Eree," she now said. "Will you fight for me? You did once. More than once. And I know there is no more fearsome warrior. Shall we not fight again, one more time, shoulder to shoulder?"

I pretended to be utterly taken aback. "You, and I, Princess? There is an ocean of blood between us."

275

"There is also an ocean of blood between us and the Roundheads. Fight for me, Helier, open that doorway for me, and I will give you your life."

"We would first of all have to come to some agreement."

We listened to a tremendous clang as a ball thudded into the portcullis, and another cheer: clearly our enemies were pleased with the effect. Culhaven sank to his knees and put his hands over his ears. "It will have to be a hasty one," Richilde said. "Tell me what you wish."

"Why, simply the lives and freedom of my companions as well as myself."

She smiled. "They are yours."

Of course we both understood that we were playing a game. She needed me, I needed her . . . at the moment. It would be a question of who stopped needing first. "Then we had best make haste," I said.

She unlocked the padlock and I shook off my chains.

"We will go up to my chamber, and find you something to wear," she decided. "Your sword is up there as well. And Lady Norton. Bulstrode, you will fetch up Dr Brewin. See that he is dressed and ready for a journey." Culhaven seemed to pull himself together and staggered towards the stairs leading down into the bowels of the castle. "Haste, Helier!" Richilde was already at the stairs.

"Helier!" Felicity panted.

"You have forgotten something, Princess," I said.

"Your mistress," she said contemptuously.

"Indeed. I will not leave without her."

"Ha!" But she stepped up to Felicity and with two strokes of the knife had her free.

Felicity slowly sat up, and rubbed herself, as if not quite believing that she was alive. "Where are her clothes?" I asked.

"I imagine they were ripped from her body. But . . ." she looked Felicity up and down. "I suppose we can find something to fit her. But we have to hurry." Indeed while we were speaking there was another fearful clang and another cheer. Richilde ran to the door and looked out. "They have penetrated the portcullis," she said. "Now all they need to do is get across the ravine. Help me close these doors, Helier." I went to her side, and we pushed the great oaken doors shut, and I dropped the crossbar in place. "We still have only minutes," she reminded me.

We ran up the stairs. Finding clothes for me was much more difficult than for Felicity, who was much the same size as the Princess. But in one of the unused chambers of the castle there was a variety of male clothing, discarded no doubt by eager lovers Richilde had summoned to her bed, and who had never left it again, at least while breathing. I did not consider this the time to reflect upon moral attitudes, and thus I was eventually crammed into a pair of breeches and a shirt which did not quite tie across my chest. Of boots, alas, I could find none to fit, but at least there was a hat with a handsome feather. While I struggled with my assorted clothing, Felicity and Richilde attended to Alicia, taking her down from the wall and dressing her as well in some of Richilde's clothes. Alicia was in a state similar to that of her husband when Bulstrode had finished with him, and did not really seem to know where she was or what was happening; I had no means of knowing how far Richilde's venom might have penetrated, and there was no time to find out. Alicia seen to, Richilde commenced filling various satchels with items she clearly regarded as important, amongst them, I noticed with interest, several bags of gunpowder. She also equipped herself with four pistols and an outsize blunderbuss, clearly intending to fight an entirely human rearguard action, if she had to. She was, of course, absolutely fearless.

Meanwhile, from the triumphant shouts across the ravine, we gathered the Roundheads were making satisfactory progress in bridging the chasm. Indeed, by looking from the window of Richilde's bedchamber, we could see them throwing ropes attached to grappling irons from one side to the other, while others were stripping off their armour to swing themselves across the crevasse. "Had I a dozen men such as yourself I would send them all to their deaths," Richilde growled.

"But as you have not, we had better hurry," I recommended. "However, there is one small matter outstanding."

"What now? Are you never satisfied?"

"The letters, Princess," I said. "You would not have me come so far for nothing?"

She glared at me, and then smiled; the contrast in expressions was exquisite. "Of course. We have a deal, have we not?" And a moment later the bundle of letters was tucked into my breeches.

In the knights' hall we found Bulstrode and Roderick. Roderick looked in much the same state as Alicia, and it was apparent to me that unless they very rapidly regained their strengths they were going to be a considerable handicap to us in our endeavour to escape. But of course there could be no question of leaving them behind. Richilde, herself carrying a flaming torch, led us through the rear door and down a steep flight of stone steps. These led in the first place to a lower level, where were situated the kitchens and pantries and storerooms. We crossed a passageway between these various departments, and reached another flight of steps, these hewn into the living rock. We had descended some twenty of these, and were, I estimated, well into the bowels of the hill upon which the castle was built, when we came upon a further passageway, some twenty yards along which was a huge, ironbound, wooden door. This was closed, as I had expected, but of course the bolt was not shot. Yet when I attempted to open it, it moved only an inch or two. Richilde set her torch in a sconce and looked at me. "It opens outwards, and has been blocked with falling rock, loosened by the explosion."

I inspected the door. But it presented no difficulties, as the screws holding the hinges were naturally upon the inside. It was a matter of ten minutes work with my knife to remove them, and then the entire door fell in. While this was going on, the noise above us grew, as the Roundheads commenced their crossing. And now we were faced with a far more serious problem, as in the opened doorway there was, as Richilde had suggested, piled a mass of stone and rubble, not to mention some fair-sized boulders. "It is part of the roof," Richilde said. "The charge could be set off from inside as well, should anyone find their way up the secret passage."

"You mean you dug your own grave," I remarked. But recriminations were even more a waste of time now, and so I set my sword aside and got to work. The others could not help me, as there was only room for one person in the restricted space. In any event none of them possessed sufficient strength to tackle the job. I pulled and I pushed, wary always of what might be above my head still waiting to come down, just as I was wary that when I did create a passage, I had to be the one occupying it. It was not possible to trust Richilde further than I could throw her – in fact, a good deal less than that distance.

But for the moment she remained always at my back, herself holding the torch, often enough her shoulder rubbing mine as she encouraged me and oversaw my progress. "By the devil my master," she declared. "You are a man amongst men, L'Eree. With you beside me, I could conquer the world."

And indeed, for those few moments, we did recapture the glorious spirit of my youth – I cannot claim it was hers – when we had faced the world together. Felicity and Bulstrode hovered just behind us, also following my progress with great interest, while Alicia and Roderick

279

sat on the ground, too weak to move. Above us the noise grew louder.

Sweat poured down my face and shoulders, soaked my shirt and breeches, and I became covered in dust which rapidly turned to mud. But then suddenly I felt a whisper of breeze on my cheeks, and a hasty flurry with my hands opened an aperture through which even I could wriggle. "Oh, L'Eree, you have saved us!" Richilde cried.

But as she spoke there came a tramping of feet on the stairs. "Do you take the upper chambers!" the Roundhead captain shouted. "The rest of you, follow me down these steps."

"Too late," Bulstrode croaked. He was a confoundedly depressed fellow.

It was time for me to make a hasty decision. If I let Richilde go, with the others, I would probably never see her again until she was again ready for my destruction, while Felicity and Brewin would not stand a chance . . . I already had to concede that Alicia was probably beyond saving. But if I did not check the Roundheads then were we all lost in any event. I picked up my sword. "I will hold them. Do you get out, Richilde."

She gazed at me, her eyes shining. "No, no, L'Eree," she declared. "We will hold them together. Bulstrode, do you get these people out. Wait for us at the grotto. Leave the weapons."

He was only too eager to obey, holding Alicia's arm to drag her through the opening, while she groaned and sighed most terribly. Felicity hesitated. "Will we see you again, Helier?"

"In a few minutes," Richilde promised.

Felicity gazed at me for a few minutes longer, then helped her brother into the passageway.

"Here's another flight of stairs, captain," said a voice from close above us. "Leads down into the mountain."

"Then that's where they will have gone."

I looked at Richilde, barely visible in the darkness,

and she looked at me. I well knew the risk I was running, as while a Roundhead sword or bullet would easily end my life, Richilde was impervious to such man-made irritations, providing, as she had told me, she could staunch the flow of blood and obtain some repleishment. Nor could I be certain that if I gained a victory she would not shoot me in the back. But at the moment her face displayed nothing but a loyal enthusiam. "We will conquer, my sweet," she assured me. "Do you get behind me."

I obeyed her, but it was a strange place for Helier L'Eree, behind a woman's skirts . . . even if she was a vampire. Although she was armed with that wicked enough looking blunderbus.

"Should I not handle that, Richilde?" I asked.

"Fie on you, Helier," she said. "Do you not suppose I can kill with human weapons as well as my own?"

We listened to feet scraping on the stairs. "Bring a torch," the leader called.

There was a moment's delay, and then the torch was passed down. By its light we could see some eight men crouched on the stairs, swords drawn. But they could not see us. "Do you charge them, L'Eree," Richilde whispered. "When I give the signal." And do you know, at that moment it never crossed my mind to disobey her?

The leader of the search party had reached the bottom of the steps, and now peered into the darkness, the torch held above his head so that it was licking the roof of the tunnel. But he could still see nothing more than a blur in the gloom of the doorway. And now Richilde spoke. "Who comes into my lair?" she asked. It was no more than a whisper, but she managed to invest it with that quality of resonance which made it appear to come from the very walls to either side.

Certainly the sergeant stopped, trembling, both sword and torch thrust forward. Richilde levelled the blunderbus, and fired. The noise in the confined space was tremendous.

But the effect was even more so, for the gun had been loaded with a variety of scrap iron as well as ball, and this hail of lead and iron swept up the passage like a gale of wind. The Roundheads were unable to take evasive action, even had they any idea what was coming at them before it hit them; thus they were utterly discomfited, and even more so when, as Richilde pinched my arm, I leapt up and charged them behind my sword. There was no room properly to swing the weapon, but it could cut and thrust, as I did, with all of my strength. Blood flew and the survivors uttered piteous screams of pain and terror as they scrambled back out of the deadly corridor, leaving behind five of their number: two had suffered from the blunderbus and three from my sword.

"To me, L'Eree!" Richilde commanded, and I hastened back to her side. "Bring the pistols," she said, and retreated through the opening in the rocks.

On the far side she knelt with the utmost composure, apparently able to see in the dark as she recharged the blunderbus. I knelt at her side, while from above us there came the most tremendous hubbub, the remnants of the advance guard declaring that they had been assailed by wizards and monsters. The captain attempted to restore some order, and courage, in his men. "They will come again," I suggested.

"And we will defeat them again. Are there any in the world can stand against you and I, Helier, when we have chosen the field?" I could not argue with that.

"So do you watch out for them, while I make some preparations," she told me, and she commenced to scrabble around in the various satchels she had had us bring down. I knew what she had in mind, and could not help but wonder what might be the outcome if she made a mistake in the darkness. Were the gunpowder to go up, I would certainly go with it. But could a vampire be destroyed by gunpowder? That was a conundrum.

However, I was very rapidly recalled to the present,

as the Roundhead captain had succeeded in rallying his men sufficiently for another attempt to be made upon the passageway, and they were again decending the steps behind their flaring torches. "They are to make another attempt," I whispered.

Richilde ceased her activities, which had carried her some distance away from me and down the passageway, to return and kneel at my side. "They will be expecting a charge this time," I said. And indeed, this was made plain by their dispositions, for by the light of their torches we could see that while there was a forlorn hope of four men well in front, these were followed by a gap of several feet before half-a-dozen more could be seen, and these were armed with muskets.

"I am not quite ready," Richilde said. "Do you engage them with pistols, Helier. There are six here, together with the blunderbus. But save that for in case they charge. We need another five minutes."

I nodded, laid down my sword, and picked up the first pistol, sighting carefully down the passageway. The advance guard had by now reached the foot of the steps, and were coming closer, trying to peer past their torches at the wrecked doorway and the rubble beyond. When they were just close enough to make out some details, I fired. Truth to tell, I am not half so efficient with a pistol as a sword, mainly through lack of practice, but in the confined space I could not miss, and although I do believe my ball struck the wall before anything else, it ricochetted into their midst and had one fellow howling that he was hit. Whereupon I promptly levelled a second pistol and this time had more success, as I hit another man in the backside as they beat a hasty retreat. "That was no ghost!" shouted the Roundhead captain, from his position of safety somewhat higher up the stairs. "Musketeers!"

"Down!" I told Richilde, as the six musketeers came down the steps, weapons at the present. I fired another pistol, but where the ball went I have no idea, and then lay down myself as the passageway became filled with noise and flying balls.

"Now charge those devils!" the captain roared.

Richilde picked up her blunderbus, and as the Roundheads came down the passageway, fired, again with devastating effect. I added my last two pistols, and our enemies were scattered the length and breadth of the corridor. "Now, L'Eree!" Richilde snapped. "To me!"

I picked up my sword, scrambled through the rubble, and followed her, for a further ten feet or so down the passage, to where she had lain her powder train. This she lit with a spark from our tinder box. "It will go in thirty seconds," she told me. "Haste!"

I ran behind her, panting, having to bend double as the roof was not very high. From behind us there came shouts as the Roundheads, having recovered themselves, could hear from my echoing footfalls that their enemies were retreating. They gave a roar and ran forward, but as they did so Richilde's powder train exploded, and for the second time this night the roof fell in. Those men who had actually reached the doorway screamed in agony, and the rest screamed in terror, while we continued on our way, in pitch darkness now. But I knew where Richilde was, and followed her, at that moment uncaring of the future.

CHAPTER 11

The passageway led downwards, ever downwards, but while the slope was steep it was not difficult to traverse, apart from the pitch blackness which caused the odd slip. We emerged some fifteen minutes later, into the darkness of the night but also the freshness of the hill air. We were in the valley beneath the castle. That I understood in a moment, partly because I could hear the rushing of the stream, and partly because to our right the village of Culhaven still burned. Richilde, indeed, never hesitating, followed the water for some hundred yards before stopping.

"There is a ford here," she told me, and holding her skirts daintily above her knees, proceeded to show me, stepping from stone to stone with a certainty which convinced me that she had used this way before. I followed her, but on the far side paused to wash my hands and face in the water, as my exertions had left me somewhat dirty. Richilde watched my ablutions in silence, waiting patiently until I was finished before leading me on again, now back into the shelter of the mountain, and a few minutes later we came upon the remnants of our party. "Helier!" Felicity gasped, throwing herself into my arms. "We had counted you lost."

"How could he be lost?" Richilde demanded. "He was with me, silly girl." Felicity made no reply; Richilde Bethlen was the one woman who had the power to reduce her to silence. Richilde stepped past her to peer at her husband, then at Roderick and Alicia.

"They're pretty done up," Culhaven said. "What they need is rest."

Richilde smiled. "They will have all the rest they can stand in a little while. It is these two we must consider."

This confirmed my worst fears, and it came as a bit of a shock, to understand that nothing had changed, after the Witch and I had fought shoulder to shoulder. "I had almost hoped it might be possible for us to be allies, for a season, even if we can never be friends," I said.

"But it is," Richilde said, most enthusiastically. "I have decided that, after all, I shall turn you into a vampire, and let you roam the ages at my side. What a pair we shall make, you and I, Helier. What a pair we already do make. But you are limited by your mortality. Would you not like to shed that nuisance? Oh, do not worry, we will take the girl with us into eternity; she is a charming little thing."

"Helier!" Felicity's voice shook.

My head followed its example. "That can never be, Richilde," I said. "We struck a bargain, back there at the castle. Therefore I give you your life. But join you in your unnatural activities? Never!"

"You, give me, my life?" Richilde sneered. "You assume powers beyond your understanding, sweet Helier. You stand there, bare-footed, in scanty and ill-fitting clothing, armed with but a sword, and probably the most wanted man in England, after the King. You have no food and no money, and you will lumber yourself with that insipid young woman. It is your own survival you should consider. Whereas I offer you eternal life and total triumph at my side. Are you that much of a fool?"

"So some would say, Princess."

"Well, then, you bring your troubles on yourself. I have offered you a place at my side. Should you refuse, you know I cannot let you live. You know too much of me, and you would in time again come after me. This I know. And this I cannot permit. Now for the last time, I command you. Nay, I implore you. Lay down your sword and come to me, and couple with me, and let me drink your blood, that I may implant the seed within you."

"And for the last time, Princess, although I know I commit a crime, I give you your life. Now take your 'husband', and begone, and leave these good people and me to fend for ourselves."

"So be it." She brought up her hand, which had been concealed in the folds of her habit, and in it was a pistol. "Fare thee well, Helier." But of course, in attempting to defeat me with a human weapon, Richilde was merely playing my game, not hers. As her finger whitened on the trigger, I was throwing myself to one side, and the bullet was whining into the darkness behind me. Nor did it hit Felicity, for she had been quick enough to throw herself the other way. Richilde stamped her foot in anger as she realised her mistake. And her danger, for I was picking myself up, still grasping my sword. "Bulstrode!" she shouted.

Culhaven gulped, but he made the only decision he could: I might be a terrible prospect, but he had not yet actually seen me in action, whereas he knew just how terrible a prospect Richilde was. Thus he drew his sword and advanced towards me, presenting as brave a face as he could, while from the confines of his coat he also produced a dagger. "Helier!" Felicity gasped.

I was not the least concerned with Culhaven; I was more interested in what Richilde was doing, as I saw her disappearing into the gloom, and beckoning Roderick and Alicia to follow her. Even more to my dismay, they obeyed her without question. "Roderick!" Felicity shouted, but her brother ignored her.

Meanwhile, Culhaven, seeing me momentarily distracted, came at me behind thrusting blade, but a single flick of my own weapon turned his aside, and he had to leap to one side to avoid disaster. "I would have you know," he panted, "that I learned swordsmanship from Bertholde of Siena, many years before you were born."

"There is your problem," I pointed out, now concentrating. "Your methods are out of date."

"But yet you see me at my strongest," he threatened. "In the middle of the night."

"As I once advised you, milord," I told him, "your strongest is the strength of a babe, compared with mine." He made another pass followed by another hasty withdrawal. But now I saw what he was at, as he again circled: he was hoping to lay his evil hands upon Felicity. "Felicity," I said. "Do you keep always behind me." She obeyed, and Culhaven panted his anger. "Now it is time to end this farce," I said. "I would have you believe, milord, that being acquainted with you has been interesting, if not edifying." Saying which I launched myself at him behind my swirling blade. He brought up his own but of course could not match me, and it was swept aside, while mine, continuing on its way, bit so deeply into his shoulder that his arm was all but severed.

He gave an almost animal-like cry of pain – sounding indeed very like a bat – and looked at the blood gushing down his side. I knew I had probably done enough to destroy him, but was not in the mood for taking chances, and so swung my blade again, to sever his head at the neck and send it spinning away into the darkness. "My God!" Felicity gasped, gazing at the still twitching trunk lying on the ground, from which blood spouted as from a fountain. "Is he truly gone?"

I placed my sword point upon his breast and drove it through him into the earth. This was reversing the accepted procedure, to be sure, but I considered this mere pedantry, in my circumstances. "He is certainly truly going," I assured her. As we watched, his body, emptying itself so rapidly of that blood which had been its vital force, and being very old indeed, dwindled into a skeleton before our very eyes.

Felicity, of course, being a doctor's sister and practised in the medical art herself, was disturbed neither by the sight of blood nor by the dwindling phenomenon, but remained intensely practical. "What are we to do now?" she asked.

"Follow the Princess, and see what can be done about Roderick and Alicia," I said. I did not dare tell her that I feared we were already too late.

However, following the Princess, in the short term, was easier said than done. The Roundheads had by now not only cleared away the rubble brought down by our explosion, but had also alerted those of their number who had remained on the far side of the ravine, and these fellows had horses. We heard both the shouts of those feeling their way through the passageway, and the hooves of those coming back down the mountain. And now, quite apart from a desire to complete their assignment, they were inspired by the necessity to avenge those of their comrades who had fallen. I seized Felicity's arm and dragged her into the shelter of some bushes, and we huddled together, scarce daring to breathe, and very thankful at once to the darkness, and the various distractions to which our pursuers were subject. "What's this?" demanded the captain, stopping very close to our hiding place.

"Looks like a headless skeleton," suggested his cornet.

"Don't be absurd! How can a man become a skeleton in a matter of minutes?"

"He must have been here more than a few minutes," the cornet argued.

"But not very much longer," the captain riposted. "Here are his sword and dagger. Both bright and new."

"Perhaps it was a woman," suggested the sergeant, clearly a chauvinist, although even accepting that it was difficult to follow his reasoning.

"Those are certainly bones, with respect, sir," the cornet

said, and there was a clang. "What is more, they are old bones. My sword went right through them."

"Let's get on with it," the captain growled. "This is no Christian business."

It was at this juncture that their presence became an absolute asset. For still lurking in the woods had been Blacking and Giles and their people. No doubt they had overseen the escape of Richilde and ourselves. But they had not then been prepared to interfere, being not unnaturally mortally afraid of the woman they had condemned to death and who had proved herself able to surmount all obstacles, especially when she had been supported by the sword of Helier L'Eree. However, with the Witch and myself separated, they would certainly have proved a nuisance to each of us, on account of their numbers. Now, assuming the Roundheads to be in full pursuit of us, they returned to the still burning houses of the village in an endeavour to retrieve at least some of their personal belongings, and thus found themselves in the way of the second wave of Roundheads, returning down the hillside.

The battle that followed was bloody but swift. The villagers had no proper arms or armour to oppose the swords and cuirasses and morions, not to mention the discipline, of the Ironsides, and the night became filled with shrieks of agony and despair, shouts of triumph and lust.

Felicity and I remained hidden while this slaughter continued: we could do nothing to help the people of Culhaven, even had we wished to do so. Thus we waited, and watched, and towards dawn saw flames rising from the castle itself. The Roundheads, having disposed of the villagers, were now returning up the hill to carry out their orders to destroy Richilde's home. They then moved some distance back up the valley, and pitched camp where they had earlier left their supply wagon.

To this they now also, with much huffing and puffing, dragged their cannon. By now the rain, which had ceased for a while during the night, was again falling in a steady drizzle. We thus spent an uncomfortable few hours, but at that we remained fortunate. One body of Roundheads had made camp. The others, those who had come through the secret passage and discovered Culhaven's body, and who were led by the captain himself, continued to beat through the trees and bushes on the lower slopes of the mountain, at the foot of which Felicity and I lay concealed. And these fellows were rewarded, for just before dawn there came a tremendous hullaballoo from not very far above us, and I recognised the voices of both Alicia, screaming, and Richilde, cursing. But even the vampire's powers were useless against a score of armed men, and so it was that we saw them being brought back down the hillside, their hands bound behind them, a most miserable and unhappy trio.

Naturally, Felicity would have attempted to rescue her brother, but I held her fast. There are limits to even what I can achieve, and twenty armed and capable soldiers were a bit much. Besides, I was content to know where Richilde was. While she, having cursed a bit when discovered, was now once again calm and resolute. Her hat had come off and her hair was wet, lying in a straight auburn stain down her shoulders, while her face was composed. She was not afraid of death, or at least, of being hanged, and was clearly relying upon the fact that the Roundheads, and their magistrates, would seek nothing more than her conventional execution. Her two companions both looked thoroughly bedraggled, but they also were not as downcast as one might have expected, which but confirmed my concern that they too no longer feared a conventional execution. Alicia, indeed, for all the rain which had her hair also an undressed mess and the mud which stained her hands and clothes, had seldom looked more beautiful – and that is saying a great deal.

They disappeared into the gloom, and once again

Felicity would have followed immediately, but once again I restrained her. "You mean to let them die?" she said angrily. "To let Roderick die?"

"I mean to rescue them," I promised her, not altogether truthfully. "But it must be done with caution, and at a time advantageous to ourselves. That is certainly not now. Patience, my sweet. This is a game I have played before."

Thus reassured, she waited with me, on the dawn.

We were both wet and chilled, and hungry. We were able to slake our thirst from the stream, but then it was necessary to consider our position. "First," I said, "we, or at least I, must obtain some more adequate clothing. And secondly, we must find some food."

"And then?" she asked. "Where will they take the demon and my brother?" She apparently no longer considered Alicia worth mentioning.

"I imagine, to Shrewsbury. But we will follow," I said. "When it is safe to do so."

Thus we again waited, shivering and starving, until the Ironsides broke camp and resumed their journey, together, we had to assume, with their prisoners. Then we left our hiding place and stole into the destroyed village and the abandoned encampment. The Ironsides had not bothered to bury the dead villagers, and we beheld some pretty horrifying sights. The Roundheads, as was their wont when fronted with those they considered as belonging to a heathen religion, had spared neither women nor child, and in most cases had clearly preceded murder with rape. Amongst the corpses, to my, and even more, Felicity's satisfaction, were to be seen the grim visages of both Giles and the man Blacking, who had so brutally defiled her. "Good riddance," she commented.

I was more interested in what we could find which could be of value and this was virtually nothing. The village was burned out, and the Roundheads had left nothing behind them. While I was fully prepared to devote the remainder of my life to the pursuit of the Witch, I knew I could not undertake such a vast task virtually naked and entirely lacking food and drink, or indeed arms, save for my sword. I therefore once again climbed up the circular road to the castle. Felicity accompanied me, but would not re-enter that place of terrible memory, preferring to wait for my return. I found crossing the chasm no great difficulty, for the Roundheads had lowered the remains of the drawbridge, and indeed, laid new planks; this had been to get the horses out before firing the place, and my only concern was that some of the stonework had become loosened in the heat and might break away.

In places, Richilde's last home – as I was determined – still burned and smouldered. But it is of course very difficult to destroy a castle by fire, unless one is prepared to devote a great deal of time and trouble to the task. The Roundheads had been in something of a hurry. And then their work had been affected by the rain. Thus while the servants' barracks and the stables had both been burned out, the knights' hall was virtually undamaged, although all the drapes had been set alight and the heat was intense. The great staircase, being made of stone, was also undamaged, and I was able to mount it, and investigate the bedchambers above. Several of these had caught fire, and others smouldered, yet my search was not without reward. I came across a considerable amount of silver coin in one of the rooms, as well as two pistols and some powder and ball, untouched by the flames or the heat. I also found a wallet attached to a belt that I was able to strap round my waist, and which provided a receptacle for the Queen's letters, which were by now, having spent the last few hours tucked into my breeches, a sorely sodden mess, the ink run and the writing all but indecipherable. But I assumed Anne would still wish them back, and from my point of view, they would be the only proof that I had carried out my mission.

293

I was even more rewarded when I descended into the cellars beneath the hall. Although the Roundheads had removed their dead for a proper Christian burial, they had left most of their accoutrements behind, and I was able to find myself some dry and slightly more salubrious clothing, as well as, most welcome, a pair of boots which must have belonged to a fellow with outsize feet, for they actually fitted me, in a manner of speaking. However, walking any distance in them would clearly be a most uncomfortable business, and I knew I had to find a horse at the earliest possible opportunity.

My greatest success, however, came when I penetrated the kitchens. The fire had not got down here, and there was a great deal of smoked and cured food available, not to mention several loaves of bread and a good many bottles of wine. I hastily filled a bag, eating while I did so, and began to feel quite human again.

These necessary tasks completed, I called out to Felicity to let her know that all was well, and then climbed to the top of the highest tower. I could not see to the west, of course, because the mountains rose higher and higher in that direction. But I did not believe the Roundheads were going west. And to the east I could see for a considerable distance, the day being clear and my height above the valley considerable. I could even look over the ridge that led to the next valley, and it was here that I made out the sun glinting from the cuirasses and helmets of a body of men. They could only be our late antagonists, and they were heading east, out of Wales. Equally I could make out the baggage wagon in which Richilde, Roderick and Alicia had been confined – and were still confined, I was certain, or the Roundheads would not be taking themselves off. Hastily I descended from my perch, collected my bag of food, and returned across the drawbridge to where Felicity waited. I explained what I had seen. "Then we must follow," she said, while eating hungrily.

She was, of course, concerned only with saving her

294

brother, but if I now felt that this could not be done I was happy to agree with her. And so off we set.

It may be supposed our task remained virtually impossible, for a variety of reasons. In the first place, the Ironsides were mounted, and we were not. In the second, supposing we did overtake them, they numbered a good forty men, and my army consisted of a man and a woman. But, as I have demonstrated more than once in my narrative, things are seldom as they first appear, either good or bad. Mounted they might be, but the Roundheads had no concept that they were being followed, and were certainly not hurrying; they were also, as a quick examination of their tracks revealed, still lumbered with their cannon, which, on the wet and muddy roads, was slowing their progress still further. They also had two beautiful women – as they supposed – to amuse themselves with, and these would have to be handed over to the magistrates once they reached Shrewsbury, so the longer they took to achieve that the better for their masculine lusts.

While, having suffered a good deal of ill-fortune over the past couple of days, Felicity and I now enjoyed a brief season of the reverse side of the coin. From my vantage point at the top of Castle Culhaven, and again looking beyond the next ridge which separated Culhaven Valley from the outside world, I had seen smoke rising into the still autumnal air. I recollected this from our outwards journey, and towards this Felicity and I now directed our steps, I having taken off my boots and slung them around my neck to make walking easier. It took us some three hours to gain our objective, which, as I had surmised, was an isolated farmhouse. Here I boldly declared us to be Royalist fugitives from Worcester, which was no lie, and further told the good farmer and his wife that we had been sought by the very Roundheads who had been this way at dawn. I do not know for certain what the farmer's political persuasions might have been, but he found my sword and pistols as persuasive as anything else in his life, and forthwith invited us to dinner, which we accepted with great pleasure. "Now tell me this, good fellow," I said, my being enhanced by several lamb chops and half a gallon of strong cider. "Had those Ironsides any prisoners with them?"

"Oh, aye, squire," our host assured me. "Two witches and a warlock."

"What did you say?" Felicity asked.

"'Tis what they told us."

"We did not see them for ourselves," the farmer's wife put in. "They were kept under guard in the wagon. But the troopers told us they were dreadful creatures, bound for the assizes in Shrewsbury, when they will assuredly be hanged."

"If not burned as well," the farmer put in.

Felicity blanched, and I was afraid that she might give us away, but she managed not to speak. "What terrible things exist in this world," I remarked. "However, as you say, the Puritans will soon settle such creatures. Now, sir, I am sure you will understand that my wife and I need to remove ourselves from this neighbourhood just as quickly, and as far, as possible. I will therefore ask you to sell us two of your horses, and some food and cider, and we will be on our way." I was thinking ahead here, to what might follow a successful *coup-de-main*, supposing we could accomplish this. My aim was then to make one of the West Country ports and thence France, and the more food we could carry with us, and thus avoid the necessity to enter any towns or villages, the better off we would be.

"No, no," the farmer said.

"We will sell you food and drink," his wife explained. "But we will not sell our horses. Why, where would we get others? It was all we could do to stop the Roundheads from taking them as remounts."

"Nevertheless, we must have two of them," I explained, drawing my sword. They goggled at this and I laid it on the table, placing beside it several of the silver coins I had taken from Culhaven Castle. "You must decide," I told them. "Either sell the horses to me, or I will take them."

They decided to sell, and I insisted upon a receipt. Whereupon Felicity and I took our leave. "Will they not send to the nearest major-general?" she inquired.

"I have no doubt of it," I agreed. "But I doubt it will make much difference to us, as before they can do that we are liable to have every Roundhead in England at our heels in any event." She reflected on this somewhat sombrely, while we rode behind our enemies.

Following the Roundhead company was not difficult, as quite apart from the tracks they were returning very much the way we had come. Indeed, when we regained the village where we had spent the night on our way to the valley, which we did by late afternoon, we learned that the Ironsides were not a march ahead of us, and had indeed debated spending the night here rather than continuing. We did not debate this at all, pausing only for a meal. I may say that this was partly because the landlord positively goggled at us, and when encouraged, told us that the Roundheads had declared me dead. But this was of less importance in the fellow's mind than that they should have had as their prisoner the ill-famed Lady Culhaven, or that my two earlier travelling companions had turned out to be her servants. But he accepted our coin, which was, of course, actually Richilde's coin. "He also will be raising the country behind us," Felicity grumbled.

"As long as it is behind us," I told her. But by now I was studying another matter, as it was obvious that the Roundheads were heading almost due east, whereas, had they been going to Shrewsbury, they would surely have turned to their right some time around now. But instead they were making for . . . Dormintsley?

I deemed it best not to raise this point with Felicity,

but in fact she realised where we were headed the day after leaving our last village – I had allowed us only a few hours bivouac during the night – it being by now late afternoon. "Why would they wish to go to Dormintsley?" she asked.

"I have no idea. Unless it is a result of something Roderick told them."

"But Aunt Edith!" she cried.

"Absolutely. We had best make haste." As if we were not already doing this.

Dusk fell, and soon it was utterly dark. We ate some of the food we had purchased at the farm, and proceeded, thankful only that the rain had stopped. "What is your plan?" Felicity asked. We were now in territory with which she was very familiar.

"I think we need to reconnoitre the situation before we can make a plan," I told her.

Our fears were entirely correct, and we discovered that Dormintsley Manor had been turned into an armed camp.

It was now quite late at night, but the house itself was a blaze of light, while parked before the front door was the wagon in which the prisoners had travelled. It was of course too much to hope that they might still be in it, but in any event it was guarded by two soldiers. I did not regard these as a great obstacle, save for the fact, as I have mentioned, that I did not suppose they were actually guarding what we sought, but were merely standing sentry duty. Equally their comrades were all within earshot, even if, our ears told us, they were having a merry night of it. "Is there a way into the house which might be unguarded?" I asked Felicity.

"There is the back door."

I followed her on a crawl around hedgerows to arrive at the rear of the house, and discovered that this door too was guarded by two soldiers. "Is there not a secret passage into the house?" I inquired. "All respectable manor houses have secret passages in and out."

"My aunt and my grandfather never found reason for one," she said.

Here was a problem. How were we to get into the house without alarming the entire Roundhead company? However, there is no problem which does not have a solution. If we could not get into the house without alarming the entire Roundhead company, then we must needs alarm them in the most convincing possible manner. "The gun!" I said.

The Roundheads had parked their cannon at the very entrance to the drive, assuming that there would be no one in the neighbourhood, either as regards courage or technical knowhow, able or willing to interfere with such a piece of destructive machinery. But as I had surmised, and now discovered to be the case when I led Felicity back to the weapon, it was not only a field piece which rested upon its caisson. I found several round shot, as well as several charges of powder, and even a tinderbox, suitably wrapped up in oiled paper to protect it from the wet. "You mean," the innocent girl said, "that if we fire this piece, they will come running out to discover what is happening, and thus we may get in?"

"Sadly," I said, "the mere firing of the piece is not likely to bring more than a few of them running out."

"Then I do not understand your plan."

"My dearest girl," I said, holding her shoulders. "There comes a time in life when one has to face facts. Do you agree?"

"Well," she said. "I suppose so. Which facts did you have in mind?"

"Simply that you have no future here in England. You are attainted traitor for associating with me, and you are attainted witch for associating with Richilde."

"I have said that I will follow you to the ends of the earth, Helier. I but worry for my brother and my aunt."

"Well, the same thing now applies to them," I pointed out. "If we can extract them from that house there can be no going back. They will have to come with us, wherever we go. Which, in the first instance, will be France."

"I understand that," she said. "But how are we going to extract them?"

"By looking facts in the face. If, as you are agreed, there can be no future for you in England, then it must really matter nothing whether you have a home in England, or not."

She gazed at me, and then at the manor house, and then at the cannon. "My God," she said. "You *are* a monster. Can you not be satisfied with the destruction of my brother's house?"

"It is your brother's life I am endeavouring to save," I said, not altogether truthfully.

She sighed. "And do you not suppose he, and my aunt, may be killed if you send a cannonball into the house?"

"I doubt that, as I would say, the hour being late, that your aunt will have retired – supposing she has not been placed under arrest by the Roundheads – and that Roderick and the ladies will be confined, either upstairs or below stairs. I propose to send a ball into the ground floor. Or more, as the case may be."

She gulped, and took refuge in practicalities. "How may two people fire a cannon?"

"I assure you, *one* person may fire a cannon, if he knows what he is about."

"And you do?"

"I have not soldiered, on and off, for twenty years without learning something of the art. So come now, give me a hand."

The cannon was parked with its muzzle pointing away from the house. With my great strength, it was not a difficult task to push the caisson round until it pointed at the great mullioned windows of the downstairs parlour, but the turning caused a certain amount of noise, damaging as it did various bushes and plants bordering the drive, and this caught the attention of the sentries. They strolled towards us, discussing the situation with each other, while Felicity and I hid in the undisturbed bushes. "Strange," commented one. "I am sure this piece was looking the other way when last I saw it."

"I have no idea," said his companion. "But I will tell you this: cannon do not move about by themselves. So you must be mistaken." Thus they went off again.

"I am terrified," Felicity confessed when they were out of earshot.

"You are not half so terrified as they are going to be in a moment," I promised her, pouring a liberal amount of powder into the touchhole before taking one of the iron balls to roll it into the muzzle, and stoke it well home with the ramrod. It took me considerably longer to light the slow match, and this had to be done with some care in case the sentries were looking in our direction and would see the spark, but at last it was done. "Stand clear," I told Felicity. She obeyed, and I ignited the powder train. The cannon roared and bucked, but the results were all I could have wished. The ball hurtled across the drive and smashed through the nearest bay window.

Instantly all was pandemonium, with men screaming and shouting and firing muskets and pistols, at no visible enemy. I ignored the racket in favour of reloading my fearsome weapon, and before the Roundheads could even think had sent another ball behind the first, to the accompaniment of more smashing and crackling, screaming and shrieking. By this time the two sentries had worked out what was happening. To give them credit, they were not cowards, and advanced towards us at a run. But they were confronting Helier L'Eree. I levelled my first pistol and fired, and the lead man dropped in his tracks. This brought the second one up short. He was fortunate in that my second pistol misfired, but before he had decided whether to advance or retreat I was upon him with drawn sword, and had despatched him a moment later.

"Helier!" Felicity gasped, and I looked up. I am bound to say that, as the events of my life have proved time and again, I am the most accomplished arsonist in history, even if most of the fires with which I have been associated have been started by other people. One thinks of Magdeburg, for example, and then Castle Hohengraffen, of various country houses which burst into flames after I had visited them, such as Marney House, very nearly Whiteladies, and of course there was Culhaven Castle. None of these had I started with my own hand, but I must take the credit for Dormintsley Maner. It having been a cold, wet and miserable day, the Roundheads had lit a fire in the drawing room, and into this fire one of my iron balls had plunged, not merely demolishing the hearth but scattering burning wood in every direction. These flaming missiles had naturally ignited all the drapes and furnishings in the room, and now there was smoke and flame everywhere. This at least had the effect of accomplishing our purpose for us. The Roundheads evacuated the building in great haste and total disorder, quite unable to understand what had happened to them, the two sentries, who might have enlightened them, being dead. Felicity and I took refuge in the bushes while the troopers ran past us, and so doing, were taken a stage further on our quest, for the cornet shouted at the captain, "What of the prisoners?"

"Ah, leave them be," the captain replied. "The fire will get to the cellars soon enough, and they were due to be burned anyway."

Felicity squeezed my arm, and I squeezed hers back. We could only be patient, crawl through the bushes, and then run for the open front doors. No one appeared to see us. There were people running to and fro in any event as the servants flooded out from their attic rooms, and most of the Roundheads had gathered at the cannon, which they were examining with great care and some apprehension, not at all sure that it hadn't been fired by some supernatural agency. To confound everything, it now started to rain again, and exceedingly heavily.

Inside the house there was a good deal of heat and even more smoke, but this was all tending to rise, finding its way up the great staircase. While I did not doubt that it would only be a short while before the roof and the upper stories came tumbling down, for the moment the cellars were clear. Felicity led the way, as she knew it better than I, holding her wet skirts high in one hand as she descended the stairs into the gloom. I paused long enough to catch hold of a torch; lighting it was no difficult matter, and thus I was able to illuminate the darkness.

"Helier!" Richilde said. "By the devil, milord, but it is good to see you. This place is growing uncomfortably warm."

Never had I seen the Princess von Hohengraffen looking so dishevelled. Her clothes were disordered and filthy, indicating that she had indeed had to suffer at the hands of her captors – not that this would have discomfited her in the least – and her wrists were bound behind her back, so that she could not reach the cords with her teeth. As Roderick and Alicia and Miss Brewin were similarly bound, I assumed this was merely Roundhead thoroughness rather than an awareness that they were dealing with the unnatural.

"Count d'Albret," the old lady gasped. "How good to see you. Felicity, you look a perfect mess." Which was a bit hard, coming from a woman who was in something of a mess herself. But her spirit was clearly undiminished.

"These are trying times, Aunt Edith," Felicity replied, kneeling beside her aunt and slitting her bonds. Having placed my torch in a sconce, I was doing the same for Richilde.

"Oh, Helier, my knight in shining armour," Alicia declared. "What would I do without you?"

"Make do with someone else," I suggested equally, releasing her in turn.

"Oh, Roderick," Felicity said, untying her brother. "Are you all right?"

"I am admirable, and the better for seeing you, dearest sis. Let me give you a hug and a kiss."

Nothing loathe, Felicity turned into his arms for the embrace, but I, although busy with Alicia, had looked up at his words, and saw to my alarm, although not altogether to my surprise, that as he spoke he gave Richilde a quick glance, and was rewarded with an almost imperceptible nod of the head. Thus as he took his sister in his arms, her cheek pressed chastely to his, he inclined his head towards her neck. "Not so fast!" I shouted, standing up and picking up my sword, which I had laid down while freeing the women.

Both turned their heads, and I saw Roderick's elongated fangs, just for a moment. But Felicity had not, being in front of him. "Helier?" she queried. "Whatever can the matter be? Oh!"

For even as she spoke, her brother had again lowered his head and kissed her neck, holding her round the waist as he did so. Not that she made any attempt to resist him, apparently finding the experience quite enjoyable, but said, "Oh!" again, while her cheeks flamed with blood.

"Roderick!" remonstrated Miss Brewin. "That is quite unseemly."

"Unseemly indeed," I agreed, and seized Felicity's wrist, to jerk her from her brother's grasp and into my own arms.

"Why, Helier!" she protested. "It was only affection."

"You think so?" I asked, aware that I was in a den of lionesses, for both Richilde and Alicia were reaching for me, fangs bared. Felicity now saw that her brother was similarly equipped, and indeed, his lips were dripping blood, as blood was trickling down her neck. She gave a little gasp, but was not sufficiently alarmed, I feared.

The vampires stared at me, and my sword, afraid to close with me, while I stared at them, for they were widely separated, and I knew that to attack one and allow another to leap on to my back and have at me would be calamitous. I was also constrained by the presence of Felicity in my arms, by a thunderstruck Miss Brewin on the far side of the room, and by the increasing heat and crashes and bangings from above us. "Mercy me," Miss Brewin remarked. "The entire house will soon be down."

Richilde smiled, a dreadful sight, for while the face remained unutterably beautiful, the spread lips were a gash of horror. "Do you not recall, sweet Helier," she said, "how you and I sat out the destruction of Magdeburg, in just such a cellar as this, consummating our love while all about us was destruction? Should we not repeat that idyll?"

"I will see you in hell, Princess," I told her.

"Oh, you will, undoubtedly. Well, then, let us end this farce. Felicity, sweet Felicity, abandon that loutish fellow."

Her hypnotic voice drifted over us like the caress of a summer's breeze, and almost as if asleep, Felicity moved my arm. "Do not go to her, I beg of you," I said.

Felicity cast me an almost curious glance, then gently freed herself and stepped away from me. I would have attempted to regain her, but that Roderick now made a run at me, fangs bared. I brought up my sword and drove it right through his body. He uttered a great scream, while blood spouted in every direction, but remained impaled upon my sword as he fell to the floor. "Murderer!" screamed Alicia, hurling herself at me.

"Murderer!" squawked Miss Brewin.

"Murderer!" shrieked Felicity, turning back, also to attack me. Richilde smiled, content with the way things were going.

I realised that, as I had endeavoured to make Felicity understand only a few minute before, it was time to look facts full in the face. These people were my enemies, with the possible exception of Miss Brewin and Felicity, and I did not know if they could ever be considered my friends after I had slain Felicity's brother and Miss Brewin's nephew. Yet did I determine to save the old lady if I could, as well as Felicity. But none of the others. Thus I placed my foot on Roderick's belly to withdraw my sword, at the same time swinging my arm to catch Alicia on the side of the head and tumble her across the floor, skirts flailing. By then Felicity had thrown herself on to my back, but I ducked and threw her in turn, right over my head, before she had the opportunity to restrain me. This was my problem, that I could not risk the slightest nip, which might infect me also with the cursed disease. This without even knowing whether or not Felicity was actually affected, from a single bite.

However for the moment I could devote myself entirely to Roderick, who was attempting to rise from the floor, notwithstanding that he had received a wound which would have been mortal to any ordinary man. But before he could gain his feet I had kicked him on the shoulder to send him sprawling again, and as I had retained hold of my sword, this now came free, so that I could swing it round my head to decapitate him. This brought a fresh scream from Miss Brewin, and a howl of anguish from Felicity, who had regained her knees, shaken by her fall but nonetheless fully alert. I was at the moment less interested in their reactions than in those of Richilde, who I had fully expected to have joined in the physical assault on me. But she had always preferred to have others do her work for her, and besides, she had herself confessed all her secrets to me, and knew that to challenge me and lose would be the end of her. Thus when I turned I saw her making for the steps leading upwards.

I gave a roar and leapt behind her, but she reached the steps before me, and scrambled to the top, which was becoming increasingly filled with smoke. I yet reached her, falling to my hands and knees as I did so, but managing to grasp the hem of her dress. She jerked away from me, and the material ripped, but being of the very best quality, it did not tear in my hands, but rather parted from the stitching at the collar, tearing down one sleeve. She gave an exclamation of annoyance, and jerked herself free as she reached the door, leaving me with the torn gown in my hands to encumber my progress. Now she slammed the door, but being not yet entirely free of the material, caught some of it as she did so. Again she jerked herself loose, this time succeeding, and thrusting the bolt home. As she did so she gave a little shriek, but the reason for this I did not at that moment understand. I tried the door, but Richilde had shot the bolt. Obviously I could break it down, but this would take some time, and now I could see that the timbers above me were cracking, and allowing smoke to enter the cellars. No doubt Richilde could cope well enough with flames, as she had demonstrated in the past, but I knew I could not, nor could Miss Brewin and Felicity. I thus returned to them. Felicity was kneeling beside the dead body of her brother. Miss Brewin was kneeling on the other side. Neither seemed the least aware of my presence.

Only Alicia was alert and lively. And as angry as only Alicia could be. "The wretch," she declared. "The foul wretch! She has abandoned me."

At that moment it was impossible to conceive that so lovely a creature, and one so bursting with ebullient life, could at the same time be a demon from hell, even if of a subsidiary order. She came to the foot of the stairs as I descended them. "Helier," she said. "I told you once, you are all that I have left. Will you take me from this place, and back to France, to be always at your side? You promised to do this."

"I promised to succour a woman who no longer exists," I said, a trifle sadly. "However, I will *send* you from this place, milady." She stared at me, and then at my sword,

307

and then uttered one of those unearthly shrieks and threw herself at me, mouth wide and fangs bared. But I still held my sword, and this I brought up to impale her with a thrust that entered her heart. She gave another shriek, and fell back down the stairs, allowing me to withdraw my dripping blade as she did so. Another swing, and she too was headless: I was becoming quite an expert at it now.

I stepped over her and stood above the two Misses Brewin. "Murderer!" hissed Aunt Edith.

"She was a vampire," I explained. "As was Roderick, sadly. Once Richilde had got to them, they stood no chance. I did what had to be done." I was addressing Felicity more than her aunt, but she made no reply, only gazed at me with enormous eyes. "However," I said, "there are more pressing matters." The cellar was now filling with smoke, the heat was intense, and the ceiling was crackling. Breathing was becoming difficult. "Unless you know of some place we can hide," I told the old lady, "where the collapsing roof will not destroy us, we are ourselves doomed." And my memory went back to Magdeburg. "Is there not a well?"

She waved her hand. "Over there."

I hurried in the direction indicated, and found exactly what I wanted, a very solid wooden trap set in the stone floor. This I raised, and looked down into pitch darkness. My torch still glowed, and with its last light I was able to ascertain that there was a ledge round the well, again as there had been in Magdeburg. "This will do very nicely," I said.

"Down there?" Miss Brewin demanded. "We'll never get out again."

"Of course we will," I assured her. "Come here." Reluctantly she obeyed, and I held her arms and lowered her down. "Can you swim?"

"Of course I cannot swim," she snapped. "I am a lady, not some farm girl."

"Then be careful not to fall in," I advised. "Keep your back against the wall. Now you, Felicity."

She stared at me as best she could, for the torch was now all but gone. "Down there in that pit, with you?" she asked.

"Have you not shared sufficient with me to know that I attack only Roundheads and vampires?" I asked.

She hesitated, then came to me, and I lowered her behind her aunt, before joining her myself, and lowering the trap above our heads. Now indeed, as we sat on the ledge in the pitch blackness listening to the roaring rumbles from above us, did my memory go back to that unforgettable experience in Magdeburg. But of course nothing is ever quite the same. Then I had been scarce more than a boy, eager to experience everything in life; now I *had* experienced everything in life. Then I had been closeted with Richilde Bethlen, and I had been innocent enough to suppose her the most marvellous woman in the world; now I could only consider that she was again free and terrible, and that when I got out of here, if I got out of here, I would have to resume my quest – certainly, I had no great desire to couple with Felicity at that moment, even had I supposed that she had the least desire to couple with her brother's executioner. At Magdeburg we had been confined for two days, fortunately having had the foresight to take some food and drink into our hiding place; now we had nothing, but our confinement was a great deal shorter, for the downpour had apparently only grown heavier, and although the fire raged for some hours, and the roof and upper floors did indeed collapse, the blaze was steadily being extinguished by the pouring rain.

Thus after no more than a few hours I discerned that the heat was abating, and so reached up and threw open the trapdoor, heaving myself up and then lifting the ladies behind us. It was now all but dawn, and we beheld a scene even more devastating than that previous dawn at Culhaven, Dormintsley Manor being reduced to nothing more than a few charred timbers, heaped in and out of the cellars. "Oh, my home, my home," Miss Brewin moaned as she looked around her.

"This is nothing more than normal, where Count d'Albret has visited," Felicity said bitterly. I could not blame her for her mood, as she was no doubt remembering the house she had shared with her brother, whose corpse, I was happy to see, together with that of Alicia, had been quite consumed in the blaze. But I had more important things on my mind. In the first place, ascertaining that the Roundheads had taken themselves off, which they had done, assuming, as the captain had remarked to the cornet, that all their prisoners would be destroyed in the fire, and in the second place, seeking some sign as to the whereabouts of Richilde.

Being an optimist, I had hoped for something, but was yet surprised by what I did find. The steps leading up from the cellars were relatively unaffected by the flames, the rain, which continued to fall in a sullen drizzle, having prevented the stone from becoming sufficiently hot to crumble, but the door at the top, where Richilde had found herself encumbered, was burned to ashes, as were the surrounding walls. Ascending these steps, however, and moving instinctively away from the ruined building towards the trees, where I felt Richilde, again instinctively, would have in the first instance sought shelter, I tripped over a shattered flower pot, landed on my hands and knees, and in the brief second before regaining my feet looked at the pot more closely. There was a discolouration on its surface. I touched this. It had dried some time before, and yet, as I have been forced to experience a great deal of bloodshed in my time, I was certain that it had been spilled only a few hours earlier.

Now this was a side of the house away from whence Felicity and I had fired the cannon, and we had certainly engaged no one in this vicinity. Yet someone had stumbled this way, fairly recently, and bleeding, quite considerably.

Hastily I crawled a few feet further, and found another dark splodge, this time upon the gravel of the walkway. Now I could no longer doubt that I had my quarry in my sights. I went towards the copse, and found two more considerable bloodstains. Richilde was losing her vital fluid at a tremendous rate. But why? I certainly had not wounded her. And then I remembered the cut inflicted on her in Culhaven Castle . . . was it only two days ago? She had bound that up, with some care, as she had explained at the time. And in a human being, after two days, the cut should have closed, and begun to heal. But as Giles had known, and as Richilde certainly knew, once a vampire has been cut, deeply, it takes a considerable time for the bleeding to be staunched, save by the most extreme of methods. These she had certainly applied, but then I recalled her little shriek when she had pulled herself free of the door! Together with her gown, she must have caught her bandage, and that had been pulled away from the wound, not only exposing it, but opening it again. The Witch was mortally wounded!

But where was she? I moved into the trees, my sword blade held in front of me, for even a dying Richilde could still be a formidable adversary. I heard a moan. "Who is there?" I asked.

There was a moment's silence, then she replied, "Helier, is it you? I had never supposed to hear so sweet a sound."

I parted the bushes, and saw her lying on the ground, a crumpled and entirely human figure, at least in appearance, surrounded by blood, which trickled steadily down her left arm.

"Helier," she said again. "Come closer. Come to me, my dearest Helier. I need your blood." I said nothing. There was nothing to say. She had lost so much blood she was too weak to move. Clearly, she would recover herself quickly enough, could she be replenished. But there was no way I could permit that. "Helier," she begged, her

311

voice now only a whisper. "How can you be so cruel to me? I, who have only ever loved you?"

I hate to confess it, but her supplication, uttered in that marvellous whisper, and added to that hypnotic power she possessed, all but had me moving to her side. But before I could commit that irrevocable folly, I heard the snapping of a twig behind me, and turning, saw Felicity coming towards us through the morning mist. Richilde saw her too. "Felicity," she cried, her voice again gaining strength. "Oh, my dearest girl. You have come to my rescue. This brute will not help me."

Felicity came up to me and would have stepped past, moving indeed as one in a trance. "No," I said, and caught her arm.

She looked at me as if I were a stranger, and I knew then the awful truth. "You cannot stop me now, Helier," she said. "Or will you slay me like the others?"

She was right in her assumption that I would be reluctant to do that. But now she overplayed her hand. I still retained my grasp on her sleeve, and thus she lowered her head, and in that instant I saw her fangs. I immediately released her, and sprang away. She faced me, teeth bared, bosom heaving. "You cannot kill me, Helier," she shouted. "You love me!" But my sword was already swinging.

Her head fell at Richilde's feet, still spouting blood. Richilde gasped, and reached for it, but I kicked it away, and she fell on to her face, vainly scrabbling at the blood soaking into the earth. Then she rolled on her side and looked up at me. "I will see you in hell, Helier L'Eree," she whispered.

She spoke no more. I stood above her for an hour, while the last of the blood drained from her body. I was prepared to take off her head as well, much as I hoped it would not be necessary. And it was not. For as with Culhaven, so with Richilde Bethlen, Princess von

Hohengraffen. When her skin had turned white, and she no longer even twitched, she dwindled before my eyes, the flesh dropping away from her bones, and I watched the most beautiful woman I had ever known become a hideous skeleton. When I touched her with my sword point, the bones themselves dwindled into dust. She had been even older than Culhaven.

I returned to where Miss Brewin remained seated on the steps to the cellars, shoulders bowed. "Have you slain Felicity as well?" she asked.

"Sadly, it was necessary."

"You are a most destructive monster," she remarked. "My home, my nephew, my niece . . . I know you will claim all of these were necessary, but would they have been necessary if you had never come here?"

I could not deny that. "What will you do?" I asked.

"I have nothing to do, save sit here and starve."

From my wallet I took the bag of silver, and gave it to her. I could do nothing less.

Being now penniless myself, it took me some time to regain France. My only asset was that the Roundheads had reported that Dormintsley House had been destroyed, together with all the miscreants in it, and that Helier L'Eree was most definitely dead. Thus I made my way back into Wales, indulged in a little bit of highway robbery, and secured sufficient funds for a passage, and so came home.

I went first to Paris, and delivered the letters to the Queen. "By our lady, Helier," she said. "I had given you up for dead." Because it was almost exactly a year since she had given me my commission. "But now . . . ask of me what you will."

It occurred to me that she had several things in mind. But I wanted none of them. "I wish only to be left in peace on d'Albret, Your Majesty."

313

"With that shrewish woman?"

"We are well suited, Your Majesty."

"Then so be it," she agreed.

In fact, Marguerite and I are entirely suited. As perhaps we were suited from the moment, more than twenty years previously, I had carried her naked body out to the little boat in Grand Havre Bay in Garnesey, and rowed out to a lifetime of adventure. And in her way, she was pleased to see me. "Why, Helier," she remarked. "You have lost weight. And your boots are leaving mud all over the floor."

I knew I was home.

And home I have stayed. When he finally regained his throne, Charles wished to summon me again to his service, but I declined. I am done with kings and cardinals and their requirements. And even with queens, and *their* requirements. Home is best, for a man who has looked into the darkest pit of hell, and lived to tell the tale.